Jill Mansell lives with her family i̶ ̶ ̶ ̶ ̶ ̶ ̶ to work in the field of Clinical N̶e̶ ̶ ̶ ̶ ̶ ̶ ̶ ̶ but now writes full time. She watches far too much TV and would love to be one of those super-sporty types but basically can't be bothered. Nor can she cook – having once attempted to bake a cake for the hospital's Christmas Fair, she was forced to watch while her co-workers played frisbee with it. But she's good at Twitter!

Just *Heavenly*. Just *Jill*.

'Bursting with humour, brimming with intrigue and full of characters you'll adore – we can't think of a better literary remedy' ★★★★★ *Heat*

'To read it is to devour it' *Company*

'A warm, witty and romantic read that you won't be able to put down' *Daily Mail*

'Slick, sexy, funny' *Daily Telegraph*

'Mansell's fiction is a happy leap away from the troubles of today' *Sunday Express*

'Jill Mansell is in a different league' *Sun*

By Jill Mansell

Jill Mansell

MIXED DOUBLES

headline
review

Copyright © 1998 Jill Mansell

The right of Jill Mansell to be identified as the Author of
the Work has been asserted by her in accordance with the
Copyright, Designs and Patents Act 1988.

First published in 1998
by HEADLINE PUBLISHING GROUP

First published in paperback in 1998
by HEADLINE PUBLISHING GROUP

This edition published in paperback in 2014
by HEADLINE REVIEW
An imprint of HEADLINE PUBLISHING GROUP

9

Cataloguing in Publication Data is available from the British Library

ISBN 978 0 7553 3259 5

Printed and bound in Great Britain by
CPI Group (UK) Ltd, Croydon, CR0 4YY

Headline's policy is to use papers that are natural, renewable and recyclable
products and made from wood grown in sustainable forests. The logging and
manufacturing processes are expected to conform to the environmental
regulations of the country of origin.

HEADLINE PUBLISHING GROUP
An Hachette UK Company
338 Euston Road
London NW1 3BH

www.headline.co.uk
www.hachette.co.uk

For Mum and Dad
with love and thanks for everything

Chapter 1

Pru was getting hassle from her spaghetti. It was playing her up. Twirling away valiantly, willing the stuff to stay on her fork, she wondered enviously what it must be like to be Liza, who seldom bothered to even glance down at her plate, yet whose spaghetti miraculously stayed put.

It was New Year's Eve, four o'clock in the afternoon and already dark outside. In Liza Lawson's Provençal-style kitchen, around the scrubbed pine kitchen table, sat Dulcie, Liza and Pru, lining their stomachs in preparation for the long night ahead.

Far too impatient to bother with Le Twirl, Dulcie had used the edge of her fork as a knife and hacked her spaghetti to bits. It might not be the done thing but it was efficient; her stomach was no longer empty and her plate was clear. Anyway, if you couldn't do the undone thing in Liza's kitchen, amongst friends, where could you do it?

Having finished eating, Dulcie pulled a battered exercise book from her bag. 'Look what my mother found the other week during a clear-out.' She held it up for them to see. Emblazoned across the cover, in loopy, eighties-style lettering, were the words PRIVATE, KEEP OUT and TRESPASSERS WILL BE PROSTITUTED.

'My little joke,' Dulcie said fondly. 'I was fifteen. Imagine.'

Resting her chin on the cupped palm of her hand, Liza grinned.

'I was never fifteen.'

'I spent ten years being fifteen,' said Pru with feeling. When

1

everyone else had graduated to tights, her domineering mother had refused to let her wear them. Pru's recurring nightmare had involved walking up the aisle in white knee socks.

'We were all fifteen,' Dulcie reminded them, 'and all at the same time. This is the whole point of having friends of your own age,' she explained with exaggerated patience, 'so you can share your experiences. Like when you had a crush on Simon Le Bon, they had one too. When you couldn't sleep at night for worrying about that huge spot on your chin, at least you knew they were worrying about their spots as well. And when you weren't sure about one or two of the facts of life, you always had someone to ask who wouldn't laugh.'

'I never had spots,' said Liza.

'And you both definitely laughed when I asked you about French kissing,' Pru pointed out. 'You told me it was to do with French letters and the boy having to wear a condom on his tongue. Honestly, it's a wonder I ever kissed anyone after that.'

Dulcie giggled, recalling her lecture on the subject and Pru's solemn belief in every word.

'Anyway,' said Liza, 'that was donkeys' years ago.' Reaching across the table, she filled their glasses with Pouilly-Fumé. 'And this is New Year's Eve. We're supposed to be making resolutions.'

'That's why I brought the book along.' Opening it, Dulcie riffled through graffiti-strewn pages. 'God, school must've been boring to make me doodle this much. Ah, here it is.' Triumphantly she showed them the list. 'January the first. My New Year's resolutions are:

1. Buy a black satin shirt (long pointed collar).
2. Snog you-know-who.
3. Do more homework, especially maths.
4. Watch *Top of the Pops* every week.
5. Keep my room tidy.
6. Buy silver nail polish.
7. Join the *Starsky and Hutch* fan club.'

2

'A black satin shirt with a long collar.' Liza pulled a face. 'Yuk.'

'The ones about doing more homework and keeping my room tidy were in case my mother had a snoop.'

Pru was looking puzzled. 'Who was you-know-who?'

'D'you know, I haven't the foggiest. I've been trying to remember. Isn't it sweet, though?' said Dulcie happily. 'When I was fifteen those were my New Year's resolutions. That was what mattered. Such innocence.'

'Things are a bit different now,' Liza mocked. 'Sixteen years later. We're ancient.'

'Go on then.' Dulcie closed the book. 'What's your resolution for this year?'

Liza's humorous dark-brown eyes flicked from Dulcie to Pru.

'Oh, I want to get married.'

She spoke with the easy confidence of one who knows all she has to do is take her pick.

'How about you, Pru?' asked Dulcie.

Pru took a gulp of wine. She thought of Phil, her husband, and the odd way he had been behaving recently. She hoped nothing was wrong at work.

'I just want to stay married.'

Dulcie was leaning her chair back on its hind legs, wondering again who you-know-who could possibly have been. It was frustrating not being able to remember. Glancing at her watch, she realised she should be making a move. Patrick would go mental if she was late home; they were supposed to be meeting friends at seven, before going on to the country club dance.

'Dulcie,' prompted Liza. 'Your turn.'

'Me?' Dulcie brought the chair back down on to all fours with a thump. 'All I want is a divorce.'

'So who's the lucky chap?' Dulcie asked Liza as they said their goodbyes on the doorstep. 'Anyone we know?'

'Haven't decided yet.' Shivering in a thin white shirt, Liza hugged herself and edged back into the hall. Glancing up, she saw a couple of moths batting furiously around the outside light like rival lovers competing for attention.

'Still road-testing, I suppose. So many men, so little time.' Dulcie was flippant. What did Liza expect, sympathy? 'Maybe it's just as well you aren't coming to tonight's bash at the club. Less competition for me.' She looked smug. 'Personally I plan on snogging as many men as I can get my hands on.'

'You'll have to catch them first.' Liza's smile was deceptively innocent. 'Do you have any idea how much garlic went into that pasta sauce?'

Dulcie's hands flew to her mouth in horror.

'I hate you,' she exclaimed. 'When I said I wanted men to fall at my feet, I meant them to be overcome with lust, not garlic fumes.'

'You shouldn't want men to fall at your feet. You've got Patrick.'

'I'm tired of Patrick!' It came out as a howl. 'Dammit, you know better than anyone how that feels! How come you're allowed to do it and I'm not?'

'I'm not married.'

'Of course you aren't! Who'd have you?'

'Come on, if you want a lift home,' said Pru, because once these two started, they could bicker for England.

'I'm coming, I'm coming. Even if my life is over.' Dulcie huffed into her cupped hands and gazed heart-rendingly at Pru. 'Can we stop off at a chemist on the way, pick up some Gold Spot?'

'Bye,' said Liza, hugging them both. She kissed first Pru's icy cheek then Dulcie's indignant one. 'And let's have a Happy New Year. May all our resolutions come true.'

When it came to people's lives, it was generally agreed that Liza Lawson's was the kind you could envy.

She was single, successful, blonde and beautiful, with dark-brown, come-to-bed-this-*minute* eyes, flawless skin and a bewitching smile.

There is little more alluring than a woman utterly at ease with her body, and Liza – a curvy size fourteen – had never experienced the slightest urge to diet. She liked herself just as she was, and everyone else seemed to as well. She'd certainly never had any complaints.

Liza's job was pretty enviable too. Her career as a food writer had received a massive boost eighteen months earlier when she had landed the plum position of restaurant critic for the dazzlingly successful *Herald on Sunday*. Now, each week, her article appeared beneath the same photograph of herself smiling provocatively up from the last page of the colour supplement, with her gold-blonde hair falling over one shoulder and the beginnings of a heavenly cleavage peeping over the scooped-out top of a low-cut black velvet dress.

Men were forever falling in love with this photograph of Liza, and writing to tell her so.

Women envied her, because if looking like that and eating for a living wasn't a dream existence, they didn't know what was.

And restaurant owners wondered frustratedly why they had never spotted Liza Lawson in their restaurants, even when they knew she'd visited them because there in the *Herald*'s glossy Sunday supplement was the review.

Waking up late the following morning, Liza made her way gingerly downstairs. Two letters lay on the mat by the front door. She stuffed them into her dressing gown pocket, put the kettle on for coffee and opened the new packet of paracetamol she had had the foresight to buy yesterday afternoon. A hangover on New Year's Day was pretty much *de rigueur*; it was just a shame the way the older you got, the more blistering the effects became.

It was also a shame she had to work today, but a deadline

was a deadline and the job had to be done. Slotting bread into the toaster – just one slice, to reassure her nervous stomach – she made coffee and hoped her appetite would recover in time for lunch.

While Liza ate breakfast she played back last night's messages on the ansaphone. One was from an old lover, calling from London to wish her a happy New Year and inviting her to visit him at any time. The second was from her sister in New Zealand, drunkenly bawling 'Auld Lang Syne' down the phone along with what sounded like an entire team of All Blacks. The third message was from someone called Alistair, sounding self-conscious but determined, shyly telling her that having for many months admired her from afar, he would be thrilled if Liza would do him the honour of accompanying him to the theatre one night.

'. . . we've never spoken, but maybe you've noticed me playing squash at the country club,' he explained falteringly. 'I'm thirty-seven, six foot two, not in bad shape . . . um, I have dark hair, grey eyes and I drive a blue Volvo. Does this ring any bells?'

'No,' said Liza, swallowing another paracetamol.

'. . . oh dear, this isn't working out.' Alistair's voice was sounding worried now. 'I don't know how else to describe myself. Look, I'll hang up. I don't live too far from you. Why don't I drop a photograph of myself through your door? Then at least you'll know—'

At that point the tape ran out, because Liza had forgotten to rewind it the night before.

'Good thinking, Alistair.' She smiled as she retrieved the envelopes from her pocket. The first was a belated Christmas card from another ex, married and with children now but from the wry postscript sounding as if he wished he weren't. 'Missing you,' Liza read at the bottom of the card. '*Really* missing you. How about dinner sometime?' And he had scrawled the number of his mobile phone.

The second envelope, hand-delivered as promised,

6

contained a small photograph of Alistair, whom she wouldn't have recognised if he'd run her over in his blue Volvo. Still, he looked perfectly presentable and considering he was shy, the note enclosed with the photo was written in a masterful hand.

'Have I made a complete pig's ear of this attempt to ask you out?' he had written with endearing candour. 'I assure you, I'm not the hopeless case you must by now think I am. A few more salient details – I'm a barrister, divorced, three children, healthy income, detached house, fond of theatre, opera, Scrabble and Maltesers. Now I'm embarrassed again – I sound like a one-man dating agency. Enough. If you would like to contact me, my number is . . . If the prospect is too awful, please throw note and photo away and pretend this never happened. But I hope you don't. Yours respectfully, Alistair Kline.'

This was the kind of thing that happened to Liza. It was the kind of girl she was.

When Dulcie accused Liza of being a flirt, Liza declared she wasn't. Men simply liked her; she didn't do anything to actively encourage them. The way she acted towards men was never contrived.

'Do I flutter my eyelashes at them? Do I flash my cleavage?' she argued. 'Do I clutch their biceps and tell them how big and strong they are? No I do not. I never do any of that. *You* do.'

This was true, Dulcie couldn't deny it.

'I'm married; it doesn't count. Anyway, that's harmless flirting. Amateur stuff. You're the professional. You don't make men think you're flirting with them, you make them think you're *in love* with them. Dammit,' protested Dulcie, 'you make the poor sods think they're the only person on the planet worth being with.'

'You're jealous.'

'Of course I'm jealous! I want to know how you bloody do it.'

7

Having witnessed the phenomenon a million times, Dulcie had an inkling. She suspected it had something to do with Liza's dark-brown eyes and the way she looked at men when she was talking to them, the way she concentrated on them with such total absorption, the way she smiled . . .

Sadly, it didn't appear to be copyable. Dulcie had tried it a few times herself on her own in front of a mirror, but – being brutally honest here – all she'd looked was constipated.

There must be an art to bewitching men, and you either had it or you didn't. Dulcie could do standard flirting – she giggled, she joked, she could make men laugh, which was something – but she was never going to be in Liza's league. Which was a shame, because it was undeniably a handy knack to have.

Yet Liza, in turn, envied Dulcie, because attracting men might never have been a problem but staying interested once she'd got them was something else again.

She didn't know why, she simply couldn't do it. Something to do with a low boredom threshold, maybe. She could adore them initially, fall head over heels in lust, love – whatever – think this is it, this is the big one . . . then after four or five weeks the old, niggling tell-tale signs would begin to surface. She'd got to know them, she was up to date with the stories of their lives, she'd heard all their best jokes. Insidiously, boredom started to set in. While they were still enraptured by Liza, Liza found herself noting – and becoming increasingly irritated by – the way they cleared their throats, scraped their forks on their dinner plates, revealed a penchant for irritating catchphrases, watched endless reruns of *Star Trek* . . .

It was a failing over which she had no control. Liza thought she must be a hopelessly shallow person, happy to pick the icing off the cake but uninterested in the sponge underneath. Once she grew tired of someone, there could be no going back. The adrenaline had seeped away, the spark was gone. Another relationship bit the dust.

It was sad. Liza sometimes wondered if she would ever meet

a man who didn't bore her witless. She so badly wanted to. She wanted to be normal, to marry someone and have children and grandchildren. She wanted to share a life with them, not a few giddy weeks. At the rate she was going, she was going to end up a sad old maid.

This was why she envied Dulcie, who might now be hell-bent on divorce but who had at least spent the last six years married to the same man.

Chapter 2

Liza pulled up outside the Songbird at one o'clock. It was a newish restaurant several miles to the west of Bath, whose delights – or otherwise – she had intended to investigate a fortnight ago but a streaming cold had put paid to that. When you were a restaurant critic, a sense of smell and fully functioning tastebuds were a bit of a must.

But the *Herald on Sunday* needed the piece in order to make the printer's deadline, and it had to be faxed through before tomorrow. Luckily, although most restaurants didn't open for lunch on New Year's Day, the Songbird did.

Liza briefly checked her reflection in the car's rear-view mirror. It was amazing the effect a nondescript mousy wig, minimal make-up and a pair of unflattering spectacles could have. She was never recognised. Never chatted up, either. No men cast admiring glances in her direction. She was so uninteresting they seldom even acknowledged her presence. She became invisible.

It was an experience that never failed to entertain Liza. Handy, too, when you didn't want the publicity-hungry restaurateurs to know who you were.

Mark was already there, waiting for her, when she entered the restaurant. An ex with whom she had stayed on friendly terms – because he might be mad about *Star Trek* but at least he shared her passion for good food – he greeted Liza with a grin and a kiss on her un-made-up cheek. A dining companion was another must-have in Liza's line of work, enabling two meals to be assessed rather than just one. It also meant the staff's curiosity wasn't aroused by the sight of a woman – albeit a mousy one – lunching alone.

'You look well,' Mark told her, when the waiter had taken Liza's sensible navy-blue mac. 'New outfit?'

She was wearing a high-necked cream blouse, brown cardigan, calf-length beige pleated skirt and sturdy lace-ups. Mark adored the subterfuge; it gave him a kick. When he shared these meals with Liza he frequently found himself on the receiving end of sympathetic glances from waitresses wondering why a good-looking chap like him should be landed with such a frump.

They were seated in a far corner and left to study their menus. An agitated-looking blonde in her mid-twenties whisked through from the kitchen, murmured something to another waiter and whisked back again. As the doors swung shut behind her, the smell of burned garlic wafted across to their table. A party of eight, evidently still going strong from the night before, piled noisily into the restaurant and bombarded the girl behind the bar with orders. A loud cheer went up as the girl fumbled and dropped a glass on the tiled floor.

This could be promising. Liza had been given a lecture at the staff Christmas party by her editor-in-chief.

'We've been getting a bit of negative feedback,' he had explained as he sloshed whisky into a half-pint mug. 'Your reviews, my darling. Too complimentary by half. Some readers are asking if the restaurants pay us to advertise them. All this crap about enchanting presentation . . . elegant sauces . . . heavenly fish dishes . . . darling, a critic has to criticise, don't you see? You need to get the claws out, bitch it up a bit. Be wicked! Think more Michael Winner, less Dana. More *Private Eye*, less *Hello!* magazine. Aim for the jugular, sweetheart. Give the readers something to smirk about. Don't be afraid to make those restaurant owners cry.'

Liza didn't want to be Michael Winner. She wasn't naturally an aim-for-the-jugular type. But she saw her editor's point and the Dana jibe had hurt.

11

In the past she knew she had tended to gloss over the occasional less-than-perfect paella, the chef's overexuberant use of salt, the insufficiently chilled vichyssoise.

Maybe she was about to have her chance to bitch it up a bit, here at the Songbird. Liza glanced across at the flustered waitress on her knees sweeping up broken glass and mentally hardened her heart. If the meal wasn't up to scratch, she decided, she would go for it.

She still had the remains of her hangover too. That would help.

To begin with, Liza chose deep-dish aubergine Parmesan torte. Which was good, if a bit on the heavy side. The accompanying tomato sauce could have done with being a little less sweet.

Bah, humbug.

Mark had Provençal fish soup. He pronounced it delicious. Liza tasted some.

'Too much saffron,' she remarked briskly. 'And the bread should be hot.'

Mark raised his eyebrows.

'Whose bed did you get out of on the wrong side this morning?'

'No one's. I'm in training to be a cow.'

The restaurant was beginning to fill up. The party of eight, seated by the window at the front of the restaurant, emptied bottles of wine at a rate of knots and sang rousing choruses of 'Why Are We Waiting?'. The flustered waitress, serving them finally, got her bottom pinched. The other girl, the blonde, came out of the kitchen and told them sharply to keep their wandering hands to themselves. Three fingers on her own left hand were adorned with blue catering plasters.

'What happened?' jeered the chief bottom-pincher. 'Don't tell me, you tried to stab the chef and missed.'

For their main course, Mark had ordered tournedos of beef with wild mushrooms and vin santo.

'Is the steak tough?' Liza asked eagerly.

'No.'

'You asked for it rare. That's not rare, it's medium.'

Mark sat back in his chair.

'I don't think I like you like this.'

'It's my job.' Narrow-eyed, she surveyed her lamb with polenta and artichokes. It looked divine, which was no good at all.

Happily, when she tasted the lamb with its herb and breadcrumb coating, she hit paydirt. The garlic they had smelled burning earlier was right here, on her plate.

The wine was good and Mark stubbornly refused to fault his sweet – which was a trio of home-made ice creams in a brandy snap basket – but Liza was well into her stride now. Her plum and apricot tart was definitely stodgy, the sweet almond pastry case way too thick. The crust around the edge, which had been doused with icing sugar in a futile attempt at a cover-up, was burnt.

'It's busy,' said Mark, valiantly defending the little restaurant. 'Must be good to be so popular.'

'It's New Year's Day.' Liza wasn't to be deterred. 'Everywhere else is shut. Anyway,' she pointed out, 'you're only saying that because you fancy the blonde.'

'I feel sorry for her. Poor thing, she's in a flap.'

'Not surprising. I'd flap too, if I had to serve up burnt offerings like this.'

'Shall we ask for the bill?'

'No way. I want to try the coffee. Wouldn't it be fab if it was instant? Oh my God—'

Liza stared at the door, opening to admit two more customers.

'What? What?'

Twisting round in his seat, Mark craned his neck to see who had come in. Liza was just glad she was wearing her glasses and mousy wig.

It was Phil Kasteliz, Pru's husband. He was laughing and holding the hand of a woman with piled-up white-blonde hair.

Her leopard-print top ended above her belly button, and a black rubber skirt began several inches below it. The amount of make-up she wore was staggering. She looked like Lily Savage, only less demure.

She wasn't Pru by a long chalk.

'That *bastard*,' Liza hissed as the waitress showed them to their table. The moment they were seated, the blonde slipped off one spiky black stiletto and began teasing Phil with her toes.

Mark looked ill at ease. He hated scenes. (It was another reason Liza had gone off him; his anything-for-a-quiet-life attitude had driven her to distraction.)

'Who is he?' He prayed it wasn't the latest man in Liza's life. She was in such a weird mood today. He prayed even harder she wasn't about to start a cat fight.

'His name's Phil. He's the pig my friend Pru's married to.' Her dark eyes narrowed to slits. 'I think I want to kill him.'

'So that isn't his wife?'

'That old bike, are you kidding? My God, the nerve of the man!'

Liza's knuckles were white around her pudding fork. Mark envisaged the headlines: RESTAURANT CRITIC PUNCTURES DINER TO DEATH.

Or: WOMAN FORKED TO DEATH.

Feeling sick, he said, 'I don't think you should cause a scene.'

Liza gave him a pitying look. 'No, I'm sure you don't.'

But for once Mark was right. Maybe it was just as well Phil hadn't recognised her, although his attention was so clearly taken up with his companion she doubted whether her disguise was even necessary. From the look of him, he'd hardly notice if the SAS stormed the restaurant and smoke-bombed the place.

Liza had never had much time for Phil Kasteliz. She wouldn't have liked him even if he wasn't an estate agent. Despite working long hours – allegedly – he always seemed to have plenty of time left over for gambling, drinking and having a laugh with The Lads.

Pru, who adored him, stoutly maintained that she didn't mind her husband's late-night excursions to Bath's clubs and casinos. Phil worked hard, she explained patiently whenever anyone dared to criticise him. He needed to relax. He wasn't the stay-at-home, watch-a-bit-of-TV and put-up-a-few-shelves type. Anyway, Pru invariably ended up saying, where was the harm? At least Phil wasn't a womaniser, she had no worries on that score. He was far more interested in roulette.

Shame it wasn't the Russian kind, thought Liza, who had never believed a word of it anyway. When you were as generally lacking in moral values as Phil Kasteliz, what would be the point in making the effort to remain faithful? It was like expecting a crack addict to throw up his hands in horror and say: Oh no, I'd *never* touch grass.

So it didn't exactly come as a surprise to find Pru's husband dabbling in adultery, but the urge to kill him was still there.

What annoyed Liza more than anything was the kind of woman Phil was with. It was shaming to Pru. Letting her down.

If he had to cheat on her, he could at least have had the decency to do it with someone who wasn't a complete dog.

'Umm . . . would you like coffee?'

The young waitress was back, escaping further hassle from the rugby types and looking closer than ever to a nervous breakdown. It occurred to Mark that any stabbing spree instigated by Liza would give the waitress just the opportunity she needed to join in.

Imagine the headlines then:

BLOODBATH AT THE SONGBIRD.

No, even snappier: BLOODBATH IN BATH.

He began to nod. Liza shook her head.

'Just the bill, thanks.'

As the waitress hurriedly began clearing their table, her hand slipped. The chargrilled pastry Liza had left on her plate slid on to the tablecloth.

'Oh God I'm sorry—'

Liza wasn't normally rude but Phil Kasteliz hadn't improved her mood. She picked up the pastry, examined it speculatively for a moment and said, 'So am I.'

On their way out they passed within feet of Phil and his lunch companion. The woman, pretending to read Phil's palm, was saying, '. . . I predict an afternoon in bed with a sexy blonde.'

Phil's answering smirk was too much for Liza to bear. Just loudly enough for him to hear – and when she was sure he couldn't see her face – she murmured to Mark, 'Yes, but where on earth's he going to find one?'

There was no denying it; when you were in the mood, writing a really bitchy review was fun. And easy, too. The six-hundred-word piece practically wrote itself.

'Was the chef at the Songbird having an off-day,' Liza tapped into her word processor, 'or a day off?'

Too cruel? Nooo.

'. . . I couldn't help noticing the management's advice to book early in order to avoid disappointment. Well, if you really want to avoid disappointment, *my* advice to you would be don't book at all.'

Unfair? Unkind? Maybe, but it was the truth.

'. . . unable to face the prospect of coffee, we left. Happily, the day wasn't totally wasted. On our way home we stopped at Reg's mobile café on the A46. Reg's egg and chips,' Liza concluded with a flourish, 'were heaven on a plate. Not a speck of burnt garlic in sight.'

True? Well, not quite. Reg's had been shut. But if he had been open, she was sure she would have enjoyed his egg and chips.

Chapter 3

Liza might have envied Dulcie her marriage but as far as Dulcie was concerned, marriage sucked.

Anyway, she had made her New Year's resolution now. And she was jolly well going to keep it.

Yes, it was a shame, especially when everyone was forever telling you how lucky you were to be married to someone as dishy and wonderful as Patrick Ross in the first place, but they didn't know what it was really like. Because what was the point of having a dishy and wonderful husband when you hardly ever got the chance to experience his dishyness because all *he* ever did was bloody work work work?

It was particularly annoying, Dulcie mused, when you had been so sure you'd hit the marital jackpot. After years of falling for the wrongest men imaginable – and boy, had she had a talent for sniffing them out – meeting Patrick had come as such a shock to the system she'd barely known how to handle him. It had taken her months to learn to trust him, to realise she didn't *need* to know how to handle Patrick, because he wasn't playing an elaborate trick on her, he actually *was* as nice as he seemed.

Weird. It took some getting used to, especially when you were as addicted to bastards as she had been. HHB, Liza had called it, as in: 'Oh, Dulcie's HHB. Hopelessly Hooked on Bastards.'

She hadn't meant to be, but somehow that was always the way Dulcie's relationships had managed to turn out. Something to do with the adrenalin rush that went hand in hand with

17

chronic insecurity, or some such crap. Reading about it once in a magazine, Dulcie had recognised herself at once. Any man who was nice to you clearly didn't deserve you and had to be a complete wimp. If, on the other hand, he lied, cheated and treated you like dirt, you obviously didn't deserve someone as fantastic as he was and were promptly desperate to hang on to him at all costs.

Except Patrick Ross hadn't been awful to her, nor was he a wimp. He had obviously never studied the rule book. Confusion all round. Patrick was witty, he was smart, he had girls drooling over him everywhere he went. Even Dulcie's parents had approved of him, which was a startling new experience for all concerned.

Patrick had carried on being charming, phoning when he said he'd phone and turning up when he said he'd turn up. He brought Dulcie presents, made her laugh and never embarrassed her at parties. Other girls, pea green with envy, continued to swoon. Dulcie's mother even looked once or twice as if she might swoon too.

It took time, but in the end Dulcie couldn't fight it any more. She resigned her membership of the HHB club and allowed herself to fall in love with Patrick Ross. She was twenty-five, he was thirty-three. She was lazy, he was ambitious. She liked chicken breast, he liked leg. She enjoyed a drink, Patrick 'Better keep a clear head, big meeting tomorrow' preferred to drive.

It was a match made in heaven. It was perfect.

For the first four years at least.

Things had only started to go really wrong when Patrick, tired of making money for the computer company for which he was working, decided to take the plunge and set up in business on his own. The hours he put in were ridiculous. He made junior doctors look like part-timers. He would leave the house before Dulcie was awake and return home just as she was crawling back into bed.

'I never see you,' she wailed one night when it all got too

much. 'You never see me with make-up on. It's not fair . . .'

'I'm sorry.' Patrick sat down on the bed and hugged her, getting moisturiser all over the lapels of his best suit. 'I know it isn't fair, but I'm doing it for us. From now on things will be better, I promise. I'll do more work from home.'

He had been as good as his word and the result had been as disastrous as Dulcie had known it would be. She'd have got more conversation out of a Madame Tussaud's waxwork. Patrick's body might be there but his mind was so occupied with work it may as well have disappeared on a round-the-world cruise.

Like a small child desperate for attention, Dulcie found herself putting three sugars in the cups of tea she took him, just to provoke a reaction. One evening, frustrated beyond endurance and having read in *Cosmopolitan* that the element of surprise could pep up a marriage no end, she danced naked into Patrick's study, threw herself on to his lap and uncorked a bottle of champagne with her teeth. Children, don't try this at home. All it achieved was foam everywhere, a chipped upper molar and a fused disk drive. All the work Patrick had been about to save was lost and he had needed to stay up all night replacing it.

Dulcie considered suing *Cosmopolitan*. Her marriage had been pepped down.

'Get a job,' Liza had suggested when Dulcie had moaned to her about how bored she was.

'Are you mad?' Dulcie looked appalled. 'The whole point of Patrick working these stupid hours is to make money. The last thing we need is me slogging my guts out as well, earning more of the stuff. That really would defeat the object.'

'You might enjoy it.'

'No I wouldn't.' Honestly, Liza had the oddest ideas sometimes.

'Okay, what about charity work? Just a few hours a week.'

'For heaven's sake,' cried Dulcie, 'aren't I already suffering enough?'

Happily, another of Liza's suggestions met with greater success.

'Why don't you come along to Brunton Manor? Give it a try?'

Brunton Manor Country Club, situated three miles outside Bath, was where Liza went to play tennis and squash. Pru, also a member, swam there two or three times a week.

Dulcie, who was to sport what Scooby Doo was to astrophysics, wrinkled her nose.

'Don't give me that look. You might enjoy it,' Liza argued.

'People say that when they try and make you eat frogs' legs.'

'And you don't have to do anything sporty if you don't want to. Brunton's a country club, not the Foreign Legion. During the day it's full of pampered housewives drinking gin and ogling the musclemen in the gym.'

Perking up considerably at this news, particularly cheered by the prospect of a little gentle ogling, Dulcie had agreed to go along and check it out.

Brunton Manor had proved a revelation. It was, quite simply, one of *the* most glamorous country clubs in England.

The old manor house itself, two hundred years old and built of honey-coloured Bath stone, was gloriously situated on the side of a hill with unrivalled views over the Langley Stoke Valley. The estate surrounding the house comprised ninety-three acres of wooded and landscaped gardens. The sporting facilities were, of course, superb.

The club prided itself on its decidedly upmarket image, and astronomical membership fees ensured it stayed that way. People liked to boast – in passing – that they belonged to Brunton; it was on a par with casually flashing a platinum Amex. If having to pay next year's fees was likely to keep you awake at night, Brunton wasn't the place for you. You went somewhere less exclusive instead.

Dulcie had fallen in love with the club at first sight. Brunton Manor was her idea of heaven.

You really didn't have to be energetic at all.

There was an endless supply of gin, as promised.

There was a sun-drenched terrace overlooking the glittering turquoise outdoor pool and – as Liza had also promised – plenty to ogle.

There was a terrific restaurant, a cinema, sunbeds, saunas and a beauty salon. There were evening discos, impromptu parties and barbecues around the pool. It was the easiest place in the world in which to while away all those surplus hours. You could watch other members puffing and sweating their way through step classes or launching themselves around the squash courts. You could jeer – quietly – at the Wimbledon wannabes playing hopeless tennis. You could admire the miraculous tanned legs of the tennis coaches. You could laze in the sun drinking Pimm's and pretending to read a book.

Perhaps best of all – and Dulcie felt in this respect it had all the comradeship of an AA meeting, not of course that she had ever been to one – you could moan freely with the other wealthy, bored housewives about your workaholic husband and know they knew exactly what you meant.

As far as Dulcie was concerned, Brunton Manor was the answer to all her prayers. Miraculously, and certainly unintentionally, it had even turned out to be economical, since every day spent lazing by the pool in a bikini was a day not spent shopping in Bath.

The phone rang. Since Patrick was in his study working – well, it was New Year's Day, a Bank Holiday, what else would you expect? – Dulcie picked it up.

'It's me,' said Liza.

'Oh well, I'm not speaking to you. That garlic totally wrecked my chances last night. Even Luigi in the wine bar pretended he couldn't come near me because he'd got flu—'

'Never mind your snogathon. I had lunch today at the Songbird and guess who was there?'

'Cliff Richard and Angela Rippon. They were holding

21

hands. No, wait, they were canoodling. Don't you love that word?' Dulcie sighed. 'Canoodle-oodle-oodling—'

'Sometimes I wonder about you,' said Liza.

'You started it. Go on then, so who was he with if it wasn't Angela Rippon?'

'Phil was there. With another woman. In a rubber skirt.'

'You mean—?'

Liza said firmly, 'She was the one wearing the skirt. And it isn't funny. She was awful.'

'Oh,' said Dulcie. 'Were they ... um ... canoodling?'

'Big time.'

'Oh fuck.'

Dulcie decided there must have been some kind of a mix-up, a typographical error, when God or whoever organised life had been organising Pru's. She was supposed to have been given a loving husband. Instead she'd been landed with a roving one.

Poor Pru, it wasn't what she deserved.

'Did he see you?'

'No.'

'So what happens now?'

'We're going to tell her.'

When the phone had rung Dulcie had been draped across the sofa watching a trashy New Year's Day-type film. Now, glancing across at the television, she saw the tear-stained heroine covering her face with her hands and sobbing: 'But I love him, I love him! Please don't do this to me ... I *love* him ...'

Dulcie thought uncomfortably that nobody loved anyone more than Pru loved Phil.

'It'll kill her.'

'She should know. It's only fair. Dulcie, we have to tell her.'

Liza wasn't a fan of dishonesty.

'Okay, you do it. If you really have to.'

'We'll do it,' Liza corrected her briskly. 'Together.'

* * *

22

Pru and Phil Kasteliz lived in a modern detached house on the outskirts of Bath, on one of those exclusive keeping-up-with-the-Joneses type of estates bristling with carriage lamps and bay trees. Anyone whose car was more than two years old was regarded with suspicion. If your curtains weren't swagged and tailed and your windows not cleaned every week you were riff-raff. If the grass on your front lawn exceeded an inch and a half in length . . . well, you were scum. Any small children, needless to say, were expected to show consideration for their neighbours and play quietly. And tidily. But preferably not at all.

It was that kind of estate.

'What if he's there?' Dulcie peered ahead as they swung into Acacia Close. Loads of roads were called that, she really must find out what it meant. She wouldn't know an acacia if it leapt up and bit her on the bum.

'He won't be. It's Wednesday, everyone's back at work. Anyway,' Liza rounded the corner and nodded at the empty drive, 'see? His car's gone.'

'I don't know if we're doing the right thing.' Dulcie was already racked with guilt. It was all right for her, she wanted a divorce. Pru didn't. 'What if you got it wrong? It could have been an innocent meeting with a client.'

'In a rubber skirt?' Liza wasn't having any of that. Her tone was dismissive. 'And with her foot buried in his crotch? Come off it, the woman was a scrubber. If anyone was the client, it was Phil.'

When they rang the bell and the gold and white front door was pulled open, Liza got something of a shock to come face to face with the rubber-skirted scrubber herself.

Chapter 4

Upstairs, Pru didn't hear the doorbell. She was bent double with the hair dryer going full blast, putting the necessary lift into her straight conker-brown hair. Luckily it was thick and there was plenty of it; with a bit of tweaking and a lot of hairspray (maximum hold, what else?) the illusion would be complete. Her ears wouldn't peep out, they wouldn't even be glimpsed. There would not be the slightest tell-tale sign that they stuck out like jug handles at all.

Pru hated it that Phil's pet name for her was Toby.

'Well, I can hardly call you jugs, can I?' he had quipped, eyeing her 32A breasts. Playfully he had tweaked her awful ears. 'Come on, Pru, where's your sense of humour! Would you prefer Dumbo?'

Pru would have preferred it if he'd stopped making perpetual fun of her ears. It was hard to have a sense of humour about something that had blighted your life since you were eleven when a group of boys in your class had asked how far you could fly.

She had tried sleeping with a scarf tied round her head, praying nightly that by morning she would wake up with miraculously flattened ears. She had even been so driven to desperation one Friday night that she had gone along with one of Dulcie's brilliant suggestions.

This had involved superglue. 'It's what Clark Gable did,' Dulcie had exclaimed, thrilled by her own cleverness. 'It'll be like instant plastic surgery, only pain free!'

As the doctor had later drily remarked, maybe they should

have practised first with UHU. They had ended up in the casualty department of Bath Royal United with Dulcie's right hand glued to Pru's left ear, Dulcie's left hand glued to a great deal of Pru's hair and Pru in floods of humiliated tears.

Dulcie's jokes that they were Siamese twins about to be separated didn't help. Three hours of serious solvent abuse and intricate work with a scalpel later, they were allowed home.

'Don't do it again,' warned the young male doctor, attempting to keep a straight face.

'Oh well,' Dulcie shrugged, 'it was worth a try. Nothing ventured, nothing gained.'

Pru, who had left most of her hair behind on the floor of the casualty department, was forced to endure the next six months with her ears on show while she sported the ultimate haircut from hell.

She jumped as the bedroom door swung open and Liza and Dulcie came in.

'Hi!' Pru switched off the hair dryer, delighted to see them. 'What are you two doing here? Hang on a sec, I've just about finished.'

'Pru, what's that woman doing downstairs?' demanded Liza.

'You mean Blanche? Hoovering, I think.' Pru reached for the Elnett and sprayed vigorously, checking her reflection in the dressing table mirror. There, magic. No ears.

But Liza, behind her, was looking grim. Pru swivelled round.

'Why, what's the matter? Don't tell me you caught her pocketing the silver spoons?'

'She's . . . your cleaner?' Dulcie sounded dazed.

Pru looked shamefaced.

'I know. Mad, isn't it? Here's me, no job, at home all day . . . and I've got someone coming in to do the housework. Honestly, it was Phil's idea. He got it into his head just before Christmas that everyone who's anyone has to have a lady-who-does. I told him it was stupid, we didn't need a cleaner, but you know

25

what Phil's like. As far as he's concerned it's another status symbol, like a Gucci belt.' She paused, frowning. 'Is everything okay? She wasn't really nicking spoons, was she?'

Liza barely knew where to start. She'd never realised Phil could sink this low.

Dulcie, needing something to occupy her hands and determined to leave Liza to do the dirty work, began investigating the make-up on Pru's pretty dressing table. As she undid the top of a pink Chanel lipstick the sound of the Hoover being switched on drifted up from downstairs.

'This Blanche person. How did you find her?' Liza realised she was prevaricating.

Dulcie closely examined a Lancôme mascara.

'From an agency. She was highly recommended.' Beginning to look flustered, Pru said, 'She lives half a mile away, on the Everton estate. She's divorced with two grown-up sons. I know she doesn't look it, but she's nearly forty . . . Oh, for heaven's sake, what's wrong? What are you going to tell me, that she's a mass murderer?'

Estee Lauder translucent powder and a swansdown puff. Nice. Dulcie picked up Pru's bottle of Youth Dew and gave herself an experimental squirt.

'Pru, I'm sorry. This isn't easy.'

Get on with it, thought Dulcie.

'The thing is . . . the thing is . . .'

This was Liza for you. All mouth and no trousers. Dulcie, who was leaning into the mirror trying out a smoky Clinique eyeshadow, said, 'What Liza's trying to tell you is that Phil's the one who's got himself a lady-who-does. Except we aren't talking vacuum cleaners and I don't think you can call her a lady.'

'That isn't fair,' Pru sounded almost angry. 'Blanche is a hard worker. Just because her clothes are a bit . . . well, a bit skimpy—'

'I'm not talking about her clothes,' said Liza.

'And she isn't only a hard worker,' Dulcie put in, 'she's fast, too.'

26

Liza took the plunge.

'Look, I saw them. Having lunch together on New Year's Day.'

Pru's face was white. 'No you didn't. Phil was working. He told me.'

'I saw them. And I heard them. He's having an affair with her.' Liza shook her head. 'I'm sorry. I wish it wasn't true, but it is.'

Dulcie thought she might buy herself one of these Clinique eyeshadows. She couldn't bring herself to look at the expression on Pru's face. Downstairs the Hoover was switched off.

Moments later there was a tap on the bedroom door.

'All done, Pru. I'm off.'

Pru rose slowly to her feet and went to the door. Liza and Dulcie exchanged alarmed glances. Liza swallowed. Dulcie held her breath.

'Blimey, are you all right, love? You're as white as a sheet.'

'I'm fine, Blanche. I'll come down with you. You'll want your money.'

Dulcie, wearing too much eyeshadow, collapsed on the bed.

'Will she kill her in the kitchen, d'you think?'

It was what Liza had had in mind at the Songbird. She moved across the room and opened the door a fraction.

'If we hear a scream, we go down,' she told Dulcie.

But all they heard was the low murmur of voices, the sound of Blanche's high heels tip-tapping across glossy parquet, and the front door slamming shut.

Dulcie and Liza raced to the window in time to see Blanche, now wearing a red leather bomber jacket over her green top and short white skirt, making her way jauntily to the end of the road.

Pru reappeared in the bedroom doorway. She watched them watching Blanche leave.

'No, I didn't say anything to her, if that's what you're wondering.'

27

'But Pru—'

'Don't. I like Blanche. She's friendly and she's good company when I'm here on my own.'

'But—'

'And I love Phil.' She was still pale but her jaw was clenched, her expression defiant. 'He's my husband and I love him. What was my New Year's resolution, can you remember?'

Of course they remembered.

'Well, I'm sticking to it,' said Pru. 'I'm going to stay married. I still don't believe what you told me about him and Blanche, but even if it is true, it doesn't have to be the end of the world. Certainly not the end of a perfectly good marriage.'

Liza had to say it.

'Pru, it is true.'

Her grey eyes bright with tears, Pru demanded, 'Did you see them actually *doing* it?'

'Practically. She had her shoes off, and her foot in his—'

'Don't say it!' Her voice rose to a shriek, her hands went up, stopping Liza in her tracks. 'Anyway, I've already told you. There are worse things a man can do than have an innocent fling. If you hadn't seen them, no one would have known anything. If you hadn't told me, I would never have found out.'

'Pru, how can a fling be innocent when you're married to the man?' Liza blurted out. 'He's cheating on you, for God's sake! I know how upset you must be, but—'

'Don't lecture me,' Pru said coldly. 'How can you possibly know how I feel? You've never had a proper relationship in your life.'

'That went well,' said Dulcie conversationally when they were back in Liza's car. 'Oh yes, I'd call that a great morning's work. A raging success.'

Liza shook her head. 'How can she stand it? How can she hear that kind of news and stay so calm?'

'She isn't calm.' Leaning across from the passenger seat, Dulcie commandeered the rear-view mirror. 'How about a spot of shopping?' she said brightly. 'I want to buy one of these eyeshadows. This colour really suits me.'

'How can you be so shallow?'

Dulcie grinned. 'Sallow? I'm not sallow, I'm tanned.'

Pru sat in the middle of the bed surrounded by photograph albums. Each album was full of pictures of herself and Phil, separately and together, at home or abroad, in Cornwall, in Tunisia, in Scotland, swimming, sunbathing, skiing, partying . . .

How can Liza and Dulcie ever understand how I feel? thought Pru, carefully turning another page and smiling at photos of Phil and herself on holiday last year in Morocco. Phil, sunburnt and peeling, was balancing a glass on his head, showing off for her benefit. And here was one of the two of them, taken by someone they had become friendly with in the hotel bar. They were dancing, and Phil's arms were clasped around her waist, and just looking at the photograph Pru was able to relive that blissful moment, experience again the feeling of utter security.

No, neither Liza nor Dulcie could ever have understood how she felt about Phil, Pru decided. Dulcie had put herself about a fair bit before settling down with Patrick, and Liza . . . well, Liza was still putting herself about.

But Pru, who had been with Phil for fourteen years, had never even looked at another man. He had been her first and only love, rescuing her from the terrors of teenage dating, and she had been more than happy to be rescued. Phil was all she wanted; he made her feel safe, she was Phil Kasteliz's girlfriend, she *belonged* to him . . .

Pru's hand trembled as she took the photograph out of its cellophane casing and looked more closely at it. Phil was her whole life. Finding out about Blanche had been horrible, of course it had, but she wasn't a complete innocent. Sometimes men did stupid things. Their hormones got the better of them, they took risks they shouldn't have . . . and were found out.

29

But it doesn't mean he's stopped loving me, thought Pru. It's a temporary weakness, that's all. I'm his wife. He still loves me best.

Slowly, she bit her tongue. Not enough to draw blood, but almost. Although it hurt, the pain was bearable.

Like this thing with Phil and Blanche, Pru thought, carefully sliding the photo back into the album. Dulcie and Liza were acting like it was the end of the world, but it didn't have to be.

She could bear this too.

Chapter 5

Telling your husband you no longer wanted to be married to him was proving less straightforward than Dulcie had imagined. When she had first envisaged the scenario, it had seemed simple. She would just deliver her speech and that would be that.

Now she was ready to do the deed, however, a problem had cropped up.

The problem was . . .

. . . timing.

It would be so much easier, Dulcie thought, if Patrick was awful. If he used her as a punchbag, blacked her eyes and sent a few teeth flying, all she'd have to do was scream, Right, that's it, get out of my life NOW.

Ditto if she found out he was having an affair.

But Patrick wasn't awful and she didn't want the break-up to be any more traumatic than it needed to be. Which was why the timing had to be right.

Before Christmas had been a no-no. That would be too cruel, too inconsiderate for words. Knowing she couldn't bring herself to do it in December was what had prompted Dulcie to make it her New Year's resolution instead. Get the festive season out of the way and do it then.

Except now it was the middle of January and Patrick's birthday loomed. His fortieth, at that. Unhappily aware that only a complete cow would wreck her husband's birthday, Dulcie realised she had to sit on her bombshell for a couple more weeks yet.

Forty. God, the more she thought about it the more terrifying it sounded. Whoever said life began at forty must have been senile. Feeling sorry for her ancient husband, Dulcie made two mugs of coffee and wandered through to the study. Patrick was tapping lists of figures into one of the computers and peering intently at the screen. It probably wouldn't be long before he started to need glasses.

'It's your birthday in ten days' time.' Dulcie perched on the edge of his desk, both hands clasped around her mug. 'What do you want?'

The least she could do, she had already decided, was buy him a really nice present.

Patrick keyed in a few more numbers.

'Don't know. Haven't given it much thought.'

'You'll be forty.'

'Better get me a Zimmer frame then.'

'Come on, I need some clues.' Something to remember me fondly by, thought Dulcie with a burst of uncharacteristic sentimentality. A gorgeous watch, perhaps? Flying lessons? A fabulous painting?

Patrick glanced up at her. He shrugged.

'I really don't know. Clothes, I guess. I could do with a couple of new shirts.'

Men, they were hopeless.

'That's so boring. What would you really, *really* like, more than anything?'

Patrick grinned. Ah, thought Dulcie, now we're getting somewhere.

'Okay.' He reached past her, picked up a copy of last month's *PC Answers*, and flipped through a few pages until he found what he was looking for. 'There you go. The new Hewlett Packard Laserjet. What a machine . . . six hundred dpi output, no less—'

'A computer!' wailed Dulcie. 'I'm not getting you a bloody computer.'

'It isn't a computer,' Patrick explained patiently. 'It's a printer.'

'Whatever, it's still a crap present.'

'Sorry, but you did ask what I wanted.' He looked resigned, then gave her hand a squeeze. 'Never mind. Just shirts then.'

'No, no. I'll get you the printer.' She could do that much for Patrick. He would have something to keep him company during the long, lonely evenings after she had left.

It was his money anyway.

Dulcie just thought how ironic it was that her parting gift to him would be a computer-type thing, when they were what had effectively destroyed her marriage in the first place.

Still, at least the present-buying problem was solved.

'What shall we do then,' she persisted, 'on your birthday?'

Patrick was trying hard to concentrate on the flickering VDU.

'You choose, sweetheart. We could go out to dinner if you like.'

They always went out to dinner on Patrick's birthdays. It wasn't going to win awards for most riveting suggestion of the year. Dulcie wished he'd say, just once, 'How about a torrid weekend away, making love under the moonlight in Marrakesh?'

Wherever Marrakesh was when it was at home. She hadn't a clue, but it certainly sounded torrid.

She remembered a discussion she had heard the other day on Talk Radio, about men hitting forty.

'Do you think you'll have a mid-life crisis?'

Patrick was used to Dulcie's startling about-turns in the middle of conversations. He drained his coffee and handed her the empty mug.

'I haven't got time for a mid-life crisis.'

'You never know.' She looked wistful. 'You might suddenly realise that all you've done is work yourself stupid while life passes you by.'

Smiling, he glanced at his watch.

'If I don't get a move on I'm likely to have a mid-morning crisis. These figures have to be faxed to Manchester by twelve. Thanks for the coffee, sweetheart.' He ruffled Dulcie's spiky dark hair. 'See you later, hmm?'

A party, Dulcie decided. That was what she would do. Hold a spectacular surprise fortieth birthday party, to show Patrick she still cared about him and to launch him painlessly into single middle-agehood.

It would ease her own guilt and be fun into the bargain, she thought happily.

And then a week or so later, when all the excitement had died down and the timing was right, she would leave.

'A party?' Bibi Ross sounded amused. 'Darling, it's a lovely idea, but we couldn't come. Too complicated for words.'

'But it's a surprise for Patrick,' Dulcie protested. 'You're his mother. You have to be there.'

'Impossible,' Bibi replied flatly. 'How can I bring James to a—'

'Don't bring James.' Dulcie had already thought of this. 'Tell him you're ill. Tell him you're going to an old girls' school reunion . . .'

Bibi visibly winced at the words 'old girl'. She shook her head.

'I can't do that. Anyway, we're already busy that night. James has invited some terribly important client and his wife round for dinner. He really has,' Bibi insisted when Dulcie gave her a look. Rummaging in her bag, she pulled out a diary. 'See, I've written it down. Friday the twenty-eighth. Dennis and Meg Haversham, seven thirty.'

It was true. Dulcie gave in with good grace.

'Well, it's a shame. You're going to miss a terrific party.'

'Never mind, can't be helped.' With some relief, Bibi snapped the diary shut. 'Anyway, you know me. Never a great one for birthdays.'

34

Bibi had more reason than most not to be a great one for birthdays. Dulcie adored her mother-in-law but the past two years had been a definite strain.

Complicated wasn't the word for it. To maintain the degree of deception Bibi had landed them with you needed your wits permanently about you. Not to mention a degree in maths.

At the age of nineteen, Bibi – christened Barbara – had met and married George Ross. At twenty, she gave birth to Patrick.

When she was forty-five, George had died of a heart attack on the golf course. Distraught, Bibi had mourned him for three years. When finally she rejoined the outside world, she vowed never again to love anyone as much as she had loved George. The pain was too great. She couldn't bear to risk losing anyone like that again.

Bowled over by her astonishing looks, many tried, but Bibi stuck to her guns. Until she met James Elliott, and realised what she had been missing all these years.

This was when the awful subterfuge had begun.

Bibi had always taken pretty good care of herself but her chief ally was her genes. Her mother had been the same. Some people can't help it, they just look older than they are. It isn't their fault.

Bibi, going to the other extreme, looked a lot younger than her years. She always had. At forty, people refused to believe she could be the mother of a strapping twenty-year-old son. At fifty, in a police line-up (heaven forbid) she could have passed for thirty-five.

At fifty-eight she met James Elliott and was astounded by the strength of her feelings for him. When, on their third date, he mentioned in passing that he was forty-three, Bibi had been stunned. James' neatly trimmed beard had fooled her; she had put him at fifty.

And she liked him so much. *Really* liked him. The prospect of losing him was unbearable.

Panicking, she told James she was forty-six.

The repercussions of her spur-of-the-moment fib had been endless. No longer could Bibi relate the story of the day her father had come home from the war. Memories of her teenage years were hastily rejigged. Her entire past had needed to be unceremoniously hauled forward a decade-and-a-bit.

And since owning up to a thirty-seven-year-old son was out of the question – 'What, you mean you had him when you were *nine*?' – Bibi had been forced to lop a few years off his age too.

Patrick hadn't been thrilled.

'Is this a joke?' he had demanded. 'Ma, you're mad. It'll never work.'

But Bibi wasn't joking. She was desperate.

'It will, it will. He doesn't suspect a thing. Anyway, you only have to be twenty-nine. I've already told James I had you at seventeen.'

Only the fact that his mother was so obviously happy again for the first time in years persuaded Patrick to go along with the ludicrous charade.

'It won't last,' he had warned her. 'You'll be caught out sooner or later.'

Bibi hugged him.

'Not if we're clever I won't.'

And, miraculously, she hadn't been caught out. Everyone played their part, all Bibi's friends kept her shameful secret to themselves and Bibi kept her passport and driving licence locked securely out of sight. She and James were a couple, happier together than any other couple she knew. From time to time, referring to the three-year age gap between them, he lovingly called her his older woman. From time to time as well, he asked Bibi to marry him.

If she could have done so without him finding out how old she really was, Bibi would have been up that aisle like a shot. As it was, she insisted she preferred living in sin.

'For God's sake, tell him,' an exasperated Patrick had urged just before Christmas. 'He'll understand. After all this time, how can your age matter? It's you he loves, not your date of birth.'

36

But Bibi flatly refused to even consider telling James the truth. She couldn't take that risk. There was too much to lose.

Besides, some ages sounded worse than others. James teased her enough about being forty-eight.

And she was sixty.

Could anything, Bibi wondered with a shudder, sound worse than that?

Chapter 6

Once Dulcie had made up her mind about the party she threw herself into organising it with enthusiasm.

She decided to hold it at Brunton Manor. Home was out of the question if the party was to be a surprise – immersed in his work he may be, but even Patrick's suspicions might be aroused by the sight of a mobile disco being set up in the sitting room and Dulcie sweating away in the kitchen sticking a million sausages on to sticks.

Anyway, sweating away in the kitchen wasn't Dulcie's forte. Eating food was more her line of country than preparing it. Far better to let the Brunton Manor catering team take care of all that.

Better still, she wouldn't have to clear up disgusting party debris the next day.

'You'll come, won't you?' said Dulcie when she rang Pru.

Pru hesitated. 'What does that mean? Who are you inviting?'

'Loads of people!'

'I mean just me, or me and Phil?'

They hadn't spoken since the awkward showdown at Pru's house. Dulcie chewed her lip.

'Whichever. Just you, if you'd prefer. Or both of you.' Ouch, she'd chewed too hard. 'Um . . . do you want to bring Phil?'

'He's my husband. Of course I'd like him to be there.' Pru sounded stilted.

'Well, that's fine.'

'But only if you're going to be nice to him. I mean it, Dulcie.

No snide remarks. No digs. Not from you and not from Liza either. I couldn't bear it. You both have to promise to behave.'

It was on the tip of Dulcie's tongue to remark that if anyone should be promising to behave it was Phil. Heroically she kept her opinion to herself.

'I promise.' Heck, she felt like a schoolgirl being told off for smoking in the toilets. 'And Liza will too. We'll both be . . . angelic. On our very best behaviour,' she assured Pru. 'We'll treat Phil like a king.'

King Rat, thought Dulcie as she put the phone down. Maybe she'd invite Rentokil along to the party. A spot of poison slipped into Phil's drink might just do the trick.

Dulcie was wrapping up the box containing Patrick's laser printer on the morning of the party when the phone rang. Armed to the teeth with Sellotape, she had used up at least three miles of foiled paper and six miles of curly ribbon. Cooking might not be her thing but if she said so herself, she wrapped a mean present.

Patrick knew what was inside the box, of course. Not trusting Dulcie to come back with the right one, he had gone to Computerworld and bought the printer himself.

Still, it was what he wanted and it was spectacularly wrapped. As soon as Dulcie had put the finishing touches to the sides she was going to cart it down to the club where he could open it tonight.

The phone was still ringing. Dulcie grabbed the receiver, fantasising briefly that it was one of their friends asking if they could bring Kevin Costner along to the party.

But life was somehow never that thrilling. It was Eddie Hammond, the manager of Brunton Manor. Sounding agitated.

'Dulcie, bit of a hitch. I'm really sorry about this—'

'What?' yelped Dulcie, all of a sudden agitated too. If the club had been burned to the ground, where would she hold the party tonight? More to the point, where was she going to spend the rest of her life?

'It's the kitchen staff, darling. Gone down like ninepins. Fingers crossed it's just a virus but the health inspector's thrown a wobbler. Until salmonella's ruled out, he's shut down the kitchen. So . . . ah . . . no food, I'm afraid, tonight.'

Uh oh, panic attack. Dulcie went hot and cold all over.

'No food?' She wanted to cry. 'What, nothing at all? Eddie, we can't have a party without food!'

'I know, I know,' he said soothingly. 'Sweetheart, I can't tell you how bad I feel about this. But you've got a few hours to go . . . that's why I rang as soon as I could. If you organise your own buffet you can bring it down here yourself. I checked with the health inspector and he said that would be fine.'

'Oh terrific. Hooray for the health inspector,' howled Dulcie. 'Maybe he'd like to whip up a couple of dozen quiches in his tea break.'

But it didn't matter how sympathetic Eddie Hammond was to her plight, there was nothing he could do to help.

So Dulcie did the only thing she could do. She phoned Liza and Pru.

Liza was out. She had driven up to London to meet her editor, Dulcie remembered as soon as she got the answering machine, and wouldn't be back before seven. Typical.

But Pru was at home, thank God. Pru with the best-stocked kitchen cupboards in Bath.

'How many guests?' she asked, cutting through Dulcie's anguished wailings.

'About a hundred.'

'Right, I'll make a start here. I can rustle up rice salad, pasta salad, stuffed baked potatoes, that kind of thing—'

'That won't be enough.' Dulcie knew she sounded ungrateful. She didn't mean to, but her heart was in her boots already. Any minute now it was going to start burrowing through the carpet.

'Of course it won't. That's why I'm doing it. Leaving you free to shop. Got a pen and paper?' said Pru, admirably unfazed by the crisis. But that was because it was all right for Pru, thought Dulcie, it wasn't her crisis. 'Now, start making a list. I'll tell you what to buy.'

God bless M&S, thought Dulcie an hour later as she steered her trolley expertly past an old dear with a basket-on-wheels. This was okay, this was fine, her heart was back in its rightful place and she was actually beginning to enjoy herself.

Buying up Marks & Spencer's food department was far more fun, too, than simply dropping in to pick up a couple of chicken tikkas and a lemon drizzle cake. Cramming a trolley with baguettes, boxes of hors d'oeuvres, bags of prawns, packets of Parma ham and twenty different kinds of cheeses was an exhilarating experience. No longer panicking, Dulcie meandered happily amongst the fresh fruit and veg, choosing the ripest Charentais melons, the reddest, glossiest strawberries . . .

A male voice in her ear made her jump.

'Can I come?'

Dulcie spun round. Good grief, it was James.

'James!'

Three lemons and a bottle of tonic were rolling around in the bottom of his wire basket. Dulcie remembered that he and Bibi had guests for dinner themselves.

James, meanwhile, was studying the contents of her overloaded trolley with interest. Grinning, he said again, 'Can I come?'

'Come where?' Dulcie prayed she wasn't blushing.

'Well, call it spooky intuition if you like, but something tells me you're having a party.' His eyes twinkled; he and Dulcie had always got on like a house on fire. 'Either that or an attack of rampant bulimia.'

Dithering mentally, she decided it would be safe to tell him the truth. He and Bibi were otherwise engaged tonight, after all.

'It's a surprise party for Patrick,' Dulcie explained. 'At Brunton Manor. All very last minute,' she added hastily, so as not to offend him. 'I only decided to do it yesterday. And yes, of course you're both invited. Eight o'clock tonight, it's going to be great . . . Patrick doesn't have a clue . . .'

She beamed up at James, waiting for him to frown and say, 'Damn, we won't be able to make it.'

Instead, beaming back at her, he said, 'That's terrific. Look, we've got a couple of dinner guests but they'll be gone by ten. They have to catch the last train to Oxford. What we'll do is drop them at the station and drive straight over. Better late than never, eh?'

Dulcie was by this time dithering in earnest. If she was going to conjure up a plausible excuse – a reason why James and Bibi couldn't possibly come to Patrick's party – she had to do it in the next few milliseconds.

She stared up at James, wide-eyed and in desperate need of inspiration . . .

Bong. Too late.

James looked concerned.

'Are you all right, Dulcie?'

'Er . . . um . . .'

'Come on, you must have everything you need by now.' Taking control of her piled-up trolley, he began steering it in the direction of the checkouts. 'The least I can do is help you load this lot into your car.'

Dulcie emptied the food on to the conveyor belt and James stood at the other end packing it into bags far more efficiently than she could have done.

The solution came to her as she was unloading the last armful of French sticks.

It was simple. All she had to do was phone Bibi and warn her. Then Bibi could either plead exhaustion or feign sudden illness.

Sudden illness might be better, then James would be worried about her. This meant he wouldn't leave Bibi at home and come along to the party by himself.

Dulcie glanced across at him, still diligently packing bags at the other end of the checkout. That was the thing about

James, he was considerate. Kind. Devoted to Bibi.

He really was a lovely man.

If Bibi could only bring herself to tell him her dark secret, they could marry.

Inspiration, like a bolt of lightning, struck for the second time. In that moment Dulcie knew what she had to do.

Because Bibi never *would* tell James.

The answer had to be, therefore, to let James find out for himself.

And what better place for it to happen than at a party, when everyone was already in carefree party mood . . . and where Bibi's little white lie could be laughed off?

Dulcie knew she was right. It was a brilliant solution. James would know the truth at last and it wouldn't make a scrap of difference to his feelings for Bibi. And Bibi would be so relieved. And grateful.

I was meant to bump into James today, Dulcie decided.

Everything happens for a reason. This is fate, taking a hand.

'I've had an idea,' she told James as they loaded the green and white carrier bags into the boot of the car. 'Bibi doesn't know yet about the party. Don't tell her, okay?'

James looked amused. 'Why not?'

'It'll be more fun! Just say it's a wedding anniversary do for friends of yours and bring her along.' Dulcie's eyes were shining. 'Then, when you walk in, it'll be extra special. A double surprise.'

Pru had worked flat out all afternoon. At five o'clock, having done as much as she could, she jumped into the bath. By six she was dressed and ready. All she had to do now was load the food into the car, take it over to Brunton Manor and help Dulcie lay everything out.

She phoned Phil's office but he was out.

'Showing a client around a few properties,' said Janet, his secretary. 'Try him on his mobile.'

No joy there either; the mobile was switched off. Instead,

43

Pru scribbled a note explaining what had happened and left it on the kitchen table. When Phil came home he could shower and change and follow her down to the club in his own time.

In one way, Pru was glad the food crisis had arisen. Coming to the rescue as she had meant Dulcie would be so grateful she wouldn't dare say anything awful about Phil. She knew she had Dulcie's solemn promise not to anyway, but a little extra emotional blackmail never went amiss.

Dulcie was already there when Pru staggered into the banqueting hall with her arms full of salad bowls.

'Hey, you look fab!' Rushing across, she helped Pru unload and gave her a hug. 'And these look brilliant too. You are an angel. Honestly, Pru, that git of a husband of yours doesn't deserve you.'

Pru leapt away as if she'd been electrocuted.

'If you're going to start—'

'I'm not, I'm not.' Dulcie grabbed her back and kissed her noisily on both cheeks. 'It's okay, I'm just getting it out of my system before jerk-of-the-year turns up.' She grinned. 'Would I say anything to upset you when you've done all this for me?'

Probably.

'Not if you don't want a bowl of rice salad over your head,' said Pru.

'Anyway,' Dulcie changed the subject, 'you do look fab. Love the dress.'

Pru was pleased. The white silk jersey was clingier than her usual style but as ever she had been too afraid of hurting the sales assistant's feelings to walk out of the shop without it. Now she was glad she'd been a wimp. Dulcie and the sales girl had been right; it was a great dress.

'Love yours too,' said Pru, cheering up. 'And the hair. Very chic.'

Pink-faced and shiny from her exertions, Dulcie was wearing an orange sweatshirt over a lime-green elongated vest. Her short hair stuck up at weird angles and she had a shopping list scrawled in mauve felt-tip up one arm.

She checked her watch.

'Half six. I'd better get a move on. Look, can you finish putting everything out? Liza's promised to turn up before seven thirty and everyone else has orders to be here by eight. I'll arrive with Patrick just after eight. Any problems, give me a ring.'

'Right.' Pru was struck by the look of excitement on her friend's face. She smiled. 'You can't wait, can you?'

'I promise you,' Dulcie declared dramatically, 'this is going to be a night to remember. And whatever happens, don't get drunk and pass out before ten o'clock.' Her green eyes sparkled. 'There are going to be a couple of late arrivals. Call it a special guest appearance.'

'Who?'

The temptation to confide in Pru was overwhelming. Manfully, Dulcie held back. Instead she held a finger to her lips.

'Ssh, not another word. Top secret.' She winked at Pru. 'After all, if you're having a party, why settle for one surprise when you can have two?'

Eddie Hammond wasn't a great one for examining his reflection but in the aerobics studio, which was mirrored from floor to ceiling on three sides, he didn't have a lot of choice. While he waited to speak to Diana, Brunton's terrifyingly fit aerobics instructor, he studied himself without much enthusiasm in the nearest of the mirrored walls.

Terrifyingly unfit was the phrase that sprang to mind.

Or maybe overweight, overstressed and over forty.

Eddie tried sucking in his stomach but all it did was make him feel dizzy, since you couldn't suck in your stomach and breathe at the same time.

He gave up, combed his fingers through his greying hair instead, briefly closed his baggy eyes and mopped his perspiring forehead with a handkerchief. No wonder he looked harassed, he thought gloomily. Who wouldn't be, faced with a

45

day like this, his first crisis since moving down to Bath and taking over the running of Brunton Manor two months earlier? His staff were still dropping like flies, the health inspector was on his tail, the publicity could be disastrous for the club . . .

Eddie's smile was rueful. It was no good, he could go on making excuses until he was blue in the face but he couldn't get away from the fact that stress or no stress, this was the way he looked. This was him. He *was* unfit, overweight and over forty. Okay, forty-five.

Let's face it, he was no Jean-Claude van Damme.

A flash of lime green and orange made Eddie jump. Dulcie, whose reflection he had glimpsed in one of the other mirrors, stopped and stuck her head around the glass door.

'Everything okay?' Eddie prayed she hadn't tracked him down in order to report some new catastrophe.

But Dulcie, thank God, was grinning.

'No problems. All under control,' she told Eddie, entertained by the sight of him studying his own reflection as intently as any teenager. 'The rest of the food's being set out and I'm off home for a bath. Didn't know you'd signed up,' Dulcie added.

'Signed up?' Eddie frowned. 'For what?'

'One of Diana's aerobics classes.' She winked. 'I can't wait to see you in a leotard.'

Amused, Eddie said, 'There's about as much chance of that as of seeing you in one.'

As he spoke, Diana and the next scheduled class spilled out of the changing room, heading down the corridor towards the studio. Dulcie, who lived in terror of waking up and finding out she'd got drunk the night before and signed up for one of Diana's classes, said, 'Help, Cruella's coming. I'll see you later.' She waggled her fingers at Eddie. 'And cheer up, okay? Everything's fine. It's going to be a night to remember.'

Chapter 7

The great advantage of surprise parties, Pru discovered with
some relief, was the way they got everyone there on time.
Instead of having to endure that awkward first couple of hours
of guests trickling in, all leaving it as late as possible because
nobody wanted to be the first, everyone had piled in through
the doors dead on five to eight.

Everyone except Phil.

Ducking out to reception at five past, Pru tried ringing home
again. No reply. Ditto his mobile.

But she didn't have time to start worrying. Dulcie and Patrick
had arrived.

'What's going on?' Patrick was looking suitably confused.
'I thought the table at Langham's was booked for eight
fifteen . . . Hello, Pru, what are you doing here? Did Dulcie
tell you it was my birthday? Come and give me a big kiss.'

'Right, that's enough,' barked Dulcie moments later. She
seized his arm. 'No time for snogging. As soon as I've booked
a sunbed for tomorrow, we're off. Pru, where's Anna?'

Pru pointed obediently in the direction of the banqueting
hall.

'Through there.'

'Do I deserve you?' Patrick murmured, wrapping his arms
around his wife as they danced to something slow and slushy.
Dulcie was looking amazing in a skin-tight little black dress
and the kind of seriously high heels he liked. Her black hair
was slicked back Valentino style. The diamond studs he had

given her for Christmas glittered in her ears. Dulcie had the figure, the looks and the legs; what's more, she knew how to flaunt them.

And she had gone to the trouble of organising a surprise party for him, even to the extent of doing all the food. Well, with a little help from Pru.

Patrick was touched.

Dulcie stuck her tongue out at him.

'Deserve me? Of course you don't.' His dark-brown eyes narrowed with amusement.

'I do love you.'

Patrick didn't say it often, he wasn't that kind of man. But Dulcie knew he did.

It was just a shame he loved work more.

'I should bloody well think so.' Reaching up, she flicked his ear lobe with her tongue. It had been so long, she'd quite forgotten how nice Patrick was to dance with. If she wasn't so excited about James and Bibi's imminent arrival she might have put the pleasurable churning sensation in her stomach down to the effect of her husband's body pressed against hers.

'Come on then.' Patrick gave her waist a pinch. 'Your turn. Only fair.'

It was a long-standing joke between them. When she said it, Patrick didn't. When he said it, she didn't.

But this was the last birthday they would celebrate together. On impulse, Dulcie gave it one final try.

'I love you too.'

Patrick looked startled.

She went on, 'But I'd love you more if you worked less.'

'Dulcie—'

He had that look on his face, the look she had come to know oh so well during the course of the last couple of years. The one, Dulcie thought bitterly, that was about to end their marriage.

'Not a lot less,' she urged, 'just a bit.'

'Sweetheart, don't you think I would if I could?' She

recognised the note of exasperation in his voice as well. They had had this argument too often in the past. The novelty had worn off. 'I'm building up a business. It's tough.'

Damn right it's tough, thought Dulcie.

'But I'm doing it for us,' Patrick went on. This was how he always justified himself; she could have recited the words by heart. Dulcie hated this bit. She hated the way he always managed to make her feel like a spoilt child. She wasn't selfish. Well, not very. She just wanted a husband she could see occasionally, and talk to. She wanted a normal married life.

'Okay, I know the rest,' said Dulcie before he could launch into the next phase of his defence. 'Let's not argue. This is your party. And we can't stay here smooching, either.'

Patrick, as keen to change the subject as she was, looked affronted.

'Why not? It's my birthday.'

'You're supposed to spread yourself around. Smooch with other women.' Dulcie detached herself from his grasp and peered around. 'Go on, there's Pru. That bastard husband of hers still hasn't turned up.'

Pru was glad she was dancing with Patrick when Phil eventually appeared. Well, she'd rather not have been there at all, but dancing with Patrick was at least better than standing on her own propping up a wall.

Not a lot better, considering it was the most horrendous moment of her life, but a bit.

Pru felt the blood drain from her cheeks. Phil was drunk. Seriously drunk.

And . . . oh God . . . Blanche was at his side.

'Shit, *shit*,' breathed Liza, startling the banker she had been introduced to only moments before. She watched in horror as Phil shambled on to the dance floor.

Blanche was wearing the infamous rubber skirt and spike heels higher than Dulcie's. Her emerald-green halter-neck top was studded with rhinestones. Despite the stilettos, she was doing a good job of keeping Phil upright.

'Pru, sorry he's late. I bumped into him in the Forester's Arms. He kept saying he was supposed to be here so I put him in my car. You won't be cross with him, will you? He's had a few, but no real harm done.'

Pru, who had never been cross with Phil in her life, stared at him. Across the room, dimly, she heard Dulcie say, 'Oh Christ.'

Blanche's ex-husband had drunk for England. She had had plenty of practice with piss-heads; compared with her ex, Phil was only tiddly. Planting him expertly upright, she turned to leave.

'Okay, Pru? I'll be off then.'

Phil took one look at the frozen expression on Pru's face and swung round like a cartoon drunk, grabbing her back again.

'No you won't. Don't go. Stay and dance.'

'Really, I can't.' Blanche shook him off.

'Come back!' roared Phil. He gestured recklessly in Pru's direction. 'Look at her, Miss Prim-and-bloody-proper . . . Blanche, I want you to stay. I don't love her, I love you. I don't *want* her any more . . . I WANT YOU . . .'

Patrick couldn't do anything – he was holding on to Pru. Instead Dulcie launched herself like a rocket across the dance floor and punched Phil Kasteliz so hard he toppled over.

'I'm sorry, I'm so sorry,' muttered Blanche, not looking at Dulcie. Evidently as strong as an ox, she hauled Phil to his feet and all but carried him out of the room. By the door, she encountered Liza.

'I shouldn't have brought him. This wasn't meant to happen. I was only trying to help.'

Liza's voice dripped with derision.

'Oh well, that's all right then. Give yourself a pat on the back, you've done your good deed for the night.'

Pru wasn't crying. She sat on a chair in the loo, eerily composed.

50

Except she wasn't composed, Liza realised as she handed her a massive brandy. How could she be? She must be in a state of shock.

'You're in a state of shock,' she told Pru.

'Am I?' Pru stared straight ahead, her gaze fixed on the hand dryer. All in white like a jilted bride, she shrugged. 'Probably.'

Liza felt uncomfortable. Weeping and wailing wasn't Pru's style but it would be far easier to deal with.

'What do you want to do?'

Another shrug. 'I don't know. Go home, I suppose.'

'Are you sure? Phil might be there. Stay with me tonight.' Liza felt rather heroic; she had been enjoying herself tremendously. Now it looked as if she was going to have to miss the rest of the party and take Pru back to her flat instead.

Dulcie cannoned through the door.

'He's gone. I just hit him again, out in the car park. And I told that stringy cow to fuck off too.' Her green eyes glittered. 'I said if she ever sets foot in your house again she's dead. Oh Pru, I'm so sorry it had to happen like this. And they could have *ruined* the party—'

She went to fling her arms around Pru, still sitting stiffly on her chair.

Pru flung the contents of her glass into Dulcie's face. At least that was her intention but her aim was off. Most of it splattered against the mirror above the basin.

'What the—?' Dulcie staggered backwards, stunned by Pru's reaction. It was like being spat at by a nun.

'You planned all this, didn't you?' hissed Pru. She began to shake. 'Wait until ten o'clock, you said, for an extra-special surprise. Two late arrivals. For God's sake, Dulcie, what did you think you were *playing* at?'

Liza stared at Dulcie. Surely she hadn't . . .

'Oh come on!' Dulcie howled, mopping helplessly at her wet left shoulder and brandy-spotted dress. 'They weren't the surprise! Do you seriously think I'd do something that crass?'

51

Nobody said anything. Dulcie stamped her foot in frustration. Some friends she had.

'Well I bloody wouldn't. What I'd planned was brilliant, the answer to a problem nobody else has had the guts to solve. And dammit' – she checked her watch – 'if we don't get out there we're going to miss the whole thing. It'll happen without me.'

Pru rose to her feet.

'Dulcie, I'm sorry. I can't believe I just did that.' She looked worried. 'Is your dress okay?'

'I can't believe you did it either.' Dulcie broke into a grin. 'And my dress will be fine. Just as well it wasn't egg flip.'

'Come on, let's go. We don't want to miss your big surprise,' said Pru with a ghost of a smile. 'What is it, a Chippendale for Liza?'

Bibi looked pretty shell-shocked when she arrived on James's arm and realised whose party he had brought her to. Rushing over to welcome them, Dulcie saw her eyes flicker around the hall in search of banners screaming: 40 TODAY!

To allay Bibi's fears and prevent her dragging James back out to the car, Dulcie greeted her with a kiss, whispering in her ear, 'Don't panic, all under control.'

She wasn't completely insensitive. It wasn't as if she was going to jump up on to the stage with a loud-hailer yelling, 'Hands up all those eligible for a bus pass.'

Oh no, that would be downright naff.

Subtlety was the key, Dulcie had decided. She wasn't going to say anything at all. Just wait for the revelation to casually slip out.

It casually slipped out sooner than she had expected. Having recovered from the Pru-and-Phil incident, everyone had taken to the dance floor with a vengeance. Dulcie and James were telling Bibi about the panic over the buffet and Dulcie's trolley dash around Marks & Spencer. Patrick returned with drinks for Bibi and James.

Suzannah Somers was the effervescent wife of one of Patrick's old rugby friends – from way back, when he'd had time to play rugby. She tapped Patrick on the shoulder.

'Hello, birthday boy! Dulcie, you don't mind if I borrow him, do you? My hopeless other half dances like a gorilla with gout.'

'Feel free.' Dulcie waved an indulgent arm in the direction of the dance floor.

The DJ was playing something weird Patrick had never heard before. Looking worried he said, 'Don't expect miracles.'

Suzannah giggled. 'Come on, you used to be a terrific dancer! Mind you, that was in the good old days. Before you turned forty.'

James gave Suzannah an odd look. Unable to help herself, Dulcie choked on her drink. Bibi turned white.

Patrick's laugh was loud and unconvincing. 'Suzannah, someone's been spiking your shandies.' Since the best course of action was clearly to get her out of earshot, he grabbed her hand and began hauling her on to the dance floor. 'Forty, ha ha ha. That'll be the day.'

At that moment the music stopped. Suzamah, by this time deeply puzzled, said loudly, 'Patrick, are *you* drunk? Of course you're forty. That's why we're all here.'

Patrick couldn't bear it. He danced with Suzannah to something by Babylon Zoo, whoever they might be. If this toe-curling situation had something to do with Dulcie – as he suspected it had – then Dulcie could sort it out.

Chapter 8

'What's going on?' said James, who was even more confused than Suzannah. 'Patrick isn't forty. He can't be. He's thirty-two.'

Bibi's stricken expression made Dulcie feel uncomfortable. This wasn't going as well as she had planned. Somehow, when she had envisaged this scenario, everyone had looked a lot happier.

Instead, Bibi looked as if she was about to pass out.

Panicking, desperate to get to the happy bit – and how could it be reached, until someone *said* something? – Dulcie gabbled, 'Now listen, James, it was just a harmless fib that got out of hand . . . and now the time's come to sort everything out, clear the air, start afresh—'

'Sort what out?' demanded James.

Dulcie attempted a merry laugh but it didn't quite come off.

Unable to stand this torture a moment longer, Bibi turned and left.

'Sort what out?' James repeated, his voice dangerously quiet.

'Look, women lie about their age, they do it all the time,' burbled Dulcie. 'You love Bibi, don't you? All she did was lop a few years off . . . What does it matter if she's older than she said she was? It's not as if she's done something really awful, like have an affair!'

'When I met Bibi she told me she was forty-six,' said James. 'Now you're telling me Patrick's forty. For pity's sake, Dulcie. How old does that make her?'

Dulcie cringed. She did her best to soften the blow.

'Nearly . . . um . . . sixty.'

'Nearly *sixty*! How near?'

Oh well, that hadn't worked. 'Er . . . that's it, really. Sixty.' Hurriedly she added, 'But only just.'

James closed his eyes. He looked as if he was having a bad dream and wanted desperately to wake up.

'Oh James, I know it's a shock, but is it really so terrible?'

Wearily, he opened his eyes. 'Thanks, Dulcie. I've heard enough.'

'But Bibi's still Bibi—'

'Stop it.'

'—and the only reason she wouldn't marry you was because she was scared of you finding out!'

'I'm not surprised.'

In desperation Dulcie cried, 'We only wanted you to be happy.'

'Really?' James studied her for a second. 'You've got a funny way of showing it.'

When he had gone, Liza and Pru joined Dulcie. Hovering not far behind her throughout the uncomfortable exchange, they had heard it all.

'Was that it?' said Liza. 'Was that your other surprise?'

Miserably Dulcie nodded.

'Oh dear.'

'I was trying to help.'

'Hmm. Somehow I don't think trying to help is your forte.'

Patrick had returned Suzannah to her husband. He came up to them, looking grim.

'Congratulations.'

'It needed to be done,' said Dulcie defensively.

'And with such style.'

'Oh shut up.' She was feeling got at. 'Anyway, James might be okay. Once he's over the shock.'

'You saw his face, Dulcie. Don't count on it.'

55

So much for marital solidarity.

'How can you be so horrible?' Dulcie longed to kick his shins. 'After all my hard work too. I organised this party for you. I wanted it to be memorable—'

'Oh, it's that all right. Nobody's going to forget this night in a hurry. Especially not Bibi.' Patrick's tone was derisive. 'You'll be lucky if she ever speaks to you again.'

But luck wasn't on Dulcie's side. Bibi did speak to her again.

She reappeared as Dulcie was helping herself to a quadruple gin and tonic and grumbling, 'Next time I say I'm planning a surprise party, just make sure you hit me over the head until I stop.'

Pru – who somewhat bizarrely was now comforting *her* – murmured, 'Bibi's back.'

For a split second Dulcie fantasised that everything was going to be all right. James had forgiven Bibi and Bibi had come back to thank her. There would be laughter and tears, emotional hugs and happy endings all round . . .

Extremely wishful thinking.

The fantasy skidded to a miserable halt the moment she turned and saw the stony expression on Bibi's pale, unlined face.

The atmosphere was horribly reminiscent of the gunfight at the OK Corral.

'Well, he's gone. I don't suppose I'll see him again, thanks to you.'

Dulcie shivered. Was it her imagination or had the central heating just been turned off?

'Bibi, I can't tell you how—'

'Sorry you are? Oh please.' Bibi spat the words out like loose chippings. 'You knew exactly what you were doing. You had to *meddle*, didn't you? You had to interfere.'

'But I—'

'You've wrecked my life, Dulcie. I'll never forgive you for this. I wish you'd never married Patrick.'

Oh no, this is too much, thought Dulcie. Glancing across at

Patrick – surely now he would come to her rescue? – she saw that she was on her own. Patrick had no intention of backing her up. He was staring grimly back at her, not on her side at all.

Fine.

'I wish I'd never married him too.' Dulcie's fingernails gouged into the perspiring palms of her hands. Well, it was the truth. She may as well say it now. She'd started so she'd finish. 'Still, we can soon sort that out. A trip to the solicitor, a quickie divorce . . . and bingo, no more interfering daughter-in-law.' To make sure Patrick understood, she turned her gaze on him and concluded bitterly, 'No more bored-to-the-back-teeth wife.'

Apart from their immediate circle the rest of the party was still going great guns. Eddie Hammond, who had been busy organising tomorrow's squash tournament, spotted Dulcie and Patrick through a gap in the crowd and came up, munching a Marks & Spencer spring roll.

'Everyone enjoying themselves? Having a jolly time?' He gave Dulcie's shoulder an encouraging squeeze. 'Darling, the food's great. You must have worked your gorgeous fingers to the bone. I hope this husband of yours appreciates all the trouble you went to.'

Bibi turned and stalked out without uttering another word.

Dulcie, not trusting herself to speak, took a gulp of her drink.

Linking her arm through Eddie's, Liza drew him diplomatically away, murmuring, 'How about a little dance?'

Dulcie went in search of a much-needed refill. Then she perched on the edge of the table upon which Patrick's laser printer was displayed and fidgeted fretfully with a strand of the blue and silver ribbon she had used to decorate it.

The trouble with spur-of-the-moment emotional outbursts, she realised, was nobody believed you meant what you said. It hadn't occurred to Patrick that she actually wanted a divorce. He thought she was just in a strop.

Well, thought Dulcie, he'll find out soon enough.

She watched him make his way towards her, still wearing his I'm-the-headmaster-and-you're-in-detention look.

'Terry and Jean are leaving. They have to get back for the baby-sitter.'

'Better go and wave them off then.'

'Are you coming?'

She felt her bottom lip jut out practically of its own accord. She was fourteen again.

'They're your friends, not mine.'

'Come on, Dulcie, don't sulk. That doesn't solve anything.'

She longed to hurl her gin and tonic in his face, but Pru had been there, done that already tonight. It was no longer original.

Besides, her glass was empty.

She watched Patrick heave a sigh. She was clearly being extra troublesome. Detention might not be punishment enough. Maybe she was going to be expelled.

'Look, you brought this on yourself,' he told her wearily.

Dulcie snapped. She jumped down from the table, gripping the sides with her fingers. Lifting it was easy.

The super-duper laser printer slid backwards and landed with a crash on the floor.

Turning, she regarded the shattered printer with immense satisfaction.

'So did you.'

Liza woke up the next morning cold and with a crowded flat. Dulcie, lying next to her, had hogged the duvet. Pru, who had taken the sofa, stood in the doorway holding mugs of tea.

'Makes a change,' Liza remarked cheerfully, 'waking up next to someone who doesn't have hairy legs.' She prodded Dulcie, who was snoring, and looked at Pru. 'How are you feeling, or is that a stupid question?'

'Headache,' grumbled Dulcie. 'Ouch.'

'Not you.'

'Okay.' When they were both upright, Pru handed them their

tea. 'Better, at least, now I've had time to think.'

Dulcie underwent a lightning replay of last night. Hell, it really had happened. The fan had been well and truly hit.

'This is it then.' She sipped and burnt her tongue. 'Here we are, all girls together. Welcome to the singles club.'

Pru plonked herself down on the end of the bed. She had been drinking tea for the last five hours.

'I'm not single.' She looked defensive.

'Oh come on,' exclaimed Dulcie. 'You can't stay with Phil! Not after what he did to you last night.'

'He didn't mean it. He was drunk, that's all.' Pru knew from experience what Phil was like after one of his infrequent benders. He would wake up feeling hopelessly sorry for himself, unable to recall much, if anything, of the night before. He would beg for Heinz tomato soup and spend the day being penitent and little-boyish. He would also be enormously affectionate towards her.

The pattern was always the same. And although she was ashamed to admit it, even to herself, while she hated the binges, Pru actually enjoyed the recovery periods after them. They made her feel wanted and secure.

'He humiliated you in front of everyone,' Liza protested, but with less force than last time. She knew when she was wasting her breath.

'My marriage is worth fighting for. Phil didn't mean those things he said last night. He won't even remember saying them.'

'You're mad,' Dulcie said flatly.

Pru looked at her.

'Are you really going to leave Patrick?'

'Too right I am.' Dulcie thought for a moment. She had stalked out of the party, hadn't she? She wasn't at home, she was here. 'I already have.'

Pru stood up, looking waif-like in one of Liza's oversized white T-shirts, but utterly determined.

'In that case,' she told Dulcie, 'you're the one who's mad.'

Chapter 9

Dulcie was in no hurry to get home. Sod Patrick, let him stew a bit longer, let the sanctimonious bastard wonder where she was.

But her conscience was pricking her on another matter. Okay, *the* other matter. Not that it had really been her fault. Her intentions had been good.

Still, Dulcie knew she would feel a lot better if she could solve at least one of the ticklish problems last night's party had thrown up.

She phoned James on his mobile.

'James, hi, it's me! Where are you?'

He didn't seem thrilled to hear from her. Somehow she could tell.

'Is that your idea of being subtle, Dulcie? If you mean am I at home tucked up in bed with Bibi, then no, I am not. I'm at the Berkeley Hotel.'

Lord, he sounded positively grim. Dulcie pulled a face and did a thumbs-down at Liza, who was getting ready to go out. Wasting no time as usual, she was meeting last night's banker for lunch.

'Right, okay, stay where you are.' Dulcie decided she wouldn't waste time either. She would be bold and assertive. She was going to force James to see sense if she had to hammer it into his head with one of her high heels.

'Dulcie—'

'Don't move, I'm on my way,' she said very firmly indeed. 'I'll meet you in the lobby in twenty minutes.'

Dulcie found herself on the receiving end of some pretty dubious attention when she made her way through reception at the Berkeley. There was no sign of James so she settled herself on a sofa by one of the long windows. Within the space of five minutes she was asked by a porter, a snooty receptionist and the manager if they could help her in any way, madam.

'I'm meeting someone,' Dulcie told the manager pleasantly. 'I'm not on the game. The reason I'm wearing this dress is because I left my husband last night, rather unexpectedly, and I didn't happen to have a change of clothes with me, okay? I stayed with a friend who's a good six sizes bigger than me and if you think I'd wear something the size of a circus tent just to keep your geriatric guests happy . . . well, you couldn't be more wrong.'

James appeared behind the manager.

'Troublemaking again, Dulcie?'

He looked awful, as if he hadn't slept for a week. The manager, glaring at Dulcie, muttered some insincere apology for an apology and melted away.

Dulcie glared after him. 'I'm not a troublemaker. He's a pompous git.'

'Well, at least try and pull your skirt down. Everyone can see your knickers.'

'Do them a power of good.' Dulcie looked truculent. 'At least I'm wearing some.'

Ignoring this, James waited until she'd managed to cover up at least a couple more inches of thigh. The black velvet dress certainly had its work cut out. He ordered coffee from a waitress and lit a cigarette.

'Can I have one?' In times of stress Dulcie always liked to smoke; it made her feel like Bette Davis. Pre-1950, of course. Before those lines and wrinkles had set in.

'No. Why are you here, Dulcie?'

'To make you see sense.'

He didn't smile.

'I'm forty-five. Bibi is sixty. For God's sake, how sensible does that sound to you?'

Déjà vu loomed. Dulcie prayed she could come up with something original, some dazzling new tack she hadn't already tried.

'Yes, but she doesn't look sixty, she doesn't sound sixty, she doesn't *act* sixty!'

Was it her imagination or was James wincing every time she uttered the s-word?

He sounded irritated. 'Obviously she doesn't, otherwise she would never have got away with it for as long as she did.'

'There you go, then.'

'Dulcie, that isn't the point. Not the whole point, anyway. Don't you see? Bibi lied to me—'

'It wasn't a lie,' Dulcie put in hurriedly, 'just a fib.'

'It was a lie. A big one. I thought we had no secrets from each other. Now I find out our whole relationship has been built on a lie. Relationships are all about *trust*, Dulcie. How can I ever believe anything she tells me now? She could be lying. She's an expert.'

'James, she wouldn't! That was her only secret, believe me!'

'Was it?' He stubbed out his cigarette with a shaking hand and immediately lit another. 'But that's the thing, Dulcie. How would I ever know?'

Phil was sprawled across the sofa when Pru let herself into the house. A half-empty bowl of tomato soup, several bread rolls and a packet of paracetamol littered the coffee table. Strewn across the floor in front of him was a sheaf of letters.

Along with almost everyone else, it seemed, Phil was still wearing last night's clothes.

He looked pretty rough, too.

'Hello.' Pru prayed she didn't sound as nervous as she felt. 'How are you feeling?'

Phil picked up one of the letters and glanced at it, avoiding Pru's gaze.

'Sick.'

'Oh. More soup?'

This was normally when he held his arms out to her, gave her his little-boy look and said sorrowfully, 'Pru, give me a cuddle. I don't feel very well.'

Instead he said, 'I meant it, you know. That stuff last night.'

'Wh-what stuff?'

'Come on, Pru! I might not be able to remember saying it, but Blanche assures me I did. Anyway, it's the truth. I'm getting out of here. I'm sorry if I showed you up in front of your friends, but you can't plan these things. Sometimes they just happen.'

Pru couldn't believe it. This wasn't what Phil was supposed to say. Oh God, this was awful, *awful* . . .

'You're moving in with Blanche?'

He shrugged. 'I suppose so. Probably. I just know I have to get out of here.'

'But . . . but . . .'

'Look, I'm sorry.' For the first time his bloodshot eyes met hers. She saw weariness in them, and guilt. 'You're going to have to get out of here too.'

'*What?*'

Phil held the letter in his hand out to her.

'Go on, take it. And don't worry,' he gestured dismissively at the others on the floor, 'there's plenty more where that came from. Help yourself, read as many as you like. Take your pick.'

Shaking violently, wondering how on earth this could be happening to her, Pru read the first letter.

Then the second.

And the third.

She read all of them, forcing herself to keep going until she reached the end.

It was unbelievable. Phil owed money everywhere. The gambling she had always taken to be a harmless pastime had clearly rocketed out of control.

'I didn't know you'd remortgaged the house,' she said stupidly.

'Why would you?' Phil, the traditionalist, had always taken care of the bills.

Well, until he'd stopped paying them and started stuffing them into the dustbin instead.

'Anyway, now you see why you have to get out.' He shrugged. 'This place is being repossessed on Tuesday.'

'But they can't—'

'Don't be so bloody naive,' Phil shouted at her. 'Of course they can. Anyway, losing the house is the least of my worries. By this time next week I could be jobless, car-less . . . minus a few other vital bits and pieces too, if that mob from the casino have their way.'

In the space of five minutes Pru had lost her home, her husband . . . her whole life.

'How much altogether?' She spoke through chattering teeth. 'How much do you owe?'

Phil shook his head. 'You don't want to know.'

'Oh God.'

'Look, it's a hiccup, that's all. I was doing okay until last summer. Then I hit a bad patch. The longer it lasted the bigger the bets had to be to cover my losses. But it'll come good again, you'll see.'

His eyes had lit up. God, thought Pru, even talking about it makes him more cheerful.

'Phil, you have to go to Gamblers Anonymous.'

'No I don't. Listen, my luck has to change soon. It *has* to. Then as soon as that happens, I'll get the house back—'

Pru's eyes brimmed with tears.

'Is this why you're doing it? You're leaving me because you're ashamed of what's happened?.' She felt a wild surge of hope. 'Phil, gambling is an illness, you mustn't blame yourself! Together we can get through this, we can get through anything—'

'You've got it wrong.' Phil shook his head. 'This isn't to

64

protect you. I'm going because I don't want to be married to you any more. I used to think you were my type. But you aren't,' he concluded coldly. 'Blanche is.'

Dulcie knew she was really going to go ahead and do it when she arrived home and Patrick, looking supremely unconcerned, said, 'Where have you been, stayed at Liza's I suppose?'

So much for passion, possessiveness, an explosion of red-blooded jealousy, thought Dulcie.

She imagined his reaction if she told him she'd spent the night being happily ravished by the Bath first fifteen. That would capture Patrick's attention all right. 'Really? What, in the clubhouse? Did you happen to get a look at their computer system while you were there?'

Explosions of red-blooded jealousy weren't Patrick's scene.

'Yes, at Liza's.' Dulcie couldn't even be bothered to make up a more riveting story. What was the point?

'Coffee?' said Patrick, when she followed him into the kitchen. 'Kettle's just boiled.'

This was his contribution towards clearing the air. It was how they overcame arguments. A bit of stilted small talk executed in an I'm-right-and-you're-wrong-but-I'll-forgive-you kind of voice, followed by a hug and a kiss. Then everything would be back to normal.

Except this time it wasn't going to happen.

'No thanks, said Dulcie, 'but I'd love a divorce.'

'Sure you wouldn't prefer a KitKat?'

Patrick had his back to her. She watched him pour boiling water into a mug. He was wearing a dark-green and white rugby shirt and his semi-respectable jeans, the ones patched together at the bum.

Oh, she was going to miss that bum.

Dulcie sat down, all of a sudden feeling terribly tired. It had been an eventful morning so far and it wasn't over yet.

'That wasn't a joke,' she said, when she finally had his attention. 'Come on, Patrick. Look at the way things have been.

This marriage isn't working, you know that as well as I do. Time to call it a day.'

It was a no-win situation. If there was anything more futile than trying to knit fog, it was persuading Dulcie to change her mind. Patrick hadn't been married to her for seven years without learning this much. Once Dulcie made a decision, that was that. Nothing he could do or say would have any effect.

He did try, but not for long. Dulcie was immovable and Patrick couldn't bring himself to beg. Pride was one reason. Another was the knowledge that – as far as Dulcie was concerned – there was no bigger turn-off in the world than a grovelling man.

So instead he had remained outwardly calm and heard her out. Oh yes, Dulcie's mind was definitely made up.

'Okay, if that's what you want,' said Patrick at last, his tone neutral. Anyway, how could he argue? She had a point, he *had* neglected her. The knowledge that he was at least partly to blame for all this had knocked him for six.

Dulcie looked at him. 'Fine, that's settled then.' She bit her lip, determined not to cry. 'Good.'

'Are you going to spend the rest of the day in there?' she shouted, hours later, outside Patrick's office.

All the computers were switched on but Patrick hadn't done a stroke of work. All he could think about was Dulcie, who wanted out of their marriage. Who, for God's sake, wanted a *divorce* . . .

He wiped his eyes, glad he'd remembered to lock the door. The last thing he needed was for her to see him like this.

'I'm busy.'

Dulcie could have kicked the door down with her bare feet. How bloody *dare* Patrick be busy?

As she turned away she said bitterly, 'What's new?'

* * *

How can this be happening to me?

Pru stood in the doorway and gazed at the bedsitting room being offered to her. It was hideous – cramped and filthy and three floors up – but it was available. She could move in straight away.

'I'll take it,' said Pru, and even the grimy-looking landlord had the grace to sound surprised.

'You sure? When from?'

'Today.' Dry-mouthed, she opened her purse and counted out the deposit from her rapidly dwindling sheaf of notes.

'And the first month in advance.' The landlord cleared his throat, salivating at the sight of cash. When he had pocketed the notes he handed Pru the key and gestured vaguely at the cracked pane of glass in the window. 'I was . . . um . . . going to get that fixed. If I did it this afternoon, you could move in tomorrow.'

God, how can this be *happening* to me?

Pru shook her head.

'I have to move in today.'

Not even mildly curious, her new landlord shrugged and headed for the stairs.

'Suit yourself.'

Suit myself, thought Pru when he had gone. Did he really think that was what she was doing?

She had to move into this dismal room and she had to move in today.

Because between Phil, the bailiffs and the building society, she didn't really have much choice.

Chapter 10

I'm single, thought Dulcie. Weird.

Technically, of course, she was still married, but separated. Morally, as far as Dulcie was concerned, that meant she was single again. And free to do as she liked.

It was exactly five weeks since Patrick's party. Yesterday he had moved out of the house and into a flat above his office in the centre of Bath. The flat was tiny but the commuting time was four seconds. It would be two if he installed a fireman's pole.

Dulcie still felt guilty about this. She had wanted out of the marriage and he was the one who'd had to find somewhere else to live. But Patrick had insisted.

'Your parents gave us the deposit for this house,' he had reminded her. 'It's more yours than mine. Anyway, you need the wardrobe space.'

He had been so damn reasonable Dulcie had wanted to hit him. If she had been expecting him to argue, to fight to save their marriage, she would have been bitterly disappointed.

Except she knew Patrick too well.

He never would.

So, it was done. She was on the market again, the sun was shining and the sky was blue.

Bring on the dancing boys. Dulcie stuck her Reeboked feet up on the chair opposite and closed her eyes, enjoying the warmth of the sun on her face and waiting for Liza to finish her game of squash. The conservatory at Brunton Manor adjoined the bar. It was where people relaxed over Perriers –

with ice if they were being decadent – after knackering themselves on the tennis courts. It was where Dulcie – in a fetching white tracksuit – relaxed over gin and tonics and a constant supply of salt and vinegar crisps.

Liza appeared looking hot and tousled but pleased with herself.

'Hammered the bitch, six one. That'll teach her to say I've put on weight. Another drink?'

Dulcie nodded. 'And more crisps. Anyway, talking of bitches,' she waved the *Herald on Sunday*'s colour supplement at Liza, 'what happened to you? In a bit of a pooey mood, were we, when we wrote this?'

Liza cringed. The edition featuring her review of the Songbird had come out last week. Every time she read it, it sounded nastier. Her editor had been thrilled – 'This is more like it, sweetheart! This is what gets people talking' – but Liza was awash with guilt. The food hadn't been perfect, but it wasn't that bad, not as terrible as she had made out.

'That was New Year's Day, the place where I saw Phil and Blanche.'

'Oh, I get it now.' Dulcie grinned. 'It's the restaurant's fault for letting them eat there. This is your revenge.'

'Of course it isn't. It was my editor's bright idea.' Liza, looking defiant, edged towards the bar. 'He wanted me to be controversial, that's all.'

Eddie Hammond, bumping into Dulcie earlier, had checked that Liza was meeting up with her for lunch. Someone had phoned, he explained, wanting to know when she would be around.

'One of Liza's besotted boyfriends,' Dulcie guessed, but Eddie had frowned. 'I don't know about that. He didn't sound besotted to me.'

Dulcie watched Liza flirting with the bar manager. He was gay, but she still flirted with him. Even more weirdly, he was flirting back.

She hoped the phone call Eddie had taken wasn't from a hit

man, hired by the furious owners of the Songbird. It's all right for Liza's editor, urging her to be controversial, thought Dulcie; his kneecaps aren't the ones at risk.

Liza made it back to their table by the window overlooking the entrance to the club. Since she could hardly put a PS in next week's column saying 'Oh by the way, that stuff I wrote about the Songbird was a bit mean, it wasn't that bad really', she chucked the magazine on to a spare chair and changed the subject.

'So how do you feel, now Patrick's gone?'

Dulcie ripped open her crisps and started crunching.

'He was never there anyway. It'll take me a year to notice the difference.'

Bravado. Liza said, 'Are you looking for someone else?'

'No *way*.' Dulcie's silver and tiger's-eye earrings – not very sporty – rattled from side to side as she shook her head. 'Play the field, that's all I want to do. This is the start of my new life. I want to celebrate by being wild and irresponsible! I'm going to have more fun – with more men – than you could shake a stick at. Please, another relationship's the last thing I need.'

More bravado. Actually, Liza amended, more like bullshit. Until Patrick, Dulcie had spent her life crashing from one wildly unsuitable man to the next. She craved excitement but she needed security.

She wasn't nearly as independent as she liked to make out.

But this wasn't the kind of thing people liked to hear about themselves. Diplomatically Liza changed the subject yet again.

'Did you speak to Pru? Is she coming up here this afternoon?'

Dulcie shook her head. 'Gone for an interview, some awful telesales thing. Can you imagine Pru selling, for heaven's sake? She won't get it.'

'She needs to get something. That bedsit of hers is an awful tip.'

'I know, I asked her to move in with me.' Dulcie, gazing out of the window, watched a dark-green Bentley turn into the tree-lined drive. Crikey, look at it, who was visiting the club, the Queen? 'It would've been ideal but Pru turned me down, said she couldn't. She's determined to stay where she is. Something to do with pride, I suppose.' Dulcie tipped back her head, emptied the last crisp crumbs down her throat, wiped her hands on her tracksuit trousers and shrugged. 'Maybe it's just as well. If I'm going to be bringing men home all the time she might feel in the way. And I don't want my style cramped, do I?'

'Mm.' Liza was no longer paying attention. She was peering out of the window along with Dulcie as whoever was driving the Bentley screeched to a halt and parked at a reckless angle in front of the entrance.

If this is the Queen, thought Dulcie, she's desperate not to miss her step class.

It wasn't the Queen.

'Blimey,' Dulcie whistled, 'I thought only old codgers drove those kinds of cars. Mayors and stuff. I wasn't expecting something like that.'

Having jumped out of the car and made his way rapidly up the flight of stone steps leading into reception, the driver was soon lost from view. Liza, who didn't ogle like Dulcie, only had time to glimpse a fit-looking boy in his early twenties with longish dark hair. If the Bentley belonged to him, the chances were he had to be either a footballer or a rock star, Liza decided. The kind that liked to be noticed and bought his old mum a Barrett home in Basingstoke.

Dulcie was already looking excited.

'I wonder who he is?'

'No idea, but I know *what* he is.'

'What? Tell me!'

Liza grinned and retied her ponytail, which had come loose.

'Far too young for you.'

Dulcie had forgotten all about Eddie's mystery phone caller. There were so many other riveting things to discuss, like Liza's latest ex-lover (was there any bigger turn-off in the world, Liza argued, than discovering that the new Mr Wonderful in your life banked with the Co-op?) and how Pru was well shot of Phil, even if she didn't yet appreciate this fact, and which clubs in Bath Dulcie should hang out in if she wanted to meet millions of seriously hunky men.

'. . . not forgetting this place, of course,' said Dulcie charitably as she ticked venues off on her fingers. 'You do get the odd one or two dishy ones who aren't married. Oh wow—'

'What?' Liza had scooped the slice of lemon out of her drink and was busy sucking it. She raised her eyebrows at Dulcie, who'd gone all glazed and stupid-looking.

Next moment Liza realised someone was standing behind her. She swivelled round, the strip of lemon peel still dangling from one corner of her mouth.

'Are you Miss Lawson?'

'That's right.' She smiled, deftly removing the peel. 'Liza, please. And we know who you are; we saw you arriving just now. You're the boy with the Bentley.'

Up close he was even more spectacular-looking than Dulcie had suspected. Hungrily she drank in every detail: yellow-gold eyes, the colour of freshly minted pound coins; thick black lashes; cheekbones to die for; a tan like peanut butter; and a narrow, fabulously cruel-looking mouth.

Cruel mouths were Dulcie's favourite kind. She loved the transformation when they broke into a smile.

Except this one didn't seem in much danger of doing that.

'My name's Kit Berenger, Miss Lawson.'

Oo-er, thought Dulcie, none the wiser but realising from the icy tone of voice that he was every bit as cross as he looked.

Liza, who recognised the name at once, stopped smiling. All of a sudden she knew what this was about.

L. B. Berenger was a Bath-based property-development company which specialised in tacking new estates on to existing picturesque villages. The people living in the villages

72

– and those whose prized views were threatened by the springing-up of these new estates – had begun campaigning furiously against the company's bulldozer approach.

In his New Year's Eve letter to her, Alistair Kline had neglected to mention that his weekends were spent leaping into the paths of Berenger's bulldozers and grappling with security guards. Far from being shy, he had turned out to be a die-hard protester. He was eloquent too, persuading Liza – as a high-profile journalist – to write to the local paper publicly denouncing L. B. Berenger's latest plans.

She hadn't minded doing that, but weekends ankle-deep in mud with only a thermos to keep her warm weren't Liza's idea of heaven. Her relationship with Alistair Kline had lasted three weeks. Quite good, for her.

'I see,' she said now, surveying what must be the son-of-Berenger. 'And you're the heavy mob, are you? Come to tell me to mind my own business and leave your family alone to make money in peace?'

Dulcie stared at Liza. What in heaven's name did she think she was up to? If this was Liza's idea of a new chat-up line, she had to be told it completely and utterly stank.

Kit Berenger clearly thought so too. His cruel upper lip curled with distaste. 'Funny, that. You think we should be ashamed of the way we make our money. Does it never occur to you to be ashamed of the way you earn yours?'

Dulcie gazed at the pair of them, totally riveted. She'd always been a sucker for a curled lip.

'Look,' said Liza, 'I'm a journalist. My job is to write the truth as I see it. The people who already live in that village would never have moved there in the first place if they'd known it was going to be turned into Milton-bloody-Keynes.'

Kit Berenger stared hard at Liza. Finally he said, 'If you're talking about West Titherton, thirty-six houses and a mini-roundabout hardly add up to Milton Keynes. Anyway, that isn't why I'm here.'

Glancing across at the chair Dulcie was resting her feet on, he reached for the colour supplement Liza had thrown down earlier. Dulcie shivered with pleasure as his tanned arm – he was wearing a denim shirt with the sleeves rolled up – brushed against her bare ankle.

Liza wished her glass wasn't empty. Now she desperately wished he was only here to harangue her about that stupid letter to the local paper.

She didn't want to hear what was coming next.

'This,' said Kit Berenger, 'is why I'm here.'

Chapter 11

Liza's jaw tightened in self-defence. Perspiration was breaking out on her upper lip. She didn't take kindly to being sneered at by a mere boy.

'Like I said, I write the truth as I see it.'

'And does it give you a kick,' Kit Berenger snapped back, 'to write this kind of vindictive crap? Do you have any idea how hurtful it can be, or is that all part of the fun?'

'I don't—' began Liza.

'No, shut up, just listen to me. What you wrote was complete bollocks anyway. I've eaten there dozens of times and there's never been anything wrong with the food. The Songbird's a great little restaurant struggling to make a name for itself, and your review was totally out of order.'

Liza already knew that, but she was damned if she was going to admit as much now. How dare this arrogant bastard give her such a public ticking-off?

'Who runs that restaurant, your girlfriend?' she demanded furiously. 'Okay, you're on her side because I gave the place a poor review and hurt her feelings. But I'm on the other side, the customer's side. When a man scrimps and saves for a month to be able to afford to park the kids with a baby-sitter and take his wife out for a meal, he doesn't want the food to be crap, does he?'

'But the—'

'No, your turn to listen to me.' Liza pointed an accusing finger at him. 'Don't you see? That's what my job's about. I try out these places and give my honest opinion of them. If a place is good, I say it's good. But I'm telling you, I ate at the Songbird on New Year's Day. And if that married couple had spent their hard-earned cash on the meal I ordered, they'd have had their big night out ruined.'

Dulcie was still ogling away quietly in the background, admiring Kit Berenger's long legs in white Levis and Timberlands. She liked his aftershave too. The wristwatch was a bit of a let-down but he was young, she could forgive him for that. Anyway, there was definitely something cool about a man driving a Bentley and wearing a purple Swatch.

Disappointing news about the girlfriend, Dulcie thought bravely, although to be honest you'd wonder if he didn't have one. And it was sweet that he cared enough about her hurt feelings to come storming over here on her behalf.

Dulcie couldn't help noticing that Liza, not at all used to being spoken to in such a manner, was looking more and more like an outraged cat whose tail has got caught in a cat-flap.

'She isn't my girlfriend,' said Kit Berenger. 'She's my cousin.'

Dulcie cheered up at once.

'And she's worked bloody hard to get that restaurant on its feet. If you had any idea of the hours she's put in—'

Liza's lips were pressed together. 'It's a tough business.'

'I know, I know. Restaurants go under all the time.' His amber eyes bored into hers. 'But humour me, okay? Just tell me when this review came out. How long since it hit the news stands?'

Liza didn't speak.

'I'll tell you. Five days,' said Kit Berenger. 'Right, next question. Bit more tricky this time. In those five days, how many people do you suppose have phoned up and cancelled their bookings at the Songbird? Hmm?'

Dulcie began to feel sorry for Liza.

Liza shook her head.

'Come on, make a wild guess,' he coaxed silkily. 'No? Give

up? Okay, I'll tell you. Eighty-two covers. Eighty-two fucking covers in five days.'

Dulcie swallowed. She didn't know what a cover was, but all the little hairs on the back of her neck were standing to attention. Kit Berenger was awesome when he was angry. He was positively lethal . . .

'So give yourself a pat on the back, Miss Lawson. As you say, it's a tough business. And now, thanks to your hatchet job, it looks as if you've singlehandedly closed my cousin's restaurant down.'

Dulcie was beginning to get seriously on Liza's nerves. If she didn't shut up soon she was going to get a squash racket jammed down her throat.

'Cruel mouths, I just love cruel mouths.' Dulcie swooned, ticking off each dubious asset on her fingers. 'Calvin Klein aftershave, that's my favourite too. Did you recognise that was what he was wearing?'

Liza was too busy smarting furiously and thinking up brilliant ripostes. It was too late now, of course, he'd gone, but there was always the horrible possibility she might one day bump into Kit Berenger again. It didn't do any harm to keep a few ripostes up your sleeve anyway. Just in case.

'. . . and he's the exact opposite of Patrick, you know. I mean, talk about gallant. Look at the way he leapt to his cousin's defence. Patrick never leapt to my defence . . . in fact he leapt as far as possible in the other direction, that's how bloody loyal and gallant he was.'

'It's the family thing. You upset Patrick's mother. He was being loyal to her.'

'Yes, but I'm his wife!' Dulcie tore open another packet of crisps. 'Well, I was. Well, still am, I suppose . . .'

Liza wondered which would be worse if you were kidnapped and held hostage in a damp cellar for five years. Solitary confinement or being made to share with Dulcie.

'. . . anyway, you have to admit he's gorgeous. Imagine the

fantastic-looking children you'd have. God, I could definitely marry someone like him . . .'

Solitary confinement, no question.

'Whatever happened to being wild and irresponsible and changing your men as often as you change your nightie?' Liza observed drily. 'What happened to celebrating a whole new life?'

'Yeah, but what a way to celebrate,' sighed Dulcie, well ensconced on Fantasy Island now. 'And who'd need a nightie?'

Pru had a whole new life and she didn't much feel like celebrating. In the space of five weeks she had exchanged a perfect home, a loving, faithful husband (ha ha), no money worries and an N-reg Golf Cabriolet for a hideous bedsit, no husband and enough money worries to float the *Titanic*.

Ironically, she would still have forgiven Phil and stood by him. Together they could have battled their way out of debt. But in the end Pru hadn't been given that option. You could only stand by a husband who wanted you there at his side, she had belatedly discovered. If he couldn't bear the sight of you, regarded you with undisguised loathing and contempt and was only interested in the new woman in his life . . . well, there didn't seem much point.

Since a car was a necessity if she was going to find work, Pru had answered a newspaper ad and bought an ancient mini for a hundred pounds. Taxing and insuring it used up the rest of her modest savings. At least they were her savings to use up, Pru reminded herself. When they had bought the house, she had been inwardly hurt by Phil's insistence that only his name went on the mortgage. Now, thanks to his greed, his debts were his alone.

In fact, Pru discovered, becoming broke in such sudden and spectacular fashion had its weird advantages. When you spent every waking moment in a blind panic, trying desperately to figure out how you were going to cope money-wise, you didn't have much time left over to feel depressed about the fact your husband had done a bunk.

She hadn't seen Phil since the day after Dulcie's party, although she knew where he was living. With Blanche.

He wasn't working either. Pru wondered if, desperate for money, he had got caught doing some dodgy deal or other and been sacked.

She wished she could hate Phil. If she did, Pru was sure it would make her feel better.

But how can I hate him, she wondered miserably, when I'd give anything in the world to have him back?

The interview had been a nightmare, no way was she going to be offered the job.

'Come on, come on,' Pru urged through gritted teeth as she turned the key in the ignition and prayed for the engine to catch. In the last month she'd had enough practice jump-starting the Mini to go on *Mastermind* ('And your specialist subject, Mrs Kastelitz . . .?') but today she was pointing uphill. Anyway, her sadistic interviewers might be smirking out of their office windows, jeering at the moron who was as hopeless with cars as she was on the phone.

They had put a headset on Pru, given her a prompt sheet and instructed her to show them what she could do.

'Come on! Give us your sales pitch . . . show some enthusiasm!' they had roared at her. 'No, no, enthusiasm not exhaustion. Right, take a deep breath and try again! Give it all you've got! Okay, that's enough.' They had rolled their eyes at each other. 'We'll let you know.'

From the safety of her car, Pru looked up at the blank windows and mouthed bravely, 'Well, fuck you.'

The engine, evidently stunned by this act of outrageous rebellion, coughed and spluttered and came to life.

Didn't want to sell crappy conservatories anyway, Pru decided, determined to stay positive. Especially not in some frightful office where every time you made a sale you were expected to jump up on your chair and go 'Yee-haa!'

She made it home . . . *home*! by five o'clock. Pru, used to a glistening, top-of-the range, fully fitted Neff kitchen, fed fifty pence into the ancient meter and made herself a mug of tea. Clutching a copy of the evening paper in one hand and a couple of digestives in the other, she climbed into her narrow bed to keep warm.

I'll be all right, thought Pru, astonished to realise that not getting the job hadn't upset her nearly as much as she'd imagined. In fact it had quite cheered her up. So what if she wasn't cut out for high-pressure telesales? There were plenty of other things she could do.

Definitely.

It was just a question of figuring out what.

Chapter 12

A fortnight later, at six thirty on a stormy Thursday morning, Pru was on her way to work when a car roared out of nowhere at her, smashing into the passenger side of the Mini and shunting it across the road into a ditch.

The road, a mile or so from Brunton Manor, was narrow and unlit. Pru screamed as the car toppled sideways and the headlights went out, plunging her into pitch darkness. The thick scarf around her neck flopped over her face. A can of Mr Sheen, catapulting off the back seat, hit her on the back of the head.

She wasn't hurt. When she had scrambled out of the car she realised she didn't have so much as a bump or a scratch on her. It was a miracle.

It was also raining stair rods.

'. . . oh thank God! You're out . . . you're alive . . .'

A man was crashing through the blackness towards her. He slithered into the soggy ditch, colliding with Pru and almost knocking her flat.

He clutched frenziedly at her arms.

'Are you hurt? Are you okay? The car just skidded—'

'I'm all right.' Pru's teeth were chattering. 'My car isn't.'

'Don't worry, I'll sort it out.'

Pru found herself being hauled none too ceremoniously back up the slope and on to the road. Bewildered, she wondered if this meant he was a mechanic, about to roll up his sleeves and start sorting it out this minute. But could he? Surely it was going to take more than a couple of spanners and a monkey wrench to get her car out of the ditch?

81

'We'll h-have to phone the p-police,' she told him, struggling and failing to control her chattering teeth.

'No need for that. I said I'd deal with everything and I will.'

'B-but you have to inform them after an ac-ac-accident.'

His voice strained, he replied brusquely, 'Look, never mind the police for now. It's Arthur I'm worried about. He needs help, fast.'

Pru was confused. Had Arthur been driving the other car? Oh God, don't say he was dead . . .

'Quick, get in.' The man, evidently frantic with worry, pulled open the passenger door of his car.

Pru shivered and braced herself, but there was no visible corpse. No visible anyone, for that matter.

Fearfully, wondering if she was being kidnapped by a madman, she turned and opened her mouth to say, 'Where's Arthur?'

Instead, getting her first glimpse of the man who had crashed into her, she exclaimed, 'Oh thank goodness, it's you!'

Eddie Hammond peered in turn at Pru. The light inside the car was dim and she was pretty damp and bedraggled but he recognised her finally as a member of the club. Hopefully this would go in his favour.

'That's right. You're one of Dulcie's friends.'

'Pru. Pru Kastelitz.' Sticking out her icy hand – and feeling idiotic – she said, 'Phew, I was starting to get worried. Thought you might be a kidnapper.'

Eddie made his way around the front of the car – a gleaming, pillarbox-red Jaguar – and climbed into the driver's seat. He restarted the engine.

'Hang on.' Looking bemused, this time Pru remembered to say it. 'Where's Arthur?'

'On the back seat.'

She swivelled round in alarm.

And saw, half-hidden beneath a rumpled tartan blanket, a golden labrador. Asleep.

'Arthur's a *dog*?'

Grimly Eddie nodded. 'He's ill. I have to get him to the vet.'

He was reversing, putting the Jag back on course. Pru, never a tremendous dog lover, said, 'What about my car?'

'I'll get it fixed.'

'But I haven't even locked the doors! I've got loads of stuff in there—'

'Flaming Nora! What's more important, Arthur's life or your . . . stuff?' Eddie stared across at his passenger, exasperated. Then, remembering he mustn't alienate her, he forced himself to smile. 'Pru, please. Let's get Arthur to the vet first. As soon as he's been seen to, I'll sort everything out with you. That's a promise, okay?'

Feeling horribly ashamed of herself, because as far as she was concerned Arthur's life wasn't nearly as important as the contents of her car, Pru nodded and gave in. She couldn't help not being keen on dogs. An unprovoked attack on her as a child by a neighbour's Alsatian had left vivid scars on her mind as well as her arm. But to be fair, that hadn't been Arthur's fault.

To make up for being heartless, Pru twisted round and took another look at the animal snoring on the back seat.

'What's wrong with him?'

'I don't know. I woke up half an hour ago and found him like that. Out cold on the kitchen floor.'

Eddie's voice wavered. For an awful second Pru wondered if he was going to cry. He was desperately worried, she realised. No wonder he had been driving like a maniac along Brunton Lane.

And then, quite suddenly, something Dulcie had mentioned in passing last week popped into her head . . .

The vet, who lived above his surgery in Primrose Hill, was used to being woken up at unearthly hours by frantic pet owners.

'He'll live,' he pronounced, when he had finished examining Arthur.

Arthur, opening a weary eye, looked appalled by the prospect and promptly closed it again.

'Thank God, thank God.' This time Eddie's eyes filled with quivering tears of relief. 'But what caused it? What did he have, some kind of convulsion?'

The vet shook his head.

'More like some kind of cognac.' Laconically he added, 'Or it could've been Scotch.'

Pru, perched on a stool a safe distance from the examination table, exclaimed, 'You mean he's *drunk*?'

The vet nodded. Eddie stared at him, dumbfounded.

'Glenfiddich,' mumbled Eddie. 'I was drinking it last night. I fell asleep in the armchair. When I woke up this morning I saw the bottle on its side. Thought I must have knocked it over with my foot.'

Arthur whined and rolled his eyes open again, the effort clearly immense.

'Oh my poor boy,' Eddie consoled him, stroking his head. 'You must feel terrible.'

'Take him home and let him have plenty of water,' said the vet. 'No Scotch with it this time. The last thing Arthur needs is the hair of the dog.'

'Right,' said Pru, when they had loaded Arthur gently back into the car, 'time to call the police.'

He gave her a pained look. 'Could we just get Arthur home first?'

Pru gazed steadily at Eddie Hammond over the Jag's glossy red roof. Then she held out her hand, palm upwards.

'I'll drive.'

He twitched visibly.

'Why?'

'Because you lost your licence last week.'

Staring back at her, Eddie said nothing. Finally, wearily, he nodded.

'Yes.'

'What was it, drink-driving?'

Eddie looked offended.

'Certainly not. Only speeding. And jumping a red light. Nothing desperate,' he went on defensively. 'No big deal. They got me on points. Three months and a bit of a fine, that's all.'

'No wonder you didn't want me to call the police,' said Pru. 'Driving when you've been banned. No insurance. Causing an accident. And how much did you have to drink last night, before falling asleep in your armchair?' She consulted her watch. 'It's only seven thirty. You're probably still over the limit.'

Wordlessly Eddie passed over the keys. He knew Dulcie but had never actually spoken to Pru before. Having assumed she was the quiet, biddable one, he was experiencing a distinct sense of unease. Right now she looked about as biddable as Rudolf Hess.

He waited until Pru was driving before trying to explain.

'I knew it was stupid of me.' All he could tell her was the truth. 'I just panicked. I thought Arthur was dying. I was desperate.'

The Jaguar was bliss to drive after the temperamental Mini; the gears were heaven on a shift-stick. Marvelling at the metronomic sweep of the windscreen wipers – no hiccups, no judders, none of those awful screeching bird-of-prey noises her own wipers liked to make – Pru flicked a sidelong glance at Eddie.

'You could have phoned for a taxi.'

Wearily he shook his head.

'Last time I did that, the bloody thing took forty minutes to turn up.'

'What about a friend? Don't you have any of those, to call on in an emergency?'

Since moving down from Manchester to Bath four months earlier, Eddie had discovered at first hand that all the guff about northerners being friendlier than southerners was true.

'Plenty, thanks.' He heard his voice sharpening but couldn't help it. 'I have plenty of friends. In Manchester. How silly of me, I suppose I should have given them a ring.'

'It was silly of you to drive.' Pru remained calm. 'You could have killed someone. You could,' she pointed out, 'have killed me.'

Eddie was beginning to wish he had. His eyes felt gritty and his head ached. He gave up.

'So what are you going to do, call the police and turn me in?'

Pru indicated left as she turned into the entrance of Brunton Manor. He looked so crushed she couldn't help feeling sorry for him.

Her voice softened. 'Is that what you think? Actually I wasn't planning to.'

'Oh.'

'Look, phone a garage. Get my car towed away and fixed.' Pru parked the Jag neatly by the side entrance to the club but kept the engine running. 'Am I insured to drive this one?'

Bit late to ask now, thought Eddie, but he nodded.

'It's covered for any driver.'

Except banned ones.

'Okay.' Briskly Pru checked her watch; she was already late for work. 'So if it's all right with you, I'll borrow this car until mine's ready.'

Eddie panicked. He felt like a smoker having his cigarettes confiscated.

'But I might—'

'Might what?' Pru's delicate eyebrows lifted. 'Need it? Oh no, you won't need it, Eddie. You're banned.'

Chapter 13

By the time Pru arrived back at the scene of the crash, someone else had got there before her. The Mini was still lying on its side in the ditch but the five bulging black bin liners she had piled on to the back seat were gone.

This was a major blow; Pru's landlord didn't know it yet, but paying the rent depended rather heavily on the contents of those bags.

Pru, who had astonished herself this morning – she'd never been that bold and assertive with anyone in her life – now felt her eyes begin to prickle with distinctly unassertive tears. All her good clothes, fifteen years' worth, had been stolen. It had taken her hours to wash, press and check everything, making sure no buttons were missing, no hems coming undone. The woman who ran the designer as-new shop in Carlton Street, the Changing Room, had been keen to take as many of Pru's outfits, with their impressive labels, as she wanted to be rid of.

Pru didn't want to be rid of any of them but it was fast becoming a question of selling either her clothes or her body, and she couldn't imagine anyone being interested just now in her scrawny frame. Selling the clothes, on the other hand, would give her enough for six months' rent.

Pru stared at the Mini's empty back seat and hanging-open doors and wondered who could have nicked them. Had a smartly dressed young businesswoman spotted the car on her way to work, stopped to make sure nobody was lying hurt, and taken a peek inside one of the bags? Maybe she'd pulled out the navy-blue Escada suit, held it up against herself and thought, 'Size 10, what a stroke of luck, let's see what else we've got here . . .' Then, clearly liking what she found, had she stowed the five bin bags in the boot of her own sporty little car and zoomed off to work, happy in the knowledge that that was her spring wardrobe sorted out?

Or had a gang of school kids found the bags, torn them open and dumped her clothes in the nearest pond in disgust?

'Don't fret about it,' Marion Hayes declared when Pru finally turned up at Beech Farm. Arriving two hours late, and in a posh car, meant Marion's curiosity was aroused. Before she started work, Pru was forced to sit down, eat Hob Nobs, drink tea and tell all.

'That's his problem, not yours.' Marion dismissed Pru's worries with an airy flick of the hand. 'Just give him an estimate stating how much the stuff was worth. He'll send it on to his insurance people. They'll pay up.'

Pru nodded and tried to look suitably relieved. She hadn't been able to bring herself to tell Marion the whole story – about Eddie Hammond being banned and therefore uninsured – not out of any sense of loyalty, but because some things were simply safer left unsaid. She didn't fancy being arrested and slung into prison for aiding and abetting a criminal.

She couldn't help wondering, either, just how suspicious Eddie was going to be when she suddenly presented him with a hefty additional bill for stolen frocks.

I mean, how likely did it sound, Pru thought gloomily, thousands of pounds' worth of designer labels being nicked from the back of a clapped-out Mini? She used to buy shoes that cost more than that car.

'Well, at least you weren't hurt,' said Marion, draining her tea and standing up as the clock in the hall struck nine. 'Time I was out of here. The cows'll be wondering when they're going to get fed. I'll leave you in peace.'

* * *

88

When Pru had finished washing up the breakfast things she scrubbed the kitchen floor. While that was drying she vacuumed through downstairs. Next she cleaned the drawing room windows. When the floor was dry in the kitchen she threw a great pile of muddy jeans into the washing machine. Then she sat down at the table to polish silver and listen to a radio phone-in on the subject of dishonesty.

'When my husband's been horrible to me,' Teresa from Tunbridge Wells was confessing with a guilty giggle, 'I wait until he's asleep and pinch a fiver out of his wallet. The next day I spend it on chocolate.'

Pru idly considered phoning up the programme to say if anyone listening had her bin bags, could they please give them back?

She imagined herself on the radio, appealing to the thief's better nature: 'The thing is, I know they're nice clothes, but please don't think I'm rich. Because I'm not, any more. I'm horribly broke.'

At this point, the presenter would enquire gently: 'Pru, if it's not too personal a question, what brought this about?'

'Well, Gary, let me put it this way. Two months ago I had a wonderful husband, a perfect home. I employed a cleaning woman. Now I have no husband, no home, and I work as a cleaning woman.'

'Pru, that's terrible. But how did it happen?'

'How did it happen? Gary, I'll tell you how it happened. Some husbands do the routine thing, they have flings with their secretaries. But my husband had to be different, Gary. He didn't even have the decency to have an affair with his secretary, oh no, he had to be different, didn't he? He had to go and do it with our cleaner.'

'Pru, are you all right?'

Pru leapt a foot out of her chair. Marion was standing in the doorway giving her an extremely odd look.

Horrified, Pru realised she was pressing a half-polished

silver candlestick to her ear, holding it like a telephone.

Hastily she pretended to be testing its temperature against her sizzling cheek. 'Oh hi! Amazing, don't you think, how the harder you rub, the warmer it gets?'

'Pru, you could have bumped your head in the crash.' Marion sounded nervous. 'Maybe you should see a doctor after all.'

Liza had never really felt guilty before. It was awful; she didn't like it one bit. She wondered how long she would have to wait until it went away.

She was doing the stupidest things too, indulging in the kind of antics usually reserved for obsessed ex-lovers. Although the Songbird was miles out of her way, Liza found herself driving past it two or three times a week. Her stomach churning, she would count the number of cars in the restaurant's tiny car park and try to figure out how many customers were inside.

Not many, by the look of things.

Once or twice she had phoned the restaurant, pretending to have dialled a wrong number, just to see if it sounded busy.

She even persuaded Dulcie to go along there one Friday evening, to report back on atmosphere and food. Dulcie dragged a protesting girlfriend with her – 'God, Dulcie, can't we go somewhere else? That place has had some terrible reviews' – and enjoyed her meal but was hugely disappointed not to bump into Kit Berenger.

'I thought he said he'd eaten there loads of times,' she complained to Liza the next day. 'I was really looking forward to meeting him again. Lying toad, I bet he never sets foot in the place. What a swizz.'

'But the food was fine?' prompted Liza, bursting for details. 'What did you have? Take me through each course.'

'I can't remember,' Dulcie protested. She gave Liza a 'you're weird' look. 'We had three bottles of Côtes de something, told each other millions of dirty jokes and had to be poured into a taxi. Isn't that good enough?'

'You are hopeless.'

'If you're so desperate to check out the food, go there yourself.' Dulcie was miffed. Honestly, do someone a favour and all you got was abuse.

'Oh right, I'll do that,' said Liza with some sarcasm. 'I'm sure they'll welcome me with wide-open arms.'

Heavens, Liza could be thick. Dulcie rolled her eyes in despair. 'Do what you did last time, stupid. Go in disguise.'

The mechanics at Joe's Autos had a great laugh when they heard what Eddie Hammond wanted them to do to Pru's car.

Joe explained to Eddie over the phone the meaning of the technical term write-off.

'Basically, when a car like this has a headlight smashed, it's a write-off. Repairing the headlight is going to cost more than the car's worth, d'you see? And I've had a good look at the damage to the passenger door, the wing, the wheel arch, the bonnet . . . it's just not worth it, Mr Hammond. You're talking five hundred quid's worth of repairs on a total rust heap.'

'I know, I know,' said Eddie with a sigh, 'but do it anyway.'

The car was ready three days later. Eddie dialled the number Pru had left with him. A spaced-out-sounding hippy answered, mumbling, 'Yeah man, like, I'll get her, okay?'

About half an hour later, Pru picked up the phone. Eddie wondered who the hippy was; a son, maybe? God help her if that was her husband.

But it was hardly the kind of question you could ask over the phone. He switched into brisk mode instead.

'Pru? Eddie Hammond. Your car's here waiting for you, all fixed and . . .' No, no, he could hardly say as good as new. '. . . um, raring to go. So if you'd like to bring back the Jag we can do a swap.'

'Right.' Pru wondered why garages always did that. When you were desperate to get your car back, it took them a fortnight just to change a wheel nut. When, on the other hand, you were enjoying yourself thoroughly, zipping around Bath in a bright-red Jaguar, they managed to carry out six months' worth of repairs in no time flat.

Full of spite, garage mechanics.

Pru bit her lip and took a deep breath. She was doing it again, daydreaming deliberately, in order to avoid doing what had to be done next. She had been putting it off for three days and now she mustn't put it off any more.

'Fine, great, I'll come up now. Thanks very much. Only the thing is, there's . . . um . . . something else I have to—'

'See you in a minute,' said Eddie, whose other phone had begun to ring. 'You know where my office is. Just come straight up.'

Eddie wondered why Pru Kasteliz was looking so twitchy. She should be pleased, he thought, to be getting her car back.

Bloody hell, thought Eddie, who had just written out a cheque to Joe's Garage for £536, if anyone around here should be twitching it's me. He handed Pru the keys to the Mini. She promptly dropped them. He watched her kneel down, her long dark hair swinging forwards as she retrieved the keys from under his desk.

'That's settled then,' he said generously, 'all sorted out and no harm done.'

Pru felt sick. She knew she should have done it over the phone. Face to face was impossible.

'What?' said Eddie when she had opened and closed her mouth a couple of times and no sound had come out.

Three days ago, she had been awash with self-confidence. Pru wondered where it had got to now she really needed it.

Maybe that was my lot, she thought despairingly, and I used it all up in one go, like Phil at the roulette table. One glorious, exhilarating surge of assertiveness . . . and then, boom. Gone.

The meek shall inherit the earth . . . as long as that's all right with everyone else.

Wimps rule, okay? No, but really, are you *sure* that's okay?

'Look, I told you I had some things in the car,' Pru blurted out, 'and you said there wasn't time to go back and lock it, so we didn't. The thing is, by the time I did get back there, my things had been stolen. So I'm sorry, but here's a list of what was taken. I spoke to my insurers but I'm not covered, so I'm afraid this is up to you as well.'

Eddie stared at Pru in disbelief. Then he stared in even more disbelief at the sheet of paper she had pushed across the table at him.

Her hands were trembling so much it could have been a bomb. It was hardly surprising they trembled, Eddie thought when he saw the size of the bill. More of a bombshell.

'You mean you want me to give you another fourteen hundred pounds?' He sounded totally baffled. 'For a bag of *old clothes*?'

'Five bags,' whispered Pru. She wanted to tell him that if she had sold them through the Changing Room, she would have got more than that, but the words wouldn't come.

'You can't be serious,' said Eddie.

Pru stared down at her fingers, scrunched together in her lap. She knew what she should be doing. She should be fixing Mr Eddie over-the-limit Hammond with a haughty glare and telling him in no uncertain terms that it wasn't her fault her car had been smashed up and spun into a ditch, that he was the one in the wrong and that if he found the prospect of reimbursing her so appalling . . . well, then she would see him in court.

Joan Collins would have done it. Joan would have carried it off brilliantly. Maybe that's my trouble, thought Pru. No shoulder pads.

'How do I know you're telling the truth?' Eddie Hammond demanded suddenly. It crossed his mind to wonder about the hippy on the phone. Was there a drug problem there? Was Pru so desperate for money to feed her son's/lover's/husband's addiction that she would do anything to raise extra cash?

He jabbed at the list with an agitated finger.

'How do I know these clothes were really stolen?'

Well, thought Pru, I could show you a few empty fitted wardrobes.

Or she could have done, if the house hadn't been repossessed.

He was right, of course. She had no way at all of proving it.

She couldn't blame him for being suspicious either.

I'm gullible, Pru thought, but even I'd have my doubts about something like this.

'It's okay, it doesn't matter.' Realising she'd started to shake, she stood up and made a dash for the door.

'Where are you going?' Eddie half rose out of his own chair, confused by the abrupt volte-face.

Quick, thought Pru, get me out of here before I start blubbing.

'Home. Thanks for getting the car fixed.' She shook her head violently. 'It doesn't matter about the clothes.'

Chapter 14

Liza took Pru along with her to the Songbird on Saturday night. She picked her up at eight o'clock.

Pru, thrilled to be invited – *anything* to get out of that bedsitter – said, 'This is a treat. I thought you'd have brought your new chap. Couldn't he make it?'

'No.' Liza slotted Sibelius into the tape deck. 'Mainly because I didn't ask him.'

Pru recognised the look on her face. Clearly, new chap was no more.

'But you said he was gorgeous last week.'

'Last week he was. This week,' Liza said heavily, 'he started asking me about my star sign. I mean, give me a break. He's supposed to be a grown man.'

It occurred to both of them, though neither said it aloud, that considering it was mid-April, so far their New Year's resolutions weren't turning out terribly well.

Entering the restaurant was nerve-racking. Liza, wigged-up and dressed-down, knew she was being irrational. No one had ever recognised her yet, so why should they suddenly start now? But that didn't stop her heart pounding like a Sally Army drum the whole time they were being greeted and seated.

Liza's eyes flickered to the left. There was the little waitress who had been in such a fluster last time. Quick flicker to the right . . . and there serving behind the bar was the attractive blonde who had tried so valiantly to keep the rugby rabble in check. Liza wondered if this was the girl whose feelings she had hurt so much, Kit Berenger's cousin.

Sweat began to prickle her scalp beneath the unflattering mouse-brown wig. She felt like a spy, a wartime secret agent desperate not to attract the attention of the enemy.

'Relax,' said Pru, 'no one's looking.'

'I know. I just don't want to be recognised.'

'It's hardly likely, if even Phil didn't spot you.'

Oh bum.

'Phil!' gasped Liza, covering her mouth in dismay. 'Shit!'

'Well, yes,' said Pru, 'I know that now.'

'I mean I can't believe I did this to you. This is where . . . and I completely forgot . . . Hell's bells, how could I be so insensitive? Why didn't you *say* something?'

Liza cringed. Then she double-cringed, realising they were actually sitting at the table where Blanche had wriggled her toes with such enthusiasm in Phil's trousered crotch.

'It's all right. I knew you'd forgotten. Anyway, it doesn't matter.' Prue shrugged. 'Why should I be bothered?'

Liza said admiringly, 'You've got brave.'

'My husband ran off with my cleaner. I live in a bug-infested bedsit. The hippy downstairs plays bloody Donovan records non-stop and apart from this dress I own precisely two jumpers, three nighties and a skirt.' Pru hesitated, looking as if she didn't know whether to laugh or cry. 'You'd be surprised; after a while you can learn to not care about quite a lot.'

Liza stared at Pru. Pru gazed back.

Pru tried hard to keep a straight face.

Liza said slowly, 'Donovan records?'

Pru nodded. Liza began to smirk. Within seconds Pru was in fits of giggles. Liza was helpless with laughter.

Holding her sides, barely able to get the words out, she said, 'This hippy of yours. Do they call him Mellow Yellow?'

Pru was giggling so much her mascara had run.

'That's right.'

They were drawing attention to themselves. The family at the next table nudged each other, watching them. With a huge effort, Liza controlled herself.

'I mean it,' she told Pru when they had both recovered. 'You are brave.'

'I'm not,' said Pru, mentally reliving the moment she had fled Eddie Hammond's office. Oh yes, that had been brave, that had been breathtakingly courageous. Give the girl a VC.

'You definitely can't stay in that bedsitter,' Liza persisted. 'Death by Donovan, imagine. Come and live with me instead.'

'What, in your one-bedroomed flat?' Pru was touched by the offer but untempted. For the first time in her life – at the age of thirty-one – she was on her own. The least she could do was learn to cope with it.

'My flat's a jolly nice flat.' Liza leapt to its defence. 'It's bijou.'

'And if I moved in, it'd be more than your style that got cramped. Thanks,' said Pru, 'but I'm fine. Really.'

They were supposed to be ordering their meal. Liza forced herself to concentrate on the menu. Every time she looked up, she realised Pru was glancing across the room.

'Right, I'll have the Stilton soufflé and the duck with kumquats. How about you?' she said finally. Pru was doing it again. 'Someone you know?'

Pru shook her head.

The blonde girl arrived to take their order. She was pretty and utterly charming and Liza, deciding she must be the cousin, wondered how she would react if she knew who'd she'd just been charming to.

'Come on, who is it?' she persisted, when the girl had left them. Pru's eyes were still darting across the restaurant.

'No idea. He just keeps looking over.'

'Fancies me. Fatally attracted to my stunning wig,' Liza smirked, 'not to mention my cardigan.' She glanced over her shoulder and found Kit Berenger staring straight at her.

'Shit.'

'It's him, isn't it?'

Liza nodded, white-faced. 'How did you know?'

Embarrassed, Pru pleated her napkin. 'Dulcie said he was gorgeous.'

'More to the point,' said Liza, 'does he know who *I* am?' But how can he, she wondered, when I'm looking like this?

'What happens now?' Pru's stomach rumbled; she hadn't eaten all day. The prospect of not staying after all almost made her want to cry.

'Right, no need to panic,' Liza announced firmly. 'I mean, let's be logical about this. He can't possibly have recognised me. And we've ordered now, so we can't leave.' Fretfully she said, 'What I don't understand is why I didn't spot him before.'

'He wasn't there when we arrived,' Pru whispered back. 'He came through that door.' She nodded at one marked Private.

The look Liza gave her was long and measured.

'So you guessed who he was straight away.'

'I didn't think it mattered,' Pru protested guiltily, 'so long as he doesn't know who you are. I didn't want to put you off your meal.'

The Songbird was a forty-seater restaurant. Tonight – and Saturdays are the busiest night of any restaurant's week – it was half full.

Or half empty, depending on your viewpoint.

Either way, it wasn't great news. Liza wondered how many of the unoccupied tables were down to her.

She couldn't fault the Stilton soufflé, which was creamy and light with an outer crust browned to perfection.

The roast duck with kumquats was brilliant too.

'This,' declared Pru, prodding her poached salmon with a fork, 'is divine.'

Liza wondered how on earth it could be physically possible to feel a pair of eyes boring into your back. She didn't need to look round, she just knew it was happening.

'If you want to leave,' said Pru heroically, sensing her discomfort, 'we can.'

Liza wanted to. The trouble was, she wanted to sample the puddings more.

'Is he still looking over?'

'Well, kind of.'

'That means yes.'

'He's standing up,' Pru murmured, watching covertly as he pushed back his chair.

'Hell's bells—'

'It's okay, he's gone through that door again, the one marked Private.'

He was away for some time. When the door finally reopened, Liza had just taken her first mouthful of almond and apricot tart. Pru, who had chosen the honey ice cream, was so carried away by its miraculous taste and texture that her eyes were closed.

'You don't mind if I join you for a moment,' said Kit Berenger, pulling out the empty chair next to Pru.

Liza wondered briefly if it was worth putting on a German accent. If he challenged her, she could simply deny everything, say she didn't know vot he was tocking about.

But really, was there any point?

She wondered instead if Kit Berenger was about to rip her wig off. It wouldn't be a pretty sight if he did; she was wearing an Ena Sharples hairnet underneath.

He didn't. He looked hard at her for several seconds. Then with his index finger he tapped the dark-blue linen tablecloth, less than an inch from Liza's wrist.

'Very good, but that was the giveaway.'

Pru stared at the tablecloth. Heavens, was there a microphone hidden beneath it? Was the table bugged?

'I heard you laughing. When I turned round I couldn't see your face.' He tapped again. 'But I saw this.'

She had always worn her watch, a man's steel Longines, on her right hand. On her little finger she wore a narrow platinum ring. Liza was so impressed by his powers of observation she almost smiled. Maybe this is it, she thought, my chance to

99

apologise and make amends, to tell him what a terrific meal we're having . . .

'I don't know what the fuck you think you're doing back here,' Kit Berenger went on icily, 'but you certainly aren't wanted. So I suggest you leave, this minute.'

'Now look—'

'Haven't you done enough damage?' he demanded, hissing the words across the table like poison darts. 'Haven't you already hurt Nicky enough?'

Liza flinched. Mortified, Pru stared down at her melting ice cream.

'This restaurant doesn't need customers like you,' said Kit Berenger, standing up. 'Come on, out. And don't start bleating about the bill because we don't want your money either.'

'Have you told your cousin who I am?' asked Liza, feeling sick. So much for making amends.

'Are you mad? Why do you suppose I want you out of here?'

'You're making a scene.'

'I am not. I'm getting rid of you before I make a scene. Because if I did,' Kit Berenger spoke through gritted teeth, 'I promise you, it'd be a bigger one than this.'

Chapter 15

Eddie Hammond's frighteningly efficient secretary had left the computer print-out of last month's renewed memberships on his desk, together with an updated list of applications to join the club. This list was growing, which was a good sign. Since taking over the running of Brunton Manor last November Eddie had worked hard to raise the club's public profile.

Only three people hadn't renewed their lapsed memberships. He flicked the edge of the print-out with his thumb, to jog his memory. The Turner girl had got married and moved to Oxford.

Well, it was a reasonable excuse.

R. Cooper-Clark had emigrated last month to work as a flying doctor in the Australian outback.

Which was an improvement. This was what Eddie called a good excuse.

The third name on the list was P. Kasteliz.

So, Eddie wondered idly, what's yours?

He found Dulcie indulging in her favourite pastime, swinging her legs on a stool in the bar and flirting outrageously with the captain of the local cricket club. The cricketer, who hadn't been married long, looked relieved to make his escape.

'You're always working,' Dulcie protested, eyeing Eddie's crumpled grey suit and loosened tie. 'You never have any fun.' She pulled a face, remembering why the words sounded so familiar. 'That's what I used to tell Patrick. Eddie, how old are you?'

'Forty-five. Too old to have fun,' he said, humouring her.

Dulcie gave him a told-you-so look.

'You men, all the same. And then you wonder why you end up on your own. I mean, you were married once, weren't you?'

Eddie nodded.

'Did you work non-stop?'

Nodding again, he caught the barman's eye and ordered a refill for Dulcie, a Scotch for himself.

'And she got more and more bored, until in the end she couldn't stand it any more,' Dulcie scolded, wagging a finger at him. 'So when was that, how long ago did she divorce you?'

Their drinks arrived.

'Cheers,' said Eddie, clinking glasses. 'Oh, she didn't divorce me. She died.'

Dulcie clapped a hand to her forehead. Slowly, it slid down her face.

'I'm sorry, I'm just so *stupid*. Does it ever happen to anyone else or am I the only one? I tell you, every time I open my mouth I manage to say the wrong thing. Honestly, I could kill myself.'

Eddie shook his head. 'That's all right. It doesn't matter.'

'But you poor thing, how terrible for you. Um . . . how did she die?'

'She killed herself.'

Dulcie was appalled. It wasn't as if she'd even wanted to know, she had simply remembered that bereaved people got upset when you tried to pretend it hadn't happened. They didn't like you changing the subject.

But this was too much. For possibly the first time in her life Dulcie didn't dare speak.

It seemed safest to keep her mouth shut and just look as sympathetic as she could.

'Sorry,' said Eddie, 'that was awful of me. I shouldn't have said it.'

'You mean it was a wind-up?' squawked Dulcie, her eyes wide. 'You total *bastard*.'

'No, no, it wasn't a wind-up.' Hastily he shook his head.

'She did kill herself. I meant I could have put it a bit more subtly. Not dumped it on you like that.'

Dulcie hung her head. 'I kind of asked for it.'

She looked so forlorn Eddie began to wish he'd stayed in his office.

'Anyway,' clumsily he patted her arm, 'that was all a long time ago. And it isn't why I'm here now. Actually, I wanted to talk to you about your friend.'

Another one bites the dust, thought Dulcie with an indulgent smile.

'You mean Liza?'

'No,' said Eddie. 'Pru.'

What people say is true; word of mouth is the best form of advertising. No sooner had Marion Hayes at Beech Farm boasted about Pru to her friends than they were on the phone bagging Pru for themselves. Within a week she was booked up with two hours here, three hours there . . . and as much extra work as she liked.

It wasn't exactly a glittering career but at least she was in demand. And cleaning other people's bathrooms all week had one major advantage; it definitely made you appreciate your days off.

Which was why, at eleven o'clock on Sunday morning, Pru was still in bed when the doorbell rang.

She buried her head under the pillows. Donovan had been bellowing up through the floorboards until the early hours.

The bell continued to ring.

Finally – because what if it was Phil? – Pru crawled out of bed and flung a dressing gown over her nightdress. Since the building didn't stretch to luxuries like intercoms and buzzers, she had to stumble downstairs and pull the door open herself.

If it was Dulcie, she thought with bleary outrage, she jolly well wasn't going to let her in. It wasn't even midday; this was too much.

It was weird, opening the door expecting to see thin,

laughing, spiky-haired Dulcie and coming face to face with paunchy, thinning-haired Eddie Hammond instead.

'Oh,' exclaimed Pru, startled by the sight of him on her doorstep and characteristically wondering what she must have done wrong. 'Is it the car, has something happened?' Her huge grey eyes grew defensive. 'That scratch on the boot was there before I borrowed it.'

'I know.' Eddie couldn't help admiring her slender figure, wrapped in an obviously expensive sage-green satin robe. 'Sorry if I woke you up. May I come in?'

Pru automatically ran her hands over her slept-on hair, checking her ears weren't sticking out. She nodded, bemused by the request, and led the way back upstairs.

'Tea? Coffee? Um . . . would you like to sit down?'

Hurriedly she swept last night's clothes off the only chair in the room. God, the place was a pit. It was horrible seeing it through a visitor's eyes. She must look a berk, too, she realised, prancing around such a dump in her best La Perla nightie. Like Zsa Zsa Gabor camping out at Greenham Common.

'Dulcie tells me she offered you a room at her house.' Eddie didn't think Pru looked a berk but he was shocked by the state of the bedsit. There was mould on the ceiling and strips of wallpaper were peeling themselves off the damp walls. 'Why didn't you go?'

Pru busied herself making coffee. She shrugged.

'I don't know . . . pride? Shame? Something like that.'

'Come on, she's your friend. What d'you think she's going to do, gloat?'

Pru turned and looked at him. Clearly Dulcie had brought him up to date with the story so far. Where gory details were concerned, holding back wasn't Dulcie's style. She couldn't exercise discretion if she was strapped to a Nautilus machine.

'She might not mean to gloat, but she'd find it hard not to say I told you so. She and Liza did warn me, you see. They told me what my husband was getting up to and I refused to believe them.'

'But still—'

'Anyway,' said Pru, handing him his coffee and sitting down on the unmade bed, 'that's not the only reason. Dulcie's still got her house. She doesn't have to worry about money. I couldn't bear to feel like the poor relation.'

Eddie shook his head.

'You've had a rough time,' he said gruffly. 'I had no idea, until Dulcie told me.'

Cheers, Dulcie, thought Pru. What could she look forward to next, she wondered, charity fundraising? Collecting tins being rattled outside Sainsbury's? Give generously to the humiliated wives appeal?

Save Pru from Poverty?

'Here,' said Eddie Hammond, 'I'm sorry about the other day, in my office. I shouldn't have doubted you.'

Pru took the cheque for fourteen hundred pounds. She bit the inside of her mouth and smiled a wry, lopsided smile.

Maybe Dulcie wasn't so bad after all.

'Thanks.'

'And I noticed your club membership had run out,' Eddie went on, handing her a card made out in her name, 'so I renewed it for you.'

Pru felt herself going red.

'The thing is . . . I can't really afford . . .'

'You don't need to,' Eddie cut in brusquely. 'It's my way of apologising. I'm not usually that crass.'

Pinker still, Pru said, 'Well, thanks.'

'My pleasure.' He cleared his throat and looked embarrassed. 'That's when you need somewhere to go, after all. When your marriage has just broken up.'

Pru giggled.

'Now you sound like Dulcie.'

'It's what she told me last night,' Eddie admitted. 'Still, it seems to work for her.'

'She's man-hunting,' Pru said simply. 'I'm not.'

* * *

'Bloody taxis,' stormed Eddie half an hour later. He peered out of Pru's second-floor window and yanked up the aerial on his mobile, jabbing out the numbers he had soon grown to know by heart. 'Hello, hello? Yes, it's me again. Where the bloody hell's my cab?'

Pru, still in her dressing gown, watched him scowl into the phone.

'I said Medwell Crescent, not Street! Just get on to him, will you, and tell him it's Medwell Crescent. What? You mean he's picked up his next call? So how long am I supposed to wait before someone—? No, I cannot hang on another twenty bloody minutes!'

The unsatisfying thing about a mobile phone is you can't slam the receiver down. Eddie, ready to explode with frustration, did the next best thing and tried slamming the aerial down instead.

It snapped off.

'This is silly.' Pru dangled her car keys at him. 'Here, go and sit in the Mini. It'll take me two minutes to get dressed.'

'Thanks,' said Eddie when she dropped him at the railway station with two minutes to spare. The Mini might be a banger but Pru knew how to handle it. She was, he had to admit, an extremely good driver.

As he struggled to open the passenger door he joked, 'Next time I need a lift, I'll phone you.'

Pru wondered if it was sitting at the wheel of a car that gave her more confidence. She said, 'Lots of people hire chauffeurs when they've been banned.'

'I know.' Eddie sighed. 'But I don't need a full-time chauffeur.'

'You could do with a part-time one. My hours are flexible,' Pru went on rapidly. 'The people I clean for don't mind when I turn up, so long as the job gets done.'

Eddie saw the quiet determination on her face. With that straight dark curtain of hair and those serious grey eyes of hers, Pru looked more like a schoolgirl than a grown woman.

106

She was painfully thin too, beneath the man's dark-blue sweater – her husband's presumably – and those battered black jeans.

'Are you volunteering?'

'I need the money,' said Pru bluntly. 'You need a driver. I could do the job.' Leaning across, she jiggled the handle Eddie hadn't been able to get to grips with, and opened the temperamental passenger door. The train he was in a hurry to catch was just pulling into the station. 'Quick or you'll miss it. Look, think it over. If you want me, give me a ring.'

Eddie grinned. 'If I *want* you . . . ?'

'Oh well,' Pru went pink again, as he had known she would, 'you know what I mean.'

'Of course I do.' He pulled himself together. 'And I've already thought about it. How soon can you start?'

The enormous slate-grey eyes widened.

'As soon as you like.'

'Terrific,' said Eddie, knocking the gearstick expertly into reverse. 'In that case, back to Brunton to pick up the Jag. We can't stand bloody trains anyway.'

'We?' said Pru.

'Arthur hates them too.'

Chapter 16

Pru was in the pool when Dulcie saw the latest notice up on the noticeboard, announcing the appointment of Brunton Manor's new tennis pro.

Dulcie's eyes flickered incredulously from the written announcement to the photograph pinned beneath it, of a blond male in tennis whites being presented with a trophy the size of a fridge.

Her heart went kerplunk. Ignoring the receptionist's indignant squawk of protest, Dulcie grabbed the photo, clutched it to her chest and raced all the way to the pool. Everyone who saw her stopped and stared; Dulcie had never been known to run before. Whatever next, sit-ups?

Pru was instantly recognisable in her daffodil-yellow swimming hat. Her head bobbed up and down as she doggy-paddled her way laboriously up to the shallow end, completing her sixteenth length. The hat was a must for Pru. If she didn't wear one, her hair would plaster itself to her head leaving her ears on show to the world. This way her long hair stayed dry. In fact, as Dulcie had once innocently pointed out, the yellow rubber cap flattened her ears so nicely, it was a shame she couldn't wear it all the time.

Personally, Dulcie wondered why Pru persisted with this swimming malarkey, especially when she was so bad at it. All swimming did, as far as Dulcie was concerned, was wear you out and totally wreck your make-up.

She crouched at the edge of the pool, waiting for Pru to reach her. It was no good yelling, trying to hurry her up; the hat wasn't only a jolly efficient ear-flattener. When it was on, Pru couldn't hear a thing.

'What?' said Pru, hanging on to the side and blinking chlorinated water out of her stinging, pink-rimmed eyes. She peered up at the photograph Dulcie was dangling in front of her nose.

'It's you-know-who,' said Dulcie triumphantly.

Pru peeled the edge of the yellow cap cautiously upwards, just enough to be able to hear but not enough to let her ear spring out.

'What?'

'You-know-who,' repeated Dulcie, her voice loaded with meaning. 'Come on, think back a bit. New Year's Eve, Pru! New Year's resolutions.'

Pru looked blank.

'I give up. Is it someone Liza might want to marry?'

Sometimes Dulcie despaired of Pru. Honestly, if this was what swimming did to your brain.

'I'm talking about *my* resolutions,' she said impatiently. 'The ones I wrote when I was fifteen, remember? Do more homework, keep room tidy, all that guff?'

Pru remembered.

'Join the *Starsky and Hutch* fan club.' She brightened. 'I forgot to ask, did you ever join? I liked Starsky best. Didn't you think he looked sexy in that wrap-around cardigan?'

'I preferred Hutch. He was gorgeous. Nobody fancied Starsky.' Dulcie was full of scorn. Seriously, was it any wonder Pru's marriage had failed? She'd always had diabolical taste in men.

Pru peered more closely at the photograph. The chap was blond and tanned, but . . .

'Dulcie, that isn't David Soul.'

'Give me strength,' sighed Dulcie. 'Did I say it was? Now listen to me. One of my resolutions was to snog you-know-who. You said who was he and I said I didn't have a clue. Right? With me so far?'

Cautiously, Pru nodded.

'Well, this is him. This is you-know-who.' Dulcie broke into an uncontrollable grin. She still couldn't believe it herself. It was the fabbest thing to happen since Pop Tarts.

Pru looked up at Dulcie, still clutching the photo lovingly like a teenager. She didn't know who you-know-who was, but he must be famous for Dulcie to have had a crush on him for so long. A rock star or something. A tennis-playing rock star like Cliff Richard.

'And you've joined his fan club?' said Pru. It sounded a bit of an immature thing to do but . . . well, this was a free country . . .

Gazing down at her, Dulcie decided they were both in need of a stiff drink.

'I haven't joined his fan club,' she told Pru. 'He's about to join mine.'

'Remember how I always used to moan about our family holidays,' said Dulcie when Pru emerged from the changing rooms at last and joined her in the bar.

'In South Wales? Tenby, wasn't it?'

Dulcie nodded. 'Bloody yacht club. Talk about mental cruelty. I should have sued my parents for dragging me along with them every summer. All day, every day, out in that sodding boat of theirs—'

'Maybe that's what put you off swimming,' Pru suggested. 'You're just generally anti-water.'

'Anyway, when I was fifteen we stayed in our usual cottage and a group of boys were renting the place next door. There were four of them and I fell in love with the best-looking one—'

'Fell in *love*?'

'Figure of speech,' said Dulcie. 'Had a crush on. Fancied like mad. His name was Liam and he was seventeen. I was sure he fancied me back but you know what boys are like when they're with their mates. We chatted on the beach a few times.

110

When they played tennis they let me be their ball girl, that kind of thing. The others used to tease Liam about me. I was so besotted I didn't even care.' Dulcie sat back dreamily in her chair. So dreamily she spilt red wine down her T-shirt. 'On our last night, he gave me a kiss on the cheek and said, "See you next year." I was so happy I almost died on the spot. I gave him my address and he promised to write to me. My parents couldn't get over me crying buckets all the way home, when I'd always hated Tenby so much. I swear, that was the best holiday of my life.'

'I don't remember this,' said Pru. 'You kept pretty quiet about it. So what happened, did he write to you?'

'Nope.' Dulcie grinned. 'I must have driven my mother mad. I kept accusing her of intercepting the post and destroying his letters. Poor Mum didn't know what I was talking about.'

'Did you write to him?'

'Not often. Only about twice a day.'

'Dulcie!'

'Don't go all feminist on me. I was only fifteen.'

'So this Liam . . . he was the one you were so desperate to snog?'

'He kissed me here.' Half closing her eyes, Dulcie touched her cheek. 'I can still remember how it felt. It was stupendous,' she looked rueful, 'but it wasn't a snog.' Then she smiled at the memory. 'Can you imagine the sheer agony of having to wait a whole year to see him again? I was crossing off the days to August. Dammit, I was crossing off the *hours*.'

'And did you?' said Pru, by this time riveted. 'Did you see him again?'

'Did I heck! The cottage was let out to a pair of geriatric spinsters. No sign of Liam or his friends anywhere . . . and God knows I spent enough time looking for them.'

'You never told us any of this.'

'What, that I was dumped?' Dulcie started to laugh. 'Excuse me, I did have some pride. I'd have told you about Liam if there'd been anything to tell.'

The photograph of Brunton Manor's new tennis pro was back up on the noticeboard, having been plucked from Dulcie's grasp by an irate receptionist.

'And now he's coming here to work,' Pru marvelled.

Dulcie hugged herself. 'It's fate.'

'It didn't work out brilliantly last time.'

'I was fifteen,' Dulcie rolled her eyes in exasperation, 'he was seventeen. I had spots and the haircut from hell – how *could* it have worked out?'

'Yes, but—'

'That's why it's fate. We're adults now. This is our second chance,' she looked smugly at Pru, 'a chance to make a real go of it. You'll see.'

Chapter 17

Pru called Terry Lambert her mystery client because she had never seen him. Terry, brother of Marion Hayes over at Beech Farm, was a solicitor who lived alone in a picturesque Bath-stone cottage high on one of the hills surrounding the city.

'I've been telling him for years to get someone in. Men, they're hopeless,' Marion had robustly declared, before phoning Terry and informing him that she had found him a cleaner.

Marion had given Pru the spare key to Terry's house. Every Tuesday afternoon Pru let herself in, spent four hours restoring order from chaos, took the money her absent employer left for her on the kitchen dresser and let herself out again.

Even if she hadn't met him, however, she felt she knew Terry Lambert quite well, having hung up his clothes, dusted his book-shelves, washed up his breakfast things and put endless CDs and videos back in their cases. Divorced four years earlier, he was in his mid-thirties, with no children. He earned a jolly good salary and drove a metallic-green Scorpio. Pru knew all this because Marion had told her. According to Marion, her brother was quite a catch: handsome, generous and kind to animals.

'Once you're back on an even keel,' she told Pru with an encouraging wink, 'you could do a lot worse, you know, than our Terry.'

Pru couldn't imagine ever getting back on an even keel, nor was she the least bit interested in getting to know another man. Anyway, kind to animals he might be, but with the best will in the world you could never classify Terry Lambert as handsome.

She didn't say this to Marion; it didn't seem polite to point out that if the photo in Terry's bedroom was anything to go by, he was half-man, half-anteater.

But the photograph of Terry and Marion with their now-dead parents was clearly of sentimental value. Whenever she polished the ornate silver frame Pru couldn't help studying it, touched by the similarities between father and son. Both had dark eyes and thick, straight eyebrows, pronounced laughter lines and mouths that curved upwards when they smiled. They also shared the same nose, big and beaky and truly attention-grabbing.

Marion, luckily for her, had followed her mother's side of the family; her eyebrows were narrow, her nose pert.

It didn't feel odd to Pru, talking to Terry Lambert on the phone, but she wondered if it was strange for him. After all, she knew a lot about her mystery client but he knew next to nothing about her.

In fact, Terry didn't appear to find it strange. He sounded charming, and thoroughly relaxed.

'. . . the thing is, I'm going to be working unpredictable hours,' Pru explained, 'so I won't always be able to manage Tuesday afternoons. If it's a problem—'

'No problem,' Terry replied easily. 'I'm at work between eight and six, five days a week, so it doesn't affect me. Come round any time you like.'

Relieved, Pru said, 'Thanks.'

'I'm the one who should be thanking you.' He sounded amused. 'I can't believe what a difference you've made to the place.'

Pru felt herself going shy. Hopeless when it came to compliments, she mumbled her goodbyes and rang off.

He had definitely sounded nice though. Maybe when the time came to start thinking about a divorce she would ask Terry Lambert to handle it.

Oh God. Divorce.

Just not yet, thought Pru, swallowing panic. Not yet.

114

Liza's editor was pleased with her. Beaming, he emptied the folder of letters on to his desk.

'Great stuff, sweetheart. Controversy, that's what we want. You caused quite a stir, you know. And these are only the ones who've bothered to write.'

Liza picked up a couple of the letters, skimmed briefly through them – one, she noticed, was addressed to Ms Superbitch – and dropped them back on to the desk.

'What are you going to do?'

'Bloody print 'em.' He reached for his jacket. 'Come on, Superbitch, I'll buy you lunch.'

Dulcie was doing her make-up when she saw Patrick's car pull up outside. She smiled at herself in the mirror, confident that she had never looked better. This was what six days of extensive sunbedding, a brilliant ultra-short haircut, an even shorter lime-green dress and the promise, at long last, of a bit of serious fun did for you.

She sincerely hoped Patrick would notice and be impressed.

He rang the doorbell like a stranger.

'What happened to your key?' said Dulcie, puzzled, as she opened the door.

He was wearing a deep-blue polo shirt and jeans. Despite the sun blazing down, Patrick never wore dark glasses, which he regarded as an affectation. Sunglasses were for cissies, according to Patrick.

Dulcie, who whipped hers on at practically the first hint of daylight, owned at least a dozen pairs. They made her feel so Hollywood.

'I wouldn't want to interrupt anything.' Patrick followed her into the hall.

'Nothing to interrupt.' Yet, thought Dulcie, because you never knew, today could be the day.

'Anyway, I just need to pick up my dinner jacket. Won't be a sec.'

We might be separated but we can still be friendly, Dulcie reminded herself. She waited at the foot of the stairs for him to come back down.

Any man looks good in a dinner jacket. Patrick had always looked gorgeous.

'Going somewhere nice?' she asked ultra-casually when he reappeared.

Patrick shrugged. 'Doubt it. Some charity thing, a dinner-dance.'

'Not like you to be vague.' Dulcie gave him a teasing look. 'Come to that, it's not like you to go to dinner-dances. You've always been *far* too busy.'

Dig, dig.

Looking deeply uncomfortable, Patrick shifted from one foot to the other.

Dulcie's intrigue deepened.

'Is it work? Or are you seeing someone else?'

His dark eyes narrowed as he gazed with intense concentration out of the hall window. Finally he said, 'It's allowed, isn't it? You were the one who didn't want us to be married any more.'

Astonished, feeling as if she'd been kicked in the stomach, Dulcie gasped, 'You *are* seeing someone else?'

Patrick shook his head.

'I'm not. I've just been invited to this thing tonight. I'm going with a girl.'

'Who' – Dulcie cleared her throat – 'who is she, anyone I know?'

Another shake. Followed by a sigh.

'Look, it feels pretty weird being single again. I'm not used to it yet. All this is down to Bibi, if you must know.'

'Oh.' Dulcie was confused.

'Some chap invited her to the dance. She hasn't been out much since . . . well, since James left . . . so she was um-ing and ah-ing a bit. Anyway, this chap happened to mention he had a daughter. Bibi said something – God knows what – about

116

me. He said how about if the four of us went together . . . and the next thing you know it's all bloody well arranged.'

The look on his face said it all. Dulcie started to giggle.

'You're double-dating. With your mother.'

'Don't laugh, it isn't funny.'

'This girl could be awful. She could be a complete dog.'

'Better bloody not be.'

Dulcie's kicked-in-the-stomach feeling had gone, magically disappeared. The thought of Patrick actually getting involved with someone else had been a bit weird, but this was okay. This wasn't involvement, this was a blind date.

'She might be stunning.' Dulcie felt she could afford to be generous. She still hoped the girl would be a dog, but only because the idea of Patrick being set up on a blind date by his own mother was such a scream. Besides, Dulcie thought smugly, if the girl was so stunning what was she doing letting her dad fix her up?

Dulcie had more important things on her mind anyway, because today was the day Liam was due to arrive at Brunton Manor.

At three o'clock this afternoon.

And he wasn't married. In a rare burst of practicality she had checked with Eddie Hammond.

It was as well to find these things out in advance, Dulcie felt. Imagine wrapping yourself dramatically around the long-lost man of your dreams, only to be peeled off and hear him say, 'Let me introduce you to the wife and kids . . .'

At ten to three, Dulcie sauntered out on to the terrace with a drink and a book – *Pride and Prejudice*, because she didn't want Liam to think she was the kind of girl who only read airport novels.

Cutler and Gross sunglasses in place and bare, freshly pedicured feet up on the chair opposite, she began to read.

The great thing about dark glasses was you could look as if you were lost in a book when in reality you weren't missing a trick. Like the sight of Imelda Page-Weston three tables away, surreptitiously spraying the backs of her knees with Tresor and making sure she had more cleavage on show than anyone else. Silly moo.

Eddie was evidently giving Liam the full guided tour, introducing him to members *en route*. By three thirty Dulcie's feverish anticipation had begun to flag somewhat. Too excited to sleep last night, too hyped-up to eat anything today, she now found herself struggling to stay awake. What with the afternoon sun beating down on her head and two glasses of Frascati nestling comfortably in an otherwise empty stomach, it was a job keeping her eyes open. Anyway, thought Dulcie with a yawn, what was the hurry? Liam wasn't paying a fleeting visit, he'd still be here next week, next month, whenever she woke up . . .

Chapter 18

The bad news about dark glasses is the way people can't tell when you're asleep.

Seeing Dulcie apparently engrossed in the book on her lap – and recalling her earlier interest in Liam's marital status – Eddie said, 'Now there's someone I must introduce you to.'

Leading the way across the terrace he announced jovially, 'Here we are, then! Dulcie, meet our new tennis pro, Liam McPherson. Liam, this is Dulcie Ross. Dulcie?' When she didn't move, he hesitated, peering down at her more closely. 'Dulcie, are you awake?'

Jerked into consciousness, Dulcie's eyes snapped open. Seeing Eddie looming over her, red-faced and shouting her name, she snatched off her sunglasses and struggled to sit upright.

Her confusion was only momentary. As she put her hand up to her mouth, checking she hadn't been dribbling in her sleep, Dulcie's gaze fixed on the tall blond figure standing behind Eddie Hammond.

Hastily she wiped her mouth. Her sunglasses clattered to the ground. Jane Austen was already lying there, face down, next to her shoes.

Bugger, bugger, thought Dulcie, this isn't how it was supposed to happen. She had planned on smiling enigmatically, like Ava Gardner, then slowly and sensually removing her glasses so that Liam McPherson could admire her for a few seconds before doing a double-take and gasping, 'My God, it's you . . .!'

From then on he would be too awestruck, too overcome by emotion to make much sense. When he eventually stopped kissing her, and she was free to speak again, Dulcie would simply say to Eddie, 'We knew each other once. A long time ago.' Then, there would be more hugs, more kissing, and hopefully a convincing explanation for his lack of correspondence after Tenby. Like his parents had suddenly emigrated to Australia, dragging Liam with them and ruthlessly ignoring his desperate pleas to stay behind . . .

Something along those lines anyway.

'Sorry, darling, didn't realise you'd crashed out.' Grunting as he bent down, Eddie retrieved her glasses. 'They aren't broken. Jane Austen, eh? Dulcie, I'm impressed. Had you down as more of a Jackie Collins girl myself. Anyway, where were we? Ah yes – Dulcie, this is Liam McPherson.'

Grinning, Liam held out his hand.

'Hi. Good to meet you.'

'Dulcie's one of our most regular . . . er, regulars,' Eddie said with some pride.

'Terrific. I hope we'll have a game soon.' Nodding in the direction of the tennis courts, Liam swished an imaginary racket. 'Are you entered for the doubles tournament, Dulcie?'

Not a flicker of recognition. Not a double-take in sight. Dulcie told herself that this was actually a good thing, because who wanted to look like a fifteen-year-old with chip-shop hair and rampant acne anyway? Not being recognised was proof that she *had* changed for the better.

It wasn't the most promising of starts, but at least she hadn't dribbled in her sleep. As she took Liam's hand – heavens, what a firm shake – Dulcie gave him her mysterious Ava Gardner smile and said, 'Actually, we've met before. Many years ago.'

'Really?'

Liam was smiling too, but she could tell he was being polite; he clearly wasn't racking his brains to remember when or where this might have been. He was a tennis pro, after all. He had once, albeit flukily, reached the quarter-finals at Wimbledon.

During his years on the circuit he must have met thousands of devoted female fans. He had probably signed so many autographs it was a wonder he had enough strength left in his arm to hold a racket.

'Sixteen years ago,' prompted Dulcie. 'In Tenby.'

Liam frowned. He'd never played a tournament in Tenby. Hang on, sixteen *years* ago . . . ?

'You were there on holiday with your friends. I was staying in the cottage next to yours.'

Light dawned.

'You're kidding me!' Liam pointed at her in amazement. 'You were the skinny little kid . . . oh, what was your surname, something totally weird . . .?'

'Fackrell,' said Dulcie. God, it was a wonder she hadn't developed a massive complex about that name. One sniggering clique at school had called her Fuckall Fackrell. Everyone else had called her Mackerel.

Marrying Patrick had been no hardship at all.

'I'm Dulcie Ross now.'

'We used to send you into the nettles to fetch our lost tennis balls,' Liam recalled. 'Your arms and legs were covered in stings but you swore they didn't hurt. And on the night before you left, the other lads bet me a fiver I wouldn't kiss you.'

Eddie roared with laughter. Dulcie tried hard to look as if she couldn't remember this bit.

'And did you?' said Eddie.

'Damn right I did. We're talking sixteen years ago. In those days a fiver was a lot of money.'

Rather beginning to regret this trip down memory lane, Dulcie decided a detour was in order. She said brightly, 'And now here we are, all these years later. How are you settling— ?'

'Hang on, didn't you write me a truckload of letters?' Looking delighted, Liam nodded his head. 'It's all coming back to me now. I think you had a bit of a crush on me, Dulcie Fackrell. Is that so?'

121

This was mortifying stuff, but what could she do, throw a tantrum? Mentally gritting her teeth, Dulcie gave in with good grace.

'Of course I did. I slaved over those letters,' she protested. 'I suppose you laughed your head off and showed them to all your friends, you heartless beast.'

'Well, maybe. It was kind of funny at the time.' Liam's grin was apologetic. 'I mean, you weren't exactly Debbie Harry, were you?'

This was true, but Dulcie still wished he'd stop harping on about it.

'I was fifteen years old.'

'Little Dulcie Fackrell.'

'Ross now,' she reminded him. Then, in case he got the wrong idea, 'I was married, but we've been separated for some time.'

It was Eddie Hammond's turn to look amazed.

'Some time?' He raised his sandy eyebrows. 'Darling, it's only been a couple of months!'

Cheers, Eddie.

'Ten weeks,' said Dulcie. 'Anyway, the marriage was over long before that. You know when things aren't right.'

'Hey, I hope you weren't upset when I never wrote back,' said Liam.

'I can't remember.' Dulcie attempted the Liza Lawson smoulder. For good measure, she quivered a provocative lower lip. 'But if I was, I forgive you.'

He grinned. 'What a relief.'

'We've both grown up since then.'

'Well, you certainly have.'

The look he gave her this time was frankly appreciative. Hooray, thought Dulcie, getting somewhere at last. She hoped Imelda was watching and taking note.

'Right,' said Eddie Hammond, rubbing his hands together in that's-enough-of-that fashion, 'we'd better be moving on. Still plenty of people waiting to be introduced. Maybe catch you later, sweetheart.'

'There is that small chance.' Dulcie nodded vaguely. As if a wagonload of wild horses stood a chance of dragging her out of the bar tonight.

'See you around.' Liam winked as he turned to leave.

'If I do bump into you later,' she casually called after him, 'I'll buy you a drink.'

'This is going to be awful.' Patrick spoke through gritted teeth as he and Bibi made their way up the crimson-carpeted staircase of the Aston Hotel, where the dinner dance was being held. They were supposed to be meeting their dates in the Kavanagh Bar, directly ahead of them. The place was heaving already. Patrick flinched as a girl with yellow teeth and popping-out eyes turned and beamed expectantly at him. Oh please God, don't let that be her . . .

'There they are,' exclaimed Bibi, veering to the left and waving.

Patrick could hardly bear to look. He felt sick, and hopelessly unprepared. He glimpsed a flash of turquoise satin, a skinny girl plastered in more make-up than a *Come Dancing* contestant.

'Not her.' Observing the expression of undiluted horror on his face, Bibi pointed past the vision in turquoise. 'The one in the red.'

Having performed the necessary introductions, Leo Berenger bore Bibi off to the bar, ostensibly to help him with the drinks but in reality to give Patrick and his daughter a few uninterrupted minutes together.

'Look, I'm really sorry about this,' sighed Claire Berenger as soon as they were alone. 'I don't know how much pressure you were put under to come here tonight, but I can guess. I'm thirty years old and my father's beginning to panic.' She paused and pulled a face. 'Actually, that's wrong. He's been panicking for the last five years. As far as he's concerned, his daughter is up there on that shelf, in serious need of dusting. I'm afraid I'm breaking his heart.'

Miraculously, Patrick felt himself begin to relax. Maybe the evening wasn't going to be quite such an ordeal after all. Claire Berenger had a sense of humour. She was no dog either. With her glossy brown hair fastened in a plait, her pale skin and clear grey eyes, she exuded health and vigour. She was attractive in an unflashy way. Her red velvet dress was plain but close-fitting enough to reveal a good figure. She looked like an off-duty gym mistress. At school, thought Patrick, she would definitely have been house prefect.

Amused by Claire's world-weary air, he said, 'Has he done this before?'

She gave him a look.

'My father's mission in life is to get me up that aisle. Then, nine months later, into the nearest maternity ward. I'm afraid his idea of sexual equality is letting the little woman choose the colour of the wallpaper for the downstairs loo.'

'I'm already married,' Patrick apologised.

'You are? Heavens, where's your wife?'

'Well, we separated a few weeks ago.'

Claire said, 'I'm sorry.' Then, keeping a straight face, she added, 'Still, my father will be pleased. He probably thinks that's my only hope now, catching some poor chap on the rebound.'

Patrick smiled, charmed by her self-deprecating manner. He had, after all, just emerged from a seven-year marriage. And they didn't come much less self-deprecating than Dulcie.

'Anyway,' Claire glanced over her shoulder, checking that her father wasn't making his way back, 'I felt I should explain. Now you needn't be embarrassed when he starts dropping hints the size of Land Rovers. All we have to do is humour him.'

She was an accountant, Patrick discovered over dinner. And an excellent cook, Leo Berenger informed him proudly. Oh yes, she knew how to cook, his daughter. She would make some lucky man a truly wonderful wife.

As their coffee was being served, Claire leaned over and

124

whispered in Patrick's ear, 'He's slipping. He hasn't told you yet about my child-bearing hips.'

She was wearing Chanel 19. Patrick breathed it in.

'We shouldn't be making fun of him. He's just a proud father.'

'Who can't wait to be a proud grandfather,' murmured Claire. 'Go on, I dare you. Tell him you've had the snip.'

Chapter 19

Dulcie was busy being vivacious at the bar when Liam McPherson finally made his way over to her corner of it.

He appeared before her, wearing a white Nike tennis shirt and black tracksuit bottoms and looking – if it were possible – even more tanned and super-fit than he had earlier.

'We meet again,' he told Dulcie with a grin.

'Amazing. Aren't some coincidences just too spooky for words?'

'What about that drink you promised me?'

'I lied,' said Dulcie. 'I don't buy men drinks. They buy them for me.'

Liam laughed.

'You have changed. You always used to buy me drinks.'

Dulcie remembered running to the corner shop, counting out her precious pocket money and dashing back to the tennis court where Liam and his friends lay sprawled on the grass, waiting.

'Cherry Corona doesn't count.'

His tone was affectionate.

'You were a funny little kid.'

She ran an index finger idly around the rim of her almost empty glass.

'Like I said, I've grown up.'

One eyebrow was raised. Liam smiled his havoc-making smile.

'Indeed. And I'm beginning to think we have some serious catching-up to do.'

While Dulcie's stomach was still churning with pleasure, he attracted the barman's eye and had her vodka and tonic topped up. Somewhat alarmingly, he ordered a pint of orange juice for himself.

'So tell me what you get up to these days. You said you were divorced, didn't you?' Liam looked sympathetic. 'Any children?'

Dulcie loved the way he spoke to her, giving her his undivided attention. It was exhilarating, being made to feel you were the most fascinating and desirable girl in the world, after years of neglect.

That was the difference between him and Patrick, Dulcie realised. Liam was interested in her as a person. He actually cared.

'Almost divorced,' she fibbed. 'And no, no children.'

He nodded and put his arm out, shielding her back from a carelessly held cigarette. Dulcie felt absurdly protected.

'Career girl, is that it? What line of work are you in?'

'No line of work,' she said with a playful smile. 'Just . . . you know, idle rich.'

'Not too idle, by the look of things.' Liam cast a professional eye over her slender body. He ran the flat of his hand over Dulcie's bare shoulder, nodding approval. 'Taking care of yourself, that's good . . . although those deltoids could do with a bit of working on. What's your regime?'

Dulcie said, 'Sorry?'

'Your keep-fit regime.' Liam tilted his head, studying her through narrowed eyes. Dulcie felt like a racehorse being given the once-over. 'Eddie said you spend a lot of time here. Are you lifting weights?'

Dulcie returned his speculative gaze. Her keep-fit regime went something like: Get out of bed . . . eat cake . . . lie in bath . . . eat chocolate Hob Nobs.

After that she generally got dressed and went out to lunch. But something told her Liam wouldn't be too impressed.

'Not every day,' she said truthfully. 'I don't actually have a . . . a regime, as such. Just a few sit-ups here, a bit of . . . um . . . jogging there.'

'Exercise,' announced Liam. 'Exercise is the key. A healthy body is a happy body, am I right?'

'Oh, yes.' Dulcie nodded, unable to tear her eyes from his muscular brown arms.

'If there's one thing I can't stand,' Liam confided, 'it's a woman who lets herself go.'

Dulcie, who would never let herself go – she would rather die than step outside her front door minus mascara – nodded more confidently this time.

'People who don't take care of themselves make me sick,' Liam went on. 'I mean, what is wrong with them? They stuff themselves with the wrong food, can't be bothered to exercise and then have the nerve to complain when their arteries clog up.'

Dulcie looked suitably outraged. Inwardly, she was experiencing mild stirrings of panic. Gosh, he was serious.

Liam's smile was rueful. 'I'm sorry, it just bugs me. I don't understand people who aren't interested in looking after themselves. I mean, if they can't be bothered to respect their own bodies, why the hell should I respect them?'

This was ominous stuff. Worse still, the harder Dulcie tried not to think about salt and vinegar crisps, the more she craved some. Hastily she changed the subject.

'Tell me about you. Tell me all about the tennis circuit. I bet it was brilliant fun . . .'

Luckily it worked. Liam finished his pint of orange juice, ordered another and began regaling Dulcie with stories. A natural raconteur with a wonderful line in self-deprecating humour, this was much better. It must be the Irish blood in him, Dulcie decided dreamily. Liam really did have it all: looks, wit and charm by the bucketload. She could gaze into those dark-blue eyes, admire that amazing body and listen to that melting Dublin-accented voice of his all night.

* * *

Leo Berenger was okay. He was polite, he was presentable and he was certainly prosperous, but it didn't take Bibi long to realise he wasn't the man for her. When there was no spark, no chemistry, it didn't matter how loaded the man was, you couldn't make it happen.

This was a shame because Leo was sixty-one, a perfectly suitable age for the suitor of a sixty-year-old widow. As they danced, Bibi forced herself to make witty conversation and to concentrate on Leo's replies, but it was hopeless. While her mouth did the talking and her ears listened, her rebellious brain was conjuring up depressing pictures of Leo Berenger, sixty-one years old and stark naked. Then it compared them with pictures of James, her darling James, so much younger and more attractive, all tanned and gorgeous and infinitely beddable.

Bibi carried on dancing, averting her gaze from Leo's and determinedly blinking back tears. She hadn't seen James for almost three months. It was no good moping; life went on.

Sadly though, not with Leo Berenger.

'Look at those two,' he said with some pride. Turning, he allowed Bibi to see Patrick and Claire at the far end of the dance floor. 'Reckon we might have started something there. They seem to be enjoying themselves, anyway.'

Every cloud . . . thought Bibi.

Patrick had been so certain the evening would be a nightmare, he couldn't get over how easy to talk to Claire Berenger had turned out to be.

Having expected the worst, he had been pleasantly surprised.

When, at midnight, the band struck up the first notes of 'We'll Meet Again' – it was that kind of band – Claire said, 'Well, we made it. You've done your duty. And if my father slips my phone number into your pocket don't worry. Feel free to chuck it in the bin; you don't have to see me again.'

Much to his amazement Patrick heard himself say, 'But I'd like to see you again.'

For a second Claire looked equally astonished. Then, endearingly, she blushed.

'You would?'

Patrick nodded. 'I would.'

'Gosh.'

He smiled briefly. 'Bit of a shock for me as well. I wasn't expecting the evening to turn out like this. I'm horribly out of practice too,' he apologised. 'The last time I asked a girl out I wore flares and drove a two-tone Cortina.'

Coincidentally, it occurred to Dulcie much later that night that the last time she'd jumped into bed with a man she didn't actually know terribly well, he'd worn flares and driven a blue and white Cortina.

That had been Patrick, of course, and she had carried on happily jumping into bed with him for years ... until his work had taken over and she'd grown used to going to bed alone while Patrick murmured 'just-finish-this' to his beloved computer and only came upstairs hours later when she was asleep.

Tonight, though, she wasn't alone. She was with Liam McPherson. Dulcie lay back, closed her eyes and deliberately didn't think of Patrick.

And after a briefly rocky start, Liam was living up to all her expectations. Her old feelings for him were as strong as ever. Better still – because even Dulcie had to confess it, it had been a bit of a one-sided relationship in the past – the attraction was now mutual.

It was so powerful you couldn't fight it even if you wanted to ... which she certainly didn't.

It was sheer chemistry.

This is more like it, thought Dulcie rapturously. This is what I need, a glorious Greek god of a man, all blond hair and rock-solid muscles, and not just some brainless hunk, either. A glamorous tennis pro, a star.

Liam had been modest, but as far as Dulcie was concerned, if the Duchess of Kent once watched from the royal box while you played on Wimbledon's Centre Court, that definitely made you a star.

'All this time and I never knew you were famous,' Dulcie murmured dreamily, lying wrapped in Liam's arms. She had never watched much tennis on television. 'I wish I could've seen you in that quarter-final.'

'Really?' Liam sounded amused. 'I've got the video around here somewhere. Want to watch it?'

Startled, Dulcie's eyes snapped open.

'What, now?'

But his hand was already travelling lazily up her warm thigh. As he began nuzzling her neck again, Liam murmured, 'Maybe later.'

Phew.

Dulcie kissed him back, glanced at her watch – 4 a.m. – and shifted herself happily into a more accommodating position. Now this was the kind of exercise regime she liked.

And goodness, what a difference it made, being with someone who, in turn, actually enjoyed being with you.

Rather than with their sodding computer.

That morning-after scenario was something else with which Dulcie was drastically out of practice.

Her first thought upon waking was: Yes! Bingo! And yah-boo-sucks to Imelda Page-Weston who had spent most of yesterday evening jealously eyeing Dulcie and Liam from afar.

Dulcie, her eyes still closed, couldn't help feeling a bit smug; this was what she'd so desperately wanted to happen, but even she had never dreamt it would happen so soon. It was like settling down on the riverbank for a long day's fishing and before you'd had a chance to unscrew your thermos, hooking and landing Jaws.

Oh, Mr McPherson, Dulcie smirked happily, this is all so sudden.

Her second thought was that something weird was going on.

The earth appeared to be moving. She opened her eyes. No, not the earth. It was the floorboards juddering. Rhythmically, every couple of seconds. There, it was happening again.

Liam's side of the bed was empty. Moments later, wriggling across the crumpled dark-blue sheet and leaning over the edge, Dulcie found out why.

He was lying with his feet tucked under the bed, doing astonishingly energetic sit-ups.

'. . . eighty-six, eighty-seven,' muttered Liam. He grinned but didn't stop when he saw Dulcie peering down at him. 'Morning, sweetheart . . . eighty-eight . . .'

'Two fat ladies,' said Dulcie.

'Ugh. Not in my bedroom, thanks.'

She sensed he wouldn't be smitten by Liza. Voluptuous curves clearly weren't Liam's thing.

This, Dulcie decided, was a definite plus. Liza's ability to reduce grown men to quivering masses of testosterone grew wearing after a while. In fact, if you didn't have a strong stomach, all that hopeless devotion could make you quite sick.

'. . . ninety-four . . . sleep well?'

Dulcie nodded. Since it was only seven o'clock she had actually been asleep for less than three hours, but so what, who cared? Was she complaining? Not on her nelly.

'You're naked,' she told him.

'Well spotted.'

Dulcie grinned. 'I couldn't very well miss it.'

'. . . ninety-nine, a hundred.' Not even out of breath, Liam leapt up and planted a smacking kiss on her mouth. 'I'll make breakfast. Do feel free, by the way.'

It took a moment to realise he was offering her his space on the floor, now he'd finished with it.

'Bit early for me.' Dulcie slid back under the duvet with alacrity.

'Saving it for later, eh?' Liam made a playful grab for one of her ankles. 'Tell you what, I'm free between twelve and one.

132

When you've finished in the gym I'll check you out, give you a game of tennis. How about that?'

Some men, thought Dulcie, gave you flowers. Some gave you chocolates. What she wanted to know was what she'd ever done to deserve a man whose idea of romance meant giving you tips on your backswing.

Chapter 20

Liza was pounced on by a starry-eyed Dulcie the moment she drew up outside the club. Dulcie, pink-cheeked with elation, dragged her through to the coffee shop.

'My God, I suppose this means you pulled the pro.' Liza resigned herself to missing her turn on the toning table.

'Did I ever,' declared Dulcie, realising she couldn't keep the stupid grin off her face if she tried. 'And he is divine, so funny and charming . . . Wait till you meet him, he's a dream come true! I'm telling you, this is the real thing. It's love.'

The housewife, bored and starved of affection, and the gorgeous, bronzed country club tennis coach. Honestly, it was such a cliché. Then again, Liza realised, things like this happened all the time. It was how they became clichés in the first place.

Recognising a bad case of lust when she saw one, she nevertheless decided to humour Dulcie.

'Good in bed?'

'The best. Oh, and the body is to die for—'

'And is it mutual?' Liza felt it was her job to strike a note of caution. 'Is he as besotted with you?'

Dulcie looked radiant.

'That's the best part, he really is! Honestly, we talked non-stop yesterday evening, then he took me back to his place . . . he's rented a fantastic flat just behind Royal Crescent—'

'And you bonked the night away.'

'We did, we did,' Dulcie agreed happily. 'It was out of this world.'

'So when are you seeing him again?'

'Midday. On the tennis courts.'

Liza raised an eyebrow. 'You're going to bonk on the tennis courts? Won't you get in other people's way?'

'We won't be bonking. He's giving me a tennis lesson.'

Dulcie tried hard to sound casual, to pull it off. Somehow, though, the words came out lacking conviction, even to her own ears. It was like hearing Linda McCartney say, 'Yum, bacon sandwich.'

Liza raised the other eyebrow and said, 'Oh dear.'

Dulcie cracked at once. You could fool a lot of the people a lot of the time, but not Liza.

'Okay, I know. He's a health freak.' She groaned and covered her face with her hands. 'What the hell am I going to do?'

Liza hid a smile. The way Dulcie made it sound, health freak was on a par with mass murderer.

'It's his job to be fit, that's all. You don't have to join in.'

Dulcie wished she could be so sure. That was the thing about Liza, she never compromised herself. If she didn't want to do something she simply didn't do it.

But Liam's idea of breakfast had been three Shredded Wheat, a handful of multivitamins the size of horse pills and a malt and wheatgerm milkshake, and although he hadn't forced the horse pills on her, he had made her eat two Shredded Wheat. Without sugar either because he didn't keep empty calories in the house.

From little hints dropped here and there, Dulcie had begun to suspect that coming clean with Liam wouldn't be the smartest thing to do. He might not be interested in a health slob, a bone-idle junk-food junkie whose idea of a really good workout was trying on ankle boots in Russell and Bromley.

'He's everything I want,' she told Liza. 'I'm not going to risk losing him. Anyway, how hard can it be, getting fit? Come on, don't laugh—'

'You aren't serious,' said Liza, wiping her eyes. 'You, of all people, a born-again Jane Fonda.'

But Dulcie wasn't to be swayed. 'You don't understand,' she cried. 'He's worth it.'

The coffee shop overlooked the tennis courts. Liza watched a tall, vaguely familiar-looking chap in a yellow and white tracksuit make his way out on to the court closest to them. Next to him walked Imelda Page-Weston, her sleek white-blonde hair shimmering in the sunlight.

'Is that him?'

Dulcie's head swivelled round. You knew it was love when just the sight of him made your heart do Skippy-the-kangaroo impressions. She watched Imelda say something to Liam and swing her racket experimentally above her shoulder. Liam positioned himself behind her and showed her how she should be doing it. He grinned and whispered something in Imelda's ear that made her shake with laughter.

You also knew it was love, Dulcie reflected, when the sight of him touching someone like Imelda made you want to bash that someone's brains out with her own Slazenger.

She realised Liza was watching her.

'He's a tennis pro. It's his job to flirt,' Liza pointed out.

'I know.'

'And there are always going to be women who flirt back.'

Fit women. Healthy women. Women who took care of their bodies.

Women who liked salad.

'I know that too,' said Dulcie, gripped by a perverse longing. That only made her want him more.

Preparing to walk out on to the court was worse than any dental appointment. Having spent an hour in the on-site sports shop, Dulcie was kitted out in a new Lacoste shirt and a staggeringly expensive pink and white tennis skirt. What with the racket as well, she'd blown quite a hole in her credit card. Still, Dulcie reasoned, she'd be saving money on junk food.

Since her stomach was growling and she no longer ate crisps, she made her way back to the coffee shop and – ignoring the astonished eyebrows of the woman on the till – virtuously bought a couple of muesli bars instead.

The trouble with muesli bars, Dulcie discovered – apart from the fact that they were disgusting – was the bits they left lodged in your teeth. Rushing to the changing room for a last nervous pee and to check her teeth in the mirror, she ran slap bang into Imelda.

Imelda, just out of the shower, was wearing an olive-green towel. She cast a look of amusement in the direction of Dulcie's pristine skirt.

'Don't tell me you've booked a lesson too.'

'I didn't, actually. It was Liam's idea,' Dulcie replied as loftily as she could.

'And you said yes,' Imelda marvelled. 'Well, well, wonders will never cease. Although you have to admit, he is gorgeous.' As she spoke, she was drying herself with the towel, giving Dulcie the opportunity to see just how toned her own body was. 'Looks like we're both after him, then,' Imelda went on, smiling as the towel dropped to the floor and she reached for her white satin bra and knickers. 'May the best girl win, eh, Dulcie?'

Dulcie stared back at her. The bra was a 36D, which didn't help. She had never liked Imelda, who was a man's woman, a woman without female friends.

Dulcie said, 'Maybe I already have.'

'Oh dear, is this my fault?' Liam laughed and shook his head at Dulcie. 'Are you that exhausted after last night?'

Exhausted wasn't the word. What Liam called a quick knock-up had felt to Dulcie like a marathon five-setter. She couldn't understand, either, why the ball wouldn't go where she wanted it to go. She'd played enough tennis at school to know she wasn't that hopeless.

Liam leapt over the net and jogged over to her. Dulcie's legs were trembling uncontrollably and she had a raging stitch in her side. Her racket, doing double duty as a walking stick, was the only thing propping her up.

'Sweetheart, you look terrible.' He was frowning now, clearly concerned. 'What is it?'

Dulcie, thinking she would just die if Imelda was sitting in the coffee shop watching her make a spectacle of herself, croaked, 'I'm sorry, I don't know what's wrong. I f-feel awful.'

Liam put his arm around her waist and helped her off the court. Dulcie was sweating, trembling, as weak as a kitten and unable to hit a ball for toffee; it wasn't hard to figure out.

'Flu,' he announced. 'That's what it is. You're going down with flu.'

Dulcie almost collapsed with relief. 'Oh I am, I am. I knew I wasn't well! Flu, that's it—'

'Home,' Liam instructed. 'And straight to bed.'

'Um, about tomorrow . . . I was going to invite you round to my house for dinner?' Dulcie began to panic at the thought of not seeing him.

But Liam shook his head.

'Sweetheart, you'll be in no state to cook dinner. I'll see you when you're better. Maybe next weekend,' he gave her waist an encouraging squeeze, 'or the week after that.'

Liza, who had caught the end of Dulcie's lesson, was in the car park chucking her squash racket and sports bag on to the back seat of her white Renault.

'This is my friend Liza,' said Dulcie, gesturing weakly.

'I'm sending Dulcie home,' Liam explained. 'She's sick.'

'You don't have to tell me,' said Liza. Honestly, what was Dulcie like? Did she seriously expect to get away with this?

Clinging on to Liam's arm, Dulcie gasped, 'We th-think it's flu.'

'Sure it's not mad cow disease?' said Liza.

Chapter 21

'How's the invalid?' Liza asked gravely when she phoned the next morning.

'Not funny,' Dulcie wailed. 'I'm telling you, flu would be a doddle next to this. I'm totally and utterly seized up.'

Since leaving school, reaching for the next custard cream had been about as energetic as Dulcie got. Hurling herself without warning around a tennis court for sixty minutes had sent every muscle in her outraged body into spasm.

'I'm in bed,' she groaned. 'I crawled to the bathroom earlier. It took me an hour to get back.'

Liza grinned. 'You need looking after. Want me to phone Liam and ask him to pop over?'

'Don't you dare. Ouch.' It even hurt holding the phone up to her ear. 'God, this is agony. I'll never walk again.'

'Can't say I didn't warn you.' Liza was cheerful and not the least bit sympathetic. 'Told you not to overdo it, didn't I? Take some paracetamol, you'll feel better in a day or two.'

'I can't get to them, they're downstairs.' Dulcie pleaded feebly, 'You could come over, couldn't you, just for a few hours? I really do need looking after. I'm helpless.'

'I think you mean hopeless. And no, sorry, I can't.' Having pulled open her wardrobe doors, Liza stood and surveyed the neatly lined-up contents. 'I've got something else on.'

The peacock-blue silk shirt, she decided rapidly. Black leather trousers and her high-heeled black ankle boots. Why not? Just because she was joining the protesters didn't mean she had to dress like one.

'Something more important than your best friend starving to death in her own bed?' Dulcie sounded hurt.

'No, but I can't back out now. If I did,' said Liza, 'then I'd really be a wimp.'

Driving towards West Titherton, Liza barely noticed the dazzling scenery, the white clouds drifting high in a duck-egg-blue sky, dappled sunlight sweeping over the rolling Mendip hills and the thousand different shades of green that made up the countryside in late spring.

She still didn't know how Alistair Kline had managed to bamboozle her into going along today. But that, Liza supposed, was what successful barristers were all about. It was their job to persuade you to agree with them, to convince you – against your better judgement – that they were right.

'It's simply a matter of following through.' Alistair had been forceful. 'You start something, you finish it. That letter to the paper generated a fair amount of publicity, if you remember. People will expect you to be there. They'd be disappointed if you didn't turn up, Liza,' he went on, his expression sorrowful. 'Disappointed in you for not caring enough to make that small effort—'

'Stop,' Liza groaned, 'this is worse than *The Waltons*. Okay, I'll do it.'

Alistair instantly reverted to a normal tone of voice. 'Great. See you there then. Ten o'clock sharp.'

She wondered despairingly how she could ever have thought he was shy.

Liza slowed as she reached the brow of the next hill. Below her lay West Titherton, a golden toy village surrounded by a patchwork of fields, some dotted with immobile black and white cows, others with clusters of sheep.

To the left of the village the protesters were already gathered at the site of the proposed new development, milling around the yellow bulldozers that stood ready, waiting to swing into action.

It was very much a last-ditch protest. The amateurish ruse of planting a rare breed of wild orchid in the path of the diggers hadn't worked. Berenger's had their planning permission and that was that. Basically, the new estate was going to be built but – the protesters were determined – not before the last drop of bad publicity for Berenger's had been squeezed out.

Parking the Renault at the roadside where everyone else had left their cars, Liza joined the rest of the group. Sixty or seventy in total, they were a mixed bag, ranging from New Agers to Nimbys (those outraged members of the middle classes who don't mind anything being built so long as it doesn't happen anywhere near them, i.e. Not In My Back Yard).

The ground was dry and the sun blazed down, but all the Nimbys were wearing Barbours and Hunter wellies. The New Agers wore holey jeans and layers of jumpers in various shades of black.

Everyone pursed their lips at the sight of Liza in her dazzling peacock-blue shirt. She couldn't have looked more out of place if she'd worn a ball gown in a butcher's shop.

Alistair bounded over to her.

'Going on somewhere, are we?' Eyeing the gold chains around Liza's neck, disappearing into her cleavage, he looked as if he were itching to tell her to do a couple more buttons up.

'Lunch with Liberace, by the look of it,' Liza heard one of the dreadlocked New Agers murmur, nudging his friend.

'Sure you won't be cold?' asked Alistair.

'I'm fine.' Pointedly Liza shielded her eyes from the sun. 'Sure you won't be warm?'

'I'm wearing three sweaters,' Alistair told her with pride, 'in case they try setting the dogs on us.'

Liza kept a straight face.

'If they set any dogs on me,' she promised, 'I'll tie their paws up with my necklaces.'

'Hmm. I don't know how you're going to climb bulldozers

in those heels.' He glanced disapprovingly at her boots.

'Alistair! I'm here, okay? Supporting the protest. I am not climbing up on any bulldozers.'

Alistair looked resigned. She wasn't taking this seriously at all. Liza had turned out to be a major disappointment, he thought sadly. All the more so since she had truly been the woman of his dreams. He adored her, he simply didn't understand how she could not be as concerned about preserving the environment as he was. Together, Alistair thought sorrowfully, they could have made an unbeatable team.

Still, she was the nearest to a celebrity they'd got and the press were kicking their heels waiting for the action to begin. Signalling to the chaps from the *Evening Post* who were eating Big Macs – any excuse to wind up the vegetarian New Agers – Alistair steered Liza towards them.

'They want a photo of you waving a placard. And make a point of telling them how committed you are to the cause,' he instructed briskly, 'despite your clothes.'

For ten minutes Liza answered questions put to her by the reporter, who sounded almost as bored as she was. Then it was the photographer's turn. He spent ages organising Liza in the foreground with a motley crew of placard-waving New Agers behind her and the bulldozers strewn with banners bringing up the rear.

He was halfway through the reel of film – and startled to find himself already half in love with Liza – when the contractors rolled up in two filthy white vans and the carefully arranged group photo promptly disintegrated.

Within seconds, the bulldozers were swarming with protestors. Minutes later the police arrived. Scuffles broke out. Alistair punched one of the bulldozer drivers on the nose.

'Want to wait in my car, love?' the *Evening Post* reporter offered, clearly worried about blood getting spattered on Liza's silk shirt. But the photographer was waving his arm, beckoning her over. A group of the less nimble protesters were staging a sit-in, blocking the path of the rumbling bulldozers.

'Come on,' bellowed the photographer, 'it'll make a great picture!'

'Do as he says,' Alistair bellowed even more loudly, from his precarious position on top of one of the diggers. 'Get over there!'

Liza hesitated. She didn't really mind joining the sit-in. She didn't even mind getting her leather trousers muddy. What did bother her was being picked up and carried away like a struggling beetle by the police . . . and being photographed in that position.

Talk about undignified.

All eyes were on the tremendous struggle in progress. Since no one's attention was on the road behind them, and the noise of the heavy machinery drowned everything else out, nobody saw or heard the dark-green Bentley purr to a halt behind the police van.

Liza was still torn between not wanting to look a wimp and not wanting to look a prat. Most of all she wished she hadn't been feeble enough to give in to Alistair's emotional blackmail. She could be playing squash now, she thought with longing, or at home working on ideas for the new food book she had just been commissioned to write.

Damn, thought Liza, even waiting hand, foot and finger on dipstick Dulcie would be fun compared with this.

'Liza, will you stop faffing around and JOIN THE BLOODY SIT-IN,' roared Alistair, kicking out at one of the contractors who was trying to grab his ankles, and pointing imperiously down at Liza.

I could just turn round and leave, she thought, willing herself to do it.

The next moment she jumped out of her skin as a weirdly familiar voice inches from her ear drawled, 'Is he your boyfriend? I'm amazed, I didn't take you for the kind of girl who'd let men boss you about like that.'

Chapter 22

Liza's heart began hammering wildly in her chest. Kit Berenger was standing next to her, arms crossed, feet apart, sunglasses in place as he calmly surveyed the scene of chaos spread out before them. He was wearing black jeans, a black and white striped shirt and that familiar aftershave.

Had it occurred to her that he might turn up today, the final day of the protest?

Of course it had.

So far, Kit Berenger had seen her sweating and out of breath after an hour on the squash court, and in her eating-out frump-of-the-year disguise. Now for the first time he was seeing how she really looked.

Liza couldn't quite bring herself to admit that this was why she had taken such care with her appearance today.

'He's not my boyfriend,' she said as calmly as she could manage, 'I don't let him boss me about, and since I'll be thirty-two next week, I'm hardly a girl.'

'Well, you're hardly an ancient old trout.'

Was there actually a flicker of a smile playing around his mouth? Sideways on, and never having seen Kit Berenger smile before, it was hard to tell.

'Anyway,' he went on, his tone conversational, 'what are you doing here, dressed up like a Christmas tree?'

Liza ignored the jibe. 'Same as everyone else. Protesting.'

'You don't look much like a protester. You've washed your hair for a start.'

Before she could move, one hand came up and touched her

blonde hair, idly following the line of the curve between her left temple and shoulder.

Liza shivered and looked up at him, but the narrow mouth gave nothing away. The eyes were still hidden behind black glasses.

'My cousin heard from your editor, by the way,' said Kit. 'Loads of people wrote to the magazine defending the Songbird. Nearly a hundred letters altogether, saying you were out of order.'

'Really,' said Liza, who had written most of them.

'They're printing a selection in next month's issue.'

'Well, there you go,' said Liza steadily. 'Looks like I was wrong and you were right.'

He took off his sunglasses. Liza waited for another smart remark. But he didn't say anything, just gazed down at her.

Alistair, meanwhile, was being dragged down from his digger by a pair of sweating policemen, one thin, one burly, like Laurel and Hardy. Mid-tussle, he spotted Liza and a tall dark-haired boy making no effort to join in the protest.

'Hey, you two! Get yourselves in front of that bulldozer, fast.'

Kit called back, 'Actually, we'd rather not.'

The next moment, as Alistair disappeared beneath a heaving mound of navy-blue serge, Kit Berenger reached out and took hold of Liza's hand. His strong fingers gripped her wrist.

'What are you d-doing?' Liza gasped, trying to snatch it away.

'Taking your pulse.' He raised a dark eyebrow. 'Hmm, fast. Very fast.'

This was even more humiliating than being hauled into a police van in struggling-beetle position, as was now happening to Alistair. Liza stared hard at the goings-on at the back of the van and pretended she hadn't heard Kit Berenger speak.

'Mine too,' he went on, releasing his grip on her wrist and offering her his own. 'Have a feel if you want.'

'No thanks,' Liza replied faintly.

'The thing is, there's something I've been wanting to do rather badly for quite a while now,' said Kit. 'Is it okay with you if I give it a go?'

Liza could barely breathe.

'Not if you're going to slap my face.'

'I don't want to slap your face.' He turned her slowly towards him, so there was no escaping the look in those extraordinary black-lashed, yellow-gold eyes. 'I want to kiss your mouth.'

This, thought Liza, is ridiculous . . .

Then she stopped thinking because it was too late now to do anything, let alone think. Kit Berenger's mouth came down on hers and Liza gave herself up to it, utterly helpless to protest. Every nerve in her body was going *zinnggg*. She was only managing to stay standing because his arms were keeping her up. The knees had gone, the stomach had disappeared . . .

Just don't stop, Liza silently begged him, willing the kiss to go on and on. Please don't stop.

'Bloody hell, it's Kit Berenger,' exclaimed the reporter, gazing in amazement at the scene confronting him as he made his way back to the car for a fag break. 'Oi, Joe, over here,' he yelled, beckoning frantically for the photographer. 'Look who's snogging Liza Lawson! Get a shot of this, for Chrissake.'

Alistair was still putting up a terrific struggle, resisting every effort to bundle him into the back of the police van. Hearing the journalist's words, he twisted round and stared in horror at Liza who appeared to be clinging to Kit Berenger for dear life.

'You bastard, take your hands off her this minute,' roared Alistair. 'Liza, what the hell d'you think you're doing? Don't you know who that *is*?'

In no time they were the centre of attention. The protesters had all stopped to watch. Joe was using up his last roll of film.

'I always say you can't beat a bit of privacy,' Kit Berenger murmured against Liza's mouth, his hand stroking the back of her neck.

When the *Evening Post* reporter had been eating his Big

Mac earlier, a group of New Agers had hissed 'murderer' at him. Now, behind her back, Liza could hear them hissing 'traitor' at her.

'I may not get out of here alive,' she said, her voice still unsteady, her whole body quivering shamelessly with lust.

'At least they're vegetarians, they won't eat you alive.'

A nightmare thought struck Liza.

'Why did you do this, to make a fool of me?'

'Come on.' Kit half smiled down at her. 'You don't really think that. I did it because it had to be done. Before we both drove each other demented.'

Liza nodded. She could no longer deny it; the chemistry was simply there between them. It had been from the word go.

'How old are you?' she asked, needing to know the worst.

'Twenty-three.'

'I'm thirty-two.' It sounded terrible. She had never been out with anyone younger than her before. Not even nine months younger, let alone nine years.

'No you aren't, you're thirty-one.'

'Only until next week.'

Kit grinned. 'A week's a long time in politics.'

The protest had by this time pretty much fizzled out. When the protesters' attention had turned to Liza and Kit, the contractors had revved up their engines and got busy with the bulldozers, to-ing and fro-ing at surprising speed as they shifted great mounds of earth.

The police van, with Alistair's outraged face glaring out of the tiny back window, bumped and jiggled its way across the churned-up ground on to the main road.

'You must be joking,' said Kit when the reporter from the *Evening Post* asked him for a quote.

'Liza?' The reporter looked not-very-hopefully hopeful.

'She doesn't have anything to say either.'

'I think I'd better go home,' said Liza, when they were alone again. She was floundering, unsure what was going to happen next. He might be nine years younger, but Kit Berenger had somehow automatically assumed control of the situation. If he were to bundle her into that dark-green Bentley of his, Liza thought with longing, and whisk her off somewhere – anywhere – to bed, she would willingly go.

'I've got a heavy day too.' Kit glanced at his watch – that ludicrous purple Swatch. 'I'm already running late. Sorry,' he smiled slightly as he led the way back to their cars, 'if I'd known this was going to happen, I could have postponed a few meetings. You'd better give me your phone number.'

He leaned against the bonnet of the Bentley and wrote the number on the back of a crumpled ten-pound note pulled from the pocket of his jeans. Liza, who couldn't bear men with namby-pamby handwriting, was passionately relieved to see how assertive he was with a pen, not nancyish at all.

As he helped her into the Renault, his lips brushed hers, thrillingly, once more.

'I'll be in touch,' said Kit.

My God, you'd better be, thought Liza, far too proud to ask when.

Chapter 23

'Did someone slip something into my cocoa?' Dulcie demanded with suitable drama two days later. 'Am I hallucinating? Or is this really a photo I see before me in the local paper – on the front page, no less – of my friend Liza snogging with the enemy?'

Liza bit her lip, gazed out of the window and said nothing.

'And you can turn that sodding answering machine off for a start,' Dulcie went on, 'because it isn't fooling anyone. We know you're in there. Dammit,' she wailed the next second, 'do you want me to *die* of curiosity?'

That, thought Liza, would be too much to hope for. Chewing her pen, she leafed irritably through the research notes she was amassing in preparation for her new book, a history of Mediterranean cookery.

'Fine, I get the message,' said Dulcie in a sing-song voice when it became clear Liza had no intention of picking up the phone. 'But don't think you can hide for ever. The minute I can walk again, I'll be over. I don't know what you've been up to,' she concluded briskly, – God, now she sounded like Joyce Grenfell on speed – 'but I'm jolly well going to find out.'

Dulcie rang off at last. Wearily, since the kitchen table might be awash with reference books but that didn't mean she was getting a stroke of work done, Liza snapped the file shut and switched the kettle on instead. For the millionth time she compulsively checked her watch.

What a hideous day. The phone hadn't stopped ringing, the poor answering machine didn't know what had hit it. The story had even been picked up by a couple of the nationals; at lunchtime a call had come through from the *Daily Mail*, who were keen to include Liza in a feature on star-crossed lovers.

'We've got a pair of besotted MPs so far – one Labour, one Tory – and a vegan who's fallen in love with a butcher,' the journalist explained with maddening cheerfulness. 'The third couple were going to be Catholic-Protestant, but to be frank,' she lowered her voice to a confiding whisper, 'your story sounds much more fun.'

Liza stood at the kitchen window, sipping lukewarm tea she didn't even want. Her so-called story might sound fun to the girl from the *Mail* but it was a lot less entertaining being on the business end, Liza could promise her that.

She gazed out at the tiny patio garden bursting with tubs of geraniums and petunias, and tried to remember if exam nerves, the real stomach-churning kind when you actually felt sick with fear, had ever been this bad.

Except with exam nerves, at least you knew when the exam would be over.

She shuddered as something alien sloshed into her mouth. Ugh, she'd forgotten to fish out the tea bag.

Uselessly Liza checked her watch again. Still only twenty-six minutes to five.

I'm a grown woman, she thought, willing herself to believe it. In four days' time I'll be thirty-two. I can handle this.

But the sick feeling showed no sign of going away.

Liza bit her lip. It was fifty-four hours since Kit Berenger had oh so casually said he would phone her.

It hadn't happened yet.

Three times a week Pru drove Eddie to Bristol, to Elmlea House, a nursing home in Clifton overlooking the suspension bridge. While she waited in the car, passing the time with one of Dulcie's eye-boggling sex-and-shopping paperbacks, Eddie disappeared inside the ivy-fronted building to visit his mother-in-law, now frail and in her late eighties but still mentally all there.

'She's a darling,' he told Pru when she had commented – quite daringly, for her – that not many men would put themselves out as much as he did for their mother-in-law.

Eddie had simply looked amused. 'It's no hardship. We're great friends. Anyway, I'm all the family she has left.'

Their regular trips to and from Bristol had proved the ideal opportunity for him to talk to Pru about his marriage. Simply and without drama, Eddie described Catherine's bizarre mood swings in the early days, and the difficulties he'd faced trying to control her when neither of them had had any idea there could be an actual medical reason for it all.

Then the petrifying roller-coaster of full-blown manic depression had taken hold. The first of many hospital admissions had given Eddie a few months' much-needed respite.

'The doctors would spend ages juggling her medication, getting it just right,' he explained to Pru, 'but as soon as she was well again, they'd discharge her. Catherine would then decide she felt so much better she didn't need the medication any more. Even if I stood over her she'd just hide the capsules under her tongue and spit them out later.' Eddie shook his head sorrowfully at the memory of those times.

'Anyway,' he went on, while Pru concentrated on the road ahead, 'it got worse. Then, twelve years ago, she ran out of the house one night when I was trying to persuade her to take her pills. She was only wearing a nightdress. My car keys were hanging up by the front door. She grabbed them, yelling that she'd had enough, and drove off. There was a high wall at the end of our cul-de-sac. Catherine must have been doing sixty when she smashed into it.' For a second Eddie's voice wavered. He cleared his throat. 'Oh well, could have been worse. At least she was killed outright.'

Pru didn't know what to say so she didn't say anything. But her grey eyes filled with tears.

'Hey, don't you cry.' Eddie sounded alarmed. 'I wouldn't have told you if I'd thought you'd cry.'

'Sorry.' Ever obedient, Pru wiped her wet face with the back of her hand.

He shook his head, half smiling as he passed her a clean handkerchief. 'I thought you were tougher than that.'

She spluttered with surprised laughter. 'Me, tough? I am the original wet lettuce!'

'That isn't true. Your marriage broke up. And in dramatic fashion,' Eddie pointed out. 'But you're coping with it.'

'Am I?' Pru sighed and blew her nose. 'Inside, I wonder if I'll ever feel normal again.' She glanced across at Eddie in the passenger seat. 'How long before you did?'

It was Eddie's turn to be stuck for words. Twelve years since Catherine's death and he still hadn't been able to bring himself to form any kind of emotional attachment. The barriers had gone up and stayed up. Well and truly up. The prospect of getting involved with someone else was still too terrifying to contemplate.

'Well . . . not long, not long at all,' Eddie lied heartily. He gave Pru a clumsy pat on the arm to cheer her up. 'You're okay. You'll be fine, you'll see.'

The book Dulcie had passed on to her this week was all bonk and no plot. Pru waded through a couple more chapters then gave up, bored. She fiddled with the car radio instead, zipping from station to station in search of something – at 7.01 p.m. – that wasn't the news. Next she tried out all the mysterious switches and buttons she'd never bothered to investigate before, unexpectedly locating the electronic wing mirror wagglers, a well-hidden lever to open the boot and an astonishingly efficient mechanism for tipping the seats back in a trice.

Whoomph, Pru was flat on her back. She pressed the switch a second time. Whoomph, upright again! What brilliant fun.

Grinning to herself, Pru catapulted up and down a few more

times. Until, mortified, she realised she was being watched.

An ancient old dear, one of the residents presumably, was standing less than six feet away. Indicating with a jab of her walking stick that she wished to say something, she moved creakily towards the car while Pru, crimson with embarrassment, slid open the driver's window.

'You'll do yourself an injury, child,' the old woman observed. 'Whatever are you playing at?'

'Trying out the seat recliner,' mumbled Pru apologetically.

'Well, it works.'

'I know. Sorry.'

The woman, who was clutching a folded-up newspaper in her free hand, peered past her into the car.

'What's that, any good?' Beadily she eyed the lurid paperback lying on the passenger seat.

The thought of this precisely spoken, autocratic old lady reading Dulcie's bonkbuster was even more blushmaking than being caught playing with the seat recliners like a three-year-old.

'No, actually, it's awful,' Pru said hurriedly. 'You wouldn't like it at all.'

'How do you know I wouldn't? I might.' The old woman's expression was challenging. 'I can see from the cover it isn't a Barbara Cartland,' she went on, almost irritably, 'which makes a change in this place, I can tell you. Wall-to-wall Barbara-bloody-Cartlands in here. Just because you're eighty they seem to think that's all you want to read.'

'This definitely isn't a Barbara Cartland.' Pru was as firm as she dared.

'Good. Well, if it's awful, you won't be wanting it. So can I have it instead?'

Pru was taken aback by the bluntness of the request. You expected to be stopped in the street by beggars and asked for spare change but you didn't expect to be faced with imperious OAPs demanding pornographic paperbacks.

As if sensing her dilemma the woman said briskly, 'I

153

promise not to have a heart attack, if it's the sex you're worried about.'

Then, when Pru still hesitated, she held out her paper. 'Go on, you can have this instead. I've done the crossword but at least you'll have something to read.'

Pru's eyes began to boggle as she saw the photograph on the front page. She grabbed Dulcie's paperback and thrust it through the open window.

'Thanks.' The old lady looked immensely pleased with her swap. 'Just one other thing.'

'What?'

'All that whizzing up and down in your seat's played havoc with your hair, child. Better do something with it; your ears are sticking out.'

'Liza, it's me. Help, you know I hate these machines . . .'

Hearing Pru's voice, Liza picked up the phone. Pru was about the only person on the planet she could bear to speak to just now, she realised. Nobody was more *au fait* with public humiliation than Pru.

'I'm here. I know, you've seen the *Evening Post*. Oh Pru, I think he did it to teach me a lesson. He kissed me in front of all those people and I practically melted on the spot. He promised to phone me and I was so sure he would,' Liza admitted brokenly, 'but he bloody hasn't.'

There was no need to pretend with Pru. Unlike everyone else, she wouldn't make sympathetic noises and all the time be madly smirking and thinking ha ha, welcome to the real world and about time too.

Pru wasn't like that. Her sympathy would be genuine. Desperate to unburden herself, Liza told her everything.

Sometimes a very old and completely trustworthy friend – which rather ruled out Dulcie – was the only person you could tell this kind of stuff to.

'I mean, you know me,' Liza rattled on. Having started, she now found she couldn't stop. 'I'm not promiscuous – well, not that promiscuous – but all I wanted to do was go to bed with him! Dammit, how could he make such a fool of me? He's nine years younger than I am, for God's sake! And every time I think of him my knees *still* turn to jelly – why am I echoing?'

As Liza's voice had risen, the echo had become more apparent.

'Um . . . I'm in the car.'

But Liza could hear someone else snorting with laughter in the background. Someone male.

'What's going on? It doesn't usually echo like that.' Her blood ran cold.

'Sorry, darling, my fault.' It was Eddie Hammond, chuckling unashamedly. 'Couldn't resist it. I switched you on to hands-free.'

Cold wasn't the word for Liza's blood now.

'You eavesdropper,' she hissed, mortified.

'Come on,' he protested, still laughing. 'Pru showed me the picture in the paper. I was curious too.'

When Liza had slammed the phone down it occurred to her that although he wasn't married, Eddie Hammond had never flirted with her.

First Eddie, now Kit Berenger, thought Liza gloomily. I must really be losing my touch.

Chapter 24

Dulcie hadn't wanted to ring Liam at the club, it seemed a bit keen, but he'd forgotten to give her his home number so she didn't have much choice.

Or much time to lose, Dulcie thought twitchily as she waited for him to come to the phone. She could just imagine what Imelda had been like over the last four days, throwing herself at Liam and making the most of Dulcie's unexpected absence. The girl was shameless and desperate. You could almost feel sorry for her.

Almost, but not quite.

Cheered by a mental image of Imelda in one of those Velcro suits you got at fairgrounds, hurling herself at a vast Velcro wall with Liam perched like Humpty Dumpty – only better-looking, of course – on top, Dulcie forgot to be nervous when he at last came to the phone.

'Hi,' she said brightly, 'I'm better! How about me cooking you dinner tonight at my place, to celebrate?'

'No more flu?' She heard the smile in his voice. He was clearly pleased to hear from her.

'No more flu,' Dulcie said with pride. 'So is that a yes?'

At Brunton Manor, Liam leaned against the receptionist's desk and grinned at the prettier of the two receptionists. She promptly went pink and smiled back. Playfully he tapped the little emerald ring on her engagement finger and pulled a mock-sorrowful face.

'Liam, are you still there?'

'Dinner sounds great.' It really did, he decided cheerfully.

And he liked Dulcie a lot, she was sparky and fun. If she was as good in the kitchen as she was in bed, he was in for a treat. 'Look, I promised to meet someone else for a quick drink at eight. Just a business thing, but I wouldn't want to let them down. Is nine-ish okay with you?'

Almost bursting with happiness – ha! Imelda hadn't got him yet – Dulcie replied triumphantly, 'Nine-ish is fine.'

Not one of life's Delia Smiths, Dulcie had nevertheless been forced during the course of her marriage to conjure up the odd decent meal or two. She even knew how to cook a proper dinner-party dinner, which might have impressed Liam if it hadn't been mushrooms fried in garlic butter followed by chicken à la crème and chocolate mousse.

The prospect of cooking something healthy was fairly daunting but Dulcie refused to be intimidated. As she had told Liza – quite often, actually – Liam was worth it. Nothing was too much trouble. If all Liam ate was roast alligator, she would happily race to the nearest swamp, catch an alligator and roast it.

Anyway, he didn't. All she had to do was grill a couple of fillet steaks, chuck a few baking potatoes in the oven and microwave a bowl of frozen peas.

It sounded simple enough but still somehow managed to take ages to do. Dulcie didn't mind, she was in love with a glorious, glamorous *vision* of a man and you had to suffer for someone as heavenly as Liam, that was only fair. She even did a bit of salad to go with it, and cut the tomatoes painstakingly into zigzag halves so they looked like lilies – albeit slightly wonky lilies – floating on an artistic lettuce and onion pond.

Dulcie wasn't asleep when the hail of gravel rattled against her bedroom window but she was buggered if she was going to get up straight away.

She heard Liam scrunching across the drive, scooping up and flinging another handful of gravel at another window further along because he didn't know which was hers. Torn between passionate relief that he hadn't stood her up after all and indignation, because – let's face it – there's late and there is late, Dulcie lay in bed for a few seconds more.

It was a retaliation, of sorts.

When she heard a shower of stones hit the bathroom window and a pane of glass go CRACK, she got up.

'There you are,' Liam exclaimed, peering up at Dulcie's spiky-haired silhouette.

'Sshh,' Dulcie hissed.

He looked alarmed. 'Why? Is your husband up there?'

'Of course he isn't.' Men, honestly. 'I was thinking of the neighbours. Anyway, what's wrong with using the doorbell?'

He looked shocked.

'It's too late to ring doorbells.' This was a hangover from Liam's rowdy teenage years. His father had gone ballistic whenever he'd forgotten his front door key. Now, standing beneath Dulcie's window, he checked his watch and offered up his wrist as proof. 'See? One o'clock.'

'You don't say.' Dulcie hadn't forgotten she was supposed to be miffed. 'Funny, I could have sworn you said you'd be here by nine. Or were you talking about breakfast?'

'I'm late,' said Liam. 'I know, I'm sorry.' He gazed up at her, utterly repentant in the moonlight. 'But I'm here now. I came all this way. Angel, you have to let me in.'

'I bloody do not,' Dulcie retorted briskly, not meaning it for a second.

'Okay, I'll climb up.' Grinning, he moved towards the drainpipe next to the porch. He stood on one of the flower-filled stone tubs and began testing the strength of the drainpipe.

'All of a sudden he's Milk Tray Man,' mocked Dulcie, but her own mouth was beginning to twitch. In all honesty, how could she resist him? Before he managed to yank the drainpipe off the wall she said, 'Okay, you win. Get down before you break a leg. I'll open the front door.'

When she did, she was naked. Liam solemnly eyed each of

her small breasts in turn, bowed his head politely and murmured in his soft Irish drawl, 'So pleased to meet you both, you're looking wonderful—'

'Berk,' said Dulcie.

When he'd finished kissing her, Liam led her by the hand into the kitchen.

'I'm starving. What's for dinner?'

'Is that a joke?' She gave him an indignant prod in the ribs. 'I fed your dinner to the foxes hours ago. You didn't seriously expect me to *save* it?'

Seeing the expression on his face, Dulcie realised he had. She marvelled at the kind of life Liam must have led, the star tennis player so used to getting what he wanted, it didn't occur to him that turning up four hours late might be considered a bit offish.

Although, actually he didn't know how lucky he was. Having stupidly imagined Liam would arrive promptly at nine, she had first grilled the steaks then put them in the oven to keep warm. By ten o'clock they had acquired the consistency of dog chews. Flinging them out through the kitchen window had been an act of mercy. If the foxes had got at them, thought Dulcie, serve them right.

'Sweetheart, it was a business meeting. I was held up,' Liam protested. In reality it had been an Imelda meeting and he had been held down, but some details were better glossed over. From what he could gather, there wasn't much love lost between the two girls.

Dulcie was on the brink of making some cutting remark about the lack of phones where he'd been when she realised how it would make her sound. Like some nagging old *wife*, she thought with a shudder, the frumpy, bitter kind whose husbands you felt most sorry for, the kind where you wouldn't blame their husbands for wanting to sneak off.

How awful, and this is only our second date. If it even counts as a date . . .

But Liam was here, and that was what mattered. When you

159

were famous, Dulcie realised, you lived by different rules. It was like inviting the Queen to tea and expecting her to pitch in afterwards with the washing-up. If you ever wanted to see her again, bunging her a pair of Marigolds and telling her to get scrubbing wasn't a smart move to make.

Liam was glad he'd made the effort to come round. Fish fingers and reheated baked potatoes might not set the pulse racing but they were an excellent source of vitamin B. Anyway, now she'd stopped sulking he had Dulcie to make his pulse race.

If he was honest, Liam preferred Dulcie to Imelda, who had spent most of the evening dropping hints the size of comets about holidays. Liam had marvelled good-naturedly at her train of thought; women were funny creatures. He'd taken Imelda to bed a couple of times, that was all. Whatever made her think he'd want to spend a fortnight with her in Phuket?

Liam's attitude to life was uncomplicated. All he wanted was to keep fit, play tennis and have as much fun as possible with the opposite sex. This, he decided, was where Dulcie definitely had the edge. He was genuinely fond of her. She was more laid-back, probably relishing her own new-found freedom, and hadn't so much as mentioned holidays. Liam, very much a 'so many women, so little time' man himself, was mystified by the female preoccupation with – yawn – monogamy and – bigger yawn – settling down.

Jesus, where was the fun in that?

With Eddie needing to be driven that morning to Swindon for a meeting at eleven which was likely to go on for hours, Pru had consulted her diary and decided to get Terry Hayes' cottage out of the way first. Ringing him beforehand to be on the safe side and getting no answer – he wasn't kidding when he said he started work early – she pulled up outside his front door at seven thirty and let herself in.

The kitchen didn't take long. When Pru had finished in there

160

she moved on to the bathroom. Terry had bought himself some new aftershave, she noticed. Ralph Lauren, Polo. Nice. And a bottle of hair-thickening shampoo. Trying to spruce himself up, Pru thought with an indulgent smile. Bless him. What's the betting he's splashed out on new underpants too?

Humming to herself, Pru fished the Hoover out from the cupboard under the stairs and hauled it upstairs. Elbowing the door open, she launched herself into Terry's bedroom. Honestly, what was it with men? Why did it never occur to them to draw back the curtains before they left for work?

The Hoover landed with a crash on the floor. Two people abruptly jack-knifed into sitting positions on the bed. Only semi-covered by the tangled duvet, they were both naked.

And neither of them was Terry Hayes.

'What's going on?' demanded the man, sitting bolt upright.

'Who's *she*?' squeaked the girl next to him, pulling the duvet up to her ears.

'I'm the cleaner.' Pru told herself not to be so silly, they couldn't possibly be burglars. In the semi-darkness she peered closely at the man, who was rather good-looking. Those heavy eyebrows and piercing dark eyes, now she came to think of it, were definitely familiar.

'Who are you?' said Pru. 'Terry's brother?'

'Pru?' The man began to relax. He grinned at her. 'I'm Terry.'

'No you aren't.' Pru hesitated, confused. This was like a John le Carré novel where the gardener suddenly whisks off his beard and turns into a KGB agent.

'Actually, he is,' volunteered the girl in the bed. 'And I've worked with him for the last four years, so I should know.'

Having taken the intrusion amazingly calmly, considering, Terry asked Pru if she wouldn't mind making them all a pot of coffee.

Ten minutes later, showered and dressed, he appeared in the kitchen.

'Sorry about barging in,' said Pru, going pink at the memory

161

as she poured the coffee into green and gold cups. 'I thought you were at work. I did ring.'

'Day off. I never hear the phone when I'm asleep.' Terry dismissed her apology with a good-natured shrug. 'Anyway, I'm curious. Why didn't you think I was me? What's my bossy sister been telling you?'

'Nothing,' protested Pru. 'Marion didn't say anything. It's my mistake. It was the photograph in your bedroom, that's all. I just assumed the chap in it was you.'

Terry's rather angular mouth twitched.

'It *was* me.'

'But—'

He tapped the side of his nose.

'Before I had this done.'

Pru winced. She'd put her foot in it again.

'You mean you had an . . . an accident?'

'No accident. You're being wonderfully tactful,' Terry looked amused, 'but there's no need. You've seen the photo, Pru. Let's be honest, I was born with one hell of a nose.'

'Oh . . . well . . .'

'Jokes? I heard them all. Witty nicknames? Honker, Concorde, Big Bird . . . I've been called everything in my time. When I was at school, the other kids made my life hell,' Terry went on. 'Then you get older, and people might stop calling you names, but you know they're still staring at you, trying to concentrate on what you're saying to them and all the time thinking: "God, *look* at the hooter on him." '

Pru couldn't stop staring either.

'So . . . so you had plastic surgery?'

'It wasn't a question of vanity.' For the first time Terry sounded defensive. 'I just wanted to look . . . normal.'

'Oh I know,' cried Pru. She understood exactly how he must have felt. 'I *know*. Did . . . well, did it hurt?'

He shrugged.

'A bit. But it was worth it. If it had hurt a hundred times more, it would still have been worth it. You see, I don't have to

162

think about my nose any more. Why are you crying?' He looked worried. 'Pru, stop it. You mustn't cry. Your nose is *fine*.'

Unable to speak, Pru raised her arms and scooped her hair away from her face.

At that moment the girl who shared both Terry's office and his bed came into the kitchen wearing his towelling dressing gown.

'Good grief.' She eyed Pru's ears with alarm. 'Shouldn't you get those seen to?'

'Karen is to diplomacy what Margaret Thatcher is to tap dancing,' Terry apologised. 'But this time I have to say she's right.'

Pru covered her ears back up again. Funny how all it had taken to overcome a lifetime's fear of surgery was a snapshot of a man with a beaky nose.

Typical, too, that all those years when money had been no object, she hadn't been able to pluck up the courage to have her ears fixed.

Now I've got the courage, Pru thought gloomily, and I can't even afford a tube of UHU.

Chapter 25

Liza lay in the bath for an hour, watching her skin shrivel and marvelling at her spectacular stupidity. It was her birthday, she was thirty-two, and she was acting like a pathetic teenager.

Damn, worse than that. She was acting like . . . Dulcie.

There had been plenty of offers over the course of the last few days, from various men eager to take her out on her birthday. Stupidly, still hoping against hope that Kit Berenger would be in touch, she had turned them all down. She had even invented ever more elaborate excuses on Kit's behalf, every time the phone rang and it wasn't him.

In the end Liza had run out of excuses. Reasonable ones anyway. The only excuse that would do now was if he were dead.

So here she was, a grown woman in the grip of a deeply embarrassing crush – an unrequited crush at that – all alone on her birthday and feeling more spinsterish by the minute.

Climbing out of the bath, Liza put on a baggy yellow sweater and a pair of pink shorts. Since it was sunny outside she took her work out into the tiny garden.

Seconds after she'd settled herself down with more reference books and a notepad, the post arrived. Sending her coffee flying, Liza raced to the door. Cards, cards, cards . . .

None of them from Kit Berenger.

Hating herself for being foolish enough to even think he might have sent one – how truly pathetic could you get? – Liza crammed her sunglasses on to her face and forced herself to work for two hours straight.

At midday she made herself another pot of coffee and phoned Mark.

'Dinner tonight. Are you still up for it?'

'I thought you were busy.'

'Change of plan,' Liza replied brightly. 'I can make it now.'

'Oh, shame, I made other arrangements.' Bemused by her call – it didn't occur to him for a second that she could actually have been stood up by another man – Mark added, 'Of course, you're welcome to join us. Suzie wouldn't mind . . .'

Dulcie was just as much of a let-down.

'I can't, I'm seeing Liam. He's mad about me,' she confided happily. 'You should have seen him last night, trying to climb in through my bedroom window! He's so romantic,' she sighed, '*so* masterful.'

Not in the mood to hear this, Liza attempted a quick getaway. 'Okay, doesn't matter—'

'Hang on! You still haven't told me what's been going on between you and Kit Berenger.'

'Terrible line, I can hardly hear you.' Liza bashed the phone against the wall a couple of times and hung up.

When the doorbell rang an hour later she was tempted not to answer it. Why bother when it was either flowers from Mark – a guilt gift to make up for not being able to see her tonight – or Dulcie determined to get the low-down on the Berenger affair.

Some affair, Liza thought miserably. Chance would be a fine thing.

The doorbell rang again. Heaving an irritated sigh, she went to see who it was. If it was flowers, she'd answer the door. If it was Dulcie she definitely wouldn't.

It wasn't Dulcie. It wasn't flowers either. And the silhouette through the stained glass was man-shaped.

Pulling the door open, Liza came face to face with Kit Berenger.

'Happy birthday.'

He was wearing a dark-green shirt with a fine crimson stripe and the most impeccably cut black suit.

'Thanks.' Liza wondered how he knew it was today.

But who cared? He was here, he was *here*.

'You could always invite me in,' Kit suggested when she didn't move.

'I thought you were going to phone.' Liza stayed where she was. 'Don't tell me, you spent the ten pounds and couldn't remember my number.'

He grinned. 'Oh ye of little faith. Actually, I learned it off by heart. And I nearly phoned, hundreds of times. Had to exert a fair amount of self-control, I can tell you.'

Liza took a deep breath. She was having to exert a bit of self-control herself, right at this moment.

'Either way, phoning would have been the decent thing to do,' she said evenly. 'If you decide you don't want to see someone again, you should still let them know.'

'Come on,' chided Kit, his tone humorous, 'you didn't think that for a second.'

Liza pulled him into the narrow hallway and slammed the door shut. They stood, inches away from each other, her dark-brown eyes fixed angrily on his yellow-gold ones.

'I *thought* I didn't think that for a second,' she almost hissed at him, 'until you didn't ring. Oh for God's sake,' she blurted out furiously, 'how could you *do* that to me?'

'Look,' said Kit, 'I thought we both needed the time to think. I don't know about you, but I don't make a habit of feeling like this about someone. It's pretty scary, if you want the truth.' He hesitated, then half smiled. 'Bloody scary, in fact.'

'It's only lust. You don't have to be scared!'

'Ah, but what if it isn't only lust?' Kit put his hands on her shoulders. 'You said yourself, I was too young for you.'

Liza smiled up at him.

'I meant I was too old for you. Anyway, it doesn't matter. We're hardly talking weddings here. What's wrong with a harmless fling?'

'Is that all you're interested in?' demanded Kit. He began to sound annoyed.

Liza was just glad he was here. The relief was overwhelming. She decided to be frank with him.

'Don't take this personally, it's just the way I am. And the age thing's irrelevant; I'm the same with everyone. I get bored quickly, that's all. So trust me, you don't have to worry about getting involved, being scared,' she told Kit, 'because it won't last long enough for that to happen.'

Inexplicably, Liza heard her voice break. She paused before finishing what she had to say. 'My relationships never do.'

He touched her mouth with one finger, tracing the outline of her full lower lip.

'How soon before you get bored?'

'Three or four weeks.' She tried to move her mouth away from his finger, found she couldn't do it. 'I'm a very shallow person.'

Kit frowned.

'A month? Is that the longest you've ever been involved with someone?'

Liza nodded, ashamed.

'Pretty much. I think I managed five weeks once.'

He shook his head.

'That's really sad.'

'I've kind of got used to it,' said Liza.

'That's even sadder.'

'Don't you dare start feeling sorry for me.'

'I'm not.' Kit grinned. 'Wouldn't dream of it. Anyway, you've met me now. Things could be about to change.'

That would be just my luck, thought Liza. After years of being left cold by endless hugely eligible men, how typical if I finally fell in love with a toyboy. How unsuitable could you get?

She didn't seriously expect it to happen. It was hardly likely. All she wanted to do was enjoy the next few weeks for what they were and accept the inevitable ending with good grace.

But for Kit's sake she pretended it was a possibility.

Smiling up at him, she said, 'Who knows? Maybe they are.'

167

Kit's eyes narrowed at once. 'Don't humour me.'

His voice sent shivers of longing down Liza's spine.

'I'm not.'

'You are. You think I'm too young to understand what makes you tick.'

Liza wished he'd stop talking. All she could think about right now was how badly she wanted him to make love to her.

That, she decided, would definitely be a birthday present worth having.

She gave him her most sensual and bewitching smile, the one that no man could ever resist.

'I'm telling you, you aren't going to get tired of me,' promised Kit, resisting it. 'I'm going to keep you interested if it kills me.'

'Really?' Liza gazed at him dreamily, her fingers itching to start unbuttoning his shirt. 'And how are you planning to do this? By hypnosis?'

'Stop looking at me like that,' Kit said with a grin. 'By not sleeping with you, for a start.'

It was the first week in June. The significance of this only struck Pru as she sat on a wooden bench outside Elmlea House in Clifton, absently flipping through the *Daily Mail*.

'Driving ban for vicar after peacocks get the chop', read Pru, but it was less alarming than it sounded. An absent-minded vicar, his thoughts on next Sunday's sermon rather than the road ahead, had managed to veer into a yew hedge and demolish thirty years' worth of lovingly tended topiary. Six sculpted peacocks had promptly been decapitated. The Morris Minor had escaped unscathed. The vicar, his licence suspended for a month, was quoted as saying, 'I feel terrible about this. Everyone in the parish knows how keen I am on birds.'

It suddenly occurred to Pru that Eddie's ban must almost be up. He had served his time, paid his penance. Any day now, surely, he'd be getting his licence back.

Pru was surprised how disappointed she felt. She would miss

driving Eddie around. Maybe she should pin up a card in her local police station, offering her services to anyone else about to be banned.

But it wouldn't be the same without Eddie.

'I know who you are now.'

Pru shielded her eyes from the setting sun and looked up to see who had spoken. Oh help, it was that bossy old woman again, the one who had commandeered Dulcie's steamy paperback.

'You're with Edna Peverell's son-in-law,' the woman announced triumphantly. 'You come here with him three times a week. Edna tells me he's a damn fine chap.'

Unable to think of anything else to say, Pru put down her paper and nodded.

'Oh yes, he is. Um . . . damn fine.'

'So what I want to know,' the old woman's eyes were shrewd, 'is what's wrong with you?'

'Excuse me?' said Pru.

'Why hasn't your chap introduced you to Edna? Too ashamed, is he? What are you, one of those topless models in your spare time?' The old lady had a laugh like a fox's bark. 'Come on, child, you can tell me. Why does he always leave you waiting outside like a wet umbrella?'

The old dear was clearly a couple of sausage rolls short of a picnic, but Pru was still flattered. She glanced down at her almost nonexistent chest.

'Hardly a topless model.'

'No, you're right. Something else then. Traffic warden? Jehovah's Witness?' She pointed her walking stick accusingly at Pru. 'Member of the SDP?'

'Actually,' said Pru, 'he's not my chap. I'm just Eddie's driver. That's why he hasn't introduced me to his mother-in-law.'

'Balls,' declared the old lady. Inching arthritically around, she jabbed her stick in the direction of one of the ivy-clad second-floor windows overlooking the car park. 'That's my

169

room up there. I've been watching the pair of you for the last six weeks. I'm not blind, you know.'

No, just dotty, thought Pru.

'How did you get on with that book?' she said, changing the subject.

'Not bad.' The batty old dear had turned towards the heavy oak front door. Preparing to leave, she paused and gave Pru a sly smile. 'Not enough sex.'

She muttered something else under her breath as she disappeared through the doorway.

'What?' Pru called after her retreating back. 'What did you say?'

'I said not enough sex.' In an oddly regal fashion, the old woman waved her walking stick briefly at Pru. Then she snorted with laughter. 'Rather like you and your chap.'

Pru didn't mention this exchange to Eddie when he returned to the car. Instead she asked him when his three-month ban was up.

Eddie gazed out of the side window at the spectacular Clifton suspension bridge, stretched across the Avon gorge.

'Did I tell you three months? That wasn't quite true,' he said, sounding awkward and still not looking at Pru. 'Actually it was . . . um . . . six.'

Chapter 26

Dulcie surveyed herself carefully from all angles in the wardrobe mirror but she still didn't look any different.

This was most annoying, because when you'd put in as much hard work as she had during the last month you expected to end up looking like an international Gladiator at least.

Still, she had to be fitter on the inside. The sweating was disgusting, the grunting and straining horribly reminiscent of childbirth and the sheer pain involved was unimaginable but if this was what it took to persuade Liam she was his kind of girl . . . well, then it was worth every grunt and strain.

Following the flu fiasco, Dulcie had realised drastic measures were now called for. Some things you could bluff your way through, others you couldn't, and attempting to pass yourself off as Bath's answer to Steffi Graf when in reality you were Bath's answer to a cross between Jo Brand and a walking Mars bar clearly wasn't on.

As a result of this, Dulcie had joined another, less sumptuous sports club on the other side of the city and had booked daily lessons with the far less desirable middle-aged tennis coach there. Biting the bullet, she had also enrolled herself in the beginners' aerobics class. If she could still walk after this, she stumbled along to the gym and pumped iron for an hour.

It had been far and away the most hideous month of Dulcie's life. The only consolation was that she was doing it where no one recognised her; she was working out at a club so un-smart she was unlikely ever to bump into anyone she knew.

171

But if hanging on to Liam McPherson involved keeping fit, Dulcie was prepared to suffer.

And now she *had* suffered, for a whole month. It was just such a bugger that it didn't show.

Maybe she could squeeze Liam half to death with her thighs. Then he'd be impressed.

Having finished her inspection in front of the mirror, Dulcie wriggled her way into a new dress, a tiny clinging thing the colour of sherbet lemons. With it, she wore flat silver sandals and understated silver jewellery. She was meeting up with Liam at Poppers, the new wine bar on Pulteney Bridge, and she wanted to look good. Poppers was definitely the kind of place people went to be seen.

'Dulcie? Are you here *on your own*?'

Turning, Dulcie came face to face with her estranged husband. Honestly, trust Patrick to make her sound like a prostitute.

'No need to panic! I promise not to flash my knickers at any strange men. Anyway,' she gave him a teasing smile, 'this is a wine bar, not a street corner. I'm allowed to be here; it's all quite legal.'

Actually, it was really nice to see him . . . until the next moment when Dulcie realised the girl doing her best to look as if she wasn't in any way connected with Patrick was connected with him after all.

'Ah, sorry. Claire, this is Dulcie. My . . . er, wife. Dulcie, Claire.'

A bit of advance warning wouldn't have gone amiss, Dulcie felt. She smiled as casually as she could at Claire and was surprised how hard it was to do. What a shame people didn't wear beepers, like little personal radars, so you always had a few minutes' notice that you were about to bump into them. That was all you'd need really, Dulcie thought, just a couple of minutes to gear yourself up, mentally prepare yourself for those awkward chance meetings. If Patrick was so clever with a computer, maybe he should give it a whirl. There had to be a market for a beeper to let you know you were about to cross paths with your husband and his new bird.

'It's really nice to meet you,' said Claire, reaching out and shaking Dulcie's unsuspecting hand. 'Look, if you two'd like to talk, I could leave you in peace for a few minutes . . .'

'No need for that.' Patrick acknowledged the diplomatic offer with a brief smile and slid an arm around Claire's waist.

Dulcie's eyes almost fell out. Public displays of affection weren't Patrick's style *at all*. For heaven's sake, it had taken her about four years to persuade him to put his arm around *her* waist.

'Anyway,' he went on, as if Dulcie had deliberately tried to change the subject, 'why *are* you here on your own?'

'I'm not on my own. I'm meeting Liam.'

'Oh? Where is he?'

'I got here early,' Dulcie fibbed.

Patrick shot her a look of disbelief.

'You're never anywhere early.'

That was the trouble with husbands; they knew you too well. Dulcie cursed Patrick for knowing her. She began elongating the fib.

'Well, I didn't mean to be early but I was over at Liza's and she had to go out so she gave me a lift. And Liam warned me he might be held up . . . someone's offered him a Lamborghini and if it looks good he'll take it for a test drive . . .'

This bit was actually true. The reason Dulcie was fibbing was to cover up the fact that Liam was over an hour late already. She just knew Patrick would disapprove.

Irritatingly, Patrick wasn't as impressed as he could have been by her casual mention of the Lamborghini. Knowing him as well as he knew her, Dulcie sensed the lip curl, the slight air of amusement. He was wondering what she thought she was doing, getting herself involved with the kind of man who drove that kind of car.

Cringing inwardly, Dulcie remembered what Steve Ellis,

the leering pro from Brunton Golf Club, had called them when Liam had mentioned he was thinking of getting one.

'Hey, major babe-magnet!'

And Liam, grinning, had replied, 'I've already got one of those.'

'He probably won't buy it,' Dulcie told Patrick and Claire. 'Not that he couldn't afford to. It's just not really his style, you know. Bit naff.'

'My father had one. He sold it last year,' said Claire. Realising her gaffe, she covered her mouth and let out a peal of laughter. Then she clutched Dulcie's arm and, still giggling, whispered conspiratorially, 'Please don't be embarrassed. You're right, of course. Too naff for words. He looked an absolute sight.'

Dulcie was trapped. By nine o'clock there was still no sign of Liam and Patrick was clearly determined to keep her talking until he turned up. Since she knew no one else there, Dulcie didn't have much choice.

She thought men were supposed to go for a particular type of woman and stick with them, but Patrick certainly hadn't; he'd managed to find someone the complete opposite of her. Furthermore – it was irritating but she couldn't help it; feeling miffed was a natural response – he definitely seemed happy with Claire.

Maybe that's all he ever wanted, the type he should have gone for in the first place, Dulcie realised. A sensible, cheerful, gosh-where-did-I-put-my-hockey-stick kind of girl. Intelligent, friendly towards everyone and with heaps of common sense. The type of person, Dulcie thought darkly, who held up her hand and said, 'No thanks, really, one chocolate's enough for me.'

She even had a real career, dammit, so Patrick's ridiculous working hours wouldn't bother her in the least. The chances were she wouldn't even notice he was never home because she wouldn't be there either, she'd still be working too.

They could be Executive Couple, thought Dulcie, and the

most annoying part of all is they wouldn't even think they were missing out on any fun, because when you're that career-minded, work *is* fun.

Willing it to be Liam every time the door was pushed open hadn't worked. By nine thirty Dulcie was growing desperate . . . and trying even more desperately to hide it.

'Looks like he's stood you up,' said Patrick, not sounding in the least sympathetic. 'Come on, we'll give you a lift home.'

How sad could you get? Dulcie suppressed a shudder – God, the *humiliation* – and gaily emptied her glass.

'Don't fuss! He'll be here any minute now,' she exclaimed. 'Anyway, this party we're going to doesn't start until midnight . . . it's at the home of one of his rock star friends, did I mention that? They live in this fantastic mansion outside Calne. Oh for heaven's sake, Patrick! Stop looking at your watch. What difference does it make if someone's a tiny bit late? Look, let me get you both another drink—'

'We've got a table booked at the Blue Bowl.' Patrick's tone was curt; he wasn't amused.

'If you'd like to, you'd be more than welcome to join us,' Claire said eagerly, her clear grey eyes reflecting genuine concern. She nodded as she spoke, so rhythmically that Dulcie wondered if someone behind her was tugging on her glossy brown plait, practising a spot of bell ringing on the nearest available rope.

Bloody, *bloody* Liam . . .

And bloody Claire, come to that, for being so caring, so jolly, jolly *nice*. Where had Patrick found her, anyway? Graduating with honours from the Jane Asher School of Charm and Utter Loveliness?

This reminded Dulcie that he hadn't told her yet how things had gone the night his mother had fixed him up.

To divert Patrick's attention from Liam's lateness, Dulcie said brightly, 'I forgot to ask, how was your awful blind date the other week, the one you were dreading so much? Total nightmare or what?'

Patrick looked at Claire. Ha, thought Dulcie, delighted. That's caught you out! Been two-timing her already . . .

Claire, in turn, looked at Dulcie. There were dimples in her cheeks.

'I don't think it went too badly, considering,' she said with a playful smile.

'But—'

'Oh, Dulcie, the awful blind date was me.'

'Where have you *been*?' hissed Dulcie when Liam finally appeared. 'For God's sake, you're two hours late!'

Liam cupped a hand over one ear and shook his head.

'Damn, I hate it when that happens.'

'Hate what?'

'That terrible noise in my ear. That nagging noise.'

'I'm not nagging,' Dulcie said crossly, 'I'm just telling you, that's all. You should have been here at nine.'

'Why, what happened?'

The blonde standing with her back to Liam suddenly giggled and swivelled round to look at him. Liam, happy to have his wit appreciated, grinned back.

'My husband and his new girlfriend were here, that's what happened,' Dulcie wailed. 'They insisted on waiting here with me until you turned up.'

Liam looked around.

'So where are they?'

'They left two minutes ago!' She almost stamped her foot.

'Phew, great timing.'

The blonde giggled again. Liam tried without much success to keep a straight face. Dulcie could have kicked the pair of them.

'It isn't funny. Dammit, they felt *sorry* for me.'

'Am I going to get this earache all night?' protested Liam.

There was an unfamiliar edge to his voice, as if he were on the verge of losing his patience. Suddenly overcome by a rush of fear – what if Liam turned round, grabbed the giggling blonde and disappeared with her out of the door? – Dulcie forced herself to calm down. Liam wasn't the type to sit alone and mope. She held a privileged position. And if she didn't want it there were plenty of other women queueing up to take her place.

'I'm sorry. It was pretty embarrassing, that's all. Forget it.'

His good humour instantly restored, Liam slid his arm around Dulcie's hips and pulled her playfully towards him.

'You mean I don't get detention from teacher?' he murmured in her ear. 'I don't have to write out a hundred lines: I must not be a naughty boy and upset Dulcie?'

She quivered helplessly. Oh, that soft, purring Irish drawl! It really should come with a government health warning . . .

'I'll let you off, this once,' she said faintly as Liam began kissing the tips of her fingers. Damn, why couldn't Patrick and Claire be here to witness this *now*?

'In that case,' his blue eyes crinkled at the corners, 'I'll let you have a ride in my new car.'

'Oh dear, I'm afraid I don't accept lifts from strange men,' said Dulcie.

'It's a Lamborghini.'

'What colour?'

'Red, of course.'

'Oh, all right then.'

Chapter 27

Liza, rubbing her eyes and pulling open the front door, protested, 'Good grief, it's only seven o'clock.'

Kit looked as if he'd been up for hours. He winked, unperturbed by the grumpy welcome.

'Do you know what today is?'

She had to think for a minute. 'Tuesday.'

'No. Well, yes,' he admitted, 'but what else?'

'I give up.'

'It's time you got bored with me.'

Liza already knew that. She smiled.

'Do I have to?'

'It's been a month,' said Kit. 'Aren't you bored yet?'

Her arms went around his neck. When she had finished kissing him, Liza looked up into his extraordinary yellow-gold eyes.

'You know I'm not. I've never been less bored.'

Or more frustrated, come to that.

'The thing is,' said Kit, reading her mind and looking amused, 'you aren't bad. I quite fancy you, in fact. Maybe we shouldn't risk spoiling things.'

'Meaning . . .?'

He shrugged.

'Well, I don't know. Maybe we should stay as we are. Platonic friends. No sex for at least the next ten years. What are you doing?'

Ask a silly question.

'Unfastening your belt.'

'Oh. Not keen, then, on my idea?'

'Not very keen, no.'

Kit kicked the front door shut and leaned back against it, his eyes fixed on Liza's face.

'What are you doing now?' he said finally.

'Just unzipping your trousers.'

'Liza.'

'Mm?'

'I love you.'

Liza looked away, unable to speak. All these years and it had happened at last. She'd heard these words so many times before, but this was the first time she'd actually wanted to hear them. Until now, they'd always made her feel sick.

'It's almost killed me, waiting this long,' Kit went on. 'I want to make love to you more than anything in the world.'

Liza quivered helplessly. She knew it was corny, but a tingling sensation actually *was* going down her spine.

She cleared her throat and nodded. 'Me too.'

'But if it's going to change things between us . . . if it's going to spoil all this . . .'

'I don't think it is,' said Liza, who had wondered the same thing herself. This time she shook her head, desperate to convince him she was right. 'I really don't think it is.'

'Tell you what.'

'What?'

Slowly, he slid the straps of her white nightdress off her shoulders.

'You don't get bored with me,' whispered Kit, his breath warm against her neck, 'I won't get bored with you.'

He was so in control. Liza wondered how on earth a twenty-three-year-old could be so self-assured. Heavens, he acted older than she did.

'Is that a promise?' she said, dry-mouthed. The need to know was overwhelming.

As he carried her through to the bedroom, Kit said, 'Cross my heart, hope to die.'

It wasn't a let-down.

Thank God.

Not that Liza had seriously expected him to be lousy in bed; it was just when you built something up so much in your mind, your expectations soared so sky-high they became almost impossible to live up to.

Anyway, thought Liza, smiling with her eyes closed, it hadn't been a let-down in any shape or form.

And she *definitely* hadn't been bored.

'By the way, my cousin wants to meet you,' said Kit, much later that morning.

Liza was admiring his brown legs. Better legs, possibly, than any she had ever seen on a man.

'Which cousin?'

'Nicky.'

'You mean from the Songbird?'

Kit mimicked her look of horror.

'Yes, from the Songbird.'

'Oh my God, does she want to kill me?'

'Don't panic, business is on the up. The restaurant isn't going to close after all.'

Liza covered her face with the duvet. Her voice was muffled.

'She must hate me.'

'Actually, she agrees with you. As soon as I said you'd eaten there on New Year's Day, it clicked. That was the day her chef turned up half-cut, apparently, and Nicky had to do most of the cooking herself.'

'Poor thing.'

'She's okay. You'll get on fine,' said Kit.

Liza rested her head in the crook of his shoulder.

'This is proper boyfriend-girlfriend stuff. Meeting the family.' She smiled at the thought. This was something else she'd shied away from over the years, simply because there hadn't seemed much point. 'Whatever next?'

'May as well mention it while we're on the subject,' Kit

said evenly. 'My father. This thing is, he—'

'Your father wants to meet me too? My God, talk about popular! How does—'

Kit put his hand gently over Liza's mouth to shut her up.

'Don't jump to conclusions. I was about to say don't expect anything like that from my father, because he absolutely doesn't want to meet you.'

'Oh.'

'No offence.'

'I'm not offended,' said Liza, deeply offended.

'Look, he's pretty old-fashioned. Upsetting Nicky didn't do you the world of good, for a start.'

'Right.' Liza nodded against his chest. She could understand that.

'Well, so basically, he wasn't thrilled when I told him I was seeing you.' Kit paused and drew breath. 'Then, when he found out how *old* you were . . .'

Liza winced.

'Don't tell me. It was scrape-him-off-the-ceiling time.'

'Like I said, he's old-fashioned. He has these set ideas. Set in concrete,' Kit amended wearily. 'You know the kind of thing. My sister's thirty so she should be married and having babies. I'm twenty-three so I should be playing the field.'

'How does he know you aren't?'

'He wants me to play the field with nineteen-year-old girls. Twenty-year-olds. I said I wasn't interested.'

'Heavens, maybe he thinks you're gay.'

'Worse still,' Kit looked down at her, 'I told him I wasn't playing the field. I told him this thing with you was serious. And, God knows, that's a first for me.'

Liza's stomach did a slow, snake-like somersault. Not normally superstitious, she was nevertheless terrified of tempting fate.

'Isn't that jumping the gun a bit?'

Kit shrugged.

'Maybe, but I meant it.'

181

Oh please, please, thought Liza, squirming with pleasure as his hand trailed down her stomach, *don't ever get bored with me.*

Everyone else always seemed to sneer at it, but Dulcie adored daytime TV. She loved the pointlessness of it all . . . the viewers' makeovers, the snippets of movie gossip, the panel of experts deciding which baked beans were the least disgusting. She also enjoyed the effortless jolly banter between her favourite presenters, the how-to-transform-a-box-room-into-a-banqueting-hall items, and the cookery slots, which Dulcie found quite soothing to watch.

Best of all though, she liked Nancy, the five-times-married resident problem-solver, who was wonderfully motherly and quite unshockable. If anyone said anything shameful or embarrassing she immediately told them in her lovely soothing voice that she understood completely because that had once happened to her too.

'Believe me, I know how you feel,' Nancy was saying now to a tearful woman who had just discovered her husband had a bit of a predilection for lacy underwear. 'Tell me, is it just the undies or does he wear frocks too?'

He did, he did, confessed the woman, between sobs. She'd found a flouncy yellow chiffon dress in the back of the wardrobe and wondered what on earth it was doing there. It was horrible, not her taste in clothes at all.

While Dulcie bit the chocolate off a jaffa cake, Nancy suggested to the woman that shopping together for clothes might bring her and her husband closer, and could also help to avoid costly mistakes.

The next caller was more up Dulcie's street.

'. . . the thing is,' pleaded Greta from Scarborough, 'I really love him, Nancy. If he left me I don't know what I'd do, I just need someone to tell me how I can keep him . . . I'll do *anything* . . .'

Dulcie ate another jaffa cake. She knew that feeling all right.

'Right, Greta. I understand completely how desperate you must be feeling,' said Nancy cosily. 'I can hear it in your voice. But first of all I have to tell you what you *mustn't* do.'

'What mustn't she do, Nancy?' enquired one of the show's presenters.

'Yes, Nancy,' said Dulcie, 'what mustn't we do?'

'Please, *please* don't be tempted into thinking all your problems would be solved if you had a baby.' Nancy sounded sorrowful. 'Because believe me, Greta, that would be the biggest mistake you could make.'

The jaffa cake was melting. Dulcie licked chocolate off her fingers and conjured up a mental picture of a tiny baby, the image of Liam, wearing tennis whites and waving a miniature racquet.

This was a possibility that hadn't so much as crossed her mind.

'It's crossed my mind,' admitted Greta from Scarborough.

'Don't let it,' Nancy said firmly.

This was like being told not to think of pink elephants. Dulcie promptly imagined Liam showing off his new son, driving him around in the Lamborghini, proudly telling everyone how fatherhood had changed his whole life . . .

'I know,' said Greta, beginning to sound a bit desperate, 'but it worked for my sister. She got pregnant and her bloke stuck by her. And she did it on purpose,' she added defiantly. 'He thought she was still on the pill but she stopped taking it.'

'Deceit and trickery,' Nancy looked sad and shook her head, 'deceit and trickery. Trust me, pet, this isn't the answer. Getting pregnant – when all you're trying to do is hang on to a man – is a recipe for disaster. You're just grasping at straws.'

Dulcie lifted up her white sweatshirt and gazed down at her flat stomach. Then she shoved the biscuit tin under the sweatshirt and surveyed the odd-shaped lump. Nancy had got rid of Greta now. She had moved on to John from Norwich who was forty-four but his mother had never let him have a girlfriend.

Dulcie knew from the tone of Greta's voice that she would go ahead and do it anyway. You could always tell when people were going to ignore Nancy's sound advice.

Dulcie pulled the biscuit tin out from under her sweatshirt, opened it and thoughtfully bit into a bourbon. There was no doubt about it, getting pregnant accidentally-on-purpose might not do the trick – but then again, what if it did? It could be a risk worth taking.

What a shame there wasn't a Predictor pregnancy kit for men, a just-pee-on-this type of thing that would reliably inform you whether the prospective father of your child might actually be quite keen on the idea.

Or, on the other hand, if he was a fully paid-up member of the run-a-mile club.

Minutes later, it came to her.

Brilliant, thought Dulcie excitedly, amazed that a solution so perfect and simple hadn't occurred to her before. Or, indeed, to Nancy.

Who needed a pre-pregnancy test? All she had to do was bend the truth a bit.

It wasn't even fibbing, it was . . . well, it was research.

Chapter 28

'You're *what*?' said Liza, horrified, when Dulcie announced her momentous news the next day out in the back garden. 'You're kidding!'

'I found out last week. Isn't it terrific?'

Dulcie beamed at them both. Pru, sitting cross-legged on the grass, looked dazed. Liza, frowning, swirled the ice cubes around in her tall glass.

'I don't know,' Liza said finally. 'Is it terrific? How does Liam feel about it?'

Feeling quite pregnant already, and weirdly protective of her nonexistent child, Dulcie decided Liza was jealous.

'I'm telling him tonight. I bet he'll be chuffed.'

Pru was shielding her eyes from the sun, peering at Dulcie's stomach.

'How many weeks are you?'

'Six.' Dulcie was firm. She had consulted her diary and committed the necessary dates to memory. She had learned her lesson from the Bibi fiasco, the lesson being: If you're going to lie, be thorough, be convincing and above all be consistent.

All the same, she was glad she had her RayBans on. It wasn't so easy fibbing to your friends.

'Morning sickness?' said Liza, giving her a slightly odd look.

'God, morning sickness!' Dulcie groaned and clutched her stomach. You didn't watch as many soaps as she had in her time without becoming something of an expert on the various

185

signs and symptoms of pregnancy. 'I've been throwing up like nobody's business—'

'Cravings?'

'Cravings!' Dulcie rolled her eyes. 'Tell me about them! Custard creams, pickled beetroot dunked in chocolate spread, peanut butter and honey sandwiches—'

'You've always eaten those.'

'I know, but then I just fancied them,' explained Dulcie. 'Now I *crave* them, totally. Morning, noon and night. And cornflakes mashed up with double cream and marmalade.'

'I read an article in the paper recently,' Liza went on. 'Some professor was saying women who crave green olives have boys, and if they go for lemons it's a girl.'

Dulcie had already decided Liam would prefer a son. To start with, anyway. She patted her stomach and said happily, 'I'm eating millions of olives. I know it's going to be a boy.'

Then because Liza and Pru were both still exchanging furtive glances, she wailed, 'Isn't anyone going to congratulate me? Come on, I'm having a baby here! Is this exciting or what?'

Pru looked away, pretending to pick a bit of grass off her shirt. Finally Liza spoke.

'It might be exciting,' she said drily, 'if it were true.'

'But it is true!'

Liza reached across and whipped off Dulcie's dark glasses.

'You might be able to do it to everyone else, but you can't lie to us.'

Oh bugger, so much for subterfuge.

'Damn.' Resignedly, Dulcie grabbed her glasses back. 'How could you tell?'

'You might be flippant,' said Liza, smiling at the expression on Dulcie's face, 'but even you aren't that flippant.'

'Plus,' Pru added, looking apologetic, 'if you really were pregnant, you wouldn't be able to keep it to yourself for an hour, let alone a week.'

'I made up the bit about the olives, by the way,' said Liza.

Feeling ganged-up on, Dulcie said nothing. She drank her glass of tonic and pulled a face. At least now the game was up, she could stick some gin in.

'Sorry.' Liza was trying not to laugh. 'What were we, the practice run?'

Dulcie nodded.

'Thought so. It's a really sick thing to do, you know.'

Since Liza wasn't Liam's greatest fan, this came as something of a shock to Dulcie; it made her sit up a bit. Hang on, was she defending him here? Was she actually on Liam's side?

'I thought you'd approve,' she protested. 'I'm being responsible, aren't I? If he's thrilled, I'll do it for real. If he isn't . . . well, then I won't.'

Pru looked at her.

'Well, don't you think it's a good idea?' said Dulcie defensively. 'I'm testing the ground first. You'd try on a dress, wouldn't you, before you bought it?'

'Except we aren't talking about a dress here,' said Liza, 'we're talking about a baby and that's a pretty major deception.' She shook her head. 'I still think you're mad.'

'Some men just need a nudge in the right direction.' Dulcie hugged her knees; she still thought it was a brilliant idea. 'Look, how did you *really* know I was lying?'

'We know you,' said Liza with a shrug.

'Okay, but Liam doesn't. He'll believe me, won't he?' Dulcie raised her eyebrows, pleading with them to be on her side. 'So long as you two back me up.'

Pru looked flustered. Subterfuge didn't come naturally to her.

'Why don't you just *ask* him if he'd like a baby?' she said with an air of helplessness.

Sometimes Dulcie wondered about Pru. Was she from the real world or not?

'Because,' she explained patiently, 'it just doesn't work like that.'

* * *

187

Kit was taking Liza away to the Lake District for the weekend. He picked her up at four o'clock and chucked her case in the back of the Bentley.

'We're going to stay at this amazing hotel,' he told her, 'surrounded by woodland. The countryside's fantastic. You'll love it.'

Liza wondered jealously who he'd taken there before. She wondered how many times he'd been there and how many girls he'd been there with.

'None,' said Kit, glancing across at her as they headed for the motorway.

'What?'

'In case you were wondering.'

'Wondering what?' Liza unwrapped a packet of fruit pastilles.

He grinned. 'The look on your face. Total giveaway.'

'I don't know what you're talking about,' she protested, but it was half-hearted.

'Five years ago, the father of my best friend from school remarried,' said Kit. 'The reception was held at Egerton Hall and I was invited along. As soon as I saw the hotel I knew this was the place for me. When I met the right girl I'd bring her here.' He paused, concentrating on the road ahead. When they had navigated round a swaying horsebox, he added casually, 'And now it's happened. You are that girl.'

'I'm thirty-two. Hardly a girl.'

Kit shrugged.

'Okay, you are that ancient old battleaxe.'

'Oh God.' Fearfully she pulled down the sun visor, studying her face in the mirror. 'What if the chambermaids think I'm your mother?'

They were approaching a lay-by. Kit braked hard and pulled in. As the trundling horsebox overtook them, he took Liza in his arms.

'Stop it,' he said firmly. 'I love you. I don't care that you're older than me. And if it bothers anyone else, then they're the

188

ones with the problem. We're talking nine years' difference here, not ninety. I mean, so what? Big deal.'

He was still kissing her when the phone rang in the car.

'Bugger,' said Kit, then he grinned and flicked a switch. 'Hooray for hands-free.'

But Leo Berenger's autocratic voice, booming through the car, stopped them in their tracks.

'Kit, you've gone off with the bloody keys to the safe.'

'Shit.' Kit's hand went to his jacket pocket. He pulled out the keys and gazed at them in disgust.

'You'll have to bring them back,' ordered Leo Berenger.

'Lucky we stopped before the motorway.' Kit winked at Liza. To his father he said, 'Forty minutes, okay?'

'We're waiting for them *now*,' roared Leo. 'Make it twenty.'

'Looks like it's meet-the-folks time,' Kit said cheerfully as he swung the Bentley into the gravelled drive. There, waiting for them on the front steps of Rowan House, was Leo Berenger. Tall, burly and ominous-looking, even from this distance. Liza wondered about hiding herself under a blanket on the back seat – except there was no blanket to hide under. There was no anything. It was an incredibly clean car.

'You should have dropped me off first.' She shivered, unable to help herself.

Kit gave her thigh a reassuring squeeze.

'Come on, he's only my father. No need to be scared, just because he can't stand the sight of you.'

'Ha ha,' said Liza, because Kit was grinning. She was glad someone found it funny.

Leo Berenger clearly didn't, when they reached him at last.

'Keys,' Kit announced, sliding open the driver's window and holding them out to his father. 'Sorry about that.'

But although Leo Berenger took the keys, he appeared not to hear his son's apology. He was too busy, instead, looking at Liza. Having rather hoped he would opt for ignoring her completely, Liza now found herself forced to return his gaze.

She tried to look friendly but not totally grovelly.

Leo Berenger's expression, by way of contrast, was on a par with slicing open a peach and finding a nest of squirming maggots inside.

Rapidly, because he couldn't very well not, Kit performed the introductions.

'I already know who you are,' Leo Berenger told Liza. 'And I daresay my son's told you how I feel about this . . . relationship.' His eyebrows were like caterpillars, his tone Yorkshire-blunt. 'But I'll say it again, just so you get the point. You all but wrecked my niece's business, and you're certainly the wrong sort for my son. I don't know what you think you're playing at, but the sooner he comes to his senses and finds himself a girl his own age—'

'Thanks, Dad, that's fine, we've got the message.'

'Because believe me, the sight of you sitting there in that car where my late wife used to sit—'

'Right,' Kit said wearily, 'I wondered when we'd get to that.'

He switched off the ignition, opened the driver's door and climbed out. Within seconds, the boot was unloaded. Carrying four cases, Kit somehow managed to open the passenger door.

'Come on,' he told Liza without emotion, 'we'll go in mine.'

It made a change, anyway. Instead of feeling old, Liza now felt about fifteen. The last time she'd been told off by a boyfriend's enraged father was when they'd been caught smoking in his garden shed.

'She might not want to go in yours.' Leo Berenger's taunting voice followed them around the side of the vast Georgian house. 'After all, it's no Bentley.'

At the back of the house, across a cobbled courtyard, an old stable block had been converted into garages. They loaded the suitcases into Kit's battered – and spectacularly untidy – slate-grey Peugeot.

'He thinks I'm a gold-digger,' Liza marvelled.

'We could really gee him up,' said Kit, slamming the boot shut, 'we could tell him you're pregnant.'

'I'm not.'

Kit's yellow-gold eyes glittered like a cat's in the dusty sunlight. He kissed Liza's warm mouth, then her neck, then her bare shoulder.

'You're not yet.'

Oh my God, thought Liza dazedly, marvelling at the effect he was having on her body. How does he do it? How can this be *happening* to me?

But when Kit drove the Peugeot around the side of the house, Leo Berenger was still standing there next to the Bentley, his arms folded across his barrel of a chest, his disapproving gaze fixed on Liza.

Kit lowered his window and said cheerfully, 'See? It's my body she's after, not your cash. Bye, Dad.'

His father didn't reply.

Making sure she spoke loudly enough to be heard, Liza said as they drove past, 'Is he really your father? Sure you weren't switched at birth?'

Chapter 29

It was one of Eddie's visiting days. Pru picked him up at five o'clock that afternoon and gave Arthur's ears a friendly scratch when he scrambled on to the passenger seat ahead of Eddie. Arthur had formed a passionate attachment to Anita, the golden retriever belonging to the caretaker at Elmlea nursing home; for the past couple of weeks he had taken to yelping with excitement every time he spotted Pru, and hurling himself into the car like a frantic commuter hailing a taxi.

'It's love,' said Eddie with a grin, shoving Arthur through to the back before he drooled over Pru's pale-green shirt.

Pru was getting used to Arthur now. As dogs went, he was okay. How he'd ever managed to get himself a girlfriend though, was beyond her. Arthur had frightfully bad breath.

'Down,' Eddie commanded as the dog's paws crept over the back of his seat. A long pink tongue lolled wetly, inches from his shoulder. For a mad moment he wished it could be Pru's tongue.

Pru, extremely glad it wasn't her shoulder, said, 'You're supposed to play it cool, Arthur. Look like you don't give a damn.'

But with dogs there was no need for all that. The second Arthur spotted the object of his desire, he would howl with joy and scrabble in desperation at the car door until he was let out. Anita, in her turn, would leap up, eyes alight with pleasure, and race across the grass towards him, Hollywood style.

None of your complicated human stuff, Eddie thought, all

this hiding your true feelings, preserving your pride and generally faffing about.

'Speaking of playing it cool,' said Eddie, 'how's it going with Dulcie and Liam?'

He only asked because Liam's new car was hard to miss and this morning he had spotted it racing out of the club's car park. Eddie hadn't paid a great deal of attention but even he hadn't been able to help noticing that the mane of blonde hair attached to the girl in the passenger seat didn't belong to Dulcie.

This is it, thought Pru, willing herself to stay calm and unflustered. This is my chance to see if I can pull it off.

'Actually, I saw Dulcie this morning. She rang Liza and me, asked us to go and see her. She's really excited' – eyes on the road, just sound normal, don't blush, *don't blush* – 'you see, she's just found out she's pregnant.'

'Good God.' Eddie sounded horrified. 'What – who's – I mean, is it Liam's?'

Pru was hating this already. She felt hot and unhappy. Fibbing might come naturally to some people but she wasn't one of them.

Except Dulcie had made her *promise*.

Pretending she was an actress playing her part on a stage, Pru nodded. Actually, it helped.

'Of course it's Liam's. She's thrilled!'

'Is Liam thrilled?'

'He doesn't know yet. She's telling him tonight. So don't say anything,' Pru warned him, 'because I shouldn't have told you.'

Eddie looked at Pru and decided not to mention the blonde in Liam's car. It was none of his business anyway. If Pru relayed this information to Dulcie – and it all ended in tears – he would only be left with the finger pointed accusingly at him.

Safer not to get involved, he thought. Hear no shenanigans, see no shenanigans, that was the way to deal with these kind of adventures.

Pru wondered unhappily why Dulcie couldn't have left

her out of it. She had lied. Successfully, too.

And it felt horrid.

On the back seat, as they sped down the dual carriageway towards Bristol, Arthur let out an impatient whine, the doggie equivalent of: 'How long before we're *there*?'

Pru may have felt terrible at deliberately deceiving Eddie, but she didn't feel as terrible as Liam did when Dulcie broke the momentous news to him that night.

In addition, her hearing appeared to have been affected.

'Christ. A baby! I don't know if this is a good idea—'

'Isn't it the most fantastic news ever?' Dulcie rattled on regardless, ignoring his less-than-thrilled expression. 'Just think, a son! You'll be able to teach him to play tennis!'

'Dulcie . . . sweetheart, sit down. Stop yakking for a minute.' Liam shook his head; he looked pained. 'The thing is, I'm not sure I'm ready to be a father.'

It was bound to come as a bit of a shock, thought Dulcie. She could understand that. She had to make allowances. When it began to sink in, the idea would grow on him. She just had to plant the right seeds.

'Nobody's ever sure they're ready for children,' she told Liam soothingly, 'but once it's happened, they wonder how they ever lived without them. Look at all your old tennis pals . . . John McEnroe, Pat Cash . . . they're *devoted* to their kids! And it makes men so attractive, too,' she enthused. 'Look at Sting, Simon Le Bon, Tom Cruise . . .'

Dulcie had worked out the best way to play it, and she was right. Even in his shell-shocked state, Liam was drawn to the sexy-but-caring image. Maybe it wouldn't be so bad; he could do it Rod Stewart style, have umpteen kids by a succession of drop-dead-gorgeous girlfriends . . .

Then he thought of the astronomical child support and shuddered.

'Look, Dulcie, we do need to think about this.' He paused, not wanting to upset her, choosing his words with care. 'We need to think about it seriously. There are other . . . well, other options, you know.'

Dulcie, her green eyes huge, gazed at him like a wounded fawn. Her lower lip began to tremble.

'How could you even *think* that?'

Her hands clutched her stomach. Liam instantly felt dreadful, like an axe murderer.

With a sigh, he supposed he was lucky this hadn't happened before. He was almost thirty-five, had been firing on all cylinders since he was fifteen . . . well, that was a pretty good innings. Okay, so he'd been let down by a faulty condom, but they were said to be only ninety-seven per cent effective anyway, weren't they? And he'd certainly used more than ninety-seven condoms in the past twenty years.

Anyway, looking on the bright side – at least now he knew he wasn't infertile.

Liam decided to give in gracefully, he may as well make the best of it. He'd been caught out, but so what? It might not be what he wanted but then neither was it the end of the world.

He relaxed, sat back in his chair and smiled at Dulcie.

'So how are you feeling?'

Dulcie hurled herself at him as joyously as Arthur had hurled himself earlier at Anita, the glorious golden retriever of his dreams.

'Oh I knew you'd be thrilled,' she cried, covering his face with kisses. 'Imagine, our very own baby! Our own future Wimbledon champion—'

'Do you feel okay?' Liam studied her face. Dulcie certainly seemed to be glowing.

'Sick.' Belatedly she remembered her long list of symptoms. 'But that's normal. Hundreds of food cravings, which the doctor says I should just go along with. Oh, and I'm tired so I have to rest a lot, mustn't do too much.'

'Really?' Liam looked alarmed.

'Otherwise your ankles swell,' Dulcie explained. 'It can be dangerous.'

He glanced at her ankles, which looked okay to him, but Dulcie was reaching down, miming them blowing up like balloons and exploding. She pulled a face and shook her head.

'That's what my doctor said. Yuk, imagine. So no more tennis, which is a real shame. Still, you have to do as you're told, don't you?' Patting her stomach, looking regretful but at the same time serene, Dulcie added caringly, 'The baby comes first.'

Never having had any involvement with pregnant women before, Liam's knowledge of the subject was largely limited to the old black and white movies he had watched on TV as a teenager. Happily for Dulcie, their attitude towards mothers-to-be was pretty much on a par with hers.

Liam racked his brains for a second and came up with, 'You'd better lie down. Shall I make you a cup of tea?'

Dulcie, who had watched a lot of the same films, happily did as she was told. This was more like it. Liam was going to turn into Cary Grant, she'd be Audrey Hepburn and together they would live happily ever after . . .

'Tea, brilliant.' She sank back on to the sofa and put her feet up. 'Actually, I'm just craving a bowl of peanut butter ice cream. There's some in the freezer.'

When he had switched the kettle on, Liam came back into the sitting room with a spoon and the tub of ice cream. He frowned as he read the list of calories per 100 mls. and the percentages of sugar and fat.

'This stuff's lethal. You'll end up the size of a sumo wrestler.'

'No I won't.' Reaching up, Dulcie grabbed the tub and the spoon. Liam watched her expertly peel off the lid and balance it on one knee.

'I'll go and get you a bowl.'

'Don't worry,' said Dulcie, swooning with pleasure, 'I'll manage like this.'

Chapter 30

Liza hated the word toyboy. She wished it didn't get to her, but it did. If you're ugly you can wear make-up, if you're bald you can wear a wig and if you're short you can wear high heels . . .

But if you're nine years older than the man in your life, Liza thought with rising frustration, there's damn all you can do about it. Because you can't wear anything to make you *younger* than you are.

It didn't bother Kit at all. He really couldn't care less.

'You have to come to the party with me,' he urged. 'What's the problem? Everyone knows I'm seeing you. Now I want them to meet you.'

The party was being held to celebrate the twenty-third birthday of one of Kit's friends. Since the weather was dazzling, it was taking place outside in the garden of his home overlooking the river. As soon as they arrived, stepping out of the taxi on Sunday afternoon, Liza began to feel twitchy.

It didn't take long for things to get worse.

Terrified of looking like mutton dressed as lamb, she had decided against wearing anything Dulcie-length. Instead, she had chosen a long, loose, topaz-yellow summer dress and strappy yellow high heels. The bad news was, her heels kept sinking into the lawn so to avoid toppling over backwards she ended up having to take them off. This meant the dress was now too long and trailed along the ground. Nobody else had made the same mistake. Everywhere Liza looked, girls in either tiny dresses or ultra-short tops and skirts showed off acres of midriff and conker-brown leg. They all seemed to have hair like spun silk that had to be continually flipped back. There wasn't a wrinkle or an ounce of flab in sight. Worst of all, hardly anyone else looked old enough to drink.

Liza felt like a Shetland pony amongst racehorses. Minus her heels, she wished desperately she'd worn her hair up, instead of loose, to give her a couple more inches. As friends of Kit stopped to chat, she fumbled in her handbag, her fingers desperately searching for a couple of stray hair combs.

She couldn't bear to look round when she heard two girls behind her, discussing her in giggly cut-glass voices.

'Is that really Kit's latest?'

'Must be. Hugh said he was bringing her.'

'My God, she looks like thingummy from *The Munsters*. Cousin It.'

More giggles. Liza was surprised they knew who the Munsters were.

'Wonder what Kit sees in her? She's hardly his usual type.'

'Oh well, you know Kit. Anything with novelty value. She won't last long.'

'It's weird though,' mused the second girl, 'when he could have anyone he likes. Me, for a start.'

'Give him time.' The first girl sounded smug. 'He will.'

It didn't help that while Liza was listening to this going on behind her, she was being subjected to some serious chatting-up from the front. A blond, rather good-looking boy called Toby was giving every impression of being bowled over.

But Liza's confidence had taken such a knock, instead of simply taking the attention for granted, she wondered if he was doing it for a bet.

Somehow she stuck the party out for the next hour and a half, hating every second but by some miracle managing to hide the fact from Kit. Having decided miserably that she was the oldest person there, Liza was hugely relieved to spot a late arrival making his way down the garden towards them.

The man, who was maybe forty, wore jeans and a blue and

198

white striped shirt. He was definitely handsome. When she saw him, one of the blonde coltish girls ran across the lawn and threw her arms around his neck.

Liza didn't care how handsome he was. She was just glad he was there. Older than her and there.

He approached Liza less than ten minutes later, while Kit was getting more drinks.

'Hi, you're Liza Lawson.' He grinned and shook her hand. 'Dominic Hunter-Greene. I'm a great fan of yours. Read you every Sunday.'

Liza chatted happily for several minutes. Kit was being waylaid at the bar by a couple of college friends but it didn't matter a bit. She was fine. Dominic Hunter-Greene wasn't chatting her up, he was simply being friendly while his young blonde girlfriend helped out with the barbecue.

'Come on, I need to sit down,' he said and Liza followed him over to a white wrought-iron table surrounded by matching padded chairs. Draped leggily across the chairs were two more mini-skirted blondes and their boyfriends, all drinking Becks and smoking Marlboro Lights.

He was clearly totally at ease with the fact that he was older than everyone else there. But then, Liza thought enviously, it was so different for men. Bag yourself a gorgeous young girlfriend and everyone goes 'wey-hey, good for you'. When a woman, on the other hand, gets herself a younger boyfriend, everyone goes 'yeugh, gross'.

'Okay you lot, park yourselves on the grass,' said Dominic.

'Not fair,' complained one of the girls.

'Yes, Dad, we were here first,' said the other.

'I don't care. This is my house and these are my chairs.' Dominic expertly tipped his daughter off hers. 'Anyway, you're young, you can sprawl anywhere you like.' Liza stiffened as he placed a protective hand on her forearm, drawing her into the conversation. 'We oldies prefer something more dignified.' He winked at Liza. 'When you get to our age, you appreciate a bit of comfort.'

Liza saw the glances exchanged by the two girls, who knew she was here with Kit.

'Who's the girl helping with the barbecue?' she said, when they had wandered off, no doubt leaving the wrinklies to it.

'Has no one introduced you?' Dominic looked despairing. 'Honestly, kids today. That's Sacha, my youngest.'

It was turning into one of those days. Feverishly planning her escape, the best excuse Liza had been able to come up with was a headache. Now, having fretted over the lack of originality, she realised her head actually was beginning to pound in ominous pre-migraine fashion.

Not knowing whether to laugh or cry, Liza tried to concentrate on the story Dominic was telling her. As soon as he finished, she would find Kit and tell him she had to get home. Her migraine attacks didn't strike often but when they happened they weren't to be taken lightly. Within minutes, Liza knew, her vision would be distorted by flashing lights, the pain would become intense, her words would begin to slur and she would start to feel horribly sick.

'I say, are you feeling all right?' Dominic leaned towards her, concerned. Liza had suddenly gone quite pale.

She forced a smile.

'Bit of a headache, that's all. I think I'm going to have to . . . oh, good grief . . .'

Liza saw who was approaching and experienced a surge of nausea. This was truly turning into the party from hell. And her vision was already starting to go.

'Surprise,' said Kit, his shirt-sleeved arm around the shoulder of yet another stunning young blonde. Only this time it was one Liza recognised.

'Nicky, this is Liza. Liza,' Kit went on, grinning broadly, 'meet my cousin Nicky.'

The flickering lights were moving like storm clouds across Liza's field of vision. Hardly able to see the girl's face, all she could do was pray her expression was friendly.

'I'm sho em-embarrassed.' Liza stumbled over the words

as the pain behind her left eye intensified. Having struggled to her feet she now realised she was in danger of losing her balance. Swaying, she clutched Kit's arm. Damn, now everyone was going to think she was pissed.

Kit was just saying, 'There's no need to be embarrassed,' when Liza abruptly let go of him and with a mumbled, 'Excuse me,' lurched past Nicky and disappeared inside the house.

Her head felt as if it was about to explode. Reaching the bathroom just in time, Liza threw up spectacularly into the toilet and stayed there, shuddering and retching, until there was nothing left to throw up.

Not until there was a discreet tap-tap and the bathroom door swung open did Liza realise she hadn't locked it properly. She moaned and grabbed a handful of loo roll to wipe her eyes with, knowing how red and hideously puffed-up her face was.

'Please, don't come in.'

'Sorry, too late.'

Within seconds Liza found herself being lifted off the floor and helped over to an uncomfortable chrome chair in the corner of Dominic Hunter-Greene's stunning silver and white bathroom. The toilet – also chrome – was briskly flushed and a box of tissues thrust into her trembling hands.

'I heard you being sick,' said Nicky Berenger. Rummaging in her handbag she produced a packet of chewing gum and a bottle of eye drops and offered them both to Liza. 'Here, these'll help. What was it, too much Pimm's?'

Liza tried to smile. God, it hurt. She gestured feebly at her head.

'Migraine.'

Nicky looked appalled.

'And there was me, thinking you were paralytic! Oh, you poor thing. My dad suffers from migraine . . . he's got special pills to take as soon as he feels an attack coming on.'

Liza managed a minuscule nod.

'Me too, but my last headache was over a year ago.' Gingerly, she smiled. 'You forget what they're like.'

'Are you two okay in there,' said Kit, minutes later, 'or are you having a fight?'

Nicky unwrapped another chewing gum and gave it to Liza, who had just thrown up again.

'She's got a migraine. I'm doing my Florence Nightingale bit. You'll need to borrow a bucket,' she told Kit, 'for on the way home.'

He looked horrified.

'We came by taxi. What driver's going to take someone carrying a bucket and bringing her boots up in the back of his cab?'

This was true.

'Okay, I'll give you a lift,' said Nicky. 'Come on.'

The migraine continued on its inexorable course. The journey home was hell. With Kit's arms around her, Liza closed her eyes and gritted her teeth against the agonising vice-like pain. She was sick twice more, luckily into the borrowed bucket. By the time they reached the flat, it was as much as she could do to mumble an almost unintelligible thank-you and let Kit carry her inside to bed.

When Liza arrived at the Songbird two days later, Nicky was perched on a stool at the bar going over next week's bookings with the chef.

'Still alive then.' She grinned when she saw Liza, then exclaimed, 'Oh, they're amazing! You didn't have to do this,' as Liza put the cellophane-wrapped mass of orange roses into her arms.

'I think I did.' Liza kissed her flushed cheek. 'You were brilliant on Sunday. I just wanted to say thank you for everything. For all your help, and the lift home.' She hesitated, summoning up the courage to say the rest. It wasn't made any easier by the chef, who clearly recognised her and was glowering away under fearsome eyebrows like Lurch from the Addams family. 'I still can't believe you're even speaking to me after I almost wrecked your business. I'm so sorry,

202

I can't tell you how terrible I felt about that.'

Nicky, her eyes gleaming, pushed back her blonde hair and gave Lurch a hefty prod in the ribs.

'Well, don't. It wasn't your fault, it was Marcel's. Wasn't it, Marcel?' she added teasingly. 'If you hadn't got legless on Newcastle Brown and turned up for work still half-cut, Liza wouldn't have been able to criticise us, would she?'

Marcel looked embarrassed. Apart from anything else, he was a Frenchman. How was he ever going to live down the humiliation of having got plastered on Newcastle Brown Ale?

Liza, who had to be in Cheltenham by midday, checked her watch.

'Look, I have to go. Thanks again for everything. See you soon, I hope.' She paused. 'And if there's ever anything I can do for you . . .'

'That's an easy one,' Nicky said promptly. 'Marry Kit.'

Liza burst out laughing.

'Any particular reason?'

Nicky's smile was mischievous as she waved an arm, encompassing the restaurant.

'Then you can hold your wedding reception here.'

Dulcie, sunbathing in the back garden on Tuesday afternoon, heard the sound of a familiar car engine. When it switched off in front of the house she experienced an odd sensation of *déjà vu*. Except it wasn't *déjà vu*, of course; the reason she knew it so well was because she used to hear it all the time.

'I'm round the back,' Dulcie yelled when she dimly heard the front door bell being rung. She chucked down her empty crisp packet and licked her fingers. 'Door's unlocked, just come through.'

Lying back on the sun-lounger, far too lazy to get up, Dulcie lifted her head and shielded her eyes in order to watch Patrick appear.

When he did, moments later, he was wearing dark-blue

chinos and a yellow shirt she hadn't seen before. She wondered if thingy had bought it for him.

The next thing Dulcie noticed he was wearing was an odd look on his face.

'Nice shirt.'

'Don't you think you should put this on?' Reaching down and picking up the top half of her pink and purple bikini, Patrick held it towards her.

Dulcie tried not to smile.

'Why? Will it stop me getting cold?'

'It'll keep you decent,' said Patrick evenly. To her amazement she realised he was keeping his eyes deliberately averted from her breasts.

'Patrick, you're my husband! You have seen them before.'

'Things are different now.'

Gosh, thought Dulcie, he sounded weird. Stunned into obedience, she took the bikini top from him. Damn, there was a mark on it where she'd spilled chocolate ice cream.

'Put it on,' repeated Patrick.

He waited until she had, before looking down at her.

'Is something wrong?' Dulcie wondered if this sudden and bizarre obsession with decency meant someone had died.

'I thought I should come over. There appear to be things we need to sort out.'

'Things? What things?'

'The divorce,' Patrick said quietly, because Dulcie clearly didn't have a clue.

Dulcie swallowed. She hadn't actually given it much thought. Okay, it had been her New Year's resolution but once she'd left Patrick it hadn't seemed important.

Then another thought struck her. Rather unpleasantly, like malaria.

He wants a divorce so he can marry Claire, Dulcie realised, stunned. And I can't object because he's been so nice to me. Now it's my turn to be nice back . . .

She managed to nod.

'Okay.'

'I've spoken to Simon,' said Patrick. Simon was a solicitor friend of his. 'Basically, if we want it over quickly and we aren't going to argue about money, the easiest thing is to go for a no-fault, two-year separation. It's simple and it costs hardly anything. Are you happy with that?'

Two years, that's fine, thought Dulcie, suddenly finding it easier to breathe. That was eighteen months away.

'Fine.'

'Right. So that's settled, we can be divorced by September.'

Dulcie sat bolt upright.

'What about the two years?'

'All you have to do,' Patrick explained wearily, 'is *say* you've been separated for two years. Then it just goes through.'

'But that isn't true! That's . . . lying!' yelped Dulcie.

'Oh dear, how terrible. How will we live with ourselves?' Patrick mocked. 'Lying. Tut tut, that would never do.'

Dulcie hated it when he was sarcastic. She swallowed her pride and lay back down again. Patrick wanted to be free of her so he could marry Claire. He didn't want to look at her bare boobs any more, he only wanted to look at Claire's.

'How is she?' said Dulcie, to prove she was a grown-up. 'Claire?'

'Fine.' Patrick nodded briefly. A muscle was going in his jaw. At last he said, 'And Liam?'

If Claire was fine, Dulcie decided, Liam was more than fine.

'Very well indeed. Brilliant.' She nodded strenuously. 'Great.'

'Congratulations, by the way.'

Dulcie looked up, startled. There was that muscle again, twitching away.

'On . . .?'

'The baby,' said Patrick.

'Oh. Right.'

Dulcie was glad she had her sunglasses on. Somehow she'd

managed to persuade herself that Patrick wouldn't get to hear about this.

She wondered how he had.

'Word gets around,' Patrick went on after an awkward pause. 'One of the girls from the office downstairs is a member of Brunton.' He cleared his throat and managed a bleak smile. 'Bit of a weird way to find out, but still . . .'

Dulcie bit her lip. She felt terrible. Half of her wanted to blurt out the truth, to tell Patrick that it was okay, she wasn't really pregnant, it was just a scam, a desperate attempt to hang on to Liam.

The other half of her knew she had to keep her mouth shut because the humiliation, the look of disdain on Patrick's face, would be too much to bear.

He's happy with Claire, thought Dulcie. The last thing I need is Patrick feeling pity for me.

She kept her mouth well and truly shut.

'Anyway, I guessed you'd be anxious to get things settled.' Dulcie nodded.

Patrick nodded too.

'Are you going to marry him?'

'I expect so.' Bloody hope so. 'Maybe. No hurry.'

'How are you feeling?'

Dulcie shrugged again. Actually, she was feeling a bit peculiar. She was lying, and for the first time in her life not enjoying it much at all.

'How am I feeling?' Dulcie forced herself to concentrate. She even managed a smile. 'Great. Bit sick . . . you know, but otherwise fine. Looking forward to the big day.'

'And Liam?'

'Oh, he's thrilled. Pleased as Punch.'

'Well, that's good news. I'm happy for you,' said Patrick, not looking it. 'You've got what you wanted. I really hope it all works out.'

'Thanks.' The sun was hot but Dulcie was suddenly cold. She couldn't quite believe she was having this stilted conversation with Patrick. She was also beginning to feel uncomfortably underdressed. Before, it hadn't mattered. Now, a few layers of protective clothing – a couple of sweaters, a pair of jeans and a thick duffel coat, say – wouldn't have gone amiss.

In a strange way too, Dulcie realised, she was miffed that he hadn't seen through the lie. Liza and Pru had, effortlessly, and they were only her friends.

I was married to you for nearly seven years, she silently accused Patrick. I'm your wife. You're supposed to know me better than anyone – so how come you can't tell I'm lying to you now?

Chapter 31

Pru was asleep when the ringing sound started. In her dream, a fire engine was racing round and round her bedsit but instead of going nee-naa nee-naa, it was making a noise like a doorbell. Then the fire engine screeched to a halt. A dozen firemen leapt out and surrounded her bed.

'There isn't room for all of you in here,' protested Pru, which, even if she didn't know it was a dream, was a pretty Freudian thing to say. 'I'm sorry, but some of you will have to wait outside.'

The fireman in charge, who looked weirdly like Eddie Hammond, said, 'Can I stay?'

'I've only got a single bed,' Pru told him, and he broke into a smile.

'Fine with me. Except you'd better answer that door bell first.'

Pru woke up, jack-knifing into a sitting position as the bell – *her* door bell – shrilled again.

She looked at the luminous green figures on her radio alarm: 3.42.

Up through the floorboards floated the voice of Donovan's greatest fan shouting blearily: 'Will somebody get that, for Chrissake?'

Pru fell out of bed and stumbled across to the window. Pulling back the flimsy curtain, she peered down to the street below.

The next second she yanked the window open so fast a shower of old paint flakes parted company with the half-rotted wooden frame.

'Phil? What are you *doing* here?'

Phil Kasteliz heard the words but was in no state to locate them. Puzzled, hanging on to the front door for support, he looked left, then right, then behind him.

'Pru?'

'Up here,' hissed Pru. He was extremely drunk, she could tell by the way his head moved in a kind of slow-motion swivel. 'Phil, go home. It's four o'clock in the morning.'

She heard him laughing to himself. Too late, Pru remembered his penchant for singing.

'It's four in the mor-ning,' warbled Phil, 'and da da da da da. Damn, forgotten the words. How does it go, Pru? It's four in the morning . . .'

He was standing unaided now, his arms outstretched as he tried to conduct her.

From below Pru's feet came the plaintive wail: 'Man, get that guy *out of here* . . .'

If Pru had been Dulcie she would have yelled back that it served him bloody well right and one night of Phil Kasteliz in exchange for all those months of drippy Donovan was a pretty good swap.

But Pru, who wasn't Dulcie, was terrified at the prospect of upsetting a neighbour, even if he was a dope-head devoted to Donovan.

'Stop it,' she yelled in a strangled whisper, waving her arms at Phil in an attempt to hush him up. 'I'm coming down.'

When she opened the front door, he tripped over the step. She practically had to carry him upstairs to her room.

'How did you find this place anyway?' Pru gasped.

Fumbling in his jacket pocket, Phil finally pulled out his wallet. He showed Pru the letter she had written to him months earlier letting him know her new address.

'Showed it to the taxi driver,' Phil confided. 'He brought me straight here.'

Pru marvelled at her own lack of response. She had written that letter with tears streaming down her cheeks. At the time,

209

she would have given anything in the world for Phil to show it to a taxi driver and be brought straight here. Fantasising that it might happen had been about the only thing that had kept her going.

And now he was here . . .

She felt nothing.

'Why?' said Pru.

'Had a row with Blanche.' Phil collapsed heavily on the bed, still clutching his wallet.

'What about?'

'She's just a bad-tempered bitch.' He shrugged and shook his head. 'Honestly, all she did was yell at me. Just because I was a bit late home.' He looked up at Pru, his eyes bloodshot. 'You never yelled at me.'

'I know I didn't.' To yell, or not to yell, thought Pru. Which was best?

'She's mad because I had a couple of drinks. Bloody cow wouldn't let me into the house.'

Phil shook his head again in disbelief and tried to fit the bulging wallet back into his pocket. When it wouldn't do as he wanted, he gave up and chucked it on to the pillow behind him.

Pru's eyes widened as the wallet fell open, revealing a great wodge of notes.

'Got something to drink, Pru? Brandy, Scotch, anything like that.'

'Nothing, sorry.' She was still staring in disbelief at the wallet.

'What?' Alarmed, Phil tried to look over his shoulder. 'What is it, a spider?'

'That money! Have you been to the casino?'

He grinned and nodded, and put an unsteady finger to his lips.

'Sshh.'

'You won?' said Pru, astounded.

'Course I won. Didn't I tell you I'd get there in the end?

Only don't tell Blanche, okay? That stroppy bitch isn't getting her hands on this. It's my money, I won it fair and square.' Phil doubled up with laughter. 'Except roulette wheels aren't square. Better say I won it fair and round, ha ha ha.'

'How much did you win?' whispered Pru, all the hairs at the back of her neck standing up.

'Don't know. Haven't had a chance to count it yet.' He laughed again. 'Bloody loads. Pru, come on, have a drink with me to celebrate. You must have a bottle hidden away somewhere.'

'Oh man, I don't believe this.'

Donovan was wearing a grubby grey T-shirt and – yuk – a pair of ancient maroon Y-fronts. He groaned and rubbed his hands over his face as if needing to convince himself Pru was real.

'I'm sorry, I know it's late,' said Pru sweetly, marvelling at her own bravery. Here she was, out of the blue, doing it again. Being Assertive.

'Whadya want, man? It's, like, the middle of the night.'

'We need something to drink.' Pru got straight to the point. 'I don't have anything. I thought perhaps you might.'

Donovan stared at her. He'd never managed to figure out what Pru was doing living above him, a posh bird in a dump like this. And now here she was, cool as a cucumber on his doorstep at four in the frigging morning, acting like one of those women who wave collecting tins under your nose, asking if he could spare a bottle or two for a good cause.

'Like what?' he said warily. ''Cause I'm fresh out of Bollinger, if that's what you're after.'

'Anything,' said Pru.

She made her way back upstairs clutching two cans of Special Brew and a half-empty flagon of cider which Donovan assured her had only been opened a couple of days ago, so it still had some life in it.

Pru only hoped, as she nudged open the door with her foot,

211

that Phil still had some life left in him. Since she'd gone to the trouble of getting him something to drink, he'd better still be awake enough to drink it.

He had, but only just. While Pru chattered brightly away to him, Phil lolled across the bed and finished off the cider. Then he opened one of the cans of lager but most of it went down the front of his crumpled white shirt. Pru mopped at the duvet cover with a towel.

'You'll look after me, won't you?' mumbled Phil, his eyes closing. 'You always looked after me.'

And look where it bloody got me, thought Pru as his head sank back on to the pillow and the can slid to the floor.

Within seconds he was snoring like a walrus, out like a light and oblivious to the tugging going on as Pru yanked his shoes off. She managed, after a struggle, to get the duvet out from under him. Then she smoothed it over his sleeping form, straightened the pillow and put the still unfastened wallet on the bedside table.

Since Phil had commandeered the bed, Pru could either sleep in the chair or on the floor.

But she didn't sleep. She couldn't. Her mind was working overtime. Her conscience was having an all-out battle with itself.

After staring at the wallet for an hour, Pru reached over and picked it up. She emptied the fat bundle of twenty-pound notes into her lap and, hands shaking, counted them.

Good grief, there was almost two thousand pounds there.

Pru looked at Phil, still snoring so loudly it was a wonder the rest of her neighbours hadn't called the police.

Two thousand pounds. Won, fair and square.

Now was that fair?

It had been a long and uncomfortable night. At eight o'clock Pru was still hopelessly undecided. She made herself a cup of tea; maybe that would help.

At nine o'clock, with Phil still dead to the world, she

212

rummaged in her purse and found a couple of twenty-pence pieces. Then she slipped out of the room and made her way downstairs to the phone box in the hall.

The number she wanted was listed in Yellow Pages.

'Hello,' said Pru, when the call was answered, 'I wonder if you can help me. I just need to know how much something costs.'

Minutes later, replacing the receiver, she crept back up the stairs and silently opened the door. This was it. It was up to fate now. If Phil was awake she wouldn't be able to do anything. If he was still asleep . . .

'Oh God, my *head*. Blanche . . . Blanche, where are you? Any chance of sticking the kettle on?'

'Blanche isn't here,' said Pru. 'Will I do instead?'

Phil rolled over, bleary-eyed and stubble-chinned. Pru was holding out a mug of tea, a plate of buttered toast and a packet of paracetamol.

Confusion reigned in Phil's brain. He rubbed his bloodshot eyes and winced.

'She wouldn't let you in last night so you came here,' said Pru.

'Christ. Did I . . . um, did we . . .?'

'No.'

'Oh, right.'

'Here, drink this.' Pru passed him the tea, popped three paracetamol out of their foil wrapper and pressed them into his free hand.

'I feel terrible,' said Phil in his penitent, little-boy voice.

'You'll feel better after some toast. I'll nip down to the corner shop, shall I, and get you some tomato soup?'

Twenty minutes later, when Phil had finished the soup, he fumbled in his jacket pocket. Pru, washing up at the tiny sink in the corner of the room that served as a kitchen, heard him locate his house keys and wallet.

'Bloody hell,' she heard him exclaim.

213

Far too flushed and scared to turn round, Pru frantically scrubbed at the pattern on the soup plate.

'What is it?'

'Eight hundred quid!'

More rustling as Phil re-counted the notes.

'Ready for another cup of tea?' said Pru, her heart going like a giant woodpecker against her ribs.

'I must have won it at the casino,' Phil marvelled, and Pru breathed again.

She dared at last to look over her shoulder at him.

'You did say something about a win at roulette.'

'Brilliant!' Phil beamed at her. 'See? I knew I was due for a bit of luck.'

'Good for you.'

'Yeah, more tea'd be great. And a couple of biscuits if you've got them.'

While Pru made the tea, he sat on the narrow bed and surveyed his surroundings.

'This place is a dump.'

'I'm getting used to it.'

Pru stirred in sugar and handed him the mug.

'Thanks.' Phil shook his head. 'Pru, I'm sorry. You don't deserve to live in a place like this.'

'It's okay.'

'You must hate me.'

'I don't hate you.' She opened the packet of custard creams she had picked up at the corner shop. 'Here, help yourself.'

'You're so . . .' Phil shook his head again, searching for the right word, '. . . so *nice*. You always were. Always forgiving me.'

Pru said nothing.

'It got on my nerves in the end,' he went on. 'Did you know that?'

'No.'

'That's why I went off with Blanche. She doesn't take any crap. Stands up for herself, Blanche does.'

214

'Right.'

'I'm just trying to explain.'

'You don't have to,' said Pru. 'It doesn't matter any more.'

He finished his tea and rose cautiously to his feet.

'Time I made a move. Blanche'll be waiting for me with a frying pan.' His smile was crooked. 'And it won't be for making bacon and eggs.'

'Well, good luck.' Pru smiled back.

At the door Phil glanced around the room again, his estate agent's eye taking in the rotting window frames and damp walls.

'I really am sorry, Toby,' he used his old nickname for her, 'about this place.'

But not quite sorry enough, Pru couldn't help noticing, to stick his hand in his pocket and maybe give her a couple of hundred pounds out of his winnings.

'Take care of yourself,' she said as Phil made his way downstairs.

He grinned, evidently at the prospect of having to avoid low-flying frying pans.

'You too, sweetheart. And thanks for putting me up.'

'My pleasure,' said Pru. ''Bye.'

Chapter 32

'You're doing *what*?' squealed Dulcie later that afternoon when Pru turned up on her doorstep and explained the situation so far.

'I saw the consultant at lunchtime. He's booked me in for surgery tomorrow morning,' Pru explained. 'The only problem is, I thought I'd be flat out, but apparently they don't do that any more, they only give you local anaesthetic.'

Dulcie's stomach cartwheeled at the prospect.

'Gross.'

'I know.' Pru pulled a face. 'So I wondered if you'd come with me. Kind of hold my hand, give me a bit of moral support.'

Dulcie was moderately squeamish but she adored *ER*. Maybe if she pretended she was watching it on telly . . .

'What's the surgeon like?'

Pru half smiled.

'Tall, dark, quite dishy actually.'

Dulcie briefly fantasised exchanging steamy looks over the operating masks with Dr Doug Ross.

'Okay, of course I'll come.'

'I might ask Liza too.'

Liza, Dulcie decided, could exchange steamy looks with someone far less attractive, one of the hospital porters maybe. She wanted to keep Doug to herself.

'We'll both be there,' she promised Pru. 'We'll have an ear each.'

'And don't tell anyone,' Pru pleaded. 'I've already spoken to Eddie. I told him a friend's invited me to stay with her at her villa in Majorca. As far as he's concerned I'm away on holiday for two weeks. That's how long the bandages have to stay on,' she added, looking embarrassed. 'I know it's stupid, but I just don't want anyone to know.'

Dulcie mimed zipping up her mouth. Then a thought belatedly struck her and she unzipped it.

'But how can you afford it? I thought you were strapped.'

Pru ran briefly through the events of last night. Dulcie listened agog. When Pru finished, she broke into applause.

'But I had no idea you were so desperate to have it done! Why didn't you say before? I could have lent you the cash.'

Pru said levelly, 'I didn't want to borrow the money.'

'Oh, right.' Dulcie's expressive eyebrows said it all. 'But you didn't mind stealing it.'

Pru looked worried.

'I only took as much as I needed, eleven hundred pounds—'

'Pru, come on, I'm joking! What am I going to do, call the police?'

'He still had eight hundred left,' Pru rattled on, as if needing to reassure herself.

'Well personally I think you're mad,' Dulcie declared. 'If it had been me I'd have nicked the lot.'

Sadly for Dulcie the surgeon spent far too much time concentrating on Pru's ears to have any left over for smouldering eye-meets with her. Performing the surgery appeared to be uppermost in his mind.

Since he was dishy, this was disappointing to say the least.

'Why should you be bothered?' said Liza, when they retired to the coffee room afterwards. 'I thought Liam was the only man for you.'

Dulcie shrugged. The thing was, she was beginning to doubt if she was the only woman for Liam. Okay, so he'd gone out and bought her an exercise-your-way-through-pregnancy video, but that had been the most romantic gesture of the past fortnight. More and more often recently, he had been phoning up to tell her he had to work late at the club.

Dulcie's fantasy – apart from the *ER*, Doug Ross-type one – that Liam would whisk her down to Mallory's and tell her to choose a dazzling, money-no-object diamond ring had so far failed to materialise. Neither had he suggested living together.

Worst of all, when Dulcie had visited Brunton Manor last week, Imelda had been wearing a horribly self-satisfied smirk of the I-know-something-you-don't-know variety.

It was hard to maintain the rosy glow of pregnancy when you suspected you were being laughed at – or even worse, pitied – behind your back.

'Here we are then,' announced the surgeon, entering the coffee room with his arm around Pru's shoulders. The pressure bandage holding her ears in place looked comical and her hair was sticking out like Ken Dodd's but she was clearly relieved the ordeal was over.

'All ready to go home,' the surgeon purred. 'Now I've explained to Pru, she has to take things easy for a few days. She needs cosseting.'

He beamed at Dulcie and Liza. He was using his jolly, be-extra-nice-to-the-private-patient voice. Dulcie decided he wasn't so gorgeous after all without his sexy operating mask; he was just a smarmy, patronising git.

'So, can I leave her in your safe hands, girls? Promise me you'll take good care of her.'

Dulcie didn't even care when she realised all his attention was on Liza. The man was practically drooling; he obviously fancied her rotten. And he was wearing a wedding ring. Unfaithful bastard.

'We can't cosset you in your bedsit,' Dulcie told Pru, who was looking horribly pale and in need of rest already. 'Come on,' she reached for her thin arm, 'you can come and stay with me.'

Telling Pru he had been banned for six months had been a panic reaction on Eddie's part, simply the only excuse he'd been able to come up with to ensure he could carry on seeing her on a regular basis. If she were no longer driving him around, he would be reduced to catching the occasional brief glimpse of her at the club.

Eddie knew it was stupid, not to mention expensive, but he didn't care. He looked forward to their time together. He could talk to Pru more easily than any other woman he knew. He could relax with her. She made him feel good.

He had felt horribly guilty when, on the phone yesterday, she had apologised over and over again for letting him down.

'I know it's short notice,' she had falteringly explained, 'but my friend begged me to go and see her . . . I'm *really* sorry to let you down like this . . .'

Pru was such a terrible liar, Eddie knew something was up. His stomach contracted with fear at the possibility that Pru might be heading off to the sun with another man . . . though if this was the case, why would she feel the need to lie? She was effectively single, she could do whatever she liked, with whoever she liked.

Eddie hated the idea but he had no right to say so. Miserably he wished Pru a happy holiday; another big lie.

At least he had his licence back. Pru wasn't inconveniencing him in the way she thought. Eddie just wished, as he drove Arthur and himself to Bristol that evening, he could stop torturing himself imagining what she might be getting up to on a sun-drenched beach in Majorca.

As he parked outside Elmlea nursing home he noticed one of the other residents, a bright-eyed old dear with a walking stick, sitting on one of the wooden benches watching him.

'No dogs inside,' she called across to Eddie when he let Arthur leap out of the car. 'Matron won't allow it; they might widdle on the lino. Then we'd have residents skidding in all directions.' She cackled with laughter. 'Fractured femurs galore.'

'I know,' said Eddie. 'I'm just letting him out for a two-minute run.'

'Two-minute widdle, more like.' Still smirking, the old dear held out a gnarled hand. 'Here, you can leave him with me. I'll look after him.'

'His name's Arthur.' Eddie passed her the lead.

'My late husband's name.' Up close, the woman's eyes were astonishing, almost kingfisher blue. 'He used to widdle everywhere too, come the end.'

Cautiously, Arthur sniffed her lisle-stockinged leg.

'Not me,' the woman told the dog briskly. 'Still continent, thank you very much.'

By the time Eddie re-emerged from the nursing home he found Arthur draped across the rest of the bench with his head on the old woman's tweed lap. He was fast asleep and snoring like a train.

'Getting more like my husband by the minute.' The woman fondly stroked Arthur's ears.

'Well, thanks for keeping an eye on him,' said Eddie.

'So where is she?'

'Who?'

'That pretty girl of yours. Dumped you, has she? All over now?'

'You mean Pru?' Eddie hesitated then said awkwardly, 'She's away on holiday. A fortnight in Majorca.'

'Why didn't you go with her?'

'Well . . . she's gone to stay with a friend. A female friend.'

The old woman's straggly eyebrows lifted in amusement.

'What, you mean she's a lesbian?'

'No. Of course not.'

'So. D'you miss her?'

'No . . . well . . .' Eddie wasn't often at a loss for words but it was pretty daunting being interrogated by an octogenarian. Flustered, he went on, 'It's only a holiday. She'll be back in a couple of weeks. Anyway, we aren't involved in that way.'

'But you wish you were,' said the old woman.

'Not . . . not necessarily—'

220

'Bull. Get a grip, man! Life doesn't last forever, you know. And you're no spring chicken.'

'Are you always this bossy?' Eddie retaliated, relieved to see that Arthur had at last opened his eyes.

The old woman gave him a long, measured look.

'I'm eighty-four years old, young man. I can say whatever I like.'

'You don't even know me.'

'Ah, but that's it, I do. You're Edna Peverell's son-in-law. What d'you think we do all day in this place, play table tennis?' Mockingly, remorselessly, she went on, 'We talk, young man. I know everything there is to know about you. And if you ask me, it's high time you got yourself another wife.'

Chapter 33

Hearing from Liam after three days of nail-biting silence made Dulcie's heart do an extra-jubilant hop, skip and jump. Just the sound of his voice on the phone – those melting Irish syllables – was enough to remind her how hopelessly smitten she still was.

'How about if I come round about eight-ish?' said Liam beguilingly. 'We could have a romantic evening together, just the two of us.'

Romantic evening? Did that, Dulcie wondered, suggest a big dazzling engagement ring to go with the rampant sex?

She glanced across the sitting room at Pru, who was lying on the sofa watching a wildlife documentary. Her hair, desperately in need of a wash, was sticking out at all angles around the bandages.

What with that, no make-up and a Julio Iglesias T-shirt, she looked a sight.

Furthermore, Dulcie remembered, she was here incognito. As far as the rest of the world was concerned, Pru was in Majorca.

'Actually, my grandmother's staying with me for a few days. It's easier if I come to you.'

'Okay.' Liam realised he would have to go through the flat first, removing any evidence of Imelda's recent stay. 'Better make it nine then, the place is a mess. I'll have a clear-up before you arrive.'

He must love me, Dulcie thought joyfully, to care about tidying up.

As the end credits of the wildlife documentary began to roll, Pru heard Dulcie wail, 'Oh *bum*,' from upstairs.

'What?' she said when Dulcie reappeared looking disconsolate.

'So much for a romantic evening. My period's started.'

'What will you do?'

Dulcie said gloomily, 'Have a headache, I suppose.'

'A what?' Liam grinned, clearly thinking it was a joke. He waited for the punchline.

'A headache. Right here.' Dulcie clutched her temple and winced. 'It's throbbing like mad.'

'I know how it feels.'

'Ouch, it really hurts. Maybe I'm getting migraine, like Liza.'

Playfully Liam pulled her on to his lap.

'Lucky I know a cure for headaches.'

His hand was travelling to the nape of her neck. In one smooth movement her dress was unzipped. Dulcie tried not to squirm with pleasure.

'I can't . . . I can't.' As the magic fingers slid lower she wriggled frantically away, gasping, 'Please don't! The doctor said I mustn't—'

Liam's hand shot out of her dress as if he'd been electrocuted.

'What?'

Phew, mission accomplished.

'The doctor.' Dulcie shook her head slightly, the reluctant bearer of bad news. Greta Garbo had done something similar in one of those films where she died at the end. 'When I saw him yesterday he said we shouldn't . . . you know. To be on the safe side.'

'Is everything all right?' Liam stared at her stomach.

'Oh yes, as long as I take it easy. Just for the next week or so.'

He was looking stunned. Touched by his concern, Dulcie gave him a reassuring kiss.

'Don't worry, everything's going to be fine. All I need is a bit of . . . of cosseting.'

Liam thought for a moment.

'I'd have said move in with me for a couple of weeks, but I suppose that isn't really on.'

Dulcie's eyes widened with excitement. She couldn't imagine why not.

'Well—'

'Not if you've got your grandmother staying with you.'

Oh. Bugger.

'No.' Disappointed, Dulcie dredged up a smile. 'I suppose not. Well, she'll just have to cosset me instead.'

It was blissful, anyway, being looked after by Liam that evening. While Dulcie lay on the sofa with her feet up, he cooked a rice, fish and vegetable casserole so healthy and bursting with vitamins it could have won a triathlon. After dinner, when Dulcie assured him her doctor had told her she must give in to her cravings, he even jogged down to the petrol station and bought her two packets of crisps and a Bounty ice cream bar.

While Liam washed up, Dulcie embarked on stage two of her plan.

'Finlay?' she suggested, holding up the book of babies' names she had bought yesterday. 'Look, it's Gaelic for fair soldier. Is Finlay better than Xavier, do you think?'

Liam wasn't wild about Xavier. As far as names were concerned, maggot was better than Xavier. Honestly, pregnant women had some funny ideas, presumably because their hormones were up the creek.

'Finlay's not too bad.' He rejoined Dulcie in the sitting room and leaned his elbows on the back of the sofa, wishing he could summon up more enthusiasm for the task. It was weird trying to choose a name for something currently the size of a centipede.

But Dulcie, it seemed, had enthusiasm to spare.

'And now, raising the Wimbledon championship trophy

proudly above his head, this year's triumphant winner . . .' she
fanfared '. . . Finlay Fackrell!'

'Jesus Christ.'

'What?' Dulcie abruptly twisted round and gazed up at him
in concern. The expression on his face was one of utter horror.
'What's wrong? Don't you want him to win Wimbledon?'

'It's not that,' spluttered Liam, 'it's . . . it's Fackrell!'

Dulcie looked wounded.

'That's my name.'

'Yes, but—'

'I'm sorry.' Dulcie tried hard to ignore the triumphant little
voice in her head yelling Bingo! 'I just kind of assumed, under
the circumstances, he'd have my name.'

Liam looked deeply uncomfortable.

'Yes, but *Fackrell*. Couldn't you stick with Ross? Finlay Ross
sounds all right.'

'But it's my married name! It's Patrick's name,' she protested,
'and this isn't anything to do with Patrick.'

Another long silence. Dulcie could feel Liam's warm breath
on her shoulder. She could smell his aftershave. Mentally she
willed him on; this was his cue, his big chance to say something
impossibly romantic, something along the lines of, 'I want my
son's name to be McPherson, I want *your* name to be
McPherson, oh, Dulcie, I can't bear it another minute . . . please
divorce Patrick and marry me . . .'

She couldn't understand why it wasn't happening. Was this
a dream opportunity or what?

Liam stood up and ruffled her short hair in an awkward let's-
change-the-subject gesture.

'Okay, you win. But if it's going to be Fackrell you can't
have Finlay. Sounds like some character out of *Sesame Street*.
You'd be better off with something plain,' he concluded off-
handedly as he disappeared into the kitchen, 'like Rob or Tom.'

When Dulcie woke up the next morning, Liam was already
out of bed and in the shower. She lay back against the pillows

225

and fantasised pleasurably about him soaping his perfect body. As soon as the week was over, she would make up for this enforced celibacy, big-time.

Reaching across for the phone, Dulcie dialled home.

'Are you okay?'

'I'm not an invalid,' protested Pru. 'Actually, I've just defrosted your fridge. Do you have any idea how many Bounty ice cream bars there are in your freezer compartment?'

'I hate running out.'

'It's a miracle you can run anywhere, the amount you eat.'

At that moment Liam appeared in the doorway, an odd expression on his face.

'Anyway,' said Dulcie, 'I'll be home soon, Granny. And don't worry about the washing-up, I'll do it when I get back.'

Pru sounded amused. 'Careful, I might hold you to that.'

'Are you all right?' said Liam when she had hung up.

'Great. Just checking up on Granny.' Dulcie waved the phone at him. 'She's fine.'

'Managed without you last night then?'

Why was he *looking* at her in that peculiar way?

'Oh, no problem.' Wondering if for some reason he didn't believe her, Dulcie began to elaborate. 'She went to bingo, actually. Won eighteen pounds fifty. Granny's always been lucky . . . last year she entered a competition on the back of a cornflakes packet and won a scuba-diving holiday in Tenerife.'

Liam, magnificently naked, pulled on a tracksuit. He didn't appear to be listening.

'I've got to get to the club.'

Dying to have a private snoop around the flat, Dulcie said brightly, 'Don't worry about me, I can let myself out.'

But he was already picking up her crumpled clothes, holding them towards her.

'I'd rather we left together.'

This was a bit of a shame but Dulcie consoled herself with the thought that maybe it was Liam's way of being romantic.

226

'Headache gone, then?' he said as the flat door slammed shut behind them.

Headache?

'Oh!' *That* headache. 'Oh, absolutely.' Relieved, Dulcie beamed up at his unsmiling profile. That must be why he'd seemed so odd; he was *worried* about her. 'Completely gone, thanks.'

But Liam still didn't smile.

'Good.'

A gleaming red Parcelforce van was just driving off as Dulcie arrived home. Missing its bumper by a whisker as she screeched into the drive, she realised with a strange pang that the driver had strong brown forearms exactly like Patrick's.

No need for that V-sign though.

Pru was in the hall clutching a parcel.

'It's for Patrick,' she said, 'marked Urgent. I had to sign for it.'

Dulcie wondered what the driver had made of Pru's bandaged head. With each passing day she was looking more and more like Frankenstein's monster.

'Some component for one of Patrick's computers.' Peering at the label on the parcel, she recognised the company's logo. Their own computer evidently hadn't been updated with his change of address.

Dulcie dumped the parcel on the hall table and made her way through to the kitchen.

'It says Urgent.'

Following her, Pru sounded agitated. Pru, Dulcie recalled, was the kind of person who felt compelled to pay the electricity bill the same day it arrived. Preferably with a first-class stamp.

'Okay, okay. Breakfast first. You make the tea and I'll defrost the doughnuts.' It was still only nine o'clock, after all. 'Then I'll take it round.'

* * *

227

When Dulcie arrived at the office, however, the doors were locked. For a Tuesday morning this was unthinkable; Patrick had to have been abducted by aliens at the very least.

Except he hadn't. When Dulcie climbed the next flight of stairs she found the door to Patrick's flat open and Patrick there, standing with his back to her, packing decidedly un-computerlike things into a holdall.

Dulcie cleared her throat and he spun round.

'Did I startle you? Sorry.'

'Dulcie!'

She half smiled.

'I've never seen you looking guilty before. What is it, a couple of kilos of heroin?'

The expression on Patrick's face was exquisite. She couldn't resist going over to the bag and taking a closer look.

A beach towel. Swimming trunks. Factor 4 Ambre Solaire. A bottle of wine *and* a corkscrew. A frisbee.

A *frisbee*, for God's sake . . .

She looked at Patrick, who had never blushed in his life.

He was blushing.

Dulcie said, 'Don't forget your bucket and spade.'

He zipped up the holdall.

'What are you doing here, Dulcie?'

She held out the parcel.

'It says Urgent. I thought you might be desperate.'

'Oh. Thanks.'

Like a small boy reluctantly unwrapping a birthday present from a great-aunt, knowing it's going to be socks, Patrick opened the package.

'If I'd known,' said Dulcie, to break the suddenly awkward silence, 'I'd have bought you a beachball instead.'

Recovering himself, as if realising he didn't have to feel guilty, Patrick held up the polystyrene box of microchips and grinned.

'No really, these are fine. Just what I wanted.'

Dulcie felt something twist and tighten in her stomach.

'You've closed the office.'

'Just for the day.'

The something, she realised, was jealousy.

'Where are you going?'

'Devon.' He glanced out of the window, at the traffic-clogged street below. 'It's hot, it's sunny. We thought we'd drive down, find a beach.'

And play fucking *frisbee*, thought Dulcie, biting her lip until it hurt.

'You and Claire?'

'Me and Claire.' Patrick nodded.

'Sure you can remember how to swim?' She mimed the breaststroke. 'It's a leisure pursuit, you do it in water. Sometimes you splash about a bit and have something known as fun. Maybe if I drew a diagram—'

'Dulcie, stop,' said Patrick, but not crossly. He was being – ugh, far worse, Dulcie realised – *patient* with her. 'You always told me I worked too hard. Well, now I'm taking a bit of time off to enjoy myself. You of all people should approve.'

Inexplicably, Dulcie's eyes filled with tears. She wanted to scream at his stupidity. He wasn't supposed to take time off and enjoy himself *now*.

'Are you crying?' Patrick looked shocked. 'You never cry.' He unzipped the holdall, pulled out the beach towel and gave it to her to wipe her eyes on. Then he smiled briefly. 'Must be your hormones.'

Wrong, thought Dulcie, it's you.

Dammit, how thick could an intelligent man get?

Chapter 34

Since she was supposed to be in Majorca where the temperature was up in the nineties, Pru realised she was going to look pretty odd if she reappeared without at least some kind of a tan.

By eleven o'clock, Dulcie's back garden had turned into a suntrap. Reassured by its total seclusion, Pru dragged one of the padded sunloungers into pole position, slathered on half a tube of Factor 8, arranged herself so as to catch the maximum number of rays, and closed her eyes.

She almost fainted twenty minutes later when a man's voice said, 'Jesus Christ, what happened to you?'

Pru opened her eyes and shrieked. Liam was standing over her looking appalled, which was fairly understandable given that she was wearing her least exotic white bra and a pair of ancient green pants.

'I wasn't asleep!' Gabbling, stalling for time, Pru sat bolt upright and tried to cover herself with her hands. Being found naked would have been better than being spotted in these pants. She peered across at the gate which led through from the front garden. 'I didn't hear the gate! How did you open it without clicking the latch?'

The wooden gate was only four feet high. Liam gave her a pitying look.

'I jumped over.'

'Oh.'

'I thought you were Dulcie.' He paused. 'From a distance.'

Highly likely, thought Pru.

'Dulcie isn't here.'

Liam was still staring at her head. Pru braced herself for the next question. In the event of emergency, she had an explanation ready. She had been in a car crash.

But Liam said, 'I thought you were supposed to be in Majorca.'

'Yes, I . . . well, I . . .'

'So what's with the bandages?'

Pru swallowed.

'I . . . had an . . .'

Accident, prompted her brain. You had an accident.

'You had an operation,' Liam suggested helpfully. 'What, to pin your ears back?'

Pru was outraged.

'Who told you? Bloody Dulcie, I suppose—'

Liam grinned.

'Relax. Lucky guess. Actually, my cousin had it done years ago. You look like she looked afterwards.' The grin broadened. 'Drove her mad not being able to wash her hair.'

Praying he'd go away wasn't doing much good. Liam was now making himself comfortable on the grass beside her sunlounger.

'Dulcie might not be back for ages.'

He shrugged. 'That's okay. I'll keep you company instead.'

'Oh.'

In contrast with Liam, Pru was feeling more and more uncomfortable. She sensed he had something to say that he hadn't yet said.

'So you're the grandmother, I take it?'

'Sorry? Oh . . . yes.' Unhappily, Pru nodded. 'I didn't want anyone to know I was here.'

A glimmer of a smile. 'I won't breathe a word.'

'Thanks.'

Liam idly picked a daisy from the lawn and rolled the stem between his finger and thumb.

'You aren't much good at lying, are you? Not as good as Dulcie.'

Oh Lord.

'I'm not sure what you m-mean,' stammered Pru.

'You know,' Liam prompted. He sounded amused. 'Fibbing. Bending the truth. Making up stories.'

Helplessly, Pru shrugged. She didn't need a mirror to know her cheeks were absolutely scarlet.

'No . . . well, I suppose I'm not great at it. I just . . . just didn't want people to know I'd had my ears done, that's all. I'm very sensitive about my ears—'

'You see,' Liam's tone, as he cut through the gabble, was conversational, 'I know Dulcie isn't pregnant.'

Pru stared at him.

'What? *How* do you know?'

He shrugged.

'How?' repeated Pru, redder than ever.

'The wonder of the double-bluff. You just told me.'

This was a nightmare. This was truly awful. Pru began to shake.

'You mean you *didn't* know? It was a *guess*?'

Again the rueful half-smile.

'Well, call it an educated one.'

'Oh shit!' wailed Pru. Dulcie was going to kill her.

'Come on, calm down. The thing is, how I react depends on the reason she's doing it,' Liam soothingly explained. 'I mean, if the whole thing was a con-trick, an attempt to trap me, I wouldn't be too pleased. But if it was just for a joke, some kind of girly bet . . . well,' he shrugged, 'I can take a joke.'

'It was, it was a joke!' The words tumbled out breathlessly. 'Of *course* it wasn't serious!'

Liam's blue eyes were cool.

'Like I said, you're a lousy liar.'

Defeated, Pru fell back on the sunlounger. Somehow her horrible green pants didn't matter any more. She watched him bat away a persistent wasp.

'So how did you guess she wasn't . . . um . . . telling the truth?'

'Put it this way. What would you think if your pregnant girlfriend spent the night with you and the next morning you found a bit of cellophane bobbing around in the loo?'

'What?'

'The kind of cellophane that comes wrapped round Lil-lets,' said Liam. 'The kind that's hard to flush away.' He paused. 'Bit of a giveaway, that.'

'Oh!' Pru breathed a sigh of relief. 'You mean Dulcie already knows you know?'

He shook his head.

'I needed time to think. I had to make sure I was right.' Again, he almost looked amused. 'Lucky you were here.'

Not lucky for me, thought Pru miserably. Somehow she knew she was going to end up taking the blame for this.

'So what will you do now?' she whispered.

Liam stretched out on the grass, knees bent, and began performing energetic sit-ups.

'What people normally do when they've had a narrow escape, I imagine,' he said. 'Celebrate.'

Dulcie arrived home fifteen minutes later. Liam had by this time progressed to one-armed press-ups. Unable to bear the look of joy on Dulcie's face when she saw him in her back garden, Pru rushed up to her room. Burdened with guilt and shame, sticky with perspiration and sun cream, she lay on her bed with the windows shut, terrified of overhearing what was going on outside.

Whatever it was, it didn't take long. Pru heard the slam of a car door and the crunch of wheels on gravel. When she dared to peer out of the window – through a crack in the curtains like some neighbourhood watcher – she saw Liam tearing off up the road in his red Lamborghini. Alone.

The door to the spare bedroom was flung open. Dulcie, barely recognisable with her face streaked with mascara and tears, erupted into the room.

Pru cringed.

233

'He's gone! He's bloody gone,' wept Dulcie, stubbing her toe on the leg of the bed and letting out a renewed howl of pain. 'Oh! Ow! I can't *bear* it . . . he's really gone.' Clutching her toe, collapsing on to the bed, she stared wild-eyed at Pru. 'And it's ALL YOUR FAULT.'

Pru couldn't handle this. Too racked with guilt to argue – she *knew* it was her fault – and too stunned by the bitterness of Dulcie's attack to even attempt to fight back, she knew she had to escape. Racing downstairs, dragging on a long red T-shirt as she went, she grabbed her bag and stumbled barefoot across the stinging gravel to her car in the garage.

So much for being cosseted.

Back at the bedsit, fusty and unaired, Pru discovered the money in the electricity meter had run out and everything in the fridge had turned to slime.

She spent two hours cleaning out the stinking fridge and frenziedly scrubbing the floor. Not having worked for the last week and a half meant she was perilously low on funds. This reduced her to fresh tears of despair.

How could I have been so stupid? she thought hopelessly. I've got new ears, and no food.

As she was washing the grimy windows, Dulcie's car rounded the corner. Pru leapt away from the window like a frightened rabbit and crouched on the floor, trembling. She wasn't up to another tirade of abuse, she just wasn't.

'Oh, Pru, I'm so sorry. Can you ever, *ever* forgive me?'

Dulcie, still looking a sight with mascara tracks dried on her cheeks, gazed miserably at Pru. 'I'm such a stupid bitch. I'm so, so ashamed of myself. It wasn't your fault, it was all mine. If you want to,' she offered in desperation, moving closer to Pru on the front doorstep, 'you can slap my face.'

Pru made a noise halfway between a sob and a snort of laughter.

'Go on,' Dulcie said humbly, 'I mean it. Hard as you like.' She offered her cheek.

'Don't be such a berk,' said Pru. 'You'd better come in.'

When they reached the bedsitter, Dulcie wrinkled her nose at the overpowering smell of bleach.

She watched as Pru filled the kettle at the sink.

'I know I'm a berk. Are you still my friend?'

'Stupid question,' said Pru, dangerously close to bursting into tears all over again. 'Lend me fifty pee and I'll make you a cup of tea.'

When Dulcie had finished shovelling coins into the meter – 'Not that you're staying here. You're coming home with me' – she delved into her massive handbag and pulled out a dark-green Jolly's carrier.

'I was going to buy you flowers, but that's what guilty husbands do when they've cheated on their wives. So I got you these instead.'

Pru opened the carrier containing six Lancôme lipsticks, four Clinique eyeshadows and seven Chanel mascaras.

'Bit of a job lot. I was parked on double yellows in Milsom Street, didn't want to get clamped,' Dulcie apologised. 'I just raced in and grabbed what I could. Still, more useful than a bunch of roses.'

'You went into Jolly's looking like that?' Pru was touched.

'Like what?'

Dulcie screamed when she saw her reflection in the mirror.

'My God, no wonder they asked me if I wanted my mascara waterproof! I'm amazed I wasn't arrested,' she said ruefully, 'for wearing make-up without due care and attention.'

Over cups of tea that tasted faintly of bleach, Dulcie told Pru just how cruel and hurtful Liam had been.

'He called me a sneaky, low-down, conniving bitch,' she said with a sigh. 'He told me I was a sad case who needed to get a life. He said I was desperate and lazy and a pathological liar, and he felt sorry for the next stupid bastard I got my claws

235

into because nobody deserved that much grief.'

'What did you say?' Pru, who would have been finished off completely by such a slating, particularly one so perilously close to the truth, marvelled at Dulcie's matter-of-fact tone. She had, it appeared, already got the worst of her misery out of her system.

'I told him he was a washed-up, over-the-hill, failed ball-basher with delusions of celebrity,' said Dulcie. 'I said he was boring and health-obsessed, with about as much personality as a salad sandwich.' She thought for a moment. 'Oh, and I told him he was crap in bed.'

Pru's eyes widened.

'Was he?'

'Of course he wasn't,' said Dulcie, 'but you always tell them that.'

'Crikey.'

'It niggles away at the back of their mind. They hate it but they can't help wondering if— Who's that?'

The doorbell was ringing.

Pru's hands flew instinctively to her bandaged ears.

'No one knows I'm here. Don't answer it.'

But Dulcie, ever curious, was already hanging out of the open window, peering down to the street below.

'Dulcie, hi!'

'It's Eddie,' Dulcie murmured incredulously.

'Don't let him in,' squeaked Pru.

'I was just passing,' Eddie called up, shielding his eyes from the sun. 'Saw the windows open. Hang on . . .'

As Dulcie watched, the front door opened. A hippy in a drooping Woodstock T-shirt emerged and Eddie grabbed the door before it could slam shut.

'Wait there,' he yelled, waving cheerfully to Dulcie, 'I'm coming up.'

Dulcie greeted him clutching a can of Mr Sheen in one hand and a pair of Pru's knickers in the other.

'How on earth could you be just passing?' she demanded,

eyeing Eddie with suspicion. 'This road isn't on the way to anywhere.'

'Well . . . you know how it is. Promised Pru I'd keep an eye on the place.' Eddie was waffling. 'Make sure it's secure . . . in case of burglars, that kind of thing.'

Dulcie's expression changed to incredulous. Would any self-respecting burglar be seen dead breaking into this hideous dump?

Eddie had taken to driving slowly past Pru's bedsit every day. He didn't know quite why, it just gave him an odd sense of comfort. When he had seen the windows open he had experienced a thrill of almost teenage proportions. Pru was home early! She was back! He was going to see her again . . . now!

Except she wasn't and he wasn't. He was being interrogated by Dulcie instead.

'Anyway,' Eddie decided the best method of defence was attack, 'what are you doing here?'

'Me? I'm polishing.' To prove it, Dulcie aimed Mr Sheen inexpertly at the peeling paint on one of the window frames. She squirted for several seconds, rubbed vigorously at the paint with the scrunched-up knickers and leapt back as a shower of brittle flakes flew at her like shrapnel, just missing her eyes.

Eddie frowned. As scenarios went, this was fairly unlikely. 'Why?'

'Pru's due back on Saturday,' Dulcie replied airily. 'I thought I'd give the place a good clean.' She gestured to the gleaming floor. 'I've been busy for *hours*.'

This was positively surreal. The idea of Dulcie scrubbing floors was on a par with Cherie Blair swigging meths from a bottle.

'Have you heard from her?' Eddie was suddenly overcome with longing, desperate for news of Pru. He hadn't had so much as a postcard from Spain. 'I thought she might have been in touch.'

But Dulcie, shaking her head, looked infuriatingly unconcerned.

'Not a word.'

'Too busy enjoying herself, I expect,' said Eddie, a brave smile concealing the inner turmoil.

'I expect.' Spring-clean evidently completed, Dulcie began closing the windows.

Out of sheer desperation, he said abruptly, 'I swear, my memory's like a sieve. I've forgotten the name of the friend she's staying with.'

'Me too.'

But Eddie noticed Dulcie was smiling to herself, the kind of secretive smile that made you want to shake the person doing it until their teeth rattled.

'What? Why are you looking like that?'

'Me?' Dulcie shrugged and looked innocent. 'I was just thinking how badly Pru needed this holiday. I bet it's doing her the world of good.' She chucked Pru's knickers over her shoulder into the sink and grinned at Eddie. 'She'll come back a different person, you'll see.'

Eddie gazed dispiritedly at the Mr Sheen-soaked knickers dangling over the hot tap. Just so long as Pru didn't come back *with* a different person, he didn't care.

'You know, I reckon Eddie's got a bit of a thing for you,' said Dulcie mischievously as she hung out of the window once more. 'He's gone, by the way. It's safe to come out now. Ooh, naughty boy. I thought he must be.'

Pru crawled out from under her bed, shuddering as a cobweb draped itself across her face.

'Must be what?'

'Driving.' Gleefully, Dulcie watched his Jag disappear around the corner. 'Tut tut.'

Pru looked worried.

'He's breaking the law.'

'And all because the lady might get burgled,' Dulcie intoned,

Milk Tray-style. She swivelled round and broke into a grin. 'He couldn't take his eyes off your knickers either. See, it must be love.'

'My Janet Regers,' wailed Pru, spotting her favourite pair hanging over the sink.

Dulcie looked indignant. 'It was an emergency, I couldn't find a duster. I had to look authentic, didn't I?'

'They're my seducing knickers,' Pru said sadly, trying to imagine a time in the dim and distant future when she might feel up to a spot of seduction. Maybe in fifty or sixty years . . .

'Take it from me, said Dulcie, 'if you want to seduce a man, the best way is no knickers at all.'

Chapter 35

One way and another, it had been an eventful day. By the time Liza arrived at Dulcie's house, Dulcie was getting stuck into her second bottle of wine. Half-smoked, irritably stubbed-out cigarettes were piling up in the ashtray, which was only brought out in moments of great crisis. The more cigarettes she smoked and the more wine she put away, the more sorry for herself Dulcie became.

'. . . and not just any old frisbee,' as she thumped the kitchen table, ash cascaded down the front of her black T-shirt, 'a *pink* frisbee with go-faster stripes round the side! I mean, can you picture it? Patrick, playing with a pink frisbee on a beach . . . on a *Tuesday*? Has Saint-sodding-Claire been slipping happy pills into his cocoa or what?'

To divert her, Liza said, 'Never mind Patrick. Tell me what happened with Liam. Careful—'

Dulcie's co-ordination had gone AWOL. Red wine splashed across the table as she tried to pour and missed. The bottle clunked against her glass, which in turn toppled over, drenching an almost full packet of Silk Cut.

The trouble is, thought Dulcie, I *do* mind Patrick. I especially mind him being happy with Claire. Forcing her attention back to Liam, she related the morning's events to Liza. Dulcie left nothing out because that was the beauty of best friends; you could moan for as long as you wanted, you never felt compelled to rush.

'All that skulking off to the other side of Bath and secretly getting fit was a waste of time,' she complained, drawing unsmiley faces in the spilled wine with her finger. 'He said he knew all along I was a fraud. I bet bloody Imelda told him. Cow.'

Liza watched as Dulcie tried inexpertly to light a sodden cigarette.

'Let her have him,' said Liza. 'You can do better than that. Okay, he looked good, but the charm was all on the surface. Where was the *real* personality?'

Dulcie gave up on the cigarette. She managed a brief smile. 'In his jockstrap.'

'There, you see?' Heartened by the attempt at humour, Liza sat back in her chair and raised her glass. 'Feeling better already. You don't need him.'

Dulcie knew that. She just wished Liam hadn't laid into her quite so ruthlessly. Those hurtful things he'd come out with . . . well, they'd *hurt*.

'I told him he was obsessed because all he cared about was boring old sport.' She kept her eyes fixed on the wet table. 'And he said at least he was obsessed about something, and didn't I ever wonder if there was anything missing in my life?'

'Like what?' said Pru.

Dulcie shrugged. 'I don't know. He just looked at me in this weird way, then he shook his head and said: "You don't do anything, Dulcie. That's your problem. You just don't *do* anything." '

'Well,' said Liza, breaking the awkward silence that had greeted this last statement – cruel, but true – 'you've got something to do now. Get Liam McPherson right out of your system and find yourself someone a hundred times better.'

'Oh right, it's that simple.' Wearily Dulcie rubbed her face. What with this morning's encounter with Patrick, followed by the Liam thing, then the fight with Pru, she didn't know if she had the energy to even think about finding herself another man. 'Tell you what, you give Brad Pitt a ring, let him know I'm unexpectedly back on the market and ask him if he'll meet me for dinner on Friday night. I'm free then.'

'What you need,' said Pru, 'is someone kind. Easy-going. Not goody-goody,' she argued because Dulcie, predictably, was already pulling I'm-going-to-be-sick faces, 'but . . . well, decent.'

'Decent!'

Pru refused to be put off. Having learned her lesson months ago, she was determined to get the message across.

'You want someone you can trust,' she said firmly. 'The kind of man who turns up when he says he'll turn up.'

'The kind who doesn't come home with lipstick on his tennis shorts,' put in Liza.

Dulcie groaned and covered her eyes. She knew, she *knew* what they were saying. It was just those words: decent, dependable, honest, trustworthy . . . linked inextricably in her mind with a vision of some bumbling, good-hearted history teacher, always eager to help, in his woolly jumper, baggy corduroys and folkweave sandals.

Men like that, thought Dulcie, decent men, simply didn't do it for her. They didn't make her heart beat faster and her stomach contract with longing. Apart from anything else, they were always ugly.

'There's nothing wrong with decent,' Pru insisted, ploughing on, refusing to give up.

Dulcie refilled her glass with Fitou and drank it quickly before it could get spilled. As she did so, it occurred to her that she did know someone decent and not ugly. Someone of whom Pru and Liza both hugely approved. Someone who had in the past been eminently capable of making her heart beat faster and her stomach tie itself in lustful knots.

Curiously, when she had bumped into him this morning, it had happened again.

Decent, mused Dulcie, turning the thought over in her mind. Like Patrick.

'Like Claire,' announced Liza, who had also been mulling the word over. Helping herself to a handful of peanuts from the bowl Pru had just placed in the centre of the table, she

242

missed the startled expression in Dulcie's eyes. 'That's what Claire is. And look how happy she's made Patrick.'

'Hang on,' Dulcie said slowly. 'How do you know he's happy?'

Too late, Liza realised she'd said aloud something she should have kept to herself.

'You said he was,' she countered with a half-hearted bluff. 'Anyway, if he's playing frisbee with her, she must make him happy.'

Dulcie sat up. She might be a bit pissed but she wasn't a total dimwit. Not completely stupid. What was going on here that she didn't know about?

Her green eyes narrowed.

'You mean you've met her?'

Liza gave up. She nodded.

'Well, only once or twice.'

Pru managed to catch the bottle of Fitou, sent reeling across the table by Dulcie's twitching elbow.

'And you didn't *tell* me?' Dulcie gazed at her in bewilderment. 'I don't get this at all. *How* did you meet her?'

It had been one of those silly situations where the longer you put off mentioning something relatively insignificant, the more significant it became. Liza wished now she'd told Dulcie straight away.

'Okay.' She hesitated. 'But the only reason I didn't say it before was because I didn't think it would last.'

Trembling, Dulcie lit a cigarette.

'Go on.'

'Her name's Claire Berenger. She's Kit's sister,' said Liza.

Dulcie screamed. The foul-smelling cigarette landed in her glass of wine.

'You lit the wrong end,' said Pru as the filter sizzled and went out.

'How could you know that and not tell me?' Dulcie shouted. Pru jumped – she hadn't had time to tell her – but Dulcie wasn't yelling at her, thankfully. She was yelling at Liza.

'I've just said, I thought it wouldn't last. There didn't seem much point.'

Liza was on the defensive. Dulcie could imagine why. She had never felt so betrayed.

'But now you know it will last, because she makes him so fantastically *happy*.' Dulcie spoke through gritted teeth. Hot on the heels of betrayal came a great surge of jealousy. She imagined the cosy dinner parties for four, Liza and Kit sitting around a candlelit table with Patrick and Claire, gossiping together, *about her*.

Laughing *at her*.

And now that I've been dumped by Liam, Dulcie felt sick at the thought, they can even feel sorry for me, too . . .

'You're supposed to be my friend,' she hissed across the table at Liza. 'I thought you were *my* friend! What's happened – did it all change while I wasn't looking?' Dulcie's eyes flashed with contempt. 'Are you Claire's friend now?'

'Don't be stupid,' said Liza defensively. 'I've met her a couple of times, that's all. She seems okay. Not dazzling, but . . . nice. You can't not like her,' she struggled to explain to a stony-faced Dulcie, 'because there's nothing to dislike.'

'I met her too, don't forget. She looks like an overgrown Girl Guide,' sneered Dulcie.

'I used to be a Girl Guide,' said Pru.

But Dulcie wasn't listening. Her overwrought imagination had moved on. Now, instead of picturing Liza and Claire having a good old girlie gossip, she saw Liza and Patrick indulging in a meaningful heart-to-heart:

'Oh, Liza, I never knew I could feel like this,' Patrick confided. 'Being with Claire is just incredible. She's made me the happiest man in the world.'

'I know, I can see she has,' Liza murmured, 'and I'm so glad for you. You deserve it, after everything you had to go through with Dulcie. You and Claire make a brilliant couple. She's lovely, Patrick. You really are the perfect match.'

'I can't believe this,' snapped Dulcie, fumbling in the soggy packet for yet another cigarette. 'I can't believe you've been sneaking off behind my back, whispering about me to my husband—'

'Oh come on.' Liza heaved an exasperated sigh. 'You don't seriously imagine I'd do that. Grow *up*, Dulcie!'

'Me? *Me* grow up?' Dulcie jabbed herself in the chest. 'Oh right, that's a good one,' she jeered. 'You're the one making an idiot of yourself with a boy ten years younger than you are, but for some reason *I'm* the one who needs to grow up!'

Liza went very still. All the colour had drained from her face. Pru, in the middle of mopping the wine-logged table top, realised this had gone far beyond the usual level of good-natured bickering.

'Okay,' said Liza, 'it's nine years actually, but point taken.' Her voice was low and not altogether steady. 'Now let me just say this. Liam might be a jerk of the first order but he was right about one thing. You definitely need to get yourself a life.'

'What—?'

'Because you are wasting the one you've got, and it isn't doing you any favours,' Liza continued remorselessly. 'What Liam said was true: you don't *do* anything. You're bored out of your skull and you don't even know it. I mean, what's the plan, Dulcie? When we're sixty and we look back over our lives, what will *you* be able to say?' Mimicking Dulcie's flippant manner, she chirruped, 'Well, I was good at shopping and brilliant at telling lies . . .'

Pru stared in horror as Dulcie, red-cheeked, leapt to her feet.

'You are a bitch,' Dulcie shouted at Liza, 'and you are *way* too old for Kit Berenger—'

'At least I'd never dream of telling a man I was pregnant—'

'He's too young for you, he's too young for you—'

'And Patrick's *definitely* well rid of you—'

'STOP IT!' shrieked Pru, launching herself across the table and pushing herself between the two of them like a boxing referee. She grabbed one of Dulcie's wrists and shook it, forcing Dulcie back into her chair. 'Just stop this AT ONCE.'

Dulcie rubbed her wrist. Ouch, it really hurt.

'Why should I? She started it.'

'I did not start it,' Liza snapped back. She glared at Dulcie. 'This is all your fault. Just because you were dumped by Liam.'

Liam. Dulcie conjured up a mental picture of him playing a brilliant backhand cross-court volley, blond hair flying, eyes flashing . . .

She closed her eyes. No, this had nothing to do with Liam.

When Dulcie didn't speak, Liza rose to her feet. Pointedly she addressed her words to Pru.

'Time to go.'

Clearly still shaken by her own bravery, Pru went with her to the front door.

Left alone at the kitchen table, Dulcie heard them murmuring together in the hall. Ah well, she was getting used to it.

She stubbed out the cigarette she'd forgotten to smoke in all the excitement, and refilled her almost empty glass.

Straining to overhear, Dulcie managed to make out Liza's words: 'No, no, I'm fine. Kit's waiting at home for me.'

Dulcie took a great slurp of wine. Raising her own voice, she called out, 'Don't forget to warm his bottle before you tuck him into bed.'

Chapter 36

Unlike Pru's bedsitter, which – as Dulcie had pointed out to Eddie Hammond – wasn't on the way to anywhere, Bibi's house was situated on the main road leading into Bath.

This meant you couldn't help passing Bibi's house even when you didn't want to.

Like today.

Dulcie felt her stomach begin to tense up as she approached the first bend in the road. One twist to the left, one twist to the right, then the traffic lights. And there, on the left if you were unlucky enough to be caught at the lights, was Bibi's house with its sloping front garden and narrow, hard-to-get-into drive.

Dulcie had a thumping headache, thanks to finishing off all the red wine Liza hadn't stayed to drink last night. She had woken up sensing something was wrong, then groaned as the awful memories seeped back.

Pru hadn't helped.

'You should apologise to Liza,' she told Dulcie.

'Oh God, why do I always have to be the one to apologise?' Dulcie wailed.

Pru hadn't stated the obvious, she had simply given Dulcie a long look.

And since in view of the Liam thing it seemed sensible to steer clear of Brunton Manor for a while, Dulcie could think of only one other sensible way to pass the time.

Go shopping.

She especially didn't enjoy passing Bibi's house today because it served as a horrible reminder of yet another occasion when she had tried to improve a situation, only to end up making it much, much worse instead.

At first, in the weeks following Patrick's eventful surprise party, Dulcie had crossed her fingers each time she approached the traffic lights, praying that when she rounded the second bend she would see James's car parked on Bibi's drive.

But this hadn't happened, which just went to show what a waste of time praying and crossing your fingers was. These days Dulcie simply hoped she wouldn't see Bibi.

Now, as the house came into view, she saw a different car on the drive.

This was interesting, because it might mean there was a new man at last in Bibi's life.

Dulcie braked, even though the traffic lights – for once in their contrary lives – were on green. A blue Renault behind her tooted irritably but Dulcie ignored it, far too intrigued by the car on the drive.

This was good news, this was promising news. If Bibi's found herself a new man, thought Dulcie, perking up at the idea, I can stop feeling guilty about James.

The lights changed to red and she drew to a halt. The driver of the Renault gave a blast on his horn in disgust.

And Dulcie realised, too late, that the car on Bibi's drive wasn't unoccupied, as she had at first thought. Those head-rests weren't head-rests at all, they were heads.

Claire Berenger hadn't only snapped up her husband, Dulcie realised miserably; she'd gone for the job lot and bagged her mother-in-law too.

Jealousy wasn't an emotion Dulcie had ever had much to do with, but she couldn't help feeling it now. It hurt too, like a serrated knife twisting in her ribs.

Unable to tear her eyes away, she watched Bibi and Claire jump out of the car, laughing and weighed down with glossy carriers. Dulcie recognised several of them; in the old days she and Bibi had indulged in delicious spending sprees, visiting all their favourite shopping haunts and stopping for lunch somewhere gossipy and glamorous. They had both enjoyed their days out together almost as much as the actual buying of the new clothes.

We always got on so well, thought Dulcie, feeling horribly bereft. Bibi was the best mother-in-law anyone could wish for. And now she doesn't need me any more. She's got herself another potential daughter-in-law, a new best friend.

The lights had changed to green again without Dulcie noticing. The blare of the Renault's horn behind her made her jump. When she lifted her foot from the clutch, the car jerked in protest and promptly stalled.

More horns were tooted. Beginning to perspire, Dulcie turned the key in the ignition. Nothing happened.

She tried again.

And again, harder this time.

Still nothing.

From the sound of it, every car in Bath was blasting its horn at her now. The prickle of perspiration had turned into a torrent of sweat. And although Dulcie couldn't bear to look, she knew Bibi and Claire would be watching with interest. Interest that would turn to amusement, no doubt, the moment Bibi recognised her car. This would make her day.

The traffic lights, almost with a shrug – 'You had your chance, you blew it' – turned back to red.

To her horror, Dulcie realised the man behind her was climbing out of his Renault. Next moment he hammered on her window, his face as shiny and purple as an aubergine.

'You stupid cow,' he bellowed. 'What the hell d'you think you're playing at? Bloody women drivers – bimbos like you shouldn't be allowed on the road!'

Dulcie wasn't up to defending herself. She was up to here with being shouted at.

She burst into tears and jumped out of the car, almost cannoning off the Renault driver's great barrel of a chest.

'The car's broken down. It won't go.' Hating herself for being such a wimp, Dulcie heard her voice go higher and higher. 'And don't yell at me because it's not my fault, okay?'

'Bloody women, nothing's ever your fault, is it?' sneered the man, whose wife had run off with a taxi driver, taken the kids with her and stung him for so much alimony his business had gone down the tubes.

Dulcie lifted her chin. Out of the corner of her eye she could see Bibi and Claire watching the goings-on.

'If you're so clever,' she said bitterly to the man, 'you have a go.'

He climbed into Dulcie's car, flicked the key in the ignition and pumped the clutch a couple of times.

The engine sprang obediently into life.

The look on the man's face was unbearable. Nobody, thought Dulcie, should be allowed to do a look like that. She wanted nothing more than to slap his horrid purple cheek.

'Here,' sneered the beastly man as he climbed out, 'think you can manage to get past the traffic lights this time, or would you like me to do that for you as well?'

Gritting her teeth, Dulcie slid back into the driver's seat. Glancing across one last time she saw that Bibi and Claire were still there, witnessing her humiliation and no doubt enjoying it hugely.

The lights turned green.

As nervous as a learner taking her test, Dulcie pulled tentatively away and made it over to the other side.

A motley bunch of teenagers on bikes who had stopped to watch the free show jeered and whistled and gave her an ironic round of applause.

And you can all get stuffed too, thought Dulcie. Her lower lip began to wobble again out of sheer relief as she drove past them and headed on into Bath.

Finding somewhere to park took for ever. By the time she had finished shoe-horning the car into a cramped space outside a wholefood café on Mortimer Street, Dulcie's yellow shirt was sticking to her back and her palms were so damp she could barely grip the steering wheel.

Since a mopping-up operation appeared to be in order, Dulcie went inside the café, ordered an orange juice and dived into the loo. There wasn't much to be done about the shirt but at least she could wash her hands, hold her wrists under the cold water tap, run a comb through her hair and quickly re-do her face.

The man behind the counter grinned at Dulcie when she reappeared.

'That's better. Been one of those mornings by the look of it.'

Nice to know you looked as dreadful as you felt, thought Dulcie, managing a brief nod in return as she paid for the orange juice.

'If you don't mind me asking,' he ventured, 'are you going to stay long?'

This is all I need, Dulcie thought resignedly. A nosy, chatty health-food freak. What's more, one with a beard.

'It's just the car,' he went on, gesturing apologetically towards the window. 'You see, I'm afraid it's blocking my garage.'

Dulcie stared at him in disbelief.

'It took me ten minutes to squeeze into that space! Why didn't you come out and tell me in the first place?'

'I'm sorry . . . I was busy in the kitchen. There is a notice . . . anyway it doesn't matter,' he hurried to reassure her. 'I don't need my car for the next couple of hours. You're welcome to stay until then.'

Dulcie wondered if anything nice would ever happen to her again, or if she truly was on the downward spiral to hell. Parking restrictions and time limits did her head in. She especially couldn't cope with them today.

'It's okay.' She resigned herself to queueing up to get into the NCP. 'I'll move the car.'

The car, however, had other ideas.

'I don't believe this, it's done it again,' yelled Dulcie, stalking back into the café and hurling her bag on to the counter. 'The bloody thing won't start!'

At table four a group of wholefood enthusiasts glanced up disapprovingly from their nut cutlets and garden-sized salads.

'Well.' On the defensive, Dulcie tugged down the hem of her short skirt. 'Sorry, but it pisses me off.'

'Rufus!' a woman's voice yelled from the kitchen. 'Two lentil and broccoli bakes.'

Rufus, his beard twitching with amusement at the expression on table four's faces, said, 'Hang on a sec,' to Dulcie, and went to fetch the order.

'Now,' he said, when the lentil and broccoli bakes had been dispatched, 'tell me what's wrong.'

Dulcie wanted to wail, Bloody everything! Instead, she rummaged in her bag.

'Look, it's okay. If I could just borrow your phone, I'll call a garage. They can tow it away and fix it.'

'Come on.' Gently, with a hand in the small of her back, Rufus guided her to the door. 'Garages cost money. At least let me have a look.'

Dulcie relayed the stalling-at-the-traffic-lights story and Rufus had another go at starting the engine, without luck.

'When did you last check the oil?'

Dulcie looked at him. Having first removed his apron, he had lifted the bonnet and was now peering underneath. As he wiped his oily hands on a piece of kitchen roll, Rufus returned her gaze.

Slowly he said, 'Okay, put it another way. *Do* you check your oil?'

It was all right for him, thought Dulcie. He was wearing a weird hand-knitted grey jersey and brown corduroy trousers. There was grey in his hair. He had a *beard*, for heaven's sake . . .

Without beating about the bush, he was a man.

She glanced down at her sunflower-yellow shirt and white

252

skirt. Her legs were brown, her sandals gold and her toenails Pomegranate Pink.

'Do I *look* like the kind of person who checks the oil?'

The dipstick was duly hauled out, wiped on kitchen roll and re-dipped.

'There is no oil in this engine,' Rufus announced gravely.

For the first time, Dulcie suppressed a smile. The way he said it sounded like No Wheels On My Wagon. She looked suitably ashamed.

'Oh.'

'I mean *really* no oil.' Rufus shook his head. 'It's a miracle the engine hasn't blown up.'

'Ah.'

He tut-tutted, then straightened up and smiled.

'My ex-wife was the same.'

Bored with lessons in car maintenance, Dulcie found herself wondering what his ex-wife looked like. Wholesome, presumably. Like Rufus, only without the beard. She tried to imagine how he would look if he shaved it off.

With a start, Dulcie realised he was still talking about oil.

'. . . a five-litre can of Castrol GTX Protection Plus. They sell it in the garage down by the river. Bit of a hike back up the hill, but that can't be helped.'

That was the trouble with these do-it-yourself types: they always wanted you to do it yourself too. Dulcie leaned wearily against the wall.

'Can't I just phone the garage, get them to do all that?'

Rufus was looking at her thin arms. In return, Dulcie wondered how old he was – around thirty-five at a guess, though with beards it was always hard to tell. Then she wondered if the grey sweater was older or younger than Rufus.

'Look, you'll never carry a five-litre can all that way. I'll go.'

'What about the café?' said Dulcie, startled.

Sounding amazingly unconcerned, Rufus said, 'You'll just have to take over until I get back.'

Chapter 37

It was like visiting your granny in hospital then suddenly being hauled into the operating theatre and told to take over while the surgeon went off for his lunch break.

Well, Dulcie conceded, maybe not quite like that, but along those lines. Luckily the café wasn't crowded so she didn't have to get into a flap. All the prices were chalked up on the blackboard behind the counter, the till was ancient and straightforward to use, and any questions Dulcie had were answered by Maris, who worked in the kitchen.

'How long have you and Rufus been together?' asked Dulcie during a quiet five minutes. She leaned against the freezer and watched Maris, who was fluffy-haired and energetic, chop a mound of onions.

Maris looked amused.

'We aren't together. Rufus's wife left him six months ago.' She wiped her eyes, streaming from the onion fumes. 'They used to run this place together, and I worked here part-time. Now it's just the two of us keeping the place going.' She finished chopping, and deftly slid the onions into a pan of sizzling oil, adding fondly, 'Bless him, he works so hard. Trying to get over his wife, that's what it is. He still misses her like mad.'

'Why did she leave?'

Dulcie wondered if it had been the beard.

'Louise? Ran off with the bank manager over the road. You wouldn't have thought it, to look at her.' Maris, clearly a gloriously indiscreet gossip, glanced at Dulcie for encouragement.

Avid for details, Dulcie said, 'What, was she the prim and proper type? Or a sour-faced old prune?'

'Hairy legs.' Maris lowered her voice. 'She never shaved them. Well, you'd have needed a lawn mower.'

'Didn't put the bank manager off,' remarked Dulcie. 'Or Rufus.'

'Poor Rufus. He adored her.' Energetically Maris stirred the sizzling onions, then reached for a Sabatier and a bulb of garlic. 'He's a lovely chap.'

'Seems nice.' Dulcie nodded. If you liked that kind of thing.

'Do anything for anyone, Rufus would. Got a heart of gold.'

'Does he drink?' said Dulcie.

'What, you mean is that why Louise left him? Noooo!' Maris looked shocked. 'Nothing like that.'

Dulcie grinned.

'I didn't mean does he get paralytic and beat up his wife. I was just asking, does he drink?'

She was busy clearing tables when Rufus reappeared ten minutes later, out of breath but beaming. He poured the oil into the engine, tried the key in the ignition and gave Dulcie a jubilant thumbs-up as the engine burst into life.

'Thanks,' said Dulcie before she drove off. 'That was really kind.'

'My pleasure.' Rufus, still pink-cheeked from climbing the hill, smiled at her over the wound-down driver's window. 'And thank you for looking after the café. Take care of this car now,' he reminded her good-naturedly. 'Try and check the oil at least once every ten years.'

'I met someone really nice today,' Dulcie told Pru over supper that evening.

Pru looked doubtful.

'You mean Liam-type nice?'

Dulcie imagined Rufus and Liam standing next to each other.

'The opposite of Liam.' She smiled, thinking that if Liam was a pin-up, Rufus was a quick-wash-and-brush-up. 'He's not a bit good-looking. Just . . . kind.'

Pru silently marvelled at this piece of information. He didn't sound Dulcie's type at all.

'Where did you meet him?'

Dulcie helped herself to more cannelloni. She offered the rest to Pru.

'He mended my car.'

'You mean he's a mechanic?'

More and more unlikely, thought Pru. But useful.

'No, I just broke down and he offered to help. He runs a wholefood café in Mortimer Street.' Dulcie scraped greedily around the edges of the dish for the best bits and added, 'He's got a beard.'

Pru was beginning to suspect a set-up. Was Dulcie serious?

'Hang on, let me get this straight. You fancy a man who isn't good-looking. He has a beard and he runs a wholefood café.' She shook her head. 'I'm getting a horrible mental picture here of David Bellamy.'

'Don't be daft, of course I don't fancy him.' Forking up her cannelloni with characteristic speed, Dulcie avoided Pru's eye. 'He's just a nice bloke, that's all. Kind.'

Pru was by this time struggling to keep a straight face.

'I see.'

'I don't fancy him,' Dulcie repeated stubbornly. 'I just like him. And you know what?'

'What?'

Dulcie had been puzzling over it all afternoon. She had only just worked it out. She gazed across the table at Pru.

'All the time we were talking, he didn't look at my boobs or my legs once.'

Remembering that she was supposed to be apologising to Liza, and taking advantage of feeling unusually saintly, Dulcie decided to ring her after supper.

'Who do you keep trying to phone?' said Pru twenty minutes later.

Still no reply. Fretfully Dulcie hung up.

'Liza. But the bloody selfish, ungrateful old bag's buggered off out.'

Maris was serving a family of six when Dulcie came into the café the next day. Up to her elbows in plates, and therefore unable to wave, she waggled her eyebrows instead and called out cheerfully, 'Rufus is in the kitchen. Go on through and tell him he owes me fifty pee.'

Rufus was wearing different clothes today. The sleeves of his blue and brown checked shirt were rolled up and he was kneading vast quantities of bread dough. There was flour in his hair and on his brown corduroys.

'You owe Maris fifty pee,' said Dulcie.

He looked delighted to see her.

'Hi! Car okay? No more problems?'

'The car's fine.' Dulcie held out the box she'd been clutching. 'Here, this is for you. Just to say thanks for yesterday.'

Rufus wiped his floury hands on a clean cloth and took the whisky.

'Glenmorangie. My word, what a treat! Dulcie, you shouldn't have. I wasn't expecting anything.'

'I know. But I asked Maris and she said you enjoyed a drop of whisky. She thought—'

'Did she indeed!' interrupted Rufus. 'In that case, the bet's off.'

Dulcie was puzzled.

'What bet?'

The doors separating the kitchen from the dining area swung open. Maris stood there grinning.

'Rufus said we'd never see you again. I said we would.'

'Unfair,' Rufus protested. 'You had inside information. That's cheating.'

Unperturbed, Maris squeezed behind Dulcie, opened the

door to the utility room and hauled out a high chair. 'Table four need this. Hang on and I'll be back in a sec.' She gave Rufus a triumphant smile and winked at Dulcie. 'For my fifty pee.'

The crash was followed by a scream, closely followed by a baby's piercing wail. As Rufus and Dulcie simultaneously rushed to the swing doors a terrible dropped-baby scenario flashed across Dulcie's mind. Her heart leapt into her throat as she tried to remember how you were supposed to do mouth-to-mouth resuscitation on a comatose toddler. She was sure she'd seen it on *ER*.

But when they catapulted through the swing doors they found the baby perched safely on his father's lap, pointing an outraged finger down at the broken bowl containing the remains of his aubergine and tomato bake.

On the floor next to the two halves of the bowl lay Maris in an undignified position. The high chair was on top of her, her scarlet knickers were on show and one arm was twisted behind her back.

Dulcie heard Rufus murmur, 'Oh thank God,' under his breath. Aloud, he said, 'Is everyone all right?'

The party of six, appearing somewhat dazed, nodded.

'I'm not all right,' Maris shouted indignantly. 'Will someone get this bloody high chair off me? Ow, my *arm*!'

Dulcie helped Rufus to lift the high chair. Maris, white-faced, gritted her teeth and tried to sit up.

'What happened?' said Dulcie.

Maris, with heavy irony, said, 'Well, I was riding my unicycle . . .'

Crouching down, Dulcie inspected the sole of Maris's sensible shoe. She peeled off a slice of aubergine and held it up.

'This is what you slipped on.'

The party of six looked uncomfortable. The baby, recognising the bit of aubergine as one he had spat out and flung down earlier, crowed with delight and made a grab for it.

'Uh-uh.' Shaking her head, Dulcie whisked it out of reach. 'This is evidence, for when we take you to court.'

The baby's father said hurriedly, 'It wasn't our fault. We didn't see him drop it—'

'Joke,' said Dulcie.

'Look, this is all very entertaining,' Maris murmured, 'and I'm sorry to spoil the fun, but my arm's hurting like hell here. I think it's broken. Any chance of a lift to hospital?'

Rufus helped her on to a chair.

'I can take you,' offered Dulcie. She brightened at the thought of all the gorgeous young doctors she might meet in Casualty.

'Sorry.' Maris looked at Rufus. 'Now I've mucked up your plans.'

'I was going to visit a friend at the hospital this afternoon,' Rufus explained to Dulcie, who was looking blank. 'My next-door neighbour actually. Poor soul's having a heart by-pass later today. She's petrified. I promised to drop in.' He paused, deep in thought. 'I suppose I could close the café.'

Without even thinking, Dulcie said, 'No need. You can take Maris to Casualty, then visit your neighbour. I'll keep things ticking over here.'

How extraordinary, she thought, listening to the words slip quite casually from her mouth. Maybe I'm having an out-of-body experience. Did I really just say that?

But Rufus was looking so delighted, she must have.

'Really, are you sure? That's great!'

Dulcie felt positively heroic, like Anna Neagle in one of those black and white Britain-at-war films. Spurred on by this, she said in a brisk, competent, Anna Neagley voice: 'Of course I'm sure. Just leave everything to me. I'll be absolutely fine.'

Chapter 38

Meanwhile, in a hotel room in Kensington, Kit lay in bed watching Liza turn herself into a frump. Having travelled up to London the night before, they had visited a West End theatre, gorged themselves on Peking duck afterwards in Soho, and walked arm in arm all the way back to their hotel, finishing the evening off with some pretty amazing sex.

Today, pleasure gave way to business. Kit had a one o'clock meeting in Highgate with the directors of a construction company hoping to win a contract with Berenger's. Liza was visiting a restaurant in Covent Garden, a celebrity haunt called Beaujolais. The maître d' at Beaujolais had recently snubbed Liza's editor, who was now hell-bent on revenge.

'That bastard turned me away,' he had told Liza furiously. 'Bloody nerve! Then, the next minute, he's welcoming Tristan Acheson with open bloody arms!' Tristan Acheson was the editor of a rival newspaper with a legendary appetite for one-upmanship. There was no love lost between the two men. 'You go there,' he went on, jabbing a pudgy finger at Liza, 'and you make sure you find fault with everything on that poncey fucking menu of theirs. I mean it, Liza. I want you to hit 'em where it hurts. Nobody turns their nose up at me.'

'Do any of your relatives work at Beaujolais?' Liza had asked Kit, as a precaution, when she had booked her table.

'What, Beaujolais in Covent Garden? That's my Aunt Isobel's restaurant.'

'You're kidding!'

Kit grinned.

'Of course I'm kidding. Don't worry, you can be as bitchy about Beaujolais as you like.'

Now, as Liza put the finishing touches to her unflattering make-up and adjusted the fringe of her wig, Kit slid out of bed and came to stand behind her. He looked at their joint reflections in the mirror.

'I have this terrible urge to undress you, take off that wig, wipe off that make-up and drag you back into bed.'

'Well, don't.' Liza drew in her breath, trying hard to ignore his warm fingers sliding inside her blouse. 'It's almost twelve already and they won't keep my table if I'm late. Anyway, you have to be in Highgate by one.'

Kit had just emerged from the shower ten minutes later when his mobile rang. Dripping and gloriously naked he answered it. The next moment, grinning, he rang off.

'That was Dan, one of the directors of BilCom. Seems they spent last night celebrating being in London away from their wives. They got totally plastered, ended up in some strip joint and ate some dodgy chicken. Apparently they've all spent the night bringing their boots up. So the meeting's cancelled.' He dropped the phone back on the bed and pinched Liza's bottom. 'Hooray for dodgy chicken.'

'What'll you do instead?' She darted out of his way as he began unfastening her skirt.

'Ah well.' Kit's yellow eyes regarded her with teasing amusement. 'Since I'm not allowed to do what I really want to do, I may as well come to Beaujolais with you.'

'I've only booked a table for one.'

Her copy of the latest MICHELIN GUIDE lay open on the dressing table. Kit found the number of the restaurant and dialled it. When he switched off the phone he said, 'There, no problem. Table for two.'

Liza did up her zip.

'Better put some clothes on first.'

* * *

261

Beaujolais was red and white, big and brash, and sported the obligatory volatile chef. A hugely popular meeting place for models and actresses, it was never without its share of paparazzi. Every so often the surly chef would erupt from his kitchen to hurl abuse at them, which kept everyone entertained. If they ever showed signs of defecting to the pavements outside other celebrity restaurants, he wooed them back with free meals.

Liza recognised the maître d' from her editor's curt description: 'Middle-aged. Ugly too. Looks like he's got a wasp down the back of his shirt and a poker up his bum.' Her brief concern, however, that he might be sufficiently appalled by her drabness to refuse her entry, was soon swept away. He couldn't have been more welcoming.

Confused, Liza murmured, 'He can't possibly have recognised me,' as they were seated.

Kit grinned.

'He hasn't recognised you.'

She looked at Kit, so handsome in an indigo shirt and beige chinos and with his dark hair still damp from the shower.

'I know,' said Liza. 'He fancies you.'

'Wrong again.' Kit grinned. He reached across and patted the tweedy sleeve of Liza's jacket. 'He fancies you.'

'I don't know how I'm going to explain this to my editor,' said Liza an hour later. Not only had the maître d' been charm itself, she had barely been able to find fault with their lunch. The menu was unpretentious, the food expertly cooked and presented with understated elegance.

'I hope the meal is to your satisfaction,' murmured the maître d', materialising at their side. Somehow he managed to ignore Kit completely.

'He was looking at your hand, to see if you're wearing a wedding ring.'

Liza didn't find it as amusing as Kit. She was beginning to get a complex about looking old. Damn, she really wished she hadn't worn her disguise today. Even being recognised would be preferable to this.

'He's still not sure about me,' Kit confided in a whisper. 'Next time he comes over I'll call you Auntie. Then he'll know the coast's clear. Bet you a tenner he asks for your phone number before we leave.'

The next moment they both turned as a girl's breathless voice squealed, 'Kit Berenger! What are *you* doing here?'

Recognising her, Kit started to laugh. Liza's heart sank. The girl, brown-eyed and with hair cut in a glossy burgundy bob, was as thin as a bit of spaghetti. She was wearing pink shorts, a minuscule black rubber waistcoat, black lacy tights and patent leather boots with spiked heels.

'Never mind what I'm doing here,' Kit told her, as she threw her arms around him, 'what are you doing wearing stuff like that?'

'Bloody old fogey,' retorted the girl, undaunted. 'What do you want me to wear, a tweed skirt and lace-ups? Oh . . . sorry.' She turned and grinned at Liza, a friendly, uncomplicated grin revealing flawless white teeth. 'Foot-in-mouth time again! I didn't mean to interrupt your meal. I was at college with Kit.' Holding out her hand she added, 'I'm Abby. Hi.'

The maître d' was hovering within earshot.

Kit said, 'Abby, this is my Aunt Elizabeth.'

As Liza dealt with the bill, Abby rushed up again.

'Hey, you two! Listen, Oliver has to get back to his office, but I'm free. How about catching up on old times over a drink? We could go to the Pyramid bar, it's just round the corner.'

As the maître d' had managed to exclude Kit earlier, so Liza found herself being ignored now. She willed him to say no.

But Kit, clearly tempted, gave Liza a 'shall we?' look in return.

'Come on, let's go for it!' This time Abby touched Liza's arm. 'They do brilliant cocktails.' Laughing, she added, 'Don't worry, we'll look after you, won't we, Kit? We won't let you get squiffy!'

'You'd be surprised,' said Kit, 'a couple of cocktails and Aunt

263

Elizabeth's a different person.' He winked at Liza in her awful wig. 'Quite a changed woman, in fact. Once she lets her hair down.'

Liza had forgotten about the photographers camped outside. As they emerged from the restaurant she found herself being elbowed out of the way. Since they were both young and strikingly attractive, Abby and Kit were the couple they focused their attentions on. Abby they recognised as an up-and-coming children's TV presenter. Kit – well, okay, maybe they didn't recognise him yet, but with those looks and that smile it could only be a matter of time.

'You two go ahead,' said Liza, when they caught up with her further down the road. 'Really, I don't feel like a drink. I'd rather just go back to the hotel.'

Kit looked at her. Abby, still clinging to his arm, pretended to be disappointed.

'Oh no! Are you sure?'

Liza nodded at Kit, signalling that she was fine, she wasn't jealous and of course he should go for a drink with Abby.

'I'm sure. I'll see you later.'

'Okay.' Brightly Abby waggled her fingers at her, just as she waved to the millions of adoring young fans who watched her Saturday-morning TV show. ''Bye, Aunt Elizabeth. You take care. See ya!'

Chapter 39

'That girl's as daft as a brush. Three years ago I told her they made rum from fermented coconuts and she *still* believes it. How she ever landed that job of hers is beyond me, although I suppose I can hazard a guess. Anyway,' said Kit, abruptly changing the subject, 'are you all right?'

Liza had washed her blonde hair – the wig always flattened it – and re-done her make-up. She had also changed into a black scoop-necked T-shirt, a clinging red velvet skirt and high heels. She looked luscious and desirable again, Kit realised, and every man in the hotel lobby was visibly lusting after her. He kissed her on the mouth and sat down next to her.

'Of course I'm all right.'

'Not peed off because of . . . you know?'

'What?'

'The old maître d' guy at Beaujolais, not making a move. Admit it,' Kit nudged her, 'you thought you'd pulled. You were gutted when he didn't ask for your phone number.'

Liza had to smile.

'When you book a table at Beaujolais, they automatically take your number. Anyway, speaking of pulling . . . is Abby an old girlfriend of yours?'

Kit shrugged.

'I went out with her for about two minutes. Got bored. She's a nice enough girl, but . . .'

Another shrug.

I'm not bored with you yet, thought Liza, watching him carefully, looking for signs. Are you bored with me?

'. . . like I said, thick as two planks,' Kit concluded with a yawn.

'I'm going down to Devon this weekend. It's my mother's birthday.'

This made him sit up.

'When did you decide this?'

'An hour ago. I rang her.' Liza nodded at the pay phone just beyond the bar. 'She was really pleased. I haven't been to see them for ages.'

'Something's wrong,' said Kit.

'Nothing's wrong.'

'Okay. I'm free this weekend. I'll come too.'

'No you won't.'

'Why not?'

'You just can't,' Liza said flatly.

He raked his fingers through his dark hair.

'But I have to meet them at some stage.'

She raised an eyebrow. 'Who says you do?'

Exasperated, Kit almost shouted, 'Liza, it has to happen sooner or later. Why not now?'

'Okay.' Liza held up one hand. She began steadily counting off on her fingers. 'We'll make a list. One, the chances are this relationship of ours won't last, so there isn't much point in meeting them. Two, they're just ordinary parents. They aren't rich or famous, or remotely glamorous. They aren't brilliantly witty and they don't tell jokes.'

'Meaning?' said Kit, stunned.

'Meaning you'd probably be bored witless.'

He shook his head. 'I can't believe you're serious.'

'Three,' Liza went on, still counting fingers, 'my mother is seventy years old, my father's seventy-two. They have traditional ideas. They want me to settle down and get married and have children. Knocking around with a twenty-three-year-old boy isn't something they'd understand—'

'Come on,' chided Kit, finally figuring out what it was she was doing. 'These aren't reasons, these are excuses. Shouldn't

266

you give your parents the benefit of the doubt? Introduce me to them and let them make up their own minds.'

'I know them. Trust me. If I rolled up with you in tow,' Liza said bleakly, 'they'd just be embarrassed.'

'I see. So they'd be embarrassed and I'd be bored.'

'Right.'

'And all this has nothing – nothing *whatsoever* to do with today.'

Liza wanted to cry. Of course it did; it had everything to do with today. She was accustomed to being in control of her life. She definitely wasn't used to feeling insecure. Lack of confidence was Pru's speciality, not hers.

And the stupid thing is, Liza realised frustratedly, nobody's making me feel like this. I'm doing it all by myself.

'I've just had enough,' she told Kit, her fingernail tracing obsessive spirals on the topaz velvet-upholstered arm of her chair. 'It's too difficult. Relationships shouldn't be difficult.'

'You're ashamed of me,' said Kit. 'Is that it? I'm an embarrassment to you?'

His yellow eyes narrowed, regarding her with mock amusement. Liza felt sick; he thought he was going to be able to coax her out of this and he couldn't. It was too late. She'd started and now she couldn't stop.

'Yes, I'm ashamed,' she said quickly, and saw that she had startled him. 'I'm embarrassed to be seen with you, okay? So it's over. I'm a grown woman, Kit. Time I found myself a grown man.'

'You missed a brilliant fight this afternoon,' Susie the receptionist said gleefully when she handed over to Bella at the end of her shift.

Bella looked interested.

'What, a punch-up?'

'Better than that. The couple booked into 201 had the most amazing slanging match, right here in the lobby in front of everyone. We were all riveted! Anyway, the woman was hellbent on finishing with him—'

267

'Hang on, room 201? I checked them in yesterday. He was gorgeous!'

Susie gave her a there-you-go look.

'That's it then, isn't it? Bet you he's been playing away and she's only just found out.'

'So how did it end? Did they make up?'

'Did Tom make up with Jerry?' Susie mimed slitting her throat. 'I'm telling you, it's over. He did his best, but there was no stopping her. She ended up yelling that she never wanted to see him again. Then she stalked out.'

'Leaving him here all on his own, you mean?' Ever hopeful, Bella's eyes lit up. 'Shall I ring his room and make sure he's okay?' She beamed. 'I bet I could cheer him up.'

The train journey back to Bath was a nightmare. Huddled in a corner seat behind dark glasses, Liza wondered if it was possible to feel more miserable than this. But it had needed to be done and she had done it. Now all I have to do, she thought unhappily, is get used to being on my own again. Pretend I never met Kit Berenger in the first place.

'Are you sure you're all right, dear?' said the nosy middle-aged woman in the next seat.

Tears were sliding out from under Liza's dark glasses. She wiped them angrily away with her sleeve.

'Fine, thanks.'

She turned and gazed out of the window but the woman began tapping her, woodpecker-style, on the arm.

'If you want to talk about it, dear, I don't mind. I'd be happy to listen.' Avidly she studied Liza's averted profile.

'All my friends tell me how sympathetic I am— Hang on, don't I recognise you? Aren't you that girl who writes about food?'

The train was crowded. Liza ended up three carriages along, squashed against a huge man in an anorak reeking of wet labrador. The smell was awful but at least he didn't interrogate her.

She couldn't cry properly until she reached home. It was over, it was all over.

There were half a dozen messages on her answering machine.

None of them was from Kit.

'Dulcie, where on earth have you been? It's eight o'clock!' wailed Pru, standing in the front doorway like an indignant wife. 'I thought you were only popping out for a pair of tights.'

Dulcie, struggling to keep a straight face, collapsed on to one of the kitchen chairs.

'I went to see Rufus, to thank him for yesterday.'

Pru recognised that smirk. Dulcie was looking ridiculously pleased with herself.

'Don't tell me, you seduced him. You've spent the entire day in bed with Mr Nice-Guy-with-a-beard.'

'Actually,' Dulcie adopted a not very convincing casual air, 'I've been working.'

'At getting the poor chap into bed, you mean.'

'I mean working in the café. Running it singlehanded, in fact.'

'Are you hallucinating,' said Pru, 'or am I?'

Dulcie could no longer contain herself. She jumped up and grabbed a bottle of wine from the fridge.

'I did, I really did,' she cried ecstatically. 'I knew you wouldn't believe me – I can hardly believe it myself – but I was brilliant! I didn't make any mistakes. Oh, Pru, you should have seen me, I did *everything*. What's more,' Dulcie's green eyes glittered as she sloshed wine into the glasses, 'I loved every minute!'

This was hard to believe, but as Dulcie continued to sing her own praises, it became apparent that she meant every word. It wasn't an elaborate set-up, or an April Fool. Quite by chance, Pru realised, and rather later in life than most people, Dulcie had discovered that work needn't be awful after all.

'I don't know where the day went,' she gabbled on, shaking

269

her head in disbelief. 'Seriously, the hours just galloped by. One minute Rufus was helping Maris into his car, and the next thing I knew, it was seven o'clock, time to close up! No thanks, better not.'

Here was another first: Dulcie holding her hand over her glass. Startled, Pru said, 'Sure?'

'The café opens at seven, for breakfast. I promised Rufus I'd be there by six.'

'Six?' squeaked Pru.

'Maris has broken her arm. She's going to be out of action for weeks,' Dulcie explained serenely. 'I offered to help out.'

'You mean . . . every day?'

'Only six days a week. They're shut on Sundays.'

It was a struggle taking it in. Pru couldn't help wondering if she'd somehow got hold of the wrong end of the stick.

'Dulcie, are you sure about this?'

Dulcie didn't reply. Instead, she studied the rim of her almost empty glass for several seconds. When she finally spoke, the jokiness, the glittering façade, was gone.

'It's what I want right now. It's what I need. Something to stop me thinking about the godawful mess I've made of my life.'

Pru experienced a twinge of alarm. This wasn't like Dulcie at all.

'Oh no, you haven't—'

'Come on, Pru. What else am I going to do with myself? If I go to Brunton I'll see Liam. If I stay here I'll only think about him.' Dulcie's eyes were sad. This wasn't the whole truth; she would mainly be thinking about Patrick. Oh, she'd been such an idiot . . .

'You know what you need,' said Pru.

Me too, thought Dulcie. A kick up the bum for being a prize wally.

Aloud, she said, 'What?'

Pru grinned.

'An alarm clock.'

Chapter 40

Having the stitches out didn't hurt a bit.

'There,' said the doctor soothingly. Finished at last, he dropped the scissors into a stainless-steel kidney bowl and reached for a mirror. 'Have a look. Tell me what you think.'

Pru looked at her wild-haired, bandageless reflection in the mirror and promptly burst into tears.

'I know, I know.' The doctor patted her on the shoulder. 'I've done a good job, if I say so myself.'

'Can I go home and wash my hair now?' sniffed Pru. It had been the longest two weeks of her life.

He smiled.

'Only if you really want to.'

Terry Lambert was in his office working his way through a pile of letters that needed signing when his secretary popped her head around the door.

'Someone to see you, Mr Lambert. A Mrs Kasteliz. She doesn't have an appointment but she wondered if you might have a few minutes to spare.'

'That's fine, Dora.' Terry Lambert carefully recapped his fountain pen. 'Please send her in.'

'Hi,' said Pru, looking smart in a white cotton shirt tucked into dark-green jeans, and with a red silk scarf around her neck. 'Thanks for seeing me.'

'My pleasure. Sit down, Pru.' Terry held the chair for her. Glancing up, he caught his secretary's eye. 'No need to wave

271

your eyebrows at me like that, Dora,' he remarked easily. 'Mrs Kasteliz is my cleaning lady.'

Tight-lipped, Dora closed the door behind her.

'Sorry about that,' said Terry. 'They know I'm involved with someone, they just don't know who. It kills the secretaries to be left in the dark. Now then, you're looking well. Good holiday?'

'Actually, that was a fib,' Pru admitted. 'I didn't really go on holiday.'

As a solicitor, Terry Lambert was nothing if not diplomatic. He leaned back in his leather chair and said, 'I see.'

Pru smiled.

'Apart from my doctor, you're the first person to see these.'

He looked faintly alarmed.

'See what?'

But Pru was scooping her hair up and away from her face. Her grey eyes shone.

'The stitches came out this morning.'

Terry broke into an enormous grin.

'They're great. You look great. Well done.'

'It's all thanks to you,' Pru said happily.

'Is that why you came here? To show me your ears?'

'Well, that too.' Pru let her hair fall back down over her shoulders. Then she took a deep breath. 'But the other reason is I want a divorce.'

Having been reduced to crossing the days off on his calendar, Eddie had come to the conclusion that this was as bad as being back at boarding school yearning for half-term. Worse, in fact, he thought now as he stood gazing out of his office window. This was like yearning for half-term and praying that during the course of the holiday you were going to be deftly relieved of your virginity.

It was Saturday. It was – he glanced at his watch – three minutes to ten. Any minute now, if all went according to plan,

Pru would rattle up the drive in her ancient Mini. She would be bronzed and relaxed from her holiday. He would tease her about the non-arrival of her postcard. She would make a fuss of Arthur and he, Eddie, would try hard not to wish it was his ears she was fondling.

And at some stage, *somehow*, he would pluck up enough courage to tell Pru Kasteliz how he felt about her.

Because he had put it off and off and there came a time when you had to brace yourself and force yourself to make some kind of move.

Because if I don't, thought Eddie, nervously thrusting his hands into the pockets of his brand-new trousers, nobody else is going to do it for me.

As she swung into the cobbled courtyard, Pru had to brake hard to avoid Liam. Dulcie, she thought briefly, would be disappointed with her.

Liam wasn't. His eyes lit up when he saw Pru.

'Terrific timing, darling! I have to get my car to the garage, some problem with the gearbox. Be an angel and follow me down, would you? Then you can give me a lift back.'

Pru glanced up automatically at the office window. There was Eddie, with his hands in his pockets, standing there watching them. At the sight of him, in his crumpled blue shirt and habitually loosened tie, something in Pru's stomach went ping.

'I can't. Eddie's expecting me.'

'Ah, never mind Eddie. He won't sack you.' Grinning, Liam followed the direction of Pru's gaze. Catching Eddie's eye he mimed opening the window then yelled up, 'Okay if I borrow her for a bit?'

Eddie didn't say it but the schoolboy riposte ran through his mind: 'A bit of what?'

He watched Pru giving the Mini's dashboard a vigorous polish with a tissue. She looked beautiful and totally absorbed in her task, as if buffing up the dashboard was more important than anything else in the world.

'All right,' Eddie said finally, and with extreme reluctance. He felt like a prisoner whose parole has been revoked at the last minute. Or maybe a schoolboy who has just been told that half-term's been postponed.

Dammit, he was ready to tell Pru how he felt about her *now* . . .

'Great. Just dropping the car off at Pargeter's. Won't be two ticks.' Liam gave him a cheerful thumbs-up before turning back to Pru. 'Meet me down there, okay?'

'Okay.'

Standing at his window, Eddie wondered what he was saying to her. Now that Liam was no longer shouting, he couldn't hear a thing.

He watched Liam pause, studying Pru in silence for a second.

'There's something different about you,' Liam told Pru. He frowned. 'Can't think what it is.'

That was the thing about Liam, she thought, he was never going to win *Mastermind*.

'New lipstick, probably,' said Pru.

Eddie, up in his office, thought agitatedly, Just stop yakking and get on with it. The sooner you're out of here, the sooner you'll be back.

Pargeter's, the ultra-smart garage catering for cars like Liam's, was on the other side of Bath. Predictably, by the time Pru pulled up on the forecourt, Liam was already leaning against the front desk, heavily engaged in chatting up the glossy blonde receptionist.

'Don't let me interrupt you,' Pru observed drily when he leapt – several minutes later – into the Mini's passenger seat.

'You didn't see what she was hiding under that desk.' Liam mimed a hugely bulging stomach. 'Seven months gone, no less.' He pulled a face. 'One way and another, I've suffered enough baby talk to last a lifetime.'

Pru concentrated on doing a U-turn against the prevailing

flow of traffic. She wondered if he'd ask her how Dulcie was.

It seemed not.

'Damn,' said Liam. 'Take the next right.'

When Pru glanced across, she saw him examining the front of his white Nike sweatshirt.

'Oil,' he sighed. 'Bloody garage, filthy place. You don't mind, do you, darling?' he added with a beguiling smile. 'My flat's only half a mile from here. Won't take me two minutes to change.'

Pru shrugged, indicated right and changed down into second gear. But Liam was still looking at her.

'Of course!' he exclaimed, so suddenly that Pru almost did an emergency stop.

'Of course what?'

'You. Your ears! The last time I saw you, they were wrapped in five miles of bandage . . .'.

'Left or right here?'

'Left.' He grinned at her, shaking his head in mock disbelief. 'And you weren't even going to tell me. Are you happy with them?'

'Very happy,' said Pru.

'I knew you looked different.' Liam sounded pleased with himself, but puzzled. 'So why aren't you showing them off?'

'I don't need to.' Pru was wearing her hair in its customary heavy bob. She knew she looked different. She also knew the only reason she looked different was because she *felt* different.

'You look great, really great.' Liam was still grinning broadly. 'Okay, we're here, pull in behind the Scimitar.'

'Don't be ages,' Pru warned him, but before she could flip open the glove compartment and get out her latest paperback, Liam's warm fingers had closed around her wrist.

'Come up with me. I'll show you my flat.'

What was wrong with etchings? wondered Pru.

'It's okay, I'm fine here.'

'Don't be silly.' Masterfully, he took the keys from the ignition. 'Anyway, I've got a present for you.'

A present? Was this a joke?

'What kind of a present?' Pru looked suspicious.

Liam winked.

'Just a little something to celebrate you getting your new ears.'

'I was invited out to Kuwait last year, to play in a pro-am tournament,' Liam explained over his shoulder as he rummaged through the chest of drawers in his bedroom. 'Everyone taking part was given a memento by the sheikh. Solid-gold razors for the blokes, earrings for the girls. Ah – here they are.'

Pru, leaning against the door frame, said, 'So what was there, some kind of misunderstanding? I mean, you don't look like a girl.'

'My mixed doubles partner,' Liam explained, 'was a very hairy lesbian. She had her heart set on a razor. On the last night she got me drunk, challenged me to a camel race and won.' He shrugged and held the leather box out to Pru. 'That was it. I was left with the earrings.'

Pru laughed.

'I can't imagine why you haven't given them to someone else.'

Liam opened the box. The earrings, pink-gold studded with diamonds, were each the shape of a stylised letter P.

'My tennis partner's name,' he said simply, 'was Paula.'

Pru stood in front of the bathroom mirror admiring her reflection. She had tucked her hair behind her ears. When she turned her head from side to side the earrings caught the light, glittering like . . . well, like diamonds.

'This is really kind of you.'

'My pleasure.' Liam moved up behind her, his breath warm on the back of her neck. Gently, he lifted Pru's dark glossy hair further away from her ears and examined the still-reddened but scalpel-fine scars.

'Your surgeon did a good job,' he told her. 'If you didn't know, you'd never know.'

His mouth was inches from her neck. Now it was moving closer. Pru, watching in the mirror, held her breath and told herself she was imagining things. Liam couldn't possibly be about to do what it looked as if he was about to do.

She let out a squeak as his warm tongue flickered against her neck.

Chapter 41

'Liam—!'

'You know, you really are an incredibly attractive woman.' He murmured the words as if confiding a tremendous secret, then dropped a kiss on to her shoulder. 'Dulcie's told me all about you and that miserable husband of yours. You know, all you need is someone to give you a confidence boost.'

Pru smothered a giggle.

'You mean—?'

'Don't get me wrong,' said Liam hastily, 'nothing serious, nothing long-term. Just, you know, a bit of fun.'

'You mean *you*?'

His dark-blue eyes met Pru's astonished grey ones in the mirror. He gave her his most irresistible smile.

'I mean exactly that. Aren't I the perfect man for the job? Come on, sweetheart, how about it? To celebrate the new you?'

Pru tried hard to imagine doing it with Liam. He was blond and blue-eyed, deeply tanned and quite extraordinarily handsome. He had wall-to-wall muscles. He was superfit. And she had heard a thousand times from Dulcie how fabulous he was in bed.

Physically, he was indeed the perfect man for the job.

Pru sighed. What a shame he had to be Liam. Anyone else with those attributes wouldn't have stood a chance of escape.

'Oh dear,' Liam murmured, teasing her. 'Big sigh. Decisions, decisions.'

His arms were sliding around her waist. Carefully, Pru extricated herself.

'No thanks, Liam.'

He looked perplexed.

'Are you sure?'

She unclipped the earrings and held them out to him.

'I'm sure.'

'What are you doing?'

'You'd better have these back,' said Pru.

Liam started to laugh.

'Keep them! I don't bribe women to sleep with me. I was only trying to do you a favour.' Still smiling, he clipped the earrings back on to Pru's ear lobes.

'Ouch.' She winced as his fingers slipped. The left one pinched like a crab claw.

'Sorry. There, that's better. Like I said, you're an attractive girl. All you need is that extra boost of confidence.'

I think you just gave me that when I turned you down, thought Pru, returning his smile. Good old Liam, you couldn't hate him. What you saw was what you got. He'd certainly never pretended to be anything other than what he was – the ultimate good-time boy.

Aloud she said, 'Thanks.'

They had been gone for almost an hour. Quite unable to concentrate on work, Eddie was pacing his office like a caged leopard when he heard the familiar sound of Pru's decrepit Mini rattling into the courtyard. In less than a second he was at the window, his hands pressed against the cold glass.

Liam was wearing a different sweatshirt, a yellow one.

He and Pru were laughing together about something.

Now Liam was leaning across, pushing his fingers through Pru's dark hair.

Eddie's stomach executed a violent double somersault. What was going *on*? Why was Liam stroking Pru's left ear in that uncharacteristically tender fashion?

More to the point, thought Eddie frantically, why the bloody hell is she *letting* him?

279

'Do you know,' said Liam, 'I've never been turned down before.'

'Oh dear.' Pru looked sorrowful. 'Have I blotted your copybook?'

He grinned. 'Bloody right. Do me a favour, will you? Keep it to yourself.'

'I won't tell. And you,' Pru reminded him, 'mustn't say anything about my ears.'

'Deal,' said Liam. He managed to yank open the passenger door. When he had climbed out, he turned and added cheerfully, 'It's our secret, sweetheart. Just between us.'

The wind had changed. Earlier when Eddie had strained to overhear Liam's conversation with Pru, he hadn't been able to catch any of it.

This time, having heard only too clearly more than he wanted to hear, he turned away from the window. There was a feeling in the pit of his stomach like a lorryload of wet sand.

So much for thinking he had a chance with Pru. Liam – God help her – had clearly got there first.

'Hi,' said Pru, appearing in the doorway still breathless from the stairs. 'I'm back.'

Her cheeks glowed pink. She looked bright-eyed and incredibly happy. Like a fresh-faced teenager in love with the school cricket captain, thought Eddie. He felt horribly old and tired in comparison.

'Hi.' He forced a smile. 'Good holiday?'

Pru's flush deepened.

'Great, thanks.'

She wasn't particularly brown, but she looked well. Eddie noticed she was wearing her hair differently, tucked behind her ears. All the better for Liam McPherson to fondle them, no doubt, he thought with a spasm of jealousy.

'Nice earrings.'

'Oh! Thanks.' Pru's eyes sparkled, and all of a sudden Eddie knew who had given them to her. The sick feeling in his stomach intensified and he sat down behind his desk, flicking abstractedly through his diary.

'Is everything all right?'

'Fine. Just fine.'

'Um . . . it's almost midday,' Pru ventured. Something was wrong but she couldn't imagine what. 'Aren't I supposed to be driving you to a meeting in Oxford?'

Eddie had cancelled the meeting. He had planned, in a surge of hopeless optimism, to whisk Pru out somewhere wonderful for lunch.

'It's been rescheduled,' he said brusquely. 'I'm seeing them on Monday instead.'

'Oh.' Pru watched him, apparently engrossed in the contents of his diary. 'So, you don't need me then?'

Yes, I need you, Eddie longed to blurt out.

He shook his head, wishing he were thirty-five again, with less paunch and more hair. He wondered if his life would have turned out differently if he'd cultivated muscles and blond highlights.

'Eddie.' She sounded hesitant. 'Have I done something to upset you?'

YES. YES. YES.

'No.'

'Okay.' Pru wasn't convinced. 'So what time on Monday?'

When he looked up, she was fiddling with one of her earrings. It occurred to him that if he wanted to, he could sack Liam McPherson. Lay-'em McPherson, he thought bitterly. But what would be the point?

'Ten thirty.'

'And roughly when will we be back?' Pru was mentally juggling her cleaning jobs. She had some serious catching-up to do after her fortnight off.

Listen to her, she just can't wait to rush home to him.

281

'Don't worry.' Eddie kept his tone even to hide the pain. 'You'll be back by six.'

'Liza, you look terrible,' said Margaret Lawson.

'Thanks, Mum.'

Liza was in the kitchen huddled next to the Rayburn, clutching a mug of tea and watching her mother peel onions for a shepherd's pie. Her offer to take her parents out to dinner had been met with the usual brisk refusal. Restaurants, according to Margaret Lawson, were a ridiculous waste of money. Anyway, she insisted, cooking for her family was never a chore. 'I enjoy it,' she told Liza. 'And shepherd's pie is your father's favourite. He doesn't care for all that fancy, faffed-about-with food.'

Liza had had this argument too many times before to think she could change their minds. She offered, they refused. That was the unalterable pattern of her visits.

She didn't want to eat out anyway.

Margaret Lawson began vigorously chopping the onions.

'I mean it. Terrible,' she declared, glancing over her shoulder at her daughter. 'You look as if you've been crying for a week.'

Wrong, thought Liza. I've only been crying for three days.

'Been sacked, have you?'

'No.'

'Pregnant?'

'No.'

'So it's man trouble,' her mother concluded, turning her attention back to the onions.

Liza didn't say anything. She had been on the receiving end of the find-yourself-a-decent-man-and-settle-down lecture almost as often as the restaurants-are-daylight-robbery one. The high turnover of men in her life and her inability to stay interested in any of them was a source of deep concern to her parents, she knew. Nothing would make them happier than to see her safely married. They weren't fussy either; any nice forty-year-old lawyer, bank manager, accountant or even architect would do.

'What was it this time, then?' Margaret persisted lightly. 'What did this one do to deserve the push? Drum his fingers on the steering wheel? Part his hair on the wrong side? Sing off-key?'

This was her mother's attempt at humour. It was her way of trying to help. And at the same time have a bit of a dig.

Liza thought of Kit and pressed her lips together. She mustn't, *mustn't* cry.

'No.'

The onions landed in the frying pan and were expertly tossed in hot butter. Margaret Lawson reached for the carrots.

'You don't want to talk about it.'

'Not really.'

'So he's married.'

God, thought Liza, when it comes to interrogation, the KGB have nothing on my mother.

As she shook her head, a single tear slid down her cheek.

'Did he finish with you?'

'No. I ended it.' She heaved a shuddery sigh. 'You don't usually ask this many questions.'

'You don't usually look like a wet fortnight in Fishguard,' Margaret Lawson replied with asperity.

Mothers. Who'd have them?

'I'm sorry,' said Liza.

The carrots were pushed to one side. Margaret Lawson wiped her hands on a tea towel and turned to face her daughter.

'Liza,' she said quietly, 'you're frightening me. Tell me what it is. Please.'

'Oh, Mum . . .'

'This one was special, was he?'

Helplessly Liza nodded.

'It doesn't matter. Just remember your father and I will still love you. Liza . . . is it that disease?'

Liza stared at her.

'What?'

Her mother's face was creased with concern.

'Do you . . . have you got Aids?'

'No!' gasped Liza, laughing and crying at the same time. She jumped up from the chair and threw her arms around her mother. 'Mum, no, of course I don't have Aids!'

Margaret hugged her back, before reverting to type.

'No "of course" about it, my girl. These things happen, and we all know how they happen. You haven't exactly led a settled life, have you?'

Liza smiled. There, she had something to be grateful for after all. She didn't have Aids.

Mini-lecture received and understood.

'He's nine years younger than me.'

The words were out before she could stop them. Amazed, Liza wondered how it had happened.

Probably because compared with Aids it didn't sound quite so terrible after all.

Chapter 42

Slowly, Margaret Lawson digested this information. She wiped her reddened hands on her apron and leaned back, thoughtfully, against the sink.

'You mean . . . he's twenty-one.'

'No.' Liza managed another weak smile. Maths had never been her mother's strong point. 'Twenty-three.'

'Oh. Still young though.'

Why am I smiling? thought Liza. Nothing's changed.

She nodded. 'I know. It would never have worked. It didn't bother me at first because I thought I'd get bored with him. Except I didn't.' She shook her head. 'But it really wouldn't have worked. I knew I had to end it. Rather now than in a few years' time . . . like cutting off a toe that's gangrenous,' she went on helplessly, her eyes filling up again. 'Better to lose a toe than the whole leg.'

'Yes, well, I can see the sense in that.'

'I just didn't realise it was going to hurt this much.' Liza sniffed, found a shredded tissue in her pocket and blew her nose.

'This young lad. What's his name?'

'Kit. Kit Berenger.'

Even the name sounded young.

'Hmm. Got a job, has he?'

'Family firm. Builders,' mumbled Liza. 'His father hates me.'

Margaret Lawson nodded.

'It's so unfair,' Liza went on. Extraordinarily, now she'd

started she found she couldn't stop. 'If he was older than me it wouldn't matter a bit. That wouldn't bother anyone.'

'I know.'

There were dark shadows under Liza's eyes. She hadn't been able to sleep.

'I shouldn't have come down here,' she mumbled. 'It's your birthday.'

'You're my daughter,' said Margaret. 'It's not often I get the chance to comfort you. Isn't that what mothers are for?'

'I don't think you can.'

'Maybe I can't.' Margaret sat down opposite Liza. 'But I do understand how you feel. I went through it too, you know.'

'*What?*'

The look on Liza's face was almost comical. Margaret smiled.

'Liza, I may be your mother but I am human. I was thirty-five when I married your father. What do you think I was doing until then, sitting up on a high shelf gathering dust?'

'Um . . . er . . .'

Well, yes.

'I was working as a secretary in London.' Margaret leaned back in her chair and gazed past Liza. 'When I was thirty I fell in love with my landlady's son. Michael, his name was. My bathroom window got broken and he came round to fix it. There was a spark between us right away. Of course, he knew how old I was, so he told me he was twenty-eight. We started seeing each other,' she went on. 'Neither of us had much money of course, but we'd meet in coffee bars, go for walks in Regent's Park, see the occasional film. We were so happy together, but I always wondered why we had to keep it a secret from his mother. Michael said she'd only make a fuss if she knew, he said she was the possessive type.'

She paused.

'And?' prompted Liza when the pause lengthened. Good grief, this was unbelievable. Her own *mother* . . .

'Oh well, she found out, of course. One of the neighbours saw us together one day in the park, holding hands. The neighbour told Michael's mother and she turned up on my doorstep that night demanding to know what I thought I was doing to her precious son.' Without realising it, Margaret Lawson was twisting her narrow wedding ring round and round her finger. 'So I tried to make her understand. I told her we loved each other and said wasn't it time she let him live his own life? He was twenty-eight, after all, I argued, hardly a little boy any more. Well, you can guess the next line. She wiped the floor with me, didn't she? Michael wasn't twent-eight at all, he was twenty-one.'

'Oh God,' gasped Liza.

Her mother's smile was dry.

'Quite. And that was that. She called me all the names under the sun, gave me a week to get out of the flat and told me never to speak to Michael again.'

'And did you?'

Margaret Lawson shook her head.

'No. I was so ashamed. I was as appalled as she was.'

'But he . . . did Michael try to contact you?'

Another weary shake.

'He couldn't have, even if he'd wanted to. I left London, moved to Bath. And a year later met your father.'

'Mum!' Liza was still struggling to take this in. It was like something out of a novel.

Her mother shrugged.

'It's in the past. This was forty years ago.'

'But . . . but you've been happy with Daddy?'

'Oh yes. Your father's a good man; of course I've been happy with him.' Her mother hesitated for a second; only her fingers moved as the wedding ring went on going round and round. She looked suddenly pale and tired. 'You just – well, I've never stopped thinking about . . . what happened. Or wondering if I would have been happier with Michael.'

* * *

287

There was only one Berenger listed in the Bath area, which was handy.

'Berenger.'

It was the voice of a man in charge. Brisk, brusque and not to be trifled with. He certainly didn't sound like a twenty-three-year-old.

'Hello. Could I speak to Kit Berenger, please,' said Margaret calmly.

'Who's speaking?'

Next to the phone was her Grattan's catalogue waiting for her to order a size fourteen ribbed cotton cardigan in shell pink.

'Margaret Grattan.'

'Hold on.'

Margaret hung on for what seemed like an hour. It was a good job Liza was in the bath. Finally, at the other end, the phone was picked up again.

'Kit Berenger speaking.'

A younger voice this time, but well-spoken and self-assured.

'Hello, Kit, my name's actually Margaret Lawson. I'm Liza's mother.'

Margaret glanced out of the sitting room window. In the garden her husband was meticulously dead-heading the gone-over peonies.

'I see.'

The voice acquired a cool edge. Instantly he was on his guard. Maybe I'm too late, she thought. Interfering with a lost cause.

'If you have a couple of minutes,' said Margaret, 'I wonder if we could talk.'

'That'll be Rose Tresilian from over the road. I promised to lend her my catalogue,' said Margaret when the doorbell rang at nine o'clock that evening. 'Answer it for me, would you, dear?'

Liza's hand flew to her mouth when she opened the door.

288

It wasn't Rose Tresilian from over the road.

'Oh my God.'

'Sorry I'm late.' Kit's hair gleamed in the porch light; his tone was carefully casual. 'I would have been here sooner, only I couldn't find my A to Z of Trezale.'

Liza was glad of the door frame, keeping her upright. She leaned against it and stared at Kit, almost afraid to blink. If he was a mirage, fine. Better a mirage, thought Liza shakily, than no Kit at all.

He was wearing a crumpled denim shirt and white jeans. There were dark shadows under his eyes, she noticed. He looked tired, drawn and somehow sexier than ever.

'Unfair,' said Liza, desperate to throw herself at him but not quite daring to. 'How come men can get bags under their eyes and look great? When it happens to women, we end up looking like Clement Freud with a hangover.'

'You haven't asked me how I found you.' Kit ignored her off-at-a-tangent ramblings.

Hesitating, Liza pushed a flopping strand of hair out of her eyes. Following her bath, she hadn't bothered to blow-dry it. Or put on any make-up.

'I think I can guess,' she replied finally. 'Only it's kind of hard to believe.'

'Your mother rang me.'

Liza nodded. She'd guessed right. It was just so unlike her mother to do such a thing.

'She isn't normally the interfering type.'

Liza sensed rather than saw him tense up.

'When you say interfering,' Kit fixed her with his unswerving yellow gaze, 'there's welcome interference and there's unwelcome interference. Liza, listen to me. I came down here because your mother told me I should. I love you and I want to spend the rest of my life with you, but you already know that. So,' he said pointedly, 'now it's up to you. If you want me to leave, I will. I'll turn around and drive back to Bath. You, meanwhile, can go inside and tell your mother she has no business meddling with your life. You can explain to her that this is an example of unwelcome interference.'

'Okay,' murmured Liza, nodding like an attentive pupil. 'And what's the other one?'

'Welcome interference.' Kit ticked the second alternative off on his fingers. 'This is the one where you realise I was right and you were wrong,' he explained, 'and so what if I'm a few years younger than you? I mean, who gives a toss, really? I don't. And your mother certainly doesn't.'

Helplessly Liza shook her head.

'No, she doesn't.'

'Anyway, you apologise to me for making the last few days possibly the worst of my life,' he continued. 'We kiss and make up and all that stuff, and you throw yourself at your mother's feet, thanking her over and over again for meddling in your life and forcing you to come to your senses.'

Having listened carefully, Liza nodded again.

'Okay. I'll have that one.'

'Sure?' said Kit.

'Definitely that one.'

'The I'm-right-and-you're-wrong one?' Kit persisted, the corners of his mouth lifting as he spoke.

'Yeah, yeah. You were right and I was wrong and I'm sorry and I love you,' murmured Liza, tears of happiness rolling down her cheeks. 'I love you so so much, you have no idea . . .'

He held out his arms and she threw herself into them. It was the best feeling, Liza thought, absolutely *the best* feeling in the world.

When Kit had finished kissing her he lifted her chin, forcing her to look at him. They were both trembling.

'Never do this to me again,' he said in a low voice, brushing Liza's wet eyelashes with his thumb. 'Promise me you won't.'

'What, no more fights, no more arguments, *ever*?'

'We can bicker. Bickering's allowed.' He shrugged. 'We're

talking about the rest of our lives here, after all. Fifty years minimum.'

'Oh, is *that* all?' mocked Liza. Reaching up, she kissed each corner of his narrow, curving mouth and wondered if it was legal to feel this happy.

'Maybe sixty. But we're not going through this again. No more it's-all-over stuff. I mean it, Liza. You have to promise me. I never want to hear you say that—'

They jumped apart as the sitting room door opened.

'Don't mind us,' said Margaret Lawson, as she and her husband reached for their coats. 'Hello, Kit, nice to meet you. Liza dear, you can't spend the rest of your life on the doorstep. Why don't you invite Kit in and make him a nice cup of tea? Your father and I are just off to the pub.'

When they had gone, Kit said, 'She winked at me.'

'This is seriously weird.' Liza shook her head in renewed amazement. 'My parents have never been inside a pub in their lives.'

'We've been Left Alone Together.' Grinning, Kit grabbed Liza around the waist. 'Just as well really, since I have this overwhelming desire to rip all your clothes off. You,' he told her as he edged her backwards, 'are about to experience the best sex of your life—'

'Not here!' gasped Liza, cornered between the grandfather clock and her mother's carved oak bookcase.

'God, you're beautiful. Even in that hand-knitted cardigan.' Playfully, Kit slid it off her shoulders. 'There, see how much I've missed you?'

'Stop it!' squeaked Liza, struggling frantically to keep both of them decent. 'I'm serious, Kit, we can't do it here. Not in my parents' house!'

Without saying a word, Kit led her by the hand across the hall, into the kitchen and out through the back door.

'I'm serious too,' he told Liza, one hand roaming beneath her T-shirt while the other deftly unfastened the button on her jeans. 'Is the garden okay?'

Outside, the air was warm and heady with the scent of late roses. They were in total darkness.

This is our grand reconciliation, thought Liza, it's supposed to be torrid and passionate and ultra ultra romantic.

As it was, things were turning out rather less glorious than she had imagined.

Getting the giggles didn't help.

'You're supposed to be gasping in ecstasy,' Kit complained.

'I can't help it. Dad mowed the lawn this afternoon, I'm covered in grass cuttings.' She clung to Kit, helpless with laughter. 'You've got leaves in your hair. And I can hear a million insecty things—'

'Ugh! What was that?' Kit winced as something weightier than an insect landed with a hideous plop on the back of his hand and leapt off again.

Their eyes had by this time adapted to the darkness.

'Frog,' squealed Liza, watching it hop into the bushes. She flinched as the wings of a moth brushed her bare shoulder.

The rasping noise of a grasshopper sounded, inches from Kit's ear. He gave up.

'Talk about coitus interruptus.'

'Insect interruptus,' said Liza, dancing her fingertips across his taut stomach.

'Bloody alfresco sex. Remind me never to try this again.'

Liza was feeling around on the grass behind him.

'I can't find my bra.'

At that moment the bushes to the left of them began to rustle ominously.

'Don't tell me,' murmured Kit, 'it's the Beast of Exmoor.'

'Sounds big.' Still hunting in vain for her favourite black bra, Liza managed to locate one of her shoes. 'Must be a dog.'

They both leapt a mile as the powerful beam of a torch snapped on.

'Right. Stay where you are! Don't move a muscle,' barked a female voice.

'Oh my God,' hissed Liza, instinctively ducking behind Kit, 'it's Mrs McKnight from next door. Oh shit shit shit—'

'Good grief,' announced the female voice, which was deep, assertive and extremely effective when it came to bossing people about; forty years in teaching had seen to that. 'Thought you were burglars! What on earth do you think you're doing in my neighbour's back garden?'

There was a horrid clammy silence. All Liza could hear was her heart beating frantically against her ribs.

'We aren't burglars,' said Kit. He reached for his white jeans and put them on.

Mrs McKnight's eyes boggled. 'You're trespassing!'

'I know. I'm sorry.' Calmly Kit found the rest of Liza's clothes and handed them to her. Molly McKnight flicked the torch in the direction of the blackcurrant bushes into which the frog had hopped earlier. Dangling from one of the higher branches was Liza's bra.

'Whatever possessed you?'

'It was a dare,' Kit said simply.

The lad was as cool as a cucumber. With merciless precision Molly McKnight swung the beam of the torch back to his girlfriend, skulking on the ground behind him, struggling frantically to get into her clothes. With her head bent and all that blonde hair tumbling over her face, it was impossible to see what she looked like.

'Is your companion going to apologise too?' The demand was brisk.

'She's Romanian.' Kit shrugged. 'Doesn't speak any English.'

'Hmmph.'

'It won't happen again.'

'I should jolly well hope not.'

'Sorry again,' said Kit, grinning as he took Liza's hand and led her towards the back gate.

Shaking her head, half amused by his chutzpah, Molly McKnight watched them go.

'Young people today, I don't know,' she sighed, just loudly enough for them to hear.

The gate clicked shut behind them.

Young people.

What utter bliss.

'I love that woman,' murmured Liza.

Chapter 43

Dulcie wondered if she was suffering from empty nest syndrome. Funny, she'd never imagined she'd miss Pru so much, but the house really did seem awfully empty.

It was early on Sunday morning and the rest of the day stretched ahead. Deeply resentful that some inner alarm clock had been insensitive enough to wake her at six – she'd never *had* an inner alarm clock before – Dulcie poured herself a fourth cup of coffee and tried not to feel sorry for herself. This was her hard-earned day off, after all. She was supposed to be enjoying it.

The trouble was, as Dulcie was belatedly discovering, enjoying yourself was more fun if you weren't on your own. And now, for the first time in her life, she was.

Patrick was busy being deliriously happy somewhere with Claire Berenger. Liam was doubtless busy being a prize stud somewhere with any number of women. Pru was working, catching up on her backlog of cleaning jobs.

And Liza . . . well, Liza hadn't spoken to her since their fight and wasn't likely to, considering the snide – and deeply unfair – remarks she'd made about Kit Berenger.

Altogether, what with avoiding Brunton Manor because of Liam – not to mention being unable to face all those women who knew what a prat she'd made of herself over him – her remaining options were limited.

I could go shopping, thought Dulcie, but even the prospect of spending money on unnecessary luxuries failed to exert its usual seductive pull.

She bit her lip and gazed out of the window. The alternatives were equally dreary.

She could – heaven help her – Go For A Nice Walk. This had always been her mother's antidote to terminal teenage boredom.

The answer was still no thanks.

Or she could have a bath, eat biscuits and lie on the sofa watching wall-to-wall rubbish on television.

At that moment the phone rang. Dulcie's spirits soared as she raced to answer it. Talk about fate.

'Hi, Dulcie? Brad Pitt speaking. You *must* come to my party . . .'

Or:

'Dulcie, hey! It's me, Sting. I'm sending the helicopter for you, okay? You're spending the day with us.'

Anything like that, really. Just something fun.

'Dulcie. Good, you're at home. All right if I drop by in about half an hour?'

Okay, so it wasn't Sting, but Dulcie still felt her heart do a clumsy somersault.

Half an hour, she thought breathlessly. I can either shower, get dressed and do my face, or lie in the bath until he gets here and saunter downstairs in a towel.

When the doorbell rang exactly twenty-eight minutes later, Dulcie sauntered downstairs in a towel. Her black hair was slicked back from her face and her wet, Floris-scented skin glistened. Her green eyes, with their ultra-white whites, were bright with anticipation and half a bottle of hastily flung-in Eye Dew.

The dark-blue velour towel, fetchingly clutched around her in a just-got-out-of-the-bath kind of way, could have been larger but it set off Dulcie's tan beautifully.

'Hi.' Patrick barely glanced at either the towel or the tan. He strode past Dulcie into the hall. 'Sorry to disturb you on a Sunday. Won't be a sec; I just need to pick something up.'

He sounded distant and briskly efficient, like a bank

manager. As she closed the door, Dulcie's suspicions were confirmed. Claire Berenger was sitting in the passenger seat of Patrick's car. When she saw Dulcie she smiled and waved.

'Off to play frisbee in the park?' Dulcie couldn't help it. The taunt slipped out as Patrick made his way through to the sitting room. Leaving a trail of wet footprints, she followed him.

'Liam not around?' Patrick countered.

'Oh ha ha,' said Dulcie bitterly. 'Please don't pretend you don't know.'

He turned.

'Don't know what?'

'Come on, your spies must have told you. It's over between me and Liam.'

He looked genuinely shocked.

'I had no idea. The girl from the office downstairs is away on holiday.'

'Funny, you'd think Liza might have mentioned it.'

Dig dig.

Patrick ignored this. 'I haven't seen Liza for weeks. When did it happen?' His eyes darkened with concern. 'God, that's terrible. I'm so sorry. How are you coping?'

Pride welled up. Defiantly, Dulcie lifted her chin. 'Fine. I've got myself a job.'

'But the baby—'

Oh hell, this wasn't going to plan at all. She'd completely forgotten about the baby.

'There isn't one.' Best to just blurt it out, she decided wearily.

But the look on Patrick's face was extraordinary.

'Oh, Dulcie . . .'

As he said her name, his voice broke. The next thing Dulcie knew, he had his arms around her. He was holding her, hugging her. She breathed in the blissfully familiar smell of his skin.

It felt wonderful, but she knew she had to get a grip. She had to start telling the truth.

'I didn't lose the baby,' Dulcie muttered, wishing the hug could go on forever. 'There never was one in the first place.'

'What?'

'I thought I was pregnant.' She kept her face buried against his chest. Oh well, she'd told enough truth for one day. 'But I wasn't. It was a mistake.'

The comforting hug was taken away. Uncertain now, Patrick stepped back and pushed his fingers through his dark hair as he always did when faced with a dilemma.

'Oh. Right. Well, sorry anyway.'

'No need,' said Dulcie. 'Liam's a jerk. He's no loss, and who wants a screaming baby anyway?' There was a huge lump in her throat but she resolutely ignored it. Pulling the dark-blue towel more securely around her she went on in a businesslike manner, 'What was it you needed? I thought you'd taken all your clothes.'

'Passport.' Patrick turned his attention to the old oak dresser, whose top drawers were crammed with a motley collection of old bills, out-of-date MOTs, rolls of Sellotape and a million rubber bands. With any luck, this was also where he'd find his passport.

Dulcie heard her voice go all high and unnatural, as if she'd just taken a furtive gulp of helium.

'Really? Going away somewhere? Anywhere nice?'

'Amsterdam.'

She said the first words that came into her head.

'Watch out; lots of prostitutes in Amsterdam.'

'I'll have Claire with me,' Patrick remarked drily, 'so maybe she'll be able to beat them off with a stick.'

He had his back to her as he searched through the drawer's muddled contents. Suffused with misery and longing, Dulcie watched him for as long as she dared. He was going away on holiday with Claire. This, from the man who regarded inter-rupting work to grab a sandwich as a waste of time.

'Hang on, I think I've seen it upstairs,' said Dulcie. She knew exactly where his passport was, filed away along with a stash of expensive half-used make-up in a silver basket on top of her dressing table.

Earlier, in the bath, she had fantasised a dozen different ways of enticing Patrick upstairs to the bedroom they had once shared.

Now, clearly, this idea was no longer on.

The bath towel had been a mistake too.

'Wait there, I'll get it,' said Dulcie.

When she reappeared, she handed Patrick the passport.

'Thanks.' He looked at her. 'Are you sure you're all right?'

Dulcie nodded.

'Of course I am.'

'And . . .' he frowned, looking doubtful, 'sorry, but did you say you had a *job*?'

Another nod.

'This I've got to see.' Patrick's smile was sceptical; it was the one he'd generally used when Dulcie had insisted on reading him his horoscope.

'It's nothing special.' She spoke with a trace of defiance. 'Just a spot of waitressing. More of a social thing, really.'

'I'd still like to see it with my own eyes.'

Dulcie, who had her image to think of, definitely didn't want him to see her sweating away in the café's cramped kitchen. She pulled open the front door.

'Mustn't keep Claire waiting. Enjoy your holiday.'

Evidently still entertained by the idea of Dulcie doing anything and actually getting paid for it, Patrick said, 'And you enjoy your job. One thing, though, Dulcie.'

'Yes?'

He grinned. 'Don't let them work you too hard.'

It was remarks like that, thought Dulcie as she closed the door, that made you wish you'd chucked your husband's precious passport down the nearest loo.

As soon as she settled herself back in the bath, the phone shrilled again. One of life's major irritations, Dulcie was reminded, was the fact that you bought a cordless phone specifically so you *could* take the thing into the bathroom with you, but you never actually remembered to bloody well do it.

By the time she reached the phone it had stopped ringing. Dripping all over the carpet as she dialled 1471, Dulcie was astounded to be told by the metallic voice that the number of the last person to ring her was Liza's.

This was frustrating, because if Liza was calling to apologise for the other night, she now thought Dulcie was out.

If I ring her back, thought Dulcie, I might have to apologise first.

Instead she dialled Liza's number, let it ring twice and hung up.

Now Liza could call 1471.

Less than a minute later, Dulcie's phone rang again.

'It's me,' said Liza. 'I'm returning your call.'

'Oh, hello,' Dulcie said airily. 'I was only returning yours.'

'You rang me.'

'You rang me first.'

'Oh what, so you want *me* to apologise for the other night?'

'Isn't that why you phoned?'

Silence. Dulcie heard a brief scuffle at the other end. Then Kit came on the line.

'Dulcie, Liza's sorry she had a go at you. I'm sure you're sorry too, for those cruel and uncalled-for remarks you made.'

Wincing, Dulcie wondered if he knew the remarks had been about him.

She cleared her throat.

'Well, I—'

'You are? Good, that's that sorted out. Now you can be friends again,' Kit announced cheerfully. 'Now, what are you doing at the moment?'

'Trying to have a bath.'

'Okay, so put the phone down and go and have one. We'll be round in twenty minutes. And make sure you're decent when we arrive.' Kit sounded amused. 'I'm far too young to cope with the sight of a middle-aged woman naked.'

300

Chapter 44

'I'm sorry I was a cow,' said Dulcie.

Liza gave her a hug.

'Me too.'

'And I'm not middle-aged,' Dulcie told Kit, who was carrying in two bottles of Bollinger.

'You are to me.' He grinned. 'But never mind, I'll let you off. If you find some glasses you can help us celebrate.'

It wasn't hard to guess what they were celebrating. Liza was looking radiant and ridiculously happy.

'You made up. You're back together.'

'Back together for good,' said Kit. 'All very Mills and Boon. Even her parents like me.'

'Good grief. How about your father?' Dulcie asked him.

'Oh well, no change there. He's a stubborn old bugger but we'll work on it. Give him a few years.'

'I can't believe you've met Liza's parents. You are honoured,' Dulcie marvelled. In the past, the rapid turnover of men in Liza's life had meant she'd never bothered.

'That's nothing,' Kit winked. 'I met their next-door neighbour too.'

Although Dulcie was glad to see them back together, she refused their offer to take her out to lunch. The sexual chemistry between them was overwhelming. They were having difficulty keeping their hands off each other and Kit was clearly dying to take Liza home to bed.

By the time both bottles had been emptied and all the gossip

301

caught up on, it was almost a relief to stand on the doorstep and wave goodbye.

Depressed and light-headed from drinking on an empty stomach, Dulcie dozed on the sofa. She woke up at four o'clock depressed and heavy-headed instead, and with a raging thirst to boot.

Worst of all, it was still Sunday. Talk about dragging on.

There was nothing on television. To pass a bit of time she meticulously painted her nails a dramatic shade of red. Only when she'd finished the third coat did she remember she couldn't work in Rufus's kitchen wearing nail polish. It all had to come off.

This time when the phone rang, it was Rufus.

'Oh hi,' said Dulcie listlessly. She was currently trying to decide whether to peel off the kitchen wallpaper just for something to do, or have another bath.

'I wondered what you were doing,' said Rufus. 'Any plans?'

'No.' Dulcie made it sound as if she'd had hundreds of offers, of course, but she'd actually wanted to stay in and go out of her mind with loneliness and boredom. 'Why?'

He said eagerly, 'I wondered if you'd like to come to the theatre with me. They're doing a special charity performance of the new Poliakoff with Brian Blessed.'

Dulcie was almost certain Poliakoff wasn't her cup of tea. And she absolutely knew she hated going to the theatre.

She frowned. 'Brian Blessed? Is he the one with the beard? I can't stand beards.'

'Okay,' Rufus replied equably, after a moment's silence. 'Are you saying you'd prefer a night in?'

'I'm saying I'd prefer the cinema.' Brightening, Dulcie said, 'The new Demi Moore film's on at the Odeon. It's supposed to be great.'

'Demi Moore? Does he have a beard?'

Dulcie hesitated, wondering if Rufus was joking.

'I'm joking,' said Rufus.

Dulcie grinned. It wasn't until they had arranged to meet

outside the cinema and Rufus had hung up that she realised what she'd said.

What was it Patrick used to murmur whenever she made one of her famous *faux pas*? 'Dulcie, are you sure you want to be a diplomat when you grow up?'

Dulcie experienced a brief pang of guilt. Rufus, bless him, hadn't said a word.

'Oh my God . . .'

Any faint hope she might have harboured that the remark had slipped by unnoticed was extinguished when Dulcie spotted him waiting for her on the pavement outside the Odeon.

'You've shaved it off!'

Rufus shrugged and looked embarrassed, as if he hadn't expected her to notice.

'I've been meaning to for ages. When I woke up this morning I just thought today's the day.'

'You look so different.' Dulcie examined his face from all angles.

Carefully casual, Rufus said, 'Different better or different worse?'

She was lost for words. The answer was neither, his face looked . . . well, naked.

But this was no time to dither. Feeling horribly responsible – because all this stuff about having done the deed this morning was clearly untrue – Dulcie reached up and touched his pink, baby-smooth jaw.

'Much, much better. It's brilliant. I love it. Really.'

Rufus flushed with pleasure. Dulcie, congratulating herself on having got away with it, grabbed his hand and dragged him into the plush crimson foyer.

'Come on, we'll be late. You don't want anything to eat, do you?' This as they sped past the popcorn and bags of sweets. 'I can't stand people stuffing their faces in cinemas; they always sound like pigs at a trough.'

Rufus, a secret popcorn addict, was already reaching into his pocket. He promptly let the wallet drop. He was out on a date with Dulcie and that was all that mattered.

'Nor me.'

'I just wanted to see this with my own eyes,' said Liza at eight forty-five the next morning.

'You and the rest of the world,' Dulcie muttered, clearing the table and signalling Liza's order for coffee and a bacon roll to Rufus as he headed back to the kitchen.

'I thought he had a beard.'

Briefly, Dulcie said, 'He did.'

Rufus emerged a couple of minutes later with Liza's breakfast. The bacon, he assured her, was locally cured and free range; it had come from a happy pig.

'He seems nice,' Liza observed when he had gone.

'He is.' Dulcie whipped out her order pad as another table clicked their fingers at her. 'Sorry, I'll have to deal with this lot.'

'You could do worse,' said Liza.

Dulcie, shiny-faced and with the harassed air of someone rushed off their feet for the last two hours, said, 'What, than Rufus?' She grinned as she moved off. 'Oh yeah, he's really my type.'

Dulcie probably wasn't Rufus's type either, Liza decided twenty minutes later, but that hadn't stopped him developing a massive crush on her.

'Of course I'm serious,' she repeated patiently, amazed that Dulcie could have remained so blithely unaware of the situation. What was she, blind? 'Look at the way he looks at you. He fancies you rotten.'

Dulcie's heart sank. Damn, she hated it when that happened. Being fancied rotten was only fun when it was mutual.

'I thought we were just good friends.'

Sorrowfully, Liza shook her head.

'You told him you weren't wild about beards, didn't you?'

304

She raised an eyebrow. 'Think about it. If some just-good-friend said it to you, would you shave your beard off?'

When Eddie and Arthur appeared in the courtyard at ten thirty, Pru was already waiting in the Jag. She was wearing a sage-green cotton shirt, a narrow black skirt and black sandals. And, Eddie noticed at once, the diamond earrings from Liam.

He felt the muscles in his jaw tighten. He'd behaved like an idiot on Saturday. Whatever Pru was getting up to was her own affair, even if it was with Liam.

It's none of my business, Eddie told himself fiercely. They're both free agents, they can do as they like.

He watched Pru emptying the ashtray of sweet wrappers and thought, I'd never have a chance with her anyway.

Arthur leapt into the car, woofing with delight and burying his nose frantically in Pru's handful of wrappers in search of any remaining trace of chocolate.

Eddie shoved Arthur over into the back seat. He decided to come straight to the point.

'Look, I'm sorry I was a moody sod. Saturday was a bad day. Can we forget it happened?'

Pru looked relieved.

'I didn't know what I'd done wrong.'

'You didn't do anything wrong.'

Bloody stupid, maybe. But not wrong.

Forgiving him instantly, Pru smiled. 'Unlike you, you mean.'

'What?' Eddie protested when she held up the sweet wrappers. 'Are you saying I'm not allowed to eat?'

'I'm saying you're not allowed to drive.'

He looked suitably abashed.

'Just practising for when I get my licence back.'

Pru made up her mind at that precise moment. The tentative plan she had formulated during her stay at Dulcie's had ground to an abrupt halt on Saturday when Eddie had gone weird on her.

But now everything was back to normal . . . well, why not?

She covered her face with her hands and sneezed.

Then she sneezed again.

'Sorry about this. Must be the moulting season.' Fishing in her bag, Pru wiped her eyes with a tissue. Between sneezes, she glanced over her shoulder at a bemused Arthur then turned apologetically to Eddie.

'It's the dog hair. Would you mind awfully if we left him behind?'

'You're allergic to Arthur?'

Pru blew her nose and nodded. Looking regretful, she said, 'It doesn't last long. Every year I get this, just for a few days. By next week I'll be fine, I promise.'

Without a word, Eddie opened the door again and shooed Arthur out. It wasn't as if the dog minded; Arthur was a great favourite around Brunton Manor, not least with Lolita, the gardener's flirtatious black and white spaniel.

Eddie, though, was hurt. He knew Pru wasn't the world's greatest dog lover but did she really hate Arthur that much?

Because those sneezes definitely weren't real.

It was late September but Oxford still teemed with tourists, particularly the American kind who appeared to love the place almost as much as they loved Bath. Pru, window-shopping to pass the time and take her mind off what she had planned for later, overheard a couple of undergraduates in a coffee shop discussing a mutual friend.

'She slept with eight men last week,' complained one. 'I mean, is that fair? At this rate she's going to work her way through everyone in college. There won't be any left for the rest of us.'

'What we'll do,' said the other, 'is put the word around that she's HIV.'

Heavens, eight men in one week. Pru, who had only slept with one man in her life, almost choked on her coffee.

One man, and that had only been Phil. Not much of a conquest quotient.

Still, these days you couldn't be too careful. Sliding out of her chair and plucking up every last molecule of courage, Pru went into Boots and bought a packet of condoms. She felt incredibly slutty doing so but – as she longed to inform the disapproving-looking old woman next to her in the queue – at least she was a safe slut.

'Good meeting?' said Pru when Eddie emerged from the Randolph Hotel at four thirty. The meeting had been held to discuss the setting-up of conference facilities at Brunton Manor.

Eddie nodded, yawned and chucked his heavy briefcase on to the back seat. One lousy cup of tea three hours earlier was all he'd been offered by way of refreshment. He could kill for a large whisky and soda, followed by steak and chips. After that, hot apple crumble and custard would fit the bill, finished off with a couple of Irish coffees and a decent cigar. Eddie had tried to appreciate the finer points of *nouvelle cuisine* but he was a Berni man at heart.

He was about to suggest this before they headed home when he remembered Pru was anxious to get back to Bath – and no prizes for guessing why. Closing his mouth again, willing himself not to imagine Pru and Liam together, Eddie fastened his seat belt, casting a surreptitious glance in the direction of Pru's slim bare legs as he did so. He'd promised she'd be home by six. Food – and his own happiness – would just have to wait.

Chapter 45

Ready. Steady. Go.

Nothing happened. Pru felt the adrenalin buzzing around her body like a million fireworks poised to go off, but every time she reached Go – and this was the seventh time she'd reached it – her courage failed her.

If she didn't act soon, she'd miss her chance completely. The M4 was already behind them. They were racing along the A46 and in less than fifteen minutes they'd be back at Brunton Manor.

Okay, this is it, Pru told herself, slowly breathing out. This time I'm really going to do it. The next side road we reach, I indicate, brake, turn off . . .

Here comes one now.

Ready. Steeeeady . . .

Her foot wouldn't do it. It stayed glued to the accelerator and the side road zipped past them. Turning her head helplessly, watching it go, Pru felt the back of her neck prickle with perspiration. Maybe a bit of casual conversation would help.

'Look, that lorry's from Andover. I don't even know where Andover is.'

Eddie, who was wondering how long this Liam thing was likely to last, grunted and said, 'Hampshire.'

Pru tried to think of something else to say about Andover but the more she thought of it, the smuttier the name sounded. She glanced, instead, at her reflection in the wing mirror. The earrings Liam had given her looked amazing; they really glittered in the sunlight.

Admiring her earrings and chattering on about nothing in particular, Pru decided, was a lot less fraught than all that Ready Steady Go business. Her heart was practically back to normal.

'Will you renew Liam's contract at the end of the season?' she asked idly.

The effect on Eddie was astonishing.

'For God's sake!' he exploded. 'Pru, I'm sorry, I know this is none of my business but you really are making the biggest mistake OF YOUR LIFE!'

Amazed, Pru said, 'What?'

'Did Liam ask you to find out?'

'No, no . . .'

'Does Dulcie know what you're up to?'

'Eddie,' she shook her head, utterly bewildered by the outburst, 'what exactly am I supposed to be up to?'

'Oh come *on*,' he seethed, the words hissing out through clenched teeth. It sounded like a radiator being bled.

'Tell me,' said Pru, 'because I don't know.'

He couldn't look at her.

'You and Liam.'

'Me and Liam what?'

This was not good grammar, but she was by this time too intrigued to notice.

'You, having an affair with him.'

'Oops.' Pru almost drove into the back of the lorry from Andover. She braked in the nick of time. 'Eddie, that isn't true!'

'I know you are,' Eddie said wearily.

'Well I know I'm not. If I was,' Pru added steadily, 'I think I'd have noticed.'

Eddie sat up. He gave her an odd look.

'Liam gave you those earrings, didn't he?'

Pru said, 'Okay, yes, he did. But I didn't have to earn them.'

Still suspicious – though more of Liam than of Pru – Eddie said, 'Why, then? Why would he give you a pair of diamond earrings?'

She shrugged.

'He doesn't know anyone else whose name begins with a P.'

The relief was phenomenal. When he rubbed his stubbly jaw, Eddie realised he was shaking.

Pru, glancing sideways at him, saw it too.

She smiled, understanding why. As if by magic, her own fears melted away. Moments later she flicked the indicator, braked and turned left, completely forgetting to go through her Ready Steady Go ritual first.

'Where are we going?'

Pru drove on, pretending not to have heard.

'Pru, this isn't a short cut.'

It was a narrow country lane bordered by hedgerows eight feet high. Pru swerved to avoid a squirrel darting across the road and drove on.

'Pru? Are you okay?'

She pulled into a gateway overlooking an empty field and switched off the ignition.

Eddie looked worried.

'Are you going to be sick?'

'No,' said Pru, 'I'm going to seduce you.'

I can't have heard right, thought Eddie. I must be hallucinating.

Pru turned to look at him.

'If you'd like me to, that is.'

Eddie felt as if he'd forgotten how to breathe. He took a huge gulp of air.

'I'm sorry, could you say that again?'

'Which bit?'

'The whole bit.'

'I'm not sure I can. Anyway, I think you heard.' Pru's courage began to fail her. What if she'd just made the most humiliating mistake of her life? 'Look, if you don't want to, just shake your head and we'll go.'

Her fingers were creeping towards the key, still swinging merrily in the ignition. Eddie launched himself across the car, grabbing her hand before she could reach it.

'Pru, are you serious?'

The look on his face told her all she needed to know.

'I've never been more serious in my life,' said Pru, touching the side of his face with trembling fingers. She leaned over and kissed him.

Eddie, still trapped by his seatbelt, fumbled to release it. He threw his arms around her and kissed her until they were both panting and out of breath.

'Oh, Pru, I've dreamed of this happening.' There was a catch in his voice. 'I've wanted to do this for so long . . .'

And then, incredibly, she was climbing across the gap between the seats. As he helped her, Eddie wondered if she could hear his heart pounding against his ribs. He kissed her neck and her chin, shifting slightly to accommodate her as she sat astride him.

'I knew I'd find a use for this one day,' said Pru, pressing the switch to recline the seat.

Eddie's hands stroked her bare brown legs and gasped as she wriggled herself into a more comfortable position.

Then he gasped again as he realised that beneath the short black skirt she was naked.

If this is a hallucination, thought Eddie wonderingly, I don't care. Just don't let it stop; whatever's happening here, *don't let it stop*.

Much later, when the first car drove past and gave them a jaunty toot, Pru buried her smile in the front of his shirt and said, 'I hope that wasn't someone who recognised your Jag.'

'I don't care.' Eddie couldn't stop grinning. 'I hope it was. I want everyone to know I've just been seduced in my car.'

'By a shameless hussy,' Pru said happily. 'I'm sorry if I frightened you half to death. I just had to do it.'

'Thank God you did. Oh, Pru, I do love you.' Eddie gave

311

her a hug. 'I've never felt this way about anyone before. I just never dreamt you'd be interested in me. I still can't believe this is really happening.' He shook his head, marvelling at the fact that it had. Then, gently pinching one of Pru's thighs, he said, 'And speaking of hussies, when on earth did you stop wearing knickers?'

She went pink.

'In Oxford. I took them off in the car outside the Randolph.'

'Good grief.'

'I got the idea from that paperback of Dulcie's,' Pru confessed. 'The one that bossy old woman nicked from me outside Elmlea nursing home.'

'Let's hope she doesn't try it out too. She could give the male residents heart failure.'

Eddie stroked Pru's ears, smoothing back her glossy dark hair.

'What?' The urge to flinch was strong, but she resisted it. Why was he looking at them in that way?

'Nothing. I like your hair like that. You've got beautiful ears.'

Pru smiled. She knew she could tell him about the surgery; he wouldn't laugh. But there was no need now. Another day.

Reluctantly she looked at her watch.

'I could stay here for ever, but we really should get back.'

Eddie didn't want to.

'Why?'

'Houses to clean,' she reminded him lightly. 'Sinks to scour, floors to scrub.'

He didn't want Pru doing that either. She shouldn't have to. She deserved so much better.

'Give it up,' he said flatly.

'Oh right, great idea, why didn't I think of that?' Pru laughed at the expression on his face. 'Why pay rent when you can live in a cardboard box?'

'Come and live with me.'

'Eddie!'

'I mean it. Please, don't laugh, I'm serious. I want you to live with me.' The words came tumbling out. He had been so unhappy for so long and Pru was everything he'd ever dreamed of. 'I want you to marry me. Oh, Pru, you'd make me the happiest man on earth. Of course, I know I'm not much of a catch . . .'

He really did mean it. Pru's eyes filled with tears.

Frantically Eddie kissed them away. 'God, don't cry! I don't want to make you cry. I love you—'

Pru wiped her wet cheeks on his shirt. How on earth could this kind, wonderful, adorable man think he wasn't much of a catch?

'—and if you really couldn't bear to l-live with Arthur,' this time Eddie stumbled on the words; this was the ultimate sacrifice, 'well, I understand. I'm sure we could find him a good home.'

She stared at him, astounded.

'Why couldn't I bear to live with Arthur?'

'You know . . . the allergy thing . . .'

Pru struggled to keep a straight face.

'I'm not allergic to Arthur. I just didn't want him leering at us from the back seat while we were . . . well, otherwise engaged. I thought we could do without an audience.'

It took a while to get themselves respectable again. Finally they were ready to leave.

'I'll drive,' said Eddie.

'That's silly. What if you get stopped?'

He flicked open his wallet and showed her his licence.

'You had it all this time.' Pru's eyes widened. 'You cheat!'

Eddie kissed her as he reached for the car keys.

'I know. But it did the trick.'

Chapter 46

As she plunged her reddened hands into the washing-up water, fishing for the last elusive teaspoon, Dulcie marvelled at the idea that only a month ago she had actually possessed nails capable of wearing polish. Twelve hours a day in Rufus's kitchen had changed her hands beyond all recognition and the rest of her had taken a bit of a battering too.

With no time for any more sunbeds, facials or mud treatments, Dulcie was feeling pale and decidedly uninteresting. Her hair, badly in need of a cut, flopped into her eyes. Finding the teaspoon at last, she held it up and studied her reflection in it.

I look like Liam Gallagher, she thought miserably, on a bad day.

Not that this seemed to bother Rufus.

It hadn't taken Dulcie long to realise that Liza had been right. Thankfully though, Rufus's crush on her was a discreet one. He was clearly the bashful type. He hadn't tried to push his luck and Dulcie, not wanting to hurt his feelings, simply pretended she hadn't noticed. When he asked her out – in extremely casual, just-good-friends fashion – she invented plausible excuses. When she mentioned in passing one day that her favourite aftershave was Eau Savage and Rufus came into the café the next morning reeking of it – rather than his usual Old Spice – she didn't say a word. And when he confided in her that he was lonely, Dulcie sympathised and pretended she wasn't.

'Finished? Great.' Rufus came charging through the swing

314

doors with a pile of dirty plates. Dumping them on the drainer, he turned his attention to the oven packed with trays of whole-wheat samosas and foil-wrapped garlic baguettes. 'It's getting busy out there. Could you take the order from table three?'

Dulcie ached all over; she actually felt as awful as she knew she looked. Praying she wasn't going down with flu, she dried her hands on a towel and reached for the order pad.

'If they're undecided,' said Rufus over his shoulder, 'push the samosas. We've got enough here to feed India.'

Wholefood cafés tend to attract a particular breed of customer, the kind that favour natural dyes and fabrics. There were usually plenty of long, droopy cotton dresses and even droopier hand-knitted sweaters in every shade of brown. The choice of perfume ranged between anything from the Body Shop, the musty tang of patchouli oil, and dope.

It wasn't difficult to spot Liam in his dazzling Persil-white tracksuit, and Imelda in a shocking-pink Lycra dress. Even if she'd been blind, Dulcie would still have been able to find her way to table three. Nobody else on the planet doused them-selves in Obsession like Imelda.

'My God, it's true!' Imelda squealed when she saw Dulcie watching them from the doorway. Giggling, she nudged Liam. 'She's really here. Dulcie, it's been ages! And you look . . . you look . . .'

Lank-haired, knackered and altogether skivvyish, thought Dulcie, who was under no illusions. At this rate she could end up giving Ruby, the maid from *Upstairs Downstairs*, a run for her money.

'Are you ready to order?' She forced herself to sound polite, loathing the way Imelda was gazing around the tiny café, as if she expected a mouse to run over her feet any minute.

Imelda waved a manicured hand dismissively in the direction of the menu.

'Nothing for me thanks, darling. We only dropped by to see how you are. Everyone back at the club's simply dying of curiosity. When they heard you'd actually got yourself a job' –

here Imelda adopted a mocking, *EastEnders*-type accent –
'in a caff, like, they thought it must be some kind of April
Fool.'

Smiling thinly, Dulcie turned her attention to Liam, who was
basking in the surreptitious attention of the other customers.
He had had his hair streaked again, and his tracksuit top was
unzipped to show off, through his T-shirt, the chiselled outline
of his tautly muscled torso. Liam was intensely proud of his
six-pack.

Dulcie was ashamed of herself for having once fallen for
that awful pseudo charm. You prat, she thought wearily. What
did I ever see in you?

'I'll have a coffee,' said Liam, 'black, and a green salad.'

'Please,' said Dulcie.

'And no free-range caterpillars.' Imelda shrieked with
laughter and squeezed Liam's knee. The smell of Obsession was
suffocating but Liam didn't seem to notice. Maybe, thought
Dulcie, he's been injected with the antidote.

'Go on then, I'll have a glass of mineral water,' Imelda said
generously. She watched Dulcie write it down. 'With a slice of
fresh lime. Got all that? Sure you can manage?'

'I'm going to spit in her water,' seethed Dulcie when she
was safely back in the kitchen.

'You are not!' Rufus looked up, startled. 'What are you
talking about? Whose water?'

When Dulcie had finished telling him, he said, 'Do you want
me to serve them?'

'What, and let them think they've got to me? No thanks.'

Table four needed clearing and the floor beneath it was
strewn with coleslaw and bits of chewed-up, spat-out radish.
Silently cursing the two small children who had left the mess,
Dulcie crawled under the table on all fours with her dustpan
and brush.

It wasn't dignified and she knew her bottom was sticking
out at a less than flattering angle, but she still had to exert
every ounce of self-control when she heard Imelda behind her

murmur to Liam, 'Darling, if this is what wholefood cafés do to you, remind me never to work in one.'

Dulcie carried on grimly sweeping up debris. When she heard Rufus's voice, saying breezily, 'Everything okay here?' and Liam replying, 'Fine thanks, couldn't be better,' she knew Rufus had come out of the kitchen to keep an eye on the situation. He was making sure she was okay.

When Rufus had gone and she had finished clearing up the mess, she rose creakily to her feet.

By this time, Imelda had thought up another jibe.

'Well, well. Now we know why you're working here,' she declared with a smirk. 'Who'd want anyone as boring and ordinary as Liam when they could have a hunk like your new boss?'

Having to listen to their sarcastic remarks about her had been bad enough, but Dulcie had gritted her teeth and willed herself not to react.

Making fun of Rufus, though, was too much.

'I think it would be nice if you apologised for that.' Glancing down at the contents of her dustpan, Dulcie now found herself wishing the children could have made a bit more mess.

Liam was smirking like a sixth-former.

'What, apologise for calling your boss a hunk?' Imelda's eyes widened in mock amazement. 'Darling, why so sensitive? Don't tell me you really are having a thing with him. You can't seriously be serious,' she affected horror, 'about a man who wears weave-your-own sandals and a Fair Isle tank top.'

Dulcie spun round and marched into the kitchen. She was back in less than three seconds with a thirteen-pint stock pot and a ladle.

The café went quiet.

'This,' said Dulcie, conversationally, clutching the stock pot to her chest and dipping the ladle in, 'is ratatouille.'

'Oh Christ,' muttered Liam, his fork clattering on to his salad plate. His chair scraped back like chalk on a blackboard.

'Dulcie, it was a *joke*,' Imelda protested lightly. 'Come on, where's your sense of humour?'

'I don't have one any more. I lost it along with my brain when I got involved with him.'

To indicate who she meant, Dulcie flicked a ladleful of ratatouille at Liam. It went splat against his chest and slid down inside his tracksuit top.

Imelda screamed and tried to dodge behind Liam but Dulcie was too quick for her. Splat went the second ladleful against the pink Lycra dress.

'Terrific shot,' someone murmured admiringly on table six.

'She's mad,' shrieked Imelda, 'someone stop her!'

'Come on, we're out of here.' Liam grabbed her by the arm and yanked her towards the door.

'Dulcie, where are you going?' shouted Rufus from the kitchen doorway, but she was already outside.

The gleaming red Lamborghini was parked across the entrance to Rufus's garage. For all Liam's obsession with exercise, he never parked his car an inch further away from his destination than was humanly possible.

Imelda was still struggling into her seat when Dulcie launched the contents of the stock pot through the open passenger door.

A tidal wave of garlicky ratatouille shot everywhere, drenching the inside of the car. It looked, Dulcie realised, pleased with the effect, like John Travolta's famous accident in *Pulp Fiction*.

And oh, how Liam loved his precious Lamborghini. Almost as much, Dulcie thought happily, as he loved himself.

'My car!' howled Liam, clawing lumps of courgette and tomato out of his hair. 'My fucking car. You *bitch*!'

'Never mind your car,' Imelda screamed, 'what about my dress?' Her voice rose another octave. 'It's a Galliano!'

'You're blocking a garage,' said Dulcie. She pointed to the No Parking sign Rufus had pinned up only last week. 'I'd move if I were you. Before you get clamped.'

318

* * *

'Sorry about the ratatouille,' she told Rufus, dumping the empty stock pot in the sink and running the taps.

'Lucky it wasn't hot.'

Dulcie pushed her sleeves up and began scrubbing the pot clean.

'I wish it bloody had been.'

She was white-faced and shaking. Rufus's heart went out to her; he knew how awful she must be feeling. When his wife had left him for the bank manager he would have given anything to have flung a pot of ratatouille in their faces. He just hadn't had the nerve.

When he saw the tears sliding down Dulcie's face, Rufus didn't hesitate. Crossing the kitchen, he put his arms around her, as he had dreamed of doing for so long.

'There, there.' He patted Dulcie's heaving back as if she were a child. 'Don't let them upset you. You deserve better than him.'

As he murmured the soothing words, Rufus wondered if they were a mistake. A naturally modest man, it felt odd to be telling Dulcie she deserved someone better when what he really meant was: someone like *me*.

On the other hand, when was he likely to get another opportunity like this? Dulcie was a woman in distress, in desperate need of comfort, and he wanted nothing more than to be the one providing it.

His heart raced. Maybe, thought Rufus, this is fate . . .

'Whmmph,' gasped Dulcie as his mouth fastened eagerly and unexpectedly on hers. She tried to pull away but it was a real sink plunger of a kiss. Rufus was giving it his all.

'Oh, Dulcie,' he breathed, when he at last came up for air. He clutched her joyfully to his Fair Isle chest. 'Forget Liam! I'd never cheat on you. I'll make you happy, I swear!'

Oh dear.

Carefully Dulcie extricated herself from his grip. Rufus was panting like a boisterous St Bernard and he had sampled the ratatouille at regular intervals during the making of it. The great wafts of garlic he was breathing all over her were strong enough to strip paint.

'I wasn't crying because I was upset.' It was hard to talk, Dulcie discovered, when you were trying to hold your own breath. 'I was just so . . . so *mad*.'

'Because he left you.' Fervently, Rufus's eyes searched her stricken face. 'But Dulcie, I wouldn't leave you. I'd never do anything to hurt you.'

This was awful. Dulcie, who couldn't tell him the real reason she had snapped, wiped her wet hands on her jeans and tried again.

'I don't want to hurt you either,' she said gently, 'but Rufus, it wouldn't work. I'm sorry.'

'Why? Why wouldn't it work?' Having finally plucked up the courage to declare himself, Rufus found the prospect of rejection unbearable. 'We could be so good together. A great team. Dammit, Dulcie, I'll *make* it work!'

Dulcie wondered what was going on beyond the kitchen door. Fifteen astonished customers had been left out there to fend for themselves for the last ten minutes.

'Table two are still waiting for their vegeburgers.'

'Sod table two,' Rufus declared frantically. 'And bugger the vegeburgers. Tell me why you think it wouldn't work.'

She knew he wouldn't understand if she tried to tell him he was just too nice. Unhappily Dulcie cast around for another reason, one he couldn't argue with.

'Okay.' Keeping her head down, she gazed at the frayed holes in her jeans. 'If you must know, I'm in love with my husband.'

'But your marriage is over.' Rufus looked bemused. 'You told me he's found someone else.'

Dulcie nodded.

'Oh, he has. And it's all my own fault, I know that. But I can't help the way I feel. I still love him.'

As she said it, she realised with a sickening jolt that it was the truth.

Chapter 47

The morning of Pru and Eddie's wedding dawned grey and cold. By midday, thunder was rattling around a charcoal sky. When the storm finally broke, halfway through the register office ceremony, the sound of rain on the windows was like gunfire, almost drowning out the solemn words of the registrar as he conducted the ceremony.

But nothing could dim the joyousness of the occasion. It was the happiest day of Pru's life, and it showed.

'Look at her,' Liza murmured. 'Can you believe this is the same girl who last New Year's Eve was so desperate to stay married to Phil?'

Dulcie smiled and nodded, because if anyone deserved happiness it was Pru, but inwardly she winced at the memory of that night. Was she the same girl who had so blithely announced that all she wanted was a divorce?

'Don't forget your resolution.' She nudged Liza. 'You're next.'

'Next to what?' said Kit when the service was over and they were splashing their way across the car park. 'What were you two whispering about in there?'

'Don't say Liza hasn't told you.' Dulcie grinned, ignoring the jab in her back from Liza's umbrella. 'Her New Year's resolution was to get married. Once a spinster reaches a certain age, you see, she starts to panic and get a bit desperate.'

'Thanks a lot,' said Liza.

'And since it's October now,' Dulcie pulled a face, 'I'd watch out if I were you. If you're not careful you could end up being It.'

* * *

Dulcie was putting on a brave face but the wedding reception –
at Brunton Manor, where else? – was something of a trial. When
Pru, making up her guest list the other week, had said longingly,
'It's a shame, I would like to have invited Patrick,' Dulcie had
felt obliged to do the decent thing. Acting as though the outburst
with Liza had never happened, as if it really couldn't matter
less, she'd replied, 'Don't be daft, if you want him, you invite
him. And Claire too.' Her intestines were frantically tying
themselves into reef knots but she gave Pru a bright smile. 'It's
fine with me.'

Delighted, Pru had added Patrick and Claire to her list. She
sucked her pen for a bit then added tentatively, 'How about
Liam?'

Dulcie gave her a meaningful look.

'Don't push it.'

When Dulcie left the reception in full flow and pushed open
the door to the ladies' loo, she came face to face with Imelda.

'Oh great,' Imelda drawled, 'it's the madwoman.'

Dulcie took comfort from the fact that at least this time she
was wearing a short navy-blue silk dress and full going-to-a-
wedding make-up. She had also had her hair cut. Imelda, on
the other hand, had clearly just come off the squash court and
was looking decidedly sweaty and dishevelled.

'Don't get mad, get even. That's my motto.'

'Ah, but who won in the end?' Imelda looked triumphant.
'I've got Liam.'

Witch.

Dulcie had been determined to maintain an air of dignified
calm, but her nerves were terribly on edge. Before she knew it
she heard herself saying silkily, 'I know, aren't you lucky? Tell
me, when he's screwing you, does he still count the number of
press-ups under his breath?'

The cloakroom door had opened behind her. Dulcie just had
time to watch with pleasure as bright spots of colour appeared

in Imelda's cheeks – so he did! – before a hand clutched her arm.

'Dulcie, there you are! Quick, they're about to cut the cake!'

'Thanks,' muttered Dulcie when they were safely out of the cloakroom.

'My pleasure.' Claire Berenger's grey eyes sparkled. 'Not that you looked as if you needed rescuing, but I thought it might be a good moment to leave.'

Awkwardly, wishing she wasn't so nice, Dulcie returned her smile.

'I'm glad you did. Are they really cutting the cake?'

'No. And I'm still dying for a pee. Come on, let's find another loo,' Claire said companionably, 'then we'll get ourselves a drink.'

In a daze of happiness, Pru watched the guests milling around her. Eddie's mother-in-law, Edna Peverell, had been too frail to leave the nursing home but upon hearing about the wedding, and with characteristic bluntness, her irascible fellow resident Marjorie Hickman had announced to Eddie on his next visit to Elmlea that she would be delighted to come instead.

'Told you he fancied you,' she had announced, waving her walking stick at Pru as she hobbled into the ballroom, resplendent in an emerald-green ruffled blouse and ankle-length tweed skirt. 'Said he'd got the hots for you, didn't I? Good grief, child, what's happened to your ears? When did you get those done?'

Pru, who was wearing her hair up, started to laugh.

'What is the old bird on about?' hissed Eddie, perplexed.

Pru shrugged.

'I'm wearing earrings. Maybe she thinks I've had them pierced.'

'And if you've got any more of those saucy books,' Marjorie declared in a loud voice, 'bring 'em with you on your next visit.'

'Doolally,' Eddie murmured to Pru. 'Totally shot away.'

323

Pru smiled to herself now as she watched Marjorie stuffing asparagus rolls from the buffet into her handbag. She saw Eddie make his way over and whisper something in her ear, and knew he was telling her she could take as much food as she liked back to Elmlea, he had already instructed the staff to make up a box.

Marjorie looked miffed; being given a food parcel wasn't half so much fun as squirrelling it away in her bag.

Glancing across at Pru, Eddie rolled his eyes good-naturedly and gave up.

I've just married the kindest, sweetest man in the world, thought Pru. Blanche was right; I have done all right for myself.

Pru had bumped into her last week. She had been loading the wedding cake into the back of the Jag when Blanche had emerged from the Sue Ryder shop. She was wearing skin-tight jeans and yellow stilettos and her hair was even blonder than Pru remembered.

'Oh . . . hello.' Blanche was only momentarily taken aback. For something to say, she had held up one of her carrier bags. 'I've just bought a pair of leggings for fifty pee.'

Pru recognised the pretty gold chain around her neck as one that had gone missing a year ago. When Phil had come home to find her sifting through the contents of the Hoover bag he had said, 'You're useless, Pru. What's the point of buying you nice things if all you're going to do is lose them?'

Blanche had taken her husband but she wouldn't have taken the chain. Pru knew Phil must have given it to her. She made sure the box containing the wedding cake was wedged securely in the boot of the car and straightened up.

'Blanche, how are you?'

Blanche half smiled. 'Oh, we're fine. Got your divorce, then. Just in time from the sound of things. Phil says you're getting married on Saturday.'

The decree absolute had come through the week before. As she stared at the all-important piece of paper, Pru had marvelled at her own lack of emotion. It was the weirdest thing, but she could barely remember how it had felt, being married to Phil.

Now, gazing at the carrier bag Blanche was holding, she recognised the distinctive label of a can of Heinz tomato soup, just visible through the thin plastic. The memories came flooding back, accompanied by a blissful sensation of release, because it wasn't her problem any more.

Blanche, meanwhile, was admiring Eddie's gleaming top-of-the range Jag.

'Nice car. Got a bit of money, this fellow, has he?'

Pru shrugged. Then she nodded.

Blanche looked envious. 'You've done all right for yourself, then.'

'Yes, I have,' said Pru, simply. Silently she added, but not in the way you mean.

'What happened to the job?' said Patrick. 'I called into that café a couple of weeks ago and the waitress said you weren't working there any more.'

Dulcie wondered if he had gone along to snigger, as Liam and Imelda had done.

'Too much like hard work,' she replied flippantly. 'I broke a fingernail.'

As soon as the words were out, she regretted them. Patrick was exchanging a 'see-what-I-mean?' look with Claire.

'Actually,' said Dulcie, 'I left because the owner developed a crush on me. It got a bit embarrassing.'

She could tell he didn't believe her.

'I don't blame you for giving it up.' Claire's tone was consoling. 'I worked in a restaurant when I was at college. Jolly hard graft.'

'Dulcie isn't much of a fan of hard graft,' Patrick remarked drily.

Dulcie was beginning to feel got at. She longed to yell, But it never bothered you before! You were the one who said I didn't need to get a job . . . you *wanted* me to stay at home!

Pride prevented her, too, from informing him that she was now working as a barmaid in one of Bath's busiest city-centre pubs, crammed with horrible yuppie types who pinched her bottom and chatted her up and gabbled non-stop into their stupid mobile phones. Because how could she boast about holding down a job at last when everyone else had been doing it for years?

Anyway, if I did tell them how vile it all was, Dulcie thought wearily, Patrick would only say in that case why did I bother?

She was damned if she was going to tell him the truth, that she was so lonely and miserable that even slogging her guts out in a stinking pub was better than moping alone at home.

To change the subject Dulcie said, 'How was Amsterdam?' and instantly regretted that too.

'Oh, we had the most fabulous time!' exclaimed Claire, her face lighting up. She clutched Patrick's arm. 'Didn't we, darling? I actually think I've managed to convert this one here to the idea of holidays,' she confided merrily to Dulcie. 'We're looking at brochures for something over Christmas and the New Year now. A real get-away-from-it-all break.' Her grey eyes shone. 'I've always wanted to visit Barbados.'

'You've got a face like a wet weekend in Weston,' Marjorie announced, plonking herself down on a chair next to Dulcie and holding her glass out to be refilled by a passing waitress. 'Friend of the bride or groom?'

'Both.' Dulcie glanced at the breast pocket of the old woman's green ruffled blouse. It was bulging with mini seafood tartlets. 'Bride mainly. Pru and I have been friends for years.'

'So you're not one of Eddie's jealous exes. Thought you might be, from the look of you.'

Dulcie smiled. Did Eddie have any jealous exes?

'No.'

'So what's the problem? Don't you approve of him?'

'Of course I do. Eddie's lovely,' exclaimed Dulcie. 'And perfect for Pru.'

Marjorie gulped down her drink and nodded in agreement.

'They look all right to me. Not that I know them well, but his mother-in-law's very fond of him.' She looked around hopefully for the waitress with the drinks tray. 'Says he's a poppet.' She snorted with laughter. 'Can't argue with that, can you? Anyone adored by their mother-in-law must be okay.'

A vision of Bibi flitted into Dulcie's mind. In the vision, Bibi was looking less than happy.

She said gloomily, 'My mother-in-law hates me.'

'Oh, so you're married, are you?' Marjorie's thin grey eyebrows went up. 'Where's your husband then?'

Dulcie pointed.

'Over there, with his girlfriend. He hates me too.'

Claire was admiring Pru's dress, which was cream lace, knee length and beautifully cut to show off her slim figure.

'You could always dye it,' she said, 'then you'd be able to wear it to other people's weddings.'

'I'll wear it to Liza and Kit's.' Pru grinned at Eddie.

Claire looked astonished.

'They're getting married? I haven't heard about this!'

'Not really. It's kind of a joke. When we made our resolutions last New Year's Eve, Liza's was to get married,' explained Pru.

Claire laughed. '*Dad* will be pleased.'

'What was Dulcie's resolution?' Patrick's dark eyes were expressionless.

Oo-er. Pru fiddled with her new, terrifically shiny wedding ring.

'Um . . . can't remember.'

'Well, who cares about Dad anyway? I *love* weddings.' Spotting Kit not far away, Claire dragged him over.

'Congratulations.' She winked at Liza. 'I hear I'm about to gain a sister-in-law.'

'Is this some kind of conspiracy?' murmured Kit.

Liza cringed.

'I didn't—'

'No, no excuses.' Claire gave her brother a playful pinch on the arm. 'Pru told me all about it. You have until the end of the year and that's an order. Otherwise,' she added soothingly, 'Liza will dump you and marry someone else and you'll regret it for the rest of your miserable life.'

'You'll never find anyone else to marry you,' Kit announced. 'Not before the end of the year.'

It was still pouring down with rain. Pru and Eddie had just driven away. All the wedding guests, who had piled out on to the steps to wave them off, had promptly belted back inside again to avoid getting drenched.

Liza and Kit were the only ones still outside but Kit had his back to the door. He kept one arm firmly around Liza's waist.

She shook her head. 'I'm sorry. I have the most embarrassing friends.'

'So I suppose I'd better do it.'

'Do what?'

There were drops of rain on Kit's eyelashes. He looked ridiculously handsome and very serious.

'Marry you.'

'Oh God, no! It was only supposed to be a joke.' Liza pulled a face. 'Don't take any notice of them . . . we don't have to get married!'

'Actually, we do. And not because your friends think we should.' He paused and lifted a strand of Liza's wet blonde hair out of her eyes. 'Because *I* do.'

'But – but we could just live together!'

'Why?' said Kit. 'Don't you want to marry me?'

Liza stared at him. What a question. Lowering her gaze, she studied the lapels of his dark suit instead. This was easier, since they didn't stare unnervingly back.

The look on her face told Kit everything he needed to know.

He smiled; she hadn't kicked up nearly as much of a fuss as he'd thought she would.

'So that's it. All settled,' he said with satisfaction. 'December all right with you?'

Dulcie had been chatting to Terry Lambert for several minutes before she realised who he was.

'I've got it now. You're the one who persuaded Pru to have her ears done.'

'Well, in a manner of speaking.' Terry looked amused. 'I wouldn't like to claim sole responsibility. We in the legal profession prefer to avoid that if we can.'

Of course, he was a solicitor, remembered Dulcie. He had handled Pru's divorce.

'Isn't dealing with endless marriage break-ups depressing?' she asked.

'Not necessarily. It isn't all slanging matches and squabbling over who gets the Monopoly set. Some couples manage to stay on good terms, which always helps.' He smiled. 'A bit of civility goes a long way.'

As she gazed across the room at Patrick and Claire, Dulcie realised it was time to prove she could be civil too. As civil as Patrick was to me when I told him our marriage was over, she thought sadly. Patrick hadn't argued or punched her or started shouting about money; he had simply moved out.

Dulcie wondered if it had been easy for him to stay civil because he hadn't felt that much for her anyway.

Imagining that this was true made her want to cry. Hastily she pulled herself together.

Either way, it's my turn to do the decent thing, Dulcie realised. Patrick hasn't put the pressure on, but that's just the way he is. And he's with Claire now. Of course it's what he wants.

As Terry offered to refill her glass, she tried not to look at his nose. He seemed charming, and he had organised Pru's divorce from Phil with admirable speed and minimum fuss.

'Maybe I could come and see you at your office,' Dulcie said casually.

Terry didn't seem surprised, he just reached into the inside pocket of his suit jacket. His brief smile as he passed her one of his business cards was sympathetic.

'You want a divorce as well?'

No, but my husband does, thought Dulcie with an ache in her chest like homesickness. And under the circumstances it seems the least I can do.

Chapter 48

The next morning Liza had to be up early. She had an appointment with her publishing editor in London at ten and a restaurant in Windsor to review at one thirty. To save time, she was wearing her frump gear and wig.

'You remind me of someone I got chatted up by yesterday,' said Kit, taking a bite out of Liza's toast as he squeezed past her in the kitchen. 'Old dear with a walking stick, kept nicking stuff from the buffet.'

'Marjorie.' Liza nodded and shoved the rest of the toast into his mouth; she was already running late. 'She told me if she was fifty years younger she'd give me a run for my money. You wouldn't believe the comments she made about your bum.'

'That's me,' said Kit with a broad grin. 'Irresistible to older women.' He grabbed Liza around the waist as she tried to rush past him. 'Hang on, I haven't had a kiss yet from my future wife.'

Liza, who was on her way to the bathroom to brush her teeth, kept her lips clamped together.

'Was that it?' Kit looked appalled. 'If that's how you kiss future husbands, forget it.'

He leaned against the door frame and watched her brushing her teeth.

'I want to see a dramatic improvement in kissing technique by this evening,' he warned.

'Who would you like me to practise on, my gay editor?' Liza spoke through a mouthful of toothpaste.

Kit grinned.

'Practise on the back of your hand. Dulcie told me yesterday it's what you used to do when you were eleven.'

'We all did!' Liza looked indignant. 'Why, what did you practise on?'

The grin broadened.

'Girls.'

From the radio in the kitchen came the sound of the eight o'clock pips. Liza groaned and brushed faster.

'God, I love the way your bottom wriggles when you do that.'

The toothbrush clattered into the basin. Liza wiped her mouth on a towel, grabbed her coat and bag from the hall and almost fell over putting on her shoes.

'I'm late late late.' Whirling around, she planted a speed-of-light kiss on Kit's face, missing his mouth by an inch. ''Bye. Back by six.'

As she raced out to the car, almost sending a pensioner flying, Kit stood in the doorway and yelled, 'What is it with you call girls nowadays? That was another crap kiss.'

Leo Berenger was at his desk when Kit turned up at nine for their meeting with a new firm of architects. The plans for the latest Berenger development, on the outskirts of Oxford, were already well underway. Leo had been studying the proposed drawings for a selection of four- and five-bedroomed Tudor-style properties since before breakfast and was impatient to bounce several ideas off his son before the architects arrived.

The last thing he needed to hear was Liza Lawson's name.

'No, *no.*' The impatient wave of his arm swept several drawings to the floor. Dammit, hadn't Kit got that woman out of his system yet? 'I don't *want* to meet her. Why the hell should I?'

Kit shrugged. He hadn't seriously expected any other reaction.

'No reason. We're getting married, that's all.'

Leo Berenger didn't go in for double-takes. Yelling 'You're

getting *what*?' wasn't his style. He simply shook his head and leaned back in his chair, his expression grim.

'When?'

'December.'

'If you do, you're a bloody fool.'

'I don't think so,' said Kit. 'I think I'm bloody lucky.'

'I suppose she's pregnant.'

'No.'

'So what's she after, a share of all this when I kick the bucket?' This time his irritated gesture encompassed the view from the windows, the offices occupying the whole of the top floor, the house itself. 'Because I tell you now, she'll have a bloody long wait.'

'Dad.' Wearily, Kit picked up the scattered drawings. Argument or no argument, the architects who had produced them would be here at any minute. 'This has nothing to do with your money. I love Liza and I'm going to marry her.'

'And nothing I say will make a blind bit of difference, I suppose.'

Was this his father's way of acknowledging and finally accepting the situation? Kit wasn't sure; all he knew was there needn't be a rift between them.

Giving him the benefit of the doubt, Kit smiled slightly and said, 'No. I'll marry her anyway.'

He got no smile in return. The expression on Leo's face was one of undiluted disgust.

'Go on then, do it. Make your own mistakes, see if I care.' He leaned forward in his chair and jabbed a solid finger at his son for emphasis. 'Just don't ever ask me again if I want to meet her.'

The meeting was over by eleven. Relieved, Kit saw the architects to their car. When he returned to the office, his father was barking instructions down the phone to one of the contractors, swigging black coffee and chewing his way irritably through a pack of Rennies.

'Okay if I disappear for an hour or two?' asked Kit, when he had hung up the phone.

'You can disappear for the next twenty years if you want to.'

Kit decided to ignore this. He reached for his jacket.

The last Rennie was noisily crunched up and swallowed. 'Don't bother sending me an invitation to the wedding, by the way.'

His father was clearly still simmering with fury, his face red, his fists clenched on the desk. Kit wondered if he was about to have a heart attack.

To placate him, and maybe lower his blood pressure a couple of notches, he said, 'Dad, it doesn't have to be like this. If you got to know Liza, you'd understand—'

'Christ almighty, what *is* this?' Leo roared, thumping the desk with his hand. 'Who d'you think we are, the bloody Waltons?'

So much for making an effort. Kit shrugged.

'Fine, have it your way,' he said shortly. 'I'll be back around one.'

Marriott's was the smartest jewellery shop in Bath, occupying a prime position on one of the smartest streets. Inside, the décor was opulent and suitably restrained, all slate-grey velvet, gleaming silver and the kind of lighting that made the most miserable diamond chip glitter like the Koh-i-noor.

Not, of course, that Marriott's went in for diamond chips, Kit thought wryly. He wasn't likely to forget this fact either, since as a child – and with Christmas approaching – he had heard his mother say Marriott's was her favourite shop. He had duly trotted along with his pocket money the following week and asked one of the assistants to show him some necklaces. Very sweetly refusing to accept Kit's seventy-three pence, the assistant had popped a Bic biro into one of Marriott's sumptuous satin-lined, slate-grey velvet boxes and sent Kit happily on his way.

Now he was browsing with rather more than seventy-three pence in his pocket, and just as well. There were some pretty startling price tags on display.

One of the assistants approached noiselessly across the plush, pale-grey carpet.

'Diamond rings . . . er, engagement rings,' Kit murmured, slightly embarrassed.

She smiled.

'Certainly, sir. How many?'

Kit relaxed and grinned back.

'Just the one, for now.'

The woman, who was in her early forties, began unlocking cabinets. She was plump but attractive, with baby-blue eyes and a dimply smile. Kit wondered how long she had worked here and if she was the one who had given him the biro in the velvet box all those years ago.

The first tray of rings was brought out for Kit's inspection. He picked up one, a fire-flashing oval solitaire, and turned it this way and that, imagining it on Liza's finger.

The assistant was wearing L'Air du Temps. She smiled at Kit. 'I know, it's a beautiful ring.'

The more he thought about it, the more he felt she could be the same woman. Kit glanced at the other customers in the shop – a smart American couple, an old man and a middle-aged woman in a crumpled green Barbour – and said, 'Have you been working here long?'

There was suppressed laughter in the assistant's eyes.

'Fifteen years. Why?'

'Sorry,' said Kit, 'it wasn't meant to sound like a chat-up line. I just wondered if—'

'Everybody FREEZE!' screamed a male voice as the door was flung open and two men in balaclavas burst into the shop.

One of the other assistants let out a terrified whimper. The American couple, like something out of a gangster movie, put their hands up.

'Nobody move!' yelled the second balaclava-ed figure,

yanking open a black leather bag and grabbing the tray of rings Kit had just been looking at. The oval solitaire disappeared into the bag along with the rest. The first man pointed a sawn-off shotgun at the assistant who had whimpered.

'Unlock the rest of the cases,' he ordered roughly. 'Go on, do it NOW.'

When the second robber had pushed past him, the rank stench of sweat had filled Kit's nostrils. Now the man had moved away he could smell L'Air du Temps again.

Jewellery and watches were being hurled into the bag. Kit's assistant watched the men, her expression petrified.

Kit, in turn, watched her trembling fingers slide with agonising slowness off the counter. He knew she was reaching for the panic button. Out of the corner of his eye he saw the shotgun swing in their direction.

'Get away from the counter!' screamed the balaclava-ed face. 'Don't touch anything!'

Since it was a silent alarm system, no one knew whether or not the button had been pressed. Kit's assistant moved as instructed towards the wall.

'Not that far! Christ, she's going for the pressure pads,' the robber yelled. He charged towards her bellowing, 'You asked for this, you stupid bitch,' and brought the butt of the shotgun down on her blonde head.

The sickening THWACK and the sound of her scream as she crumpled to the floor was awful.

'Des, for fuck's sake get a move on,' yelled the robber, turning his back on Kit for a split second.

Kit hurled himself forward, rugby-tackling him to the ground and knocking the gun out of his hands. Everyone in the shop watched it shoot across the carpet, ricochet off one of the ebony cabinets and slither to a halt at the feet of the other robber.

Kit watched him pick up the gun and take aim. He heard the woman in the green Barbour exclaim, 'Don't do this, *please* don't do it!'

He heard the muffled voice of the man on the ground snarling, 'Just kill the bastard.'

As he turned his head, still in that same split second, Kit saw the blonde assistant struggling to sit up. Blood was pouring from her head, the collar of her white shirt glistened crimson and one of her dark-blue shoes had come off.

Kit turned back. He still had his arms around the legs of the robber he had tackled to the ground.

'Let go of him,' yelled the one with the gun.

'Jesus Christ,' screamed the American woman, gibbering with fear, 'can't somebody *do* something?'

Kit watched the man's eyes through the holes in his balaclava; they were wild with terror and panic.

Des, in turn, stared at the two figures on the ground, at the brother he idolised – only just out of Strangeways after a five-year stretch for armed robbery – and at the dark-haired boy clinging to him like a bloody leech, preventing his escape.

In the distance, Des heard the faint sinister wail of police sirens.

The American bitch was right; somebody had to do something.

He cocked the gun. Then, his finger shaking, he pulled the trigger.

Chapter 49

If there was anything less alluring than a frumpy wig, it was a wet frumpy wig. Liza, admiring her reflection in the ladies' room of the Queen of Puddings in Windsor, resisted the temptation to run a comb through the straggly mess. The condescending manner of the maître d', who clearly regarded her as some kind of eccentric bag lady and wasn't bothering to conceal his distaste, deserved a special mention, she felt.

Otherwise the Queen of Puddings couldn't be faulted. The chef, a young Australian who had previously trained under Michel Roux, had a sublimely light touch. Liza had given the flash-fried smoked salmon with lime sauce top marks and the roast gigot, pink and tender, had been served with possibly the best potatoes – baked with olive oil, garlic and sage – she had ever eaten in her life.

Looking forward to a pudding, a buttermilk bavarois with raspberry coulis, Liza made her way back to the dining room. She saw the maître d' mutter something under his breath to one of the young waiters and knew she was being talked about. He was probably warning the boy to keep an eye on the cutlery, make sure none of it walked.

When the phone rang, M'sieur Pierre answered it.

'You wish to speak to Liza Lawson?' He frowned. 'I'm sorry, madam, we have nobody of that name dining in our restaurant.'

'Yes you do.' Dulcie took a steadying breath. 'Please, just get her.'

'Excuse me, are you referring to Liza Lawson the restaurant

338

critic?' As he spoke, M'sieur Pierre swept a practised eye over the female diners.

'Yes, yes, that's the one.'

'But I'm afraid you're mistaken. I can assure you we don't have Liza Lawson here. Let me check the bookings for tomorrow—'

'She's *there*,' Dulcie almost screamed. 'Wearing a wig, looking like a librarian. Just get her to the phone, will you? Tell her it's an emergency. A real emergency.'

When Liza put the phone down she was trembling uncontrollably. How could something like this have happened? How could Kit have been – oh God – *shot*?

She stared blindly at the row of multicoloured liqueur bottles lined up on the shelf above the bar, struggling to take it in, unaware of the maître d' hovering ecstatically behind her.

'Miss Lawson, my profound apologies . . . I didn't recognise you . . . may I say what a pleasure it is to welcome you to our restaurant . . .'

Kit's been shot.

She was gazing up at the liqueurs. Eager to oblige, M'sieur Pierre reached for one of the bottles. 'May I offer you a glass of strega, Miss Lawson? With our compliments, of course. Or maybe you would prefer a Courvoisier?'

'I'm sorry.' Like a zombie, Liza moved past him. She picked up her bag, then reached for her still-wet and deeply unfashionable raincoat.

Open-mouthed, M'sieur Pierre watched the heavy wooden door swing shut behind her. Through the window he saw her race through the pouring rain to her car.

'She's done a bunk! You let her scarper without paying,' exclaimed the young waiter, delighted to witness stuck-up M'sieur Pierre getting his come-uppance at long last.

'It's not a problem,' M'sieur Pierre replied with dignity. 'That was Liza Lawson.'

'Oh yeah! What makes you think that?'

'There was a phone call for her.'

The waiter smirked. He drooled over Liza Lawson's photograph in the paper every week. That blonde hair, that smile, that *cleavage* . . .

'Nah, take it from me, that wasn't Liza Lawson.'

M'sieur Pierre began to look discomforted. The waiter's pleasure was complete.

'A scam, that's what that was,' he announced happily. 'Sorry, mate, you've been had.'

It was four o'clock when Liza reached the Bath Royal United Hospital. Dulcie was waiting for her in the entrance lobby.

'They're still operating. We just have to wait. Oh, Liza, it's so awful . . . come and sit down, I'll get you a coffee from the machine.'

Liza didn't want to sit down, nor did she want a coffee, but a man with a camera was hovering, clearly trying to figure out if this white-faced woman with the terrible hair and clothes could really be Liza Lawson. She allowed Dulcie to lead her round the corner to a seat.

'How did you hear about it?'

'Leo Berenger rang his daughter. Claire rang Patrick. Patrick rang me. Luckily,' said Dulcie, 'I remembered the name of the restaurant you told me you were visiting. I didn't want to wait until you got home in case it was . . . it was . . .'

She bit her lip. Liza nodded. She knew Dulcie meant in case it was too late.

The photographer from the local paper reappeared.

'Are you Liza Lawson?'

'No she isn't,' snapped Dulcie. 'Piss off.'

Liza was spilling coffee all over the floor; it simply wouldn't stay in its plastic cup.

'Isn't there somewhere else we could go? Where are Leo and Claire? Maybe they've heard something by now.'

Dulcie looked doubtful.

'They're in the relatives' waiting room. I don't know if we

340

should. Patrick told me Kit's father's in a terrible state.'

They both jumped as a flashbulb went off. Grabbing Liza's half-full cup of coffee, Dulcie flung the tepid remains in the direction of the photographer's groin. Without even bothering to look at him she seized Liza's arm.

'Okay, come on. I can't go in but I'll show you where it is.'

Liza didn't go in either. When she knocked on the door it was opened by Leo Berenger. He stood in the doorway and she saw the terrible grief in his bloodshot eyes.

From the look of him Liza expected him to roar, but when he opened his mouth the words hissed out quiet and deadly.

'You. You can get out of here. Haven't you done enough damage already?'

'I just wanted—'

'I don't care what you want,' said Leo Berenger. 'First you tried to destroy my family. Now you've destroyed my son. Isn't that enough?'

Horrified, Liza watched the tears streaming down his face.

'But—'

'You killed him as surely as if you'd pulled the trigger yourself.' Leo Berenger's voice was barely above a whisper. 'So just go.'

That night, as Claire wept in his arms, Patrick tried to imagine how he would feel if she were to die. To be literally here one moment and gone the next.

She was good and kind, humorous and intelligent, hard-working and successful. She was liked by everyone because there was nothing about Claire Berenger for anyone to dislike. If she were to disappear from his life he would miss her, of course he would.

Feeling horribly disloyal, Patrick stroked her shining hair and tried to imagine how he would feel if Dulcie died.

Frivolous Dulcie, who was wilful and tactless, scatty and impetuous, not in the least hard-working and an incurable meddler to boot. Plenty of people, in their time, had raised their eyebrows in amazement at the antics of Dulcie Ross.

But . . .

But she was also generous, wildly loyal to her friends, beautiful and wickedly funny. Dulcie may have been bored by him but he had never, ever been bored by her. Nor, for so much as a single moment, had he stopped loving her.

As he bent to kiss Claire's hair, Patrick knew which of the two of them he would miss the most.

Chapter 50

'Over here, gorgeous! Five tequila and blackcurrants, five bottles of Pils and a packet of pork scratchings when you're ready.'

Talk about the height of sophistication. And this was two thirty on a Wednesday afternoon.

It was only the first week in December but in the Cat and Mouse, Christmas was being celebrated early.

'Oh, and one other thing,' said the lad with the bleached blond hair. He pulled his wallet out of the pocket of his blue Armani jacket.

Dulcie was busy flipping the lids off the bottles of Pils.

'What?'

'A date with you.'

She glanced up.

'On your bike.'

'No, I'm serious. Tomorrow night, anywhere you like.' The boy grinned at her. Flicking his fringe out of his eyes he waved his wallet. 'Don't worry, I've got plenty of this. We could have a wild time.'

He was twenty if he was a day.

'Don't you have to be in bed by nine?'

Too late, Dulcie realised her mistake. His grin broadened.

'My mother always told me if I'm not in bed by midnight, to give up and come home.'

'Oh ha ha.'

'Go on,' he urged, 'you're just my type.'

'I'm too old for you.'

'That's all right, I go for older women.'

'I meant mentally,' said Dulcie, pouring the last tequila. 'That'll be sixteen pounds seventy.'

'Last chance,' offered the boy, waving a twenty-pound note under her nose in what was presumably a beguiling manner, a hint of things to come. He wheedled, 'You can keep the change.'

'No thanks.'

His lips curled in disgust. 'Huh, didn't want to go out with you anyway. I only said it for a bet.'

Wondering for the millionth time why she was working in this dump with these idiots – and knowing the answer – Dulcie dropped the change into his sweaty hand and glanced past him.

'Next please.'

'I'm next . . . oh!'

Until that moment all Dulcie had been able to see was a perma-tanned arm poking out from behind pork scratchings, clutching a tenner. Then she caught a waft of Obsession and Imelda's head popped into view.

'What can I get you?' said Dulcie, wiping her hands on her jeans and realising she didn't even have the energy any more to be bitchy to Imelda.

'You're working *here* now?' Evidently taken aback, Imelda forgot to be bitchy too. Well, almost. 'What is it with this urge, all of a sudden, to get a job? Did you lose a ton of money with Lloyd's or something?'

Fifty people were going frantic, waiting to be served. Since Imelda always drank G and T, Dulcie stuck a glass under the Gordon's optic.

'No, I just decided there was more to life than the country club. It was time to move on.'

'To *this* place?' Imelda raised immaculately plucked eyebrows and glanced around the Cat and Mouse, clearly unimpressed.

Dulcie shrugged and shovelled ice cubes into the glass.

'Why not? You're here.'

'Christmas shopping with my sister.' Imelda indicated another section of the pub. 'She's over there, waiting for me. Better make that two gin and tonics. Plenty of ice, please.'

Imelda had actually said please!

'Christmas shopping.' Dulcie suppressed a shudder. 'I can't bear the thought.'

Gosh, this felt strange, exchanging polite social chit-chat with Imelda and not a pot of ratatouille in sight.

By the look of her, Imelda was finding the situation equally odd, but if Dulcie – of all people – was managing to be civil, then so could she.

Clearing her throat, she rested her elbows on the bar and lowered her voice.

'How is Liza coping?'

'As well as can be expected.' Dulcie was used to being asked. She dropped slices of lemon into each glass and shrugged. 'Not great. How does anyone cope, when something like that happens?'

'Poor Liza. It must be terrible for her. Is she still staying with you?'

'No, that was just for the first few weeks. She's down with her parents now, in Devon. I think she needed to get away from Bath.'

'Oi! Any danger of getting served in this place?' demanded a bolshie-looking man in a brown suit.

Dulcie gave him a saccharine smile.

'I'll be with you in just a moment, sir.'

'Sorry, I'm going to get you the sack.' Imelda looked rueful.

Dulcie handed over her change. 'I won't get sacked. The slimeball manager fancies me rotten and I'm the hardest worker he has.' And speaking of slimeballs . . . 'How's Liam, by the way?'

'Oh, we broke up. Well, it was pretty mutual,' said Imelda, not very convincingly.

'Some of us are dying of thirst over here,' yelled another irritated customer.

'. . . we were heading in different directions . . .'

'Sixteen pints of best and a medium sherry, *when* you're ready.'

'. . . wanting different things out of life . . .'

'You mean he dumped you too,' said Dulcie. To her amazement she found herself actually feeling sorry for Imelda.

Imelda's shoulders drooped, but she managed a flicker of a smile.

'Yeah. Bastard.'

'Bastard,' Dulcie agreed, nodding sympathetically. How stupidly they'd both behaved, vying with each other over such a total waste of space. 'Who's he moved on to now?'

'Fifi Goodison-Blake.'

'You're kidding! That nymphet! How old is she, *seventeen*?'

'And a half,' said Imelda. 'Disgusting, isn't it?'

Fifi, a promising tennis player, was the impressionable daughter of Betsy, a long-standing member of the club. Even though she was a nymphet, Dulcie felt sorry for her. She remembered all too well how Liam had first broken her own, frantically pounding teenage heart.

Well, chipped the edges a bit anyway.

'Poor kid,' she mused, 'she'll be devastated when it's over.'

Imelda picked up her drinks.

'And it isn't as if she'll be able to cry on her mother's shoulder,' she said, unable to resist sharing the latest bit of gossip with her erstwhile rival. 'Rumour has it he's having it off with Betsy on the quiet too.'

Robert and Delia Cresswell were social workers; they lived in a three-storey Georgian townhouse with three children and seven cats, and nobody collected friends like Robert and Delia.

They were *people* people, endlessly enthusiastic, interested in everyone and so essentially good-hearted that rebuffing them made anyone who tried it feel a complete heel.

It was a kind of blackmail, but it was extremely efficient blackmail. When Robert and Delia held one of their legendary parties, they invited everyone they knew. And everyone turned up.

James spotted Liza across the crowded drawing room. For a split second he wondered how long it had been since he'd last seen her, then it came back to him. The night of Patrick's fortieth birthday, when he had walked out on Bibi. The surprise party to end all surprise parties, thought James. Christ, how could he forget?

Now, Liza was wearing a plum-coloured crushed-velvet dress and her thick blonde hair, tumbling over her shoulders, had grown longer since January. Otherwise, to the casual observer, she looked as untroubled and effortlessly sexy as ever.

Only when James moved closer did the difference become apparent. The pain might be carefully concealed but it was still there.

Liza, he realised, had been dragged into a heated discussion with a group of Delia's fellow social workers about the various vegetarian restaurants in Bath. Alarmingly critical and determined to prove they knew just as much about food as Liza, they were now arguing loudly about the relative merits of buffalo and ordinary mozzarella.

James watched Liza's dark eyes glaze over. Sympathising totally, he reached past the noisiest of the social workers and touched her arm.

He was rewarded by her face lighting up.

'James! How lovely to see you.'

'Need rescuing?' he murmured as he kissed her cheek, and felt Liza's answering nod.

'Thanks.' She breathed a sigh of relief when he had extricated her from the circle. 'Phew. The great mozzarella debate. I couldn't have taken much more of that.'

James shook his head. 'What are you doing here?'

'If you know Robert and Delia, you know why I'm here,' Liza said with a wry smile. 'Since I've known them, they've invited me to every party they've had. I'm actually staying with my parents at the moment, down in Devon, but I drive back

347

every week to keep an eye on the flat. Delia spotted me and insisted I came along here tonight. The more I tried to tell her I didn't feel up to it, the more convinced she became that a party was what I needed to buck me up.'

Poor Liza, fallen helpless victim to Robert and Delia's bulldozer approach.

'And has it?'

'Of course it hasn't. But they meant well,' said Liza. 'It's my own fault anyway for being too much of a wimp to say no.'

She had lost some weight, James noticed. The famously voluptuous figure had been pared down, that mesmerising cleavage had shrunk. Being thinner didn't particularly suit her, but since he knew she hadn't done it on purpose he didn't point it out.

'I read about you and Kit Berenger in the paper, of course. I was so sorry to hear about . . . you know, what happened.'

James felt awkward; it was always hard to know what to say. But Liza simply nodded. She understood.

'He was the love of my life, James. You know what I used to be like. Kit changed all that. Then, suddenly, something like that happens . . . and he's gone. There was nothing I could do about it. I never even had a chance to say goodbye.'

There was a catch in her voice. She was pale and not far from tears, he realised, but determined not to break down in public.

'Come on.' James took her hand. 'You've done your duty. I'll drive you home.'

'It's okay, I'm not going to cry.'

'Do you *want* to stay?'

Wearily Liza smiled and shook her head.

'Oh no. I'd definitely prefer to go home.'

Outside, frost glistened on the road. Their breath came out in white puffballs of condensation and hung in the air before them. Shivering, Liza waited at the top of the steps for James to find whatever he was searching for in his coat pocket.

Finally, pulling out his keys, he aimed at a blue Mazda parked twenty yards down the road on their right. The central locking beeped and clicked open.

'You don't have to drive me home,' said Liza.

'Don't be silly.'

'Really, there's no need.'

James led her gently but firmly down the flight of stone steps and pointed her in the direction of the Mazda.

'Liza, don't argue. It's no trouble. I want to drive you home.'

She took the keys from him, zapped the car and locked it again.

'Dear James,' Liza's smile was affectionate, 'you're a gentleman, but what I mean is, there's *really no need*.' She patted the railings in front of the house they were just passing. 'I live here.'

They chatted easily together in the kitchen of Liza's flat while she made coffee and poured each of them a brandy.

'I met the Cresswells at the opening of an exhibition at the Pelican Gallery,' James explained. 'Robert introduced me to Delia's sister. You know what they're like when it comes to matchmaking.'

Liza knew.

'Did it work?'

'No,' said James simply. 'Oh, she was a nice enough girl. But she just . . .'

She just wasn't Bibi.

Liza poured the coffee and carried the cups through to the sitting room. James followed with the glasses of brandy.

As she reached down to switch on a red shaded lamp, Liza said, 'Do you still miss her?'

Bibi's name hadn't been mentioned but James didn't need to ask who she meant.

He still missed Bibi terribly.

He looked at Liza, and shrugged.

'All the time.'

They sat down next to each other on the sofa. With her left hand, Liza pleated and repleated the velvet hem of her dress.

'Are you involved with anyone else?'

'No.' He shook his head.

'I spoke to Patrick last week. Bibi isn't seeing anyone either.'

James's heart leapt, then fell again. It was what he wanted to hear, of course. But then again . . .

'What's the point?' Wearily he stirred sugar into his coffee. 'Even if I do still love her – and God only knows how she feels about me – what would be the point? She's still thirteen years older than I am.' He sounded resigned. 'She'll *always* be thirteen years older than me.'

'Tell me what you're afraid of,' Liza said bluntly. 'No, hang on, I'll tell you. You're afraid that in ten or twenty years' time Bibi will either go loopy and need looking after, or die.' She paused, fixing James with her steady gaze. 'So what am I, spot on?'

It was impossible to lie to Liza. James had had long enough to think about it now. He had got over his initial outrage at being deliberately deceived.

'I suppose so.' Reluctantly he nodded.

'But in the meantime you're miserable and Bibi's miserable,' Liza went on, 'and the whole of this last year has been a waste.'

'Look, I know what you're saying. I just—'

'Please, James. I wasted time too, agonising over the fact that I was older than Kit.' She shrugged. 'And look what happened.'

'I know, I know.'

'If you have a chance to be happy, take it,' Liza told him, 'and sod what might happen in twenty years' time. Believe me,' she said simply, 'life's too short.'

It was midnight when James finally made a move to leave. Opening the front door to let him out, Liza rubbed her arms as the icy night air swirled into the hallway.

In the dim porch light, she saw the flecks of silver glinting in James's neat dark beard. They hadn't been there last year. She reached up and touched the soft bristles.

'You're going grey.'

He pulled a face.

'Thanks a lot.'

'No, it suits you.'

'I've spent the last year feeling pretty grey.'

'You could do something about that,' said Liza.

'What, Grecian 2000?'

'I mean get in touch with Bibi.'

James reached for her hand. He held it for a few seconds then kissed her fingertips, breathing in the faint oriental scent of her perfume.

'You're thinking something,' said Liza. 'What are you thinking?'

'How beautiful you are. And how desirable.' He smiled and shook his head, marvelling at the fact that he was able to say the words aloud. 'I was thinking that if things had been different, if it hadn't been for Bibi . . . and Kit . . . I wonder if we could have got together.'

'How weird, that's what I was thinking too.'

'And?'

'Well,' said Liza, 'with my track record, I'd say it would definitely have been on the cards. But there again, with my track record . . .' She bit her lip and smiled.

'. . . we'd have lasted all of two weeks.' James finished the sentence for her.

'Who knows, maybe even three.'

He grinned.

'Three. I'm flattered.'

Liza's mouth was inches away from his own. He could have kissed her, but he didn't.

'It's better this way.' Liza was still smiling but her teeth were starting to chatter. 'Friends last longer than lovers.'

Across the road, a group of partygoers who had spilled out

of Robert and Delia's house were now piling noisily into their cars.

'You're shivering. Time I was gone,' said James. He gave Liza a hug.

She returned the hug and kissed him fondly on the cheek.

'Have a good Christmas.' Giving him a meaningful look, she added, '*Make* it a good Christmas.'

James wondered what kind of a Christmas Liza could look forward to this year. He nodded, feeling desperately sorry for her.

'You too.'

Chapter 51

There were two weeks to go and everyone within a fifty-mile radius of Bath had decided to do *all* their late-night Christmas shopping tonight.

At least that was how it felt to Dulcie. The streets were crammed with frenzied spenders, the queues to even get inside some of the shops were diabolical. Worst of all, there was no point in giving up and going home, because from now until Christmas Day itself, it was only going to get worse.

Dulcie, stuck in the middle of this mayhem, wasn't sure what she was experiencing but it was some kind of rage.

Not road rage, because this area of the city was pedestrianised.

Not trolley rage, because she didn't have a trolley. Although one would have come in incredibly useful.

Maybe Yule rage, thought Dulcie, battling her way through BabyGap and cracking her ankle on a pushchair being steered by a hopeless learner.

Grimly, she elbowed a stockbroker type out of the way and bagged a brilliant Santa scarf for her three-year-old god-daughter. The last pair of matching mittens had just been snatched up by the scowling stockbroker. Dulcie watched him fling them into his wire basket, on top of a pile of other clothes. Her fingers itched. Polly would love a pair of mittens to match the scarf . . .

Oh no, that's sick, thought Dulcie, horrified by the thoughts flashing through her mind. What kind of pond life was she to even think of doing something so—

'Are you going to stand there all day?' hissed the stockbroker, ramming the basket against Dulcie's hip as he barged past.

She whisked the mittens out of the basket and out of sight. The irritable stockbroker headed for the queue at the till and Dulcie melted away in the opposite direction. Two minutes later, while she was investigating denim dungarees, she heard a bellow of fury over by the till.

'Who the buggering hell has made off with my sodding gloves?'

He didn't sound so much like a stockbroker now.

Dulcie kept her face averted. She didn't want to get embroiled in a nasty attack of mitten rage.

By seven thirty Dulcie was carrying fifteen bags, her arms were practically out of their sockets and the soles of her feet hurt so much they burned.

Queueing in a newsagent's for a can of Coke, she overheard a woman say there had been a pile-up outside the Blenheim Street car park. Apparently the place was gridlocked, no one was getting in or out.

With a sigh Dulcie paid for two cans of Coke, carried them outside and looked around for somewhere to sit down. She may as well rest her feet and wait for the car park to unblock itself before heading back to the car.

A Salvation Army band was playing 'God Rest Ye Merry Gentlemen' in the centre of the precinct, and all but one of the benches around them were full. Limping, Dulcie lugged her bags over to the only bench that wasn't, and realised her mistake two seconds too late.

'Here, let me give you a hand with those,' said the boy who was the only other occupant. From a distance he'd looked okay, but now she was close up, Dulcie saw the mousy matted dreadlocks, the filthy clothes and the bottle of Tennant's Export sticking out of his coat pocket. He smelled awful and – oh help – something furtive was going on in the vicinity of his lap.

Dulcie tried to hang on to her bags but they were out of control, slithering in all directions. Leaning over, the boy helped her to pick them up. She wondered if he was about to do a runner, make off with her Christmas shopping, and if he did would he be pleased with the Penhaligon's bluebell soap and foaming bath oil?

'Been buying presents?' His tone was conversational.

Dulcie nodded, flipped the ring pull of the first Coke, and determinedly didn't look at his trousers.

'Wish I had money to buy presents.' His tone was sorrowful. 'Some Christmas we'll be having this year.'

'Mm,' said Dulcie.

'Couldn't spare a few coppers, could you? Not for me,' the boy assured her earnestly, 'for my dog.'

Daring to look at last, Dulcie saw that the movement in his grubby lap was in fact a squirming beige puppy. Relieved that he hadn't been exposing himself to her, she fished around in her pocket for change.

'Sixty-five pence?' The boy gazed at the coins in the palm of his hand. He looked disappointed. 'I mean thanks, but I'm not going to be able to buy little Squatter much of a Christmas present with that, am I?'

Dulcie was beginning to feel like a plague victim. She appeared to be sitting in the middle of the Bermuda Triangle; everyone was giving her bench an extraordinarily wide berth. Some were shooting her sympathetic glances. Others, observing her predicament, were clearly thinking: *sucker*.

She took her purse out of her handbag and opened it while the boy looked on, his eyes bright with interest. She had, of course, used up the last of her change buying the cans of Coke.

Hating herself, knowing she was being half conned, half intimidated, Dulcie gave him a fiver and prayed he'd go away.

The boy grinned, revealing surprisingly white teeth, and tucked the rolled-up note into his sock.

'The thing is,' he said chattily, 'if you can afford a fiver, you can afford a tenner.'

'What?'

'That wouldn't be too much to ask, would it?'

'This is called pushing your luck,' said Dulcie.

'It's called trying to get by. Come on, look at you,' the boy drawled, indicating the fifteen glossy carrier bags with a grubby thumb. 'Look at the places you shop. How can it be fair, eh? You've got everything and I've got nothing. So tell me, how can that be fair?'

The Salvation Army band, having stopped for a breather, now picked up their instruments and launched into a jaunty version of 'O Come All Ye Faithful'.

'You haven't got nothing.' Dulcie had to raise her voice to make herself heard over the sound of the brass instruments oompa-ing away with gusto. 'You've had a fiver from me and you're not getting any more, so just leave me alone, okay?'

The façade of friendliness had gone now. His eyes were cold as he jeered at her.

'Oh help, I'm *sooo* scared.'

Damned if she was going to be the one to get up and leave, Dulcie stared back. If he'd been one of the yuppie types at the Cat and Mouse, she would have told him exactly what she thought of him by now. But because he was hungry and homeless, she couldn't bring herself to do it.

Which was weird, because *he* could.

'Go on, you can afford it. Don't be such a selfish bitch,' he snarled. 'Give me a tenner and I'll go.'

'There are two policemen over there,' Dulcie lied coolly. 'Shall I tell them you're harassing me, demanding money with menaces?'

He snorted with laughter.

'Menaces! I'll deny it. I'll tell them you were harassing *me*.'

'Oh right. And who do you think they'll believe?' Dulcie retaliated. 'The woman with everything, or a repulsive little creep like you?'

'You can't call me that,' said the boy, stunned by the derision in her voice. 'I'm homeless.'

'I can call you anything I like,' Dulcie snapped back, 'because you're a git.'

He went, loping off with his Tennant's Export in one hand and the wriggling puppy in the other. As he made his way across the precinct to the off-licence he turned and winked at Dulcie, and mouthed, 'Worth a try.'

Dulcie stayed where she was. The encounter had depressed her; she wasn't proud of the way she'd reacted to the beggar's taunts. I'm just a horrible person, she thought wearily. No wonder Patrick prefers Claire.

The Salvation Army band played on, and when a young girl came round shaking a tin, Dulcie slid a tenner in. Anyone who wore one of those unflattering bonnets, she decided, deserved all the help they could get.

'That's really kind of you,' whispered the girl in the bonnet, and all of a sudden Dulcie wanted to cry. She shook her head.

'No it's not.'

The girl moved on. Dulcie took another swig of Coke. What had the beggar called her, a selfish bitch?

Well, that was true enough.

His bitter, accusing voice rang again in her head: 'You've got everything,' and Dulcie felt a lump expand in her throat.

I don't, she thought, feeling horribly sorry for herself. I used to have everything, but I don't any more.

A mother with two young children came and sat on the bench. Dulcie shifted her bags to make room for them.

'Mum. Mum, I'm thirsty, can I have a Coke?' clamoured the boy.

'Me too, Mum, I'm thirsty too,' his younger sister chimed in.

The woman, who had just eased off her shoes with a groan of relief, closed her eyes and groaned again.

'Robbie, we've just sat down. Can you wait five minutes?'

Dulcie wasn't a mother but even she knew this was a request doomed to failure.

'Nooo! Mum, I'm thirsty *now*.'

'So am I, so am I, Mum, so am I-I-I!'

'Oh God,' croaked their mother, wearily fumbling around for her shoes. 'Okay, okay.'

'Here, they can have this one.' Dulcie leaned across and offered the woman her second can. 'I bought two but I'm not thirsty any more.'

'Are you sure?' The woman's gratitude was overwhelming. 'Oh, thank you so much. You've saved my life! That's really kind of you.'

Another really kind. Two really kinds, thought Dulcie, and one selfish bitch.

The children fought over the Coke and guzzled it down, while the woman waggled her pop-socked feet, making the most of five minutes' rest.

Dulcie watched the brass players shake spit out of their trumpets and ready themselves for the next carol.

'I know this one,' exclaimed the girl next to her on the seat, swinging her legs in excitement. 'It's "Silent Night". We sing it at playgroup. I'm nearly four,' she informed Dulcie proudly. 'We're having a navitivy play next week and I'm an angel.'

'Really?' said Dulcie. 'That's brilliant. I've always wanted to be an angel.'

The girl jumped off her seat and stood in front of Dulcie.

'I'll sing it for you,' she announced, eyes shining. 'Si-lent night, Ho-ly night, All is calm, All is bright . . .'

Not to be outdone, her brother joined in, his clear, true soprano ringing out in the cold night as he guided his young sister's reedy warble through the second and third verses.

Dulcie had to swallow hard as he soared into the descant; she'd always had a weakness for descants. She watched the two of them singing their hearts out and felt her bottom lip begin to quiver. What in heaven's name was the matter with her today?

'. . . sleep in heavenly pee-eace, sle-ep in heavenly peace,' concluded Robbie and his sister, romping home well ahead of the band.

Dulcie plastered a bright smile on to her face and applauded. 'That was terrific. Thank you!'

'Couple of show-offs,' said their mother with a grin.

'Guess what Father Christmas is bringing me,' chirruped her daughter, 'a Barbie and a bicycle.'

'With stabilisers,' Robbie interjected brutally. 'My bike won't have stabilisers.'

'And he's bringing it on his sleigh and the reindeers are going to help him get it into our chimney.'

Robbie was looking superior, as if he was itching to tell his sister Father Christmas didn't exist. Noticing this, their mother forced her feet back into her too-tight shoes and stood up.

'Right, you two, we've got a bus to catch. And Robbie, sshh.' Ruffling her son's hair and raising her eyebrows in mock despair, she said to Dulcie, 'Have you got any?'

Children, presumably. Not buses, Dulcie decided.

She shook her head.

'No, I haven't.'

'Lucky you,' said the woman, plainly not meaning it. She smiled. 'Thanks again for the Coke. 'Bye. Merry Christmas.'

For the second time that evening, shoppers gave Dulcie's bench a seriously wide berth. They glanced out of the corners of their eyes at the woman sitting on it and hurried past determined not to get involved.

Dulcie saw them and didn't care. She carried on sobbing, unable to help herself. She didn't know why it was happening, she just knew she couldn't hold it in a minute longer.

Tears streamed unstoppably down Dulcie's icy cheeks. They ran down her neck and soaked into her black polo-necked sweater. She searched blindly in her coat pockets for a tissue and pulled out something soft and knitted instead.

Dulcie stared at what she saw. That was it; she'd really hit rock bottom now. You couldn't sink much lower than shoplifting Father Christmas mittens from BabyGap.

'Honestly, it's a bit much,' hissed an irritated middle-aged woman to her friend. 'I mean, why doesn't somebody do something about her? That's what we pay our taxes for, isn't it?'

'It's all care-in-the-community these days,' tut-tutted her friend, 'but what good does it do them? I bet she'd far rather be in a nice psychiatric hospital than out in public like this.'

'Poor thing.' The first woman's voice softened. 'You can't help feeling sorry for her.'

Her friend chivvied her along. 'Come on, Jean, don't get involved. I told Edward we'd be home by nine.'

Bibi, who had overheard this conversation, glanced briefly over her shoulder to see who the two women were talking about.

She stopped dead in her tracks when she saw it was Dulcie.

Dulcie, in turn, thought she was hallucinating when she looked up and saw, through a haze of tears, Bibi standing two feet in front of her.

Chapter 52

But Bibi was definitely real. Recalling the last time they had faced each other – the night of Patrick's fortieth birthday, the night she had managed . . . oh God . . . to ruin Bibi's life – Dulcie covered her face and flinched away.

'Dulcie, whatever's happened?'

Bibi's voice, when it came, was gentle. She crouched down in front of Dulcie and peeled away one of her hands.

Dulcie kept the other one clamped over her eyes.

'Sweetheart, you can't sit here like this. Tell me what's wrong.'

Between gulps and shuddering sobs, Dulcie muttered something under her breath.

Bibi leaned closer.

'What was that?'

'I s-s-stole something from B-B-BabyGap,' whispered Dulcie. She pushed the mittens, by this time soggy with tears, into Bibi's hands. 'I d-didn't mean to. It w-was an accident.'

'Oh, Dulcie, of course it was an accident! You'd never do anything like that on purpose.' Bibi shook her head, her forehead creased with concern. 'Did they call the police? Were you arrested? Darling, don't cry, we'll tell them you aren't the shoplifting type.'

Dulcie couldn't imagine for the life of her why Bibi was being so nice. She wiped her streaming nose on her sleeve and said weakly, 'I wasn't caught. Nobody saw me do it. I found them in my pocket just now. Have you got a tissue?'

Bibi never went anywhere without her Handy Andies. She

unzipped her bag and gave Dulcie the whole packet.

'But if you weren't caught,' she frowned, 'why are you crying?'

'I don't know.' Dulcie blew her nose and shrugged. 'I'm j-just miserable. I've made a complete and utter balls-up of everything. Dammit, I'm a walking j-j-jinx.'

'If you were jinxed,' said Bibi, trying to cheer her up, 'you'd have been caught pinching those mittens. There, you see? You weren't, were you? That's something to be grateful for, for a start.'

It didn't work.

'But what am I going to do?' sniffed Dulcie. 'It's too late to go back and pay for them now. Everywhere's shutting.'

Bibi peered at the damp price ticket. All this fuss over six pounds fifty.

'I could pop in there tomorrow,' she offered, 'explain what happened and give them the money. Or you could send them a cheque.'

Dulcie wiped her mascara-stained eyes and sighed.

'Okay, I'll do that.'

Bibi straightened up.

'And are you just going to carry on sitting there,' she eyed the pile of carriers from Casa Pupo, Jolly's, Janet Reger and Diablo, 'like an upmarket bag lady?'

'I'll go home in a minute.'

'Or we could stop off at Leander's if you like.'

Dulcie looked up at her, astounded.

'You mean go for a drink? What, both of us . . . together?'

Bibi smiled.

'Well, we could sit at opposite ends of the bar if you preferred, but I think you need to talk to someone about whatever's troubling you.' She paused, then bent down to pick up Dulcie's bags. 'And now we've broken the ice . . .'

Leander's wine bar was dimly lit and not too busy. It also had plenty of tables tucked away in secluded corners where bedraggled, mascara-stained women could hide without frightening the other customers.

Bibi beamed at the waiter and ordered vodka and tonics, then turned to Dulcie.

'They still do that amazing white chocolate ice cream. How about it?'

Dulcie shook her head. She was too depressed to eat ice cream.

'No thanks, just a drink's fine.'

'You used to have both,' chided Bibi. 'Always. Darling, you were the queen of ice cream! Come on, just have a little bowl . . .'

Every time she thought she'd stopped crying, Dulcie started again. She was getting through Bibi's Handy Andies at a rate of knots.

'I'm sorry,' she blubbed, 'it's because you're being kind. I still can't believe you're even speaking to me.'

Bibi's expression softened. She and Dulcie had always been so fond of each other. She gave her daughter-in-law's icy fingers a squeeze.

'I've missed you,' she said simply.

More tears dripped down Dulcie's cheeks.

'Oh, Bibi, I've missed you too. I'm so, *so* sorry about James. I didn't mean to—'

'I know you didn't. You meant well.' Bibi patted her hand reassuringly. 'It was a good plan; it just didn't quite come off.'

The young waiter brought their drinks and a bowl of the famous ice cream for Dulcie. She smiled damply and thanked him. This had been one of her and Bibi's favourite pit stops during their shopping blitzes, and he had remembered she liked extra wafers and extra-extra roasted almonds.

Unless of course it's Bibi's face he remembers and he's getting me muddled up with someone else . . .

'I expect you come here with Claire now,' she said bravely, to prove to Bibi how civilised she could be.

'No.' Bibi looked surprised.

363

'But . . . the two of you do go shopping together. I saw you, that . . . er, time outside your house.'

'Oh, we went once.' Bibi nodded, remembering. 'Patrick had mentioned you and I used to shop together so Claire offered to go with me. That was all.'

Dulcie was intrigued by the lack of detail. Bibi was to gossip what Joan Rivers was to face lifts.

So intrigued she forgot to cry, Dulcie took a mouthful of ice cream instead and said, 'And?'

Bibi sighed.

'Oh Lord, I'm supposed to be impartial.'

'Don't be impartial, it's boring.' Dulcie loaded one of the wafers with ice cream and decided she was hungry after all. 'Tell me why you only went shopping with her once.'

'Oh, it was a disaster.' Bibi came clean. 'I did my best, Dulcie, really I did, but what can you do with a girl whose idea of splashing out is two pairs of tights and a navy cardigan from Littlewoods?'

Dulcie gazed at her, speechless with pleasure.

'She's very keen on value for money,' Bibi went on, 'and comfortable clothes that won't fall apart after five minutes. And she likes to decide in advance exactly what she needs to buy, because it saves time.'

'Saves time . . .' Dulcie echoed faintly.

'I've never met anyone so efficient.' Bibi shook her head and looked sorrowful. 'The whole trip lasted ninety-five minutes.'

'Good grief.'

'She's a lovely girl,' Bibi added hastily, 'don't get me wrong. Absolutely charming.'

'Just not shopping-compatible.' Dulcie nodded to show she understood, valiantly forcing herself not to say anything bitchy.

'That's it. We might not be shopping-compatible but she's still terribly nice.'

'Oh yes, I know what you mean. Terribly, *terribly* nice.'

'Mmm.'

'For example, that amazingly ugly man over there with the huge wart on the end of his nose makes me want to start telling Quasimodo jokes,' said Dulcie, 'but if Claire was here now, I just know she'd say, "Oh, I didn't even notice that massive wart, I was just thinking what lovely kind eyes he has." '

'She would,' said Bibi solemnly. 'She certainly would. Claire was the one, actually, who told me that you hadn't meant to split me and James up. She said I should make things up with you, heal the—'

'Oh please!' wailed Dulcie. 'Pass the sick bag. I've heard enough about Saint jolly-nice Claire for one night.'

Bibi watched Dulcie – now well on the road to recovery – scrape her bowl.

'More ice cream? More vodka?'

'Yes please.'

'Feeling better?'

Dulcie nodded.

'I was so jealous,' she admitted shamefacedly, 'when I saw the two of you together.'

'It was nothing. Just a one-morning stand,' said Bibi with a grin.

'Still, Patrick seems happy enough with her.'

Bibi attracted the attention of their waiter. When she'd re-ordered, she shrugged.

'That's men for you. Talk about going from one extreme to the other.'

Was this a compliment or not? Dulcie was still trying to puzzle it out when Bibi went on casually, 'I mean, look at James. One minute he's with me, the next he's having a fling with some mini-skirted blonde in her twenties.'

Dulcie squirmed, her skin prickling with guilt.

'Oh God.'

'Doesn't matter. It didn't last long anyway.'

'How do you know?'

'He's living in the flat above Margaret Taylor, in Devenish House.' Bibi managed a slight smile. 'She's kept me up to date with his . . . er . . . comings and goings.'

More guilt, a great tidal wave of the stuff this time. I did this, thought Dulcie. It's all my fault.

'Do you still miss him terribly?' Her voice was small.

Bibi said nothing for a moment. She studied her immaculately polished nails. Then she nodded.

'Yes.'

'But . . . have you tried contacting him? I mean, have you seen him at all?' Dulcie persisted.

'Of course I haven't.' Bibi's eyes were full of pain but she spoke with dignity. 'What would be the point of that? Dulcie, *I* didn't end it. James was the one who dumped me.'

But there were a million other things to talk about. The conversation moved on. Unhappily for Dulcie it didn't take long to get around to Liam McPherson.

'Anyway,' said Bibi when they had finished discussing Pru and Eddie's wedding, 'while we're on the subject of perfect men, what happened to that dishy tennis pro of yours?' She lowered her voice. 'And what was all this I heard about you expecting a baby?'

Dulcie swallowed hard. She wasn't proud of that little piece of deception. God, she did some stupid things sometimes.

Bibi was looking at her with a mixture of concern and sympathy.

'We don't have to talk about it if you don't want to, darling. But sometimes it helps.' She paused then said delicately, 'Was it a miscarriage, or did you . . .?'

'I wasn't pregnant. I just pretended to be,' Dulcie confessed with a sigh. What the hell, she may as well admit everything. Bibi knew her well enough; she wasn't likely to be too shocked by the depths to which her errant daughter-in-law was capable of sinking.

Bibi looked confused.

'You mean . . .?'

'I was desperate,' said Dulcie bleakly. 'Liam was up for it

with any woman who so much as smiled at him in the street. He couldn't keep his tracksuit bottoms on if his life depended on it. But you hear about some men who are totally transformed when they become fathers,' she ploughed on, avoiding Bibi's gaze, 'and I thought, what if Liam's one of them? What if it jolts him into realising he doesn't want to lose me?'

'You hoped he'd turn into Mr Ever-Faithful.'

Dulcie nodded.

'That was the plan. It didn't work, of course. And then he found out, so it was all over between us anyway.' She sat back in her chair and groaned. 'I wasn't upset about losing him. I didn't even care by that time. I just can't get over the fact that I did something so awful, so pathetic and underhand. I'm so ashamed . . . I still can't believe I thought it was a reasonable thing to do.'

'Oh Dulcie, an unfaithful lover is enough to drive anyone to desperation,' Bibi said consolingly. She leaned closer. 'Look on the bright side. At least you didn't shoot him.'

Dulcie dredged up a smile.

'No, there is that.'

'And at least you weren't really pregnant.'

Dulcie's smile did an abrupt U-turn and disappeared.

'No, I know.'

'Oh darling, what's wrong?' Bibi looked alarmed.

It sounded ridiculous, but Dulcie knew she had to say this too.

'Those children I told you about, the ones who sang "Silent Night" to me,' she faltered, trying to explain. 'It made me realise how much I do want a family . . . and then I thought what if God decides to punish me for pretending to be pregnant? What if he makes sure I never have children of my own?'

'Sweetheart, you can't possibly think that!' exclaimed Bibi, before Dulcie's eyes could fill up again. 'Heavens, I'm sure God has more on his mind than your latest bit of plotting. I mean, what were you doing really?' she argued. 'Just sussing

367

Liam out, seeing if he'd make a good husband and father. If you look at it that way, it's a perfectly sensible thing to do.' With a reassuring smile, Bibi tapped her forehead. 'Like most of your bright ideas, darling. If they come off, fine. Everybody's happy.'

'And if they don't,' Dulcie concluded ruefully, 'they're not.'

By the time they reached the car park it was almost empty. Dulcie gave Bibi a lift home.

'I'm so glad we're friends again,' said Bibi when they pulled up outside her house.

'So am I.'

Bibi gave her a kiss and opened the passenger door. 'Now all we have to do is sort you out and cheer you up.'

'I will cheer up, I promise.'

Dutifully, Dulcie produced a convincing smile. Even admitting she was depressed made her feel bitterly ashamed. Compared with Liza, what the hell did she have to be depressed about?

On her own again in the car, Dulcie switched on the radio. Whitney Houston was belting out: 'And eye-eye-eye will always love yoooooooou.' Vividly Dulcie recalled the party she and Patrick had held at the house a couple of years ago, when all the furniture had been pushed back and everyone had got spectacularly legless on the punch she had concocted. She remembered Bibi and James dancing to this song, this very song. Bibi, her arms thrown around James's neck, had smiled dreamily up at him and he had bent his dark head and kissed her . . .

And I, Dulcie recalled with startling clarity, yelled out, 'Ugh, no lovey-dovey stuff allowed in this house! Less of the snogging if you don't mind.'

She waited until the song came to an end, drove up to the traffic lights and signalled left.

Then she changed her mind – luckily there were no other cars around – and signalled right instead.

Chapter 53

'Good grief.' James looked astonished when he opened his front door. 'Dulcie. Is something wrong?'

Yes, something's wrong, thought Dulcie, but not in the way you think.

'I haven't wrapped the car round a lamp post, if that's what you mean. I just needed to talk to you.' She spoke brightly, as if the last year hadn't happened. 'Okay if I come in?'

Bemused, James stood to one side and Dulcie slid past him, heading for the sitting room. The television was on. The coffee table in front of the sofa was littered with Christmas cards, an address book, a half-empty pack of M&S prawn sandwiches and an even emptier tumbler of Scotch.

James's suit jacket was flung over the back of a chair. He had undone the top button of his green and white striped shirt and loosened his tie. Dulcie watched him spin the top off a bottle of Glenfiddich and refill his glass. He paused and glanced up.

'Drink?'

'Better not. I'm driving.'

James frowned slightly.

'You look terrible.'

About to get indignant Dulcie realised she still had mascara all over her face.

'Can I use your bathroom?'

He shrugged.

'Be my guest.'

In the bathroom – rather nicely done out in mulberry and

jade green – Dulcie washed her face, which at least stopped her looking like a madwoman, and pressed James's wrung-out flannel over her puffy eyes. Next, she checked out the toiletries on show and had a brisk rummage through the bathroom cabinet.

No sign of any girlie stuff. Promising.

'Better,' James remarked when she returned to the sitting room. He had made her a coffee in the meantime. As she spooned in sugar, Dulcie couldn't help wondering if he'd heard her clunking around in his bathroom cabinet.

'Thanks.'

The cards had been pushed to one side, to make way for the tray.

'Well, I'm fairly sure you didn't knock on my door just to ask if you could use my bathroom.' James raised his tumbler, drank, and gave her a quizzical look. 'So why are you here?'

'I came to say sorry.'

'You said it before.'

'You didn't want to hear it last time,' said Dulcie. 'Now I'm trying again.'

James stood with his back to the fireplace. He was studying her, apparently deep in thought, and rubbing the heel of his hand over his close-cut beard.

It occurred to Dulcie that he was the only man she knew who had a beard she actually liked.

'Fine. Okay,' he said at last. 'It's in the past. What is this anyway, some kind of guilt trip? A quest for absolution? You can't rest until everyone whose lives you ever meddled with has forgiven you?'

That was another thing about James, Dulcie remembered, his dry sense of humour. As in Sahara-dry. It wasn't always easy to know when he was joking. For instance, he definitely sounded serious now, but wasn't there just the teeniest hint of amusement in his eyes?

Best to grovel, she decided, to be on the safe side.

'Something like that,' Dulcie admitted. 'I know what I did was wrong.' She glanced up at James. 'But I wasn't the only one.' His dark eyebrows went up a couple of millimetres.

'Oh?'

'Bibi made a mistake, not telling you how old she was. My big mistake was letting you find out.' Bluntly, no longer penitent, she concluded, 'And finishing with Bibi was yours.'

James shook his head.

'Oh, Dulcie, you haven't changed.'

'Actually, I have.' She risked a wry smile. 'You wouldn't believe it.'

'Tell me why you're really here.'

Finishing her coffee first, Dulcie put the cup back down on the tray and picked up a handful of the envelopes James had already addressed.

'Sending me one this year?' she enquired idly.

'You won't find your name on any of those. Come to think of it,' said James, side-tracked, 'how did you know I was living here?'

Dulcie shrugged and carried on shuffling through the cards.

'Just clever. Sending one to Bibi?'

When James didn't reply, she looked up. His mouth was set in an ominously narrow line.

'Is that why you're here?'

'It's a good enough reason, isn't it?' Dulcie decided to just go for it; she – or rather Bibi – had nothing to lose. 'James, I saw her today. And she isn't happy. She misses you. And you *know* you miss her. I mean, talk about screamingly obvious.'

James said slowly, 'You drove over here to ask me to send Bibi a Christmas card?'

'Don't you see?' Dulcie babbled on, really getting into her stride now. 'You tried to forget her, you tried going out with other women – well, more like teenagers from what I hear – but it didn't work, it couldn't work, because they *just weren't Bibi.'*

371

'Hang on, did Liza tell you this?' James was looking bewildered.

'No, Bibi did.'

'*Bibi . . . ?*'

'Doesn't matter.' Impatiently Dulcie brushed the interruption aside. She was on a mission; all she needed now was for James to do as he was told. 'Now look, you were the one who finished with her, so it's up to you to make the first move.'

'Can I get you another drink?' James's mouth twitched with amusement as he topped up his own glass once more. He sat down on the arm of the sofa and watched Dulcie sort frenziedly through the box of as yet unwritten-on Christmas cards.

'No thanks. Here, this one. And here's a pen.'

She was holding a glossy cherub-laden card towards him. She had even helpfully opened it out, and was pointing with his pen to the place where he should write.

'My mother used to do that to me when I was seven.'

'Please,' said Dulcie. 'It's a start, don't you see? Bibi's speaking to me again. If she can break the ice with me, you can break the ice with her.'

But James was shaking his head and turning away. Dulcie couldn't believe it. This was his chance – he *couldn't* turn it down now!

The silver Sheaffer fountain pen went whistling past James's head and ricocheted with a CLACKKK off the wall.

'How dare you!' Dulcie leapt recklessly to her feet, cracking both shins against the edge of the coffee table. 'How bloody *dare* you?' she yelled, outraged. 'How can you be so stupid, so stubborn, so . . . so . . . oh hell, what's that?'

Gasping with pain, doubled up and clutching her poor bruised shins, Dulcie collapsed back on the sofa. James had taken another envelope, already stamped and addressed, down from the fireplace. Wordlessly he held it out to her.

'It's for Bibi, isn't it?' she groaned, feeling stupid. 'God, James, you are *so* annoying. Why wasn't it down here with the rest of them?'

372

He grinned and tapped the address book on the coffee table.

'These are the people I need to look up.' Then, pointing to the other slim stack of envelopes propped up on the fireplace, he added simply, 'And these are the ones I don't.'

'Does it give you a huge amount of pleasure to watch me make an idiot of myself?'

'Huge isn't the word for it.'

'Is my card up there, then?' said Dulcie, ever the optimist.

'Ah,' James's grin broadened, 'have to wait and see.'

They had another drink. By this time it was getting on for ten o'clock.

'You'll be so glad you did this,' Dulcie told him reassuringly. 'I mean it, when Bibi gets your card, she'll be able to send you one back. Then you can either phone her or accidentally-on-purpose *bump* into her ... I can arrange that if you want me to, I could have a—'

'Dulcie, don't you think you should give up on the arranging front?' James commented drily. 'Wouldn't it be an idea to let people make their own arrangements from now on?'

Dulcie pulled a face. She was raring to go.

'I know, I know, but you men are so hopeless at this kind of stuff. If we leave it to you, you'll take months to do anything. Trust me, do it my way and I could have this whole thing sorted out by ... well, maybe even by Christmas!'

'What if I don't want it all sorted out by Christmas?'

'You see?' Dulcie was ready to explode with frustration. 'That's *exactly* what I mean. James, *please* – oh!'

She gazed down at her car keys, which had just landed unexpectedly in her lap. James was putting on his jacket and looking masterful. He slid Bibi's card into his inside pocket, switched off the television and indicated with a brief business-like gesture that Dulcie should shift herself, pronto, in the direction of the front door.

Smiling at the uncomprehending look on her face, he said quietly, 'What if I want to sort it out now?'

Three massive Scotches had given James just enough Dutch courage to do what he had been wanting to do for months. When Dulcie pulled up outside Bibi's house for the second time that evening she leaned across and gave him a kiss on the cheek.

'Go for it.'

'Wish me luck.'

'You don't need luck. The two of you belong together.'

'Yes, well. Thanks for the lift.' James reached for the door catch before what felt like a nasty attack of stage fright could get a grip.

He appeared to be one Scotch short of total confidence.

'Got the card?' said Dulcie.

He patted his pocket.

'Er . . . yes.'

'What a waste of a stamp.'

Beginning to panic, James wondered if this was wise. Maybe he should post the thing first after all.

Dulcie realised what was going on. He needed encouragement. Reaching past him, she flipped open the passenger door.

And pushed him out.

There were lights on inside the house and Bibi's car was there on the drive but nobody was answering the doorbell.

James began to feel sick. Did this mean she was too engrossed in the man who was in there with her to come to the door? Or that she had seen him climbing out of Dulcie's car and was now hiding upstairs, cursing her daughter-in-law for getting it so spectacularly wrong *again*?

Dulcie had, of course, driven off and left him to it. To get home, he would have to flag down a passing cab. Taking a deep breath, James rang the doorbell one last time.

Finally, he heard the sound of footsteps running downstairs – ha, so she'd been in bed with him, had she? – and Bibi's voice calling out, 'Who is it?'

Should he? Shouldn't he? James hesitated.

'Hello, who's there?'

Bloody Dulcie, taking off like a bat out of hell, leaving him stranded . . .

'Bibi, it's me.'

The door was flung open. Bibi stood in the doorway, visibly stunned.

She had been in the bath, James realised. Her ash-blonde hair was up in a loose topknot and damp tendrils framed her face. Her skin glowed from the heat of the bath and she was clutching the front of her white dressing gown with both hands, clinging to the lapels as if for dear life.

'James! This is . . . this is . . .'

'Unexpected. I know.' He took a deep breath. Desperate to appear cool, he pulled the envelope from his inside pocket, realising too late that his hands were trembling. 'Christmas card. Thought I'd deliver it in person.'

'There's a stamp on it.'

James smiled slightly. 'I know, but what the hell. I was passing.'

Peering over his shoulder, Bibi said, 'Where's your car?'

'Ah . . . I was passing in someone else's car.'

He couldn't tear his eyes from her face. She didn't look a day older than she'd ever looked. God, she was beautiful . . .

'Well, it's nice to see you again.' Bibi knew she sounded like a travel agent greeting an old customer. She hesitated, at a complete loss. Did James mean he was literally dropping the card off before jumping back into someone else's car – whoever Someone Else might be – or could she invite him in for a drink?

'Gosh, this is a coincidence!' Her heart was pounding. Confused, she heard herself beginning to babble. 'You'll never guess who else I bumped into today! Extraordinary really, after all this time—'

'Dulcie,' said James. Bibi was as nervous as he was. Quite suddenly he knew everything was going to be all right. 'I was passing in Dulcie's car.'

Bibi closed her eyes for a second, and leaned her head against the door. When she opened her eyes once more, she said shakily, 'That girl, don't tell me. I suppose she's been interfering again.'

James smiled and nodded and moved towards Bibi. He cupped her face in his hands and said in a low voice, 'Oh yes, she's been interfering again.'

As Bibi fell into his arms and lifted her mouth to his, she murmured back, '*Thank God* . . .'

Chapter 54

You knew a lot had happened in the last year, Dulcie thought wryly, when the first person to greet you at a party, shouting, 'Oh brilliant, you're *here*!' was Imelda.

But that was life for you. Since Liam had become a thing of the past, it had seemed a bit pointless carrying on such high-octane rivalry. Neither Dulcie nor Imelda had had the heart to maintain their feud. Some men, they decided, simply weren't worth it.

'Mwah mwah.' Imelda clutched her now, air-kissing both cheeks and looking overjoyed to see her. 'Quick, take your coat off and I'll buy you a drink. You're missing out on all the fun . . . I've just met *the* most gorgeous chap . . .'

It was still weird, though. Definitely weird.

But having been promised by Eddie that this year's Christmas Eve party at Brunton Manor would be the best ever, Dulcie had felt obliged to turn up. Her half-hearted attempt at an excuse had been briskly squashed by Pru.

'Don't be silly, of course you're coming,' she had scolded. 'And don't give me any rubbish about wanting to avoid Liam because he won't even be there. He's skiing in Zermatt.'

In the end Dulcie had decided to make the best of it. Sometimes you just had to put on your party face and best frock, drum up a bit of enthusiasm and go for it. Maybe – who knows? – if she tried hard enough, she might end up having a good time after all.

It was already ten o'clock; she was one of the late arrivals. Pausing at the entrance to the packed ballroom, Dulcie surveyed the throng. Imelda, having barged on ahead, was over at the bar buying drinks and flirting outrageously with a huge fair-haired rugby type. All the bar staff were wearing furry antlers. The ballroom had been decked out in silver and white and the DJ was wearing a Father-Christmas-meets-Jean-Paul-Gaultier fur-trimmed red PVC cape and matching jockstrap.

The dance floor bulged with guests leaping around like lunatics to Slade's 'Merry Christmas Everybody'. Bellowing out the few words they knew, they were clearly well away.

Dulcie felt horribly sober. She hoped Imelda was getting her a large one.

Pru, spotting her from the dance floor, came over and gave her a hug. The difference with real friends, thought Dulcie, was their kisses actually touched your cheeks.

'Thank goodness, I thought you weren't coming,' Pru yelled above the noise.

Dulcie smiled. 'Oh no, I'm here. With my new best friend.'

Pru glanced over her shoulder, in the direction of Dulcie's brief nod. Imelda was making her way towards them with two glasses held triumphantly aloft.

'Hmm. Just so long as you don't forget your old best friends.'

'Don't worry.' Dulcie's tone was dry; Imelda had phoned her up three times in the last week. 'She's single, I'm single. She's only doing it because she's desperate for someone to go around with.'

'Here we are!' Imelda plonked a brimming glass into Dulcie's hand. 'Cheers! Look, I'll be back in a sec, okay? That dishy guy over at the bar's just asked me to dance.'

Dulcie wondered if a grown man sporting a bow tie that lit up and spun around like a Catherine wheel could ever truly be described as a dish.

'Is that the gorgeous one you were talking to earlier?'

'No, I've lost him.' Imelda shrugged and grinned. 'Never mind, this one will do nicely until I find him again.' Her eyes lit up. 'He's a doctor, too. Dreamy or what?'

'I bet he's a porter,' said Dulcie. 'Porters always tell girls they're doctors.' Unable to resist the dig, she added, 'What did the other one tell you he was? Airline pilot, polo player or something in the SAS?'

Imelda wrinkled her nose.

'Bit of a disappointment, actually. He said he was unemployed.'

'I spoke to Liza this afternoon,' said Dulcie when Imelda had sashayed off. 'Couldn't persuade her to come along. She's driving down to Devon tonight, spending Christmas and New Year with her parents.'

'And Eddie and I will be up in Manchester with his family over the New Year,' said Pru. 'I mean, I'm looking forward to it, but it won't be the same. We'll miss our usual get-together.' She looked worried. 'I feel awful, as if we're abandoning you. What will you do this year, made any plans yet?'

'Don't worry about me, I'll be fine,' Dulcie said firmly. 'If she isn't off playing doctors and nurses, I'll go out with Imelda. Or if I really want to have fun,' she added with forced cheerfulness, 'I can work a double shift in the pub.'

Eddie came up to them, grinning and waving a fax. He kissed Dulcie and give the fax to Pru to read.

'How are you, darling? Oh dear, I know I shouldn't laugh, but this just came through from Zermatt.'

'What is it?' asked Dulcie curiously as Pru began to giggle.

'It really isn't funny.' Eddie tried hard to sound severe. 'Poor Liam—'

'What *is* it?' demanded Dulcie, making a grab for the sheet of paper.

'He sent it from his hospital bed. He's in traction,' said Pru. 'Apparently he fell off a ski lift and broke both his legs.'

'I told him skiing was dangerous,' said Eddie, 'but he assured me he was an expert. He said only people who were unfit had accidents.' He shook his head, brushing away tears of laughter. 'I told him only idiots slide down mountains on skis. Lazing around on a hot beach – now that's *my* idea of a holiday.'

Until that moment, Dulcie had cheered up. Now she experienced a pang of misery.

'That's what Patrick's doing right now. He's in Bali,' she struggled to sound normal, 'with Claire.'

Pru frowned.

'I don't think he is.'

'Well, somewhere like that. Bali ... Barbados ... somewhere hot and exotic. Not Skegness,' Dulcie added bitterly, 'that's for sure.'

'No, I mean I don't think he's away. He phoned me this morning. Asked me if you were going to Roger and Abby Alford's party tonight.'

'Roger and Abby Alford?' Bewildered, Dulcie said, 'I haven't seen them for years!'

'Well,' Pru shrugged, 'I said no, anyway. I told him you were coming here.'

Imelda was still on the dance floor, all but undressing her dishy doctor. Dulcie bought herself another drink and found a wall to lean against; she picked abstractedly at the polish on one of her thumb nails and tried without much success to ignore the horrid lurching sensation in her stomach.

It had come as a shock, discovering that Patrick had actually reached the stage where he wanted to avoid her. Pretty obviously, he was only prepared to go to the Alfords' party if he knew for sure that she wouldn't be there.

I've really lost him now, thought Dulcie miserably. He doesn't even want to be friends any more.

'Cheer up, it might never happen.'

'Oh fuck off.' Dulcie didn't even bother to look up. She was studying her thumb nail, with its unattractive picked-off burgundy polish. Really, tonight was turning into one disaster after another.

'Dulcie!' exclaimed the voice, half-amused, half-shocked, and this time she recognised it.

She gave Rufus a hug. He was looking somewhat out of place

in his blue woolly sweater and a pair of worn-at-the-knee fawn corduroy trousers, but his eyes were bright and he was evidently delighted to see her.

'I'm sorry, I thought I was about to be chatted up by a prat.' Dulcie smiled and touched his bristly cheek. 'You're growing your beard back! What on earth are you doing here?'

'I know, hardly my scene. Some friends dragged me along.' He sounded abashed. 'And now I look an idiot. I must say, I didn't realise it was going to be quite so smart.' He indicated Dulcie's jade-green satin dress and added admiringly, 'Not like you, of course. You look fantastic. I'd ask you to dance, but I'd only show you up.'

He was right. Over his woolly shoulder, Dulcie saw a group of Brunton Manor regulars – a particularly snotty group – nudging each other and smirking. She took Rufus's hand and led him past them, saying loudly as they went '. . . darling, that's the whole point of *being* a multi-millionaire, you can get away with wearing anything you like.'

They danced to George Michael's 'Last Christmas'.

'Oh Lord, was that your foot? Sorry . . . oops, done it again . . . sorry!'

But it was so nice to see him again, Dulcie didn't even mind her toes being broken.

She grinned at Rufus. 'Ever thought of taking up wine-making? You'd be brilliant at trampling grapes.'

He looked anxious. 'Would you rather sit down?'

'No, you might get the hang of it in a minute. Anyway, you've cheered me up. Tell me what's been happening in the café. Tell me what you're doing for Christmas.'

Tell me anything to stop me thinking about Patrick . . .

'Aargh!' yelped Dulcie as Rufus whirled her round, managing to step on both feet at once and – astonishingly – trying to pull the front of his baggy sweater over her head. Half suffocating beneath the scratchy wool she screeched, 'What's going on?'

'Shh, stay there, don't let her see you,' he hissed urgently.

'That blonde over there – she's the one you splattered from head to foot with ratatouille . . .'

Standing slightly away from the dance floor, surrounded by noisy revellers setting off party poppers, Patrick watched Dulcie. She was laughing and chattering away, clearly enjoying herself and not in the least bothered by the fact that the object of her attentions appeared to have at least three left feet.

A pretty young girl not long out of her teens brushed past, making deliberate contact. She smiled mock-apologetically up at Patrick, giving him his cue to say something in return.

Patrick pretended not to notice and carried on watching Dulcie, who was now affectionately stroking her partner's beard. Since she had always loathed beards, this was less than promising. She certainly seemed fond of this one.

Patrick, tight-lipped with disappointment, wondered if coming here tonight had, after all, been a huge mistake.

'Hi!' The girl who had just brushed past him was back, making eye contact for all she was worth and waving a menthol cigarette. 'Got a light?'

Dulcie was being twirled rather over-ambitiously around in circles when she thought she saw Patrick.

At first she thought she might be imagining it, maybe suffering a lack of oxygen to the brain as a result of all that centrifugal force. She dug her heels in and stopped twirling. Caught off-guard, Rufus almost fell over.

'Sorry, was I going too fast?'

'Just felt a bit dizzy,' murmured Dulcie. It was true. Her heart was racing too. She craned her neck, searching the sea of faces around the dance floor, seeking out the only one that mattered.

Then she saw him again and her heart did a tremendous swallow dive. It hadn't been a hallucination after all.

'Had enough?' panted Rufus.

'Um . . . sorry?'

382

Rufus saw her staring at someone in the crowd. The expression on her face was unmistakable.

His face fell.

'Have you seen someone you like?'

'What?' Dulcie shook her head and forced herself to concentrate. Then she smiled at Rufus.

'Well, you could put it like that.'

Chapter 55

'Hello, you,' said Dulcie.

'Hello,' said Patrick, dry-mouthed.

'You're here.' Oh help . . . inane, *inane*. 'I mean, I thought you were going to the Alfords' party.'

Patrick, who had never had any intention of going to the Alfords' party – chiefly because they weren't having one – shook his head slightly.

'Decided against it. Too far to drive.'

So where's Saint Claire? Dulcie longed to blurt out. Why isn't she with you?

But she couldn't bring herself to say it, didn't dare. It might break the spell.

Instead she nodded, quite unable to remember where Roger and Abby Alford lived.

'Oh definitely, much too far to drive. Much easier to come here. Er . . . how's . . . how's work?'

Good grief, thought Dulcie, am I a contender for Sparkling Conversationalist of the Year or what?

Her only consolation was that at least this was her husband she was making a fool of herself in front of. At least Patrick knew her, knew she could do better than this. If he'd been a total stranger he'd be off like a shot.

'Excuse me, sorry to bother you again, but I just wondered if you had the time?'

Dulcie turned and looked at the young girl gazing besottedly up at Patrick. She recognised the expression on Patrick's face too; he looked trapped and faintly uncomfortable.

He'd always been hopeless at being chatted up.

'It's ten past eleven,' said Dulcie, reaching over and consulting Patrick's watch on his behalf. She gave the girl a brief smile. 'Time you picked on someone your own age.'

'This is my wife,' Patrick cut in hurriedly as the blonde girl, looking indignant, opened her mouth to reply. 'She bought me this watch last Christmas . . .'

'Oops,' Dulcie announced cheerfully when the girl had flounced off. 'Don't say I upset her.'

'Sorry about the wife bit.' Patrick sounded embarrassed. 'It was just to get rid of her.' He hesitated, wondering what his next move should be. 'Do you need a drink?'

Dulcie was easing off one of her shoes, seeing if she could still wriggle her trampled-on toes.

'I need crutches. Rufus isn't much of a dancer.'

Patrick wondered where Rufus had got to. He forced himself to sound casual.

'Who is he, new boyfriend?'

'God, no!' Dulcie shook her head so hard her earrings rattled. 'New boyfriend? Definitely not! And yes, I'd love a drink.'

When Patrick had been served, they moved away from the bar to a less crowded area by the entrance to the ballroom. Still dying to know where Claire was, Dulcie was about to open her mouth when Patrick said, 'Sorry, you asked me how work was going.'

Oh yes, that inspired conversation-opener. One of the all-time greats, along with 'What about this weather we've been having lately?' and 'Where did you get that tie?'

But Dulcie, succumbing to the gin, was finally beginning to relax. She tilted her head to one side.

'Well, to tell you the truth, I'm amazed you're here. I mean, it is only half past eleven on Christmas Eve. I'd have thought you'd still be in your office, slaving away over your computer, up to your eyes in work . . .'

'I sold the business.'

'. . . and what about tomorrow? Don't tell me you're taking Christmas Day off too. Good grief, Patrick, is this any way to build an empire? Does Bill Gates take time off on Christmas Day? How can you . . . you . . . you did *what*?'

Dulcie's voice faltered and died as – at long last – his words sank in.

He shrugged.

'I sold the company.'

'But . . . but when?'

'Signed the contract yesterday afternoon.'

Aware that she was asking the wrong questions in the wrong order but unable to do a thing about it, Dulcie said inanely – as if she cared – 'Who to?'

'An American company: MegaCorps, in Dallas. They made an offer to buy me out . . . and I said yes.' Patrick spoke casually as if the decision had been effortless, the simplest in the world to make. 'They want me to work for them, do some freelance design stuff—'

'You're going to work in *America*?' Dulcie felt sick. Within milliseconds her brain conjured up images of Patrick and Claire moving into their new home, a Southfork type of house with a huge pool and lots of cowboys striding about in stetsons, calling Claire ma'am and lassoing anything that mooed.

Dulcie blinked but the mental image wouldn't go away. Now she saw Patrick and Claire hosting their annual barbecue, joining in the hoedown, cheering on the riders in the rodeo and hoisting excited children up on to their shoulders . . . children with Patrick's good looks, Claire's saintly temperament and high-pitched Texan accents you could grate ice on . . .

'No.' Patrick's voice dragged her back to earth. 'God, I wouldn't live in Dallas if you paid me.' Firmly, he shook his head. 'I'm staying here.'

Just as well, thought Dulcie, light-headed with relief. He'd be useless at hoeing-down.

'But why?' she finally managed to say. 'What made you

decide to sell the company after you worked so hard to build it up?'

Patrick shrugged again.

'I just thought it was time to take a break. Work isn't the be-all and end-all; there are more important things in life. So that's it, from now on I'm going to keep the hours down, take things easy and enjoy myself.'

Dulcie stared at him, white-faced, wondering if she could possibly be hearing *these* words issuing forth from *this* mouth.

She wanted to hit him.

'What?' said Patrick. 'Why are you looking at me like that?'

Dulcie spoke through gritted teeth.

'That's what I spent the last five years telling you to do. How many *times* did I say you shouldn't be working so hard? But did you take a blind bit of notice? Like hell you did. You *ignored* me—'

'I know, I know,' Patrick cut in. He held up his hand. 'I made a mistake. You were right and I was wrong. There, does that make you happy?'

Was he serious?

Oh yes, *great*, thought Dulcie wildly, I spend five years telling you not to work so bloody hard, you take *no* notice at all, our marriage goes down the tubes, then you meet the girl of your dreams and decide you needn't work so hard after all . . . and you seriously expect me to be *happy*?

The urge to slap was overtaken by the urge to grab Patrick by the lapels, shake him until his teeth rattled, scream hysterically and call him a lot of names, stupid, selfish bastard being the least of them.

Either that or change the subject.

'Oh yes, ecstatic,' said Dulcie, tight-lipped. 'So where's Claire tonight?'

Off ministering to the poor, probably. Visiting orphans and sick children, something saintly like that. Well, the world needed another Princess Di.

'Bali.'

Dulcie nodded. Of course, he'd had to stay behind to sign the contract. Bored already with the subject of Saint Claire, she said dully, 'When are you flying out, tomorrow?'

Patrick shook his head.

'I'm not going.'

'Oh.' Dulcie felt her heart begin to accelerate. 'Why not?'

'It's over. We aren't seeing each other any more.'

'Oh!' By this time her heart was in serious overdrive. In a ridiculous high-pitched voice, she heard herself saying again, like a parrot, 'Wh-why not?'

Patrick shrugged, avoiding her gaze. His dark eyes were absolutely expressionless.

'It didn't feel right, I suppose. She didn't do anything wrong, I just knew we weren't going anywhere. Claire's a lovely girl, but in the end I suppose I realised she just isn't my type.'

Dulcie was glad she was leaning against the wall. She was in serious danger of keeling over.

'But . . . why not?' She stared up at Patrick, desperately searching his face for clues. He still wasn't looking at her. He was, Dulcie realised, concentrating on a particularly riveting patch of wallpaper instead.

'It's hard to explain.' He combed his fingers through his hair, pushing it back from his forehead.

Oh God, Dulcie thought helplessly, I love your eyebrows *so much*.

'Try.'

'Well,' Patrick sounded reluctant, 'she's always in a good mood. Always cheerful.' He sighed and shook his head. 'Always happy to go along with anything anyone suggests. God, this is ridiculous . . . what am I saying?'

Unable to stop herself, Dulcie suggested, 'That Princess Perfect leaves you cold?'

Heavens, he actually smiled!

'I suppose so. When someone's always the same, there are

388

never any surprises.' Patrick cleared his throat. 'I suppose what I'm trying to say is, it just felt . . . well, predictable.'

Dulcie bit her lip. Oh, hooray for predictable!

'So how did Claire take it when you told her it was over?' As if I care! 'No – hang on, don't tell me – she took it wonderfully well. Like a trouper, like a real star.'

'She did, actually.' Patrick looked as if he was trying not to laugh. As Dulcie turned and began heading in the direction of the entrance hall he called out, 'Where are you going now?'

'Follow me and find out.'

Outside the main doors, at the top of the stone steps, he caught up with her. It was an icy night. The grounds glistened with frost and when Dulcie spoke, clouds of condensation hung in the still night air.

'Hang on to this.'

'Hang on to what?' Patrick wondered why her hands were behind her back. The next moment he heard the hiss of a zip being undone, and Dulcie's jade-green satin dress landed in a shimmering pool at her feet.

'Dulcie—'

'Sshh!'

Patrick stood and stared as she skipped down the flight of steps, made for the fountain in the middle of the circular gravel drive, kicked off her shoes and jumped in.

The fountain was still flowing, but only just. Icicles had formed from the spouting stone statues and a thin film of ice on the surface of the water crackled and broke up as Dulcie danced in the pale moonlight.

By the time Patrick reached her she was soaked and shivering but her eyes were as bright as stars.

'P-p-predictable enough for you?' said Dulcie, through teeth that chattered like castanets. Heavens, she hadn't expected ice-cold water to be quite this ice-cold. Even her eyelashes were going numb . . .

She almost fainted with relief when Patrick scooped her out

of the fountain, threw his suit jacket around her shoulders, lifted her into his arms and began to carry her back up the steps.

'You are completely mad.'

'I love it when you're m-masterful,' Dulcie murmured. 'You Tarzan, me Jane.'

'Mad.'

She grinned. 'Better than boring. No – sorry, what was the word you used? The polite way of putting it? Ah yes . . . predictable.'

'Frostbite, that's what's predictable.' Patrick pushed through the doors. 'Which way's the sauna?'

Chapter 56

Once they were inside the sauna, Dulcie – still in his arms – watched him turn the dial up to maximum.

'I s-suppose I ought to get out of these w-wet things.' Her teeth were still chattering dramatically.

Patrick glanced down at her wet, brown, goose-pimply body and sodden peacock-blue bra and knickers.

'Don't they have any towels in here?'

The towels were kept in the linen cupboard next door. Dulcie opened her eyes wide.

'Can't remember where they keep them.'

At least the sauna was heating up fast. Patrick put Dulcie down on one of the wooden benches, sat down beside her and loosened his tie.

'Am I underdressed or are you overdressed?' she said lightly. If she could persuade him to take his clothes off too, maybe—

'Dulcie.' He turned to look at her, his tone neutral. 'Why did you jump into the fountain?'

Help, thought Dulcie, nitty-gritty time. Here we go.

'Why did I jump into the fountain?' Uh oh, doing the parrot thing again. 'Well, to prove I wasn't boring. I mean, how many frozen fountains do you suppose Claire's had a close encounter with in the last twenty years?'

Patrick ignored this. He undid the top button on his white shirt.

'But why,' he said slowly, 'did you need to prove it?'

Dulcie took a deep breath.

'Because leaving you was the stupidest thing I ever did in

391

my life. Because I miss you terribly. Because I still love you,' she went on, her voice suddenly developing a bit of a wobble. 'I love you and I wish we'd never split up.'

She flinched as Patrick stood up. He had his back to her now, his body half obscured by the swirling clouds of steam, his dark head slightly bent. He was engrossed in yet another wall, it appeared. This time a pine-panelled one.

'How long have you felt like this?' he said finally, still turned away from her.

'Months.' Struggling to be honest, Dulcie thought back. 'Five, six months, I suppose. I tried not to,' she added resignedly, 'but it just kept getting worse.'

She saw Patrick shaking his head. Then he turned.

'So why didn't you do anything about it? Why didn't you tell me?' He spoke quietly. 'Dulcie, it's not like you to keep your feelings to yourself. If you want something, you don't normally stop until you get it.'

Dulcie was beginning to feel at a horrible disadvantage. She'd told him everything, blurted out the lot, and bloody Patrick had ignored it. She'd done the whole humiliating I-still-love-you bit, and here *he* was, playing twenty sodding questions.

And it wasn't easy to know for sure, what with all the steam swirling around, getting denser by the second, but he didn't actually look that happy about it.

'Come on,' Patrick said irritably when Dulcie didn't reply, 'you didn't say a word. Why not?'

She glared back at him.

'It was all Claire's fault! If she'd been a cow I could have done it . . . she wouldn't have known what had hit her.' Dulcie bit her lip and thought how much fun it had always been, sparring with Imelda. 'You see, you can bitch about a bitch,' she went on, struggling to explain, 'but you can't fight someone who makes Mother Theresa look like Cruella de Vil. Anyway,' she sighed heavily, 'everyone kept saying how terrific the two of you were together, how good she was for you. I felt like the bad fairy – I half expected everyone to start hissing and booing whenever I walked into a room. And you were so happy and settled with Claire . . . I suppose I just thought you didn't deserve the hassle. I felt like I'd done enough damage,' she concluded with a look of resignation. 'From now on, the least I could do was keep out of your way.'

For a long moment Patrick didn't say anything. He couldn't. He gazed at Dulcie – in her peacock-blue bra and knickers and with her spiky dark hair still dripping wet from the fountain – and marvelled at her logic. It simply hadn't occurred to her that he might have welcomed the hassle . . . that hassle from his beautiful, wilful, impulsive estranged wife was what he might have been longing for more than anything else, ever since the day she had walked out of his life.

'You've changed,' he said at last.

Dulcie hung her head, unsure whether this was good or bad. 'I know.'

A furious hammering on the door made them both jump.

'Dulcie! Dulcie, is that you in there? For heaven's sake, what are you up to? What's going *on*?'

It was Imelda's voice. Tempted though Dulcie was to say nothing, she knew Imelda would only persuade Eddie to unearth the master key.

'Nothing,' she called back. 'Just . . . felt like a bit of peace and quiet, that's all. Somewhere to sit down . . . on my own . . .'

'Ahem,' Imelda coughed, 'I've got your dress here.'

'Oh.'

'Someone found it outside, at the top of the steps.'

'Ah.'

'Kind of the nineties version of Cinderella's slipper,' Imelda remarked archly.

'Mm.'

'And someone else saw you being carried into the sauna.'

'Did they?'

'Quite masterfully, by all accounts.'

'Really.'

393

'So tell me who you're with,' shrieked Imelda, 'and what you're doing in there!'

'Oh be serious, what do you think we're doing in here?'

'But . . . but *who with*?'

'Haven't the foggiest,' shouted Dulcie, 'he won't tell me his name.'

They heard Imelda's footsteps go click-clacking off down the corridor. Patrick frowned, trying to place her voice. It had definitely sounded familiar.

'Is she blonde?' he asked Dulcie.

Good heavens, he was looking interested! What was this, ditch the old girlfriend and wheel on the new?

'You wouldn't like her,' Dulcie said hurriedly. 'She's not your type. She's even more boring than Claire.'

Amused, Patrick said, 'Don't you mean predictable?'

'You'd hate her.' Rattling on, Dulcie ticked each point off on her fingers. 'She gets her legs waxed every Monday at ten thirty . . . plucks her eyebrows every Thursday night . . .'

Still trying to identify the voice, Patrick said, 'Does she have terrific legs?'

'. . . a bucket of fat liposuctioned out of each thigh every September . . .'

'How old is she, around thirty?'

'. . . has her face lifted every April.' Dulcie shook her head sorrowfully. 'She might look thirty but she's really seventy-three.'

'Oh well,' said Patrick, 'sounds like you're right, then. Definitely not my type.'

'Oh hell, listen to me! I'm lying again . . . being a bitch,' Dulcie blurted out. 'Dammit, none of those things are true. I didn't even mean to say them – they just came out!'

'Dulcie—'

'Oh, it's no good,' she wailed, burying her face in her hands, 'Talk about a hopeless case . . . I was so sure I could do it . . . tell the truth, always be nice . . . and how long did I last? About thirty seconds, that's how long. God, I'm pathetic.'

'Dulcie, are you crying?'

'No wonder you weren't bothered when we split up.' Dulcie's voice broke. She kept her fingers clamped over her eyes. 'I bet you were glad to get rid of me. I'm just an all-round hideous person—'

'Dulcie, I know you aren't crying.' Reaching over, Patrick prised her fingers away from her face.

'See?' She stared at him, dry-eyed and anguished. 'I'm still doing it, even now.'

'Why?'

'Because I don't know why you're here,' Dulcie yelled, 'and it's driving me MAD!' She stopped and hung her head. This time she was speaking the truth. Quietly, avoiding his gaze, she whispered the words again. 'Because I don't know why you're here.'

Looking at the ground, she didn't see it coming. When it happened, the kiss caught her totally unawares.

Delirious with joy, Dulcie clung to him. Now the tears running down her cheeks were real. She never wanted the kiss to end, she wouldn't *let* it end . . .

'You're strangling me,' said Patrick gently.

'Sorry.' She hid her face in his neck, breathing in the heavenly, unique Patrick-type smell of him. God, if Calvin Klein could bottle that smell . . .

'Okay,' Patrick's mouth was against her hair, 'shall I tell you what you are?'

In an instant Dulcie's blood ran cold. The kiss had made her think everything was going to be all right; it had made her happy. Now, clearly it was time for the pay-off.

Her voice was muffled.

'Will I like it?'

'Probably not.'

But he was going to say it anyway, so what choice did she have?

Dulcie shrugged. 'Go ahead.'

'You're tactless.'

Pressed tightly against his shoulder, Dulcie nodded.

'Hopelessly impatient.'

Nod.

'You never think before you act.'

Nod.

'You eat far too many salt and vinegar crisps.'

Dulcie frowned. How could anyone eat too many salt and vinegar crisps?

'And you're always *so sure* you know best,' he went on.

Another nod.

'The trouble is, despite all that,' Patrick said slowly, 'you're still my type.'

'Dulcie, Dulcie, guess what?'

Imelda again. Like the Terminator, she was back.

Dulcie smiled at Patrick, rolled her eyes and carried on unbuttoning his white shirt.

The hammering on the door redoubled.

'DULCIE, SPEAK TO ME AT ONCE THIS IS AN EMERGENCY.'

'Probably found a bit of cellulite,' whispered Dulcie. She finished removing Patrick's shirt, crumpled it into a ball, flung it over her shoulder and called out, 'What?'

'We-ell, I've just managed to find out who that gorgeous man was, the one I was drooling over earlier.' Imelda sounded excited.

Some emergency.

'And?' said Dulcie, unfastening Patrick's trousers and deftly pulling the belt out through the loops.

'You'll never believe this . . . it's your ex-husband!'

Dulcie and Patrick looked at each other.

Dulcie said, 'What?'

'I know, isn't it a scream! Talk about great minds think alike! But listen, it's all over between you two – I mean, that's ancient history now – so you wouldn't mind if I have a crack at him, would you?'

Dulcie tried not to smile.

Patrick pulled her towards him, unfastened her wet bra and lobbed it in the general direction of his shirt.

'I don't know,' Dulcie called out. 'You might not be his type.'

Patrick's trousers joined the growing pile of clothes on the floor.

'Ha! Bet I am.' Imelda sounded smug.

Tiring of the interruption, Patrick glared through the swirling steam at the door.

'Go away,' he told Imelda bluntly, 'you're not.'

'You should be nicer to her,' murmured Dulcie when Imelda had stalked off.

'Why?'

'She's got my dress.'

In the dim distance, a clock struck twelve. They heard people cheering, hooters hooting and a lot of party poppers going off like fireworks.

'Happy Christmas,' said Patrick, tracing the outline of his beautiful wife's mouth with one finger.

Dulcie's eyes were closed. She couldn't imagine a happier Christmas than this. And the weird thing was, maybe they really had needed this year apart, because how else could they have discovered that the grass wasn't necessarily greener on the other side?

I've changed, thought Dulcie, I've grown up.

And Patrick? Well, he's changed too. He's realised that working too long and too hard isn't always the most important thing in life, and that sweet, kind, saintly, *perfect* women aren't necessarily the kind you want to share your life with, that sometimes a slightly imperfect one is more fun . . .

By this time there were no more clothes left to take off. With a bewitching smile, Dulcie pushed Patrick gently down on to the floor and slid, naked, on top of him.

'Now give me my present,' she said.

* * *

397

'It's no good,' sighed Pru.

Eddie reached across the bed to her. She was wearing the indigo satin bra and knickers, the topaz-and-emerald bracelet and the kingfisher-green shirt he had given her, and the bedroom was strewn with presents, glossy wrapping paper and ribbons. It was eleven o'clock on Christmas morning, the sun was streaming in through the windows, and Pru was looking worried.

'Look, I won't be offended.' Eddie rushed to reassure her. 'If you don't like anything you can take it back to the shop. Which one's no good anyway? Is it the bracelet?'

Pru smiled at him.

'I told you, the bracelet's perfect. I love all my presents. It's Dulcie I'm worried about. She just vanished last night . . . How do I know she's all right?'

Eddie stroked the back of her neck. The skin was like warm silk but the muscles beneath it were knotted with tension. He had been looking forward, more than anything, to spending the day alone with Pru, but if she wasn't happy, he wasn't happy.

He shifted Arthur out of the way, leaned over and picked up the phone.

'What's her number?'

'*You're* going to ring Dulcie?'

'If you invite her over, she'll only say she doesn't want to be a gooseberry,' Eddie explained. 'If I do it, she'll know we both want her here.'

Love and gratitude shone in Pru's grey eyes.

'You are brilliant.'

She watched Eddie dial and listen. Less than a minute later he replaced the receiver.

'What?' said Pru, more agitated than ever. 'No reply? Oh God, what if she's done something stupid?'

'Message on the machine.' Eddie cleared his throat and attempted an impression of Dulcie: ' "Hi! Happy Christmas – I'm afraid I can't come to the phone right now because I'm having totally fantastic sex with my husband, but if you'd care

398

to leave a message I'll get back to you. Don't hold your breath, though – we shall definitely be busy for some time." '

Pru stared at Eddie.

'I don't understand. Dulcie's having totally fantastic sex with her husband? With *Patrick*?'

'Well.' Eddie shrugged. 'That's what it says.'

'But . . . But . . .'

He dialled again and held the receiver out to Pru.

'Here, you have a listen. It's either an old message,' Eddie said with a grin, 'or a very new one.'

Chapter 57

The comforting thing about staying with your parents was you could slob around just as you'd done as a teenager and they weren't shocked.

It was mid-afternoon on New Year's Eve and miserable outside. Liza, stretched out on the sofa and eating Sugar Puffs out of the packet, was watching the closing minutes of *Brief Encounter* and wishing that just this once Celia Johnson would throw her library book at her dreary husband and run off into the black and white sunset with Trevor Howard.

Margaret Lawson appeared in the sitting room doorway, drying her hands on a kitchen towel.

'Silly woman, should have grabbed her chance while she had it,' she observed briskly. 'Should have gone off with the doctor.'

Liza scooped out another handful of Sugar Puffs and crammed them into her mouth.

'Careful,' said Margaret Lawson, 'you're getting them on your new jumper.'

Liza was wearing the turquoise and white zigzag-patterned jumper because her mother had knitted it for her and when someone gives you a jumper for Christmas you have to wear it, even if it does make you look like Roger Whittaker. Personally Liza felt a few Sugar Puffs dotted here and there amongst the zigzags didn't go amiss.

'Molly McKnight's having a few friends round to her house this evening.'

'Didn't know she had that many,' said Liza. Heavens, now

she even sounded like a teenager. It must be the Sugar Puffs.

'Well, she's invited us,' said her mother, 'if you'd like to go.'

Molly McKnight's booming voice still made Liza quail. Nothing had ever been said, but she had an uncomfortable feeling her parents' eagle-eyed next-door neighbour knew exactly what had been going on in the back garden that night.

'I don't think so.' Liza didn't want to socialise anyway. The whole point of coming down here to Devon had been to avoid other people and the need to put on a brave face. Especially on New Year's Eve.

'Not even for an hour or two?' Her mother looked disappointed. 'We wouldn't have to stay until midnight.'

'Mum, you and Dad go. I'll be fine. Honestly, I'd rather be on my—'

'No, no,' Margaret Lawson cut in hurriedly, 'we wouldn't dream of doing that. Goodness, it was only a suggestion – you know us, we're just as happy staying here.'

Liza hid a smile. So her mother had read the article in this morning's *Mail* too, the one about more people committing suicide on New Year's Eve than on any other night of the year.

'Mum, I'm not going to kill myself.'

Margaret Lawson tried to react as though the thought hadn't crossed her mind.

'Liza, what an idea! Of course you're not. I'm just saying we don't want to go to one of Molly's silly parties anyway. They're fearfully dull. All she ever talks about is education cuts and bringing back the birch. And she serves home-made wine.'

When the doorbell rang an hour later, Liza was too engrossed in *The Great Escape* to answer it. Maybe this time Steve McQueen could squeeze a few extra revs out of his bike and make it over that wire fence.

Vaguely she heard her mother, still busy in the kitchen, mutter, 'Now who's that at the blasted door?'

401

Moments later, the sitting room door swung open. A great waft of aftershave filled the room. Liza, who was delving into a newly opened box of Cheerios, twisted round to have a look at whoever had just walked in.

She froze in mid-delve when she saw who it was.

'Oh my God.'

'I've got the Bentley outside,' Leo Berenger announced. When Liza didn't react he heaved an irritated sigh. 'Well, come on then, woman, get a move on, will you? We haven't got all bloody day.'

'I phoned your friend Dulcie,' he said brusquely. 'She told me where you were. What are those things stuck to your front?'

'Sugar Puffs.' Liza picked them off her sweater. Far too agitated to eat them – her stomach was churning like a washing machine – she clutched them in the palm of her hand.

'That's a terrible sweater.'

'Thanks. I already know.'

The Bentley raced on along the narrow country lanes. Leo Berenger clearly didn't like to hang about. If he was doing sixty miles an hour now, thought Liza, toes curling, what kind of speed was he planning on when they hit the motorway?

She gazed out of the window at the stark black outlines of the trees whizzing past and wondered if this was really happening.

'We flew back from Washington this morning.' Leo interrupted her muddled thoughts.

So that's where he'd taken Kit. Liza breathed out slowly, forcing herself to relax. Her toes were now gripped with cramp.

'Why Washington?'

'The doctors here couldn't make me any cast-iron promises. Kit's insides were a mess.' As he spoke, Leo kept his gaze on the road ahead. 'This surgeon was recommended to me. He's one of the best thoracic guys in the world . . . and Kit was in a bad way,' he added grimly. 'He needed the best.'

402

'But he's going to be all right?' whispered Liza.

Leo Berenger nodded.

'It's been a rough couple of months. He's been through a hell of a lot, but they reckon he'll make a full recovery.'

The relief was indescribable.

Liza gazed down at the gluey mess of crushed Sugar Puffs in her hand. Light-headed, she addressed Leo Berenger's grim profile.

'Okay. So . . . so why am I here with you now?'

He blasted his horn at an old woman dithering in a Morris Minor, then leaned across and lit a cigarette.

'I blamed you for what happened,' he said finally, with characteristic bluntness. 'If Kit had died, I daresay I'd have carried on blaming you. But he didn't die. He's come through it, thank God. And he's still as bloody stubborn as his father.' At this point Liza caught a glimmer of a smile. 'All he talked about – when he *could* talk – was marrying you. Trying to tell him to forget you,' Leo said gruffly, 'was about as effective as persuading the Pope to use a condom.' He cast a sidelong glance at Liza. 'In the end I realised one of us had to give way.'

She shook her head, still dazed by what was happening.

'I don't imagine giving way is your style.'

Leo Berenger's smile was brief. He indicated left and swung on to the M5.

'Kit's been through enough. And nothing on earth was going to make him change his mind about you. I can't keep the two of you apart any longer.' He paused, cleared his throat and said reluctantly, 'I'm sorry I didn't let you know where he was, but . . .'

'I understand. You were only doing what you thought best.' Shades of Dulcie, thought Liza; always so sure she was doing the right thing, more often than not getting it horribly wrong.

'He's my son. He means everything to me. I love him.'

'I know. I do too.'

A sign flashed past: Bath 85 miles.

'It'll be another hour yet.' Leo put his foot down. 'Grab some sleep if you want to.'

As if. Liza bit her lip, trying hard not to smile.

'I won't sleep,' she said.

The nurse hired by Leo to look after Kit while he was still bedbound met them at the bottom of the staircase.

'He's been asleep for the last hour,' she told them. 'The flight tired him out. If you want to wait down here I'll let you know when he wakes up.'

'Could I see him anyway?' Liza was trembling, holding on to the banister. 'I'll be quiet.'

The nurse glanced at Leo Berenger. He nodded.

'You go on up,' he told Liza. 'Turn right at the top of the stairs. Third door on the left. Pauline, you can make me a coffee.'

Behind her, Liza heard Pauline saying with exaggerated patience, 'Mr Berenger, my job is to take care of your son. I'm not employed to run around making you coffee.'

'All right, all right,' Leo sounded irritable, 'make one for yourself then. And just do one for me as well while you're there.'

Liza opened the door, slid noiselessly into the bedroom and closed the door again behind her.

Kit was still asleep.

A splayed-open Dick Francis paperback lay on the chair pulled up next to the bed. Removing it, Liza sat down and gazed at Kit's face.

He was thinner, and paler, but she had expected that. What she hadn't imagined was that he would look even more heart-stoppingly handsome than she remembered. Every curve and angle of his face seemed somehow more perfect. His hair seemed glossier and thicker. Even his dark eyelashes seemed longer.

Liza realised she was holding her breath. She mustn't disturb him. Still shaking, she leaned forward, closer to the bed.

Kit opened his eyes.

He blinked.

'Are you having an affair with Noel Edmonds?'

'No.'

'So why are you wearing one of his jumpers?'

The smile was the same. It was still quirky and totally irresistible, and it still had the ability to make her stomach turn helpless somersaults.

Liza sat up, pulled the turquoise and white zigzagged sweater over her head and put it on the bedside table.

'That's better.' Kit eyed her vest, appreciating the way the black Lycra clung to her golden breasts.

'I'd be careful if I were you,' said Liza, her voice not quite steady. 'If I tell my mother you commented on my jumper she'll knit one for you too.'

Kit smiled again. Then he reached for her hand.

'Are you really here?'

'I'm really here.'

'How?'

'Your father came down to Devon. We've just driven back.'

'My father.' Kit sounded amused. He shook his head slightly. 'Can you believe that man? He *kidnapped* me. Did you even know I was in America?'

'No. No one knew,' said Liza. 'Not even the police. They were mad as hell.'

'I couldn't even phone you.' Kit stroked her hand. 'I tried to bribe the nurses but he'd got to them first. It was like being in Colditz. I swear, I used to dream of tunnelling out.'

'You're out now,' whispered Liza.

He reached up and touched the side of her face. She leaned against his hand, knowing he could feel the pulse hammering frantically away in her jaw.

'Something else I used to dream about. Kissing you again.'

'Are you up to it?'

'I don't care if I'm bloody up to it or not. Just get on with it,' Kit murmured. 'It's New Year's Eve, isn't it? Kissing the woman you love is what you do on New Year's Eve. Except' – he hesitated – 'hang on, let me take that Sugar Puff out of your hair first . . .'

If you enjoyed

MIXED DOUBLES

look out for the new Jill Mansell novel

THREE AMAZING THINGS ABOUT YOU

Out in January 2015

You can order
THREE AMAZING THINGS ABOUT YOU
now

www.headline.co.uk
www.jillmansell.co.uk

headline
review

Jill Mansell

THE UNPREDICTABLE CONSEQUENCES OF LOVE

In the idyllic seaside town of St Carys, Sophie is putting the past firmly behind her.

When Josh arrives in St Carys to run the family hotel, he can't understand why Sophie has zero interest in letting *any* man into her life. He also can't understand how he's been duped into employing Sophie's impulsive friend Tula, whose crush on him is decidedly unrequited.

St Carys has more than its fair share of characters, including the charming but utterly feckless surfer Riley Bryant, who is besotted with Tula. Riley's aunt is superstar author Marguerite Marshall. And Marguerite has designs on Josh's grandfather . . . who in turn still adores his glamorous ex-wife, Dot . . .

Just how many secrets can one seaside town keep?

Just *Heavenly*. Just *Jill*.

Acclaim for Jill Mansell's fabulous bestsellers:

'Bursting with humour, brimming with intrigue and full of characters you'll adore' ***** *Heat*

'You'll fall in love with the characters in this lovely tale' *Sun*

'A warm, witty and romantic read' *Daily Mail*

978 0 7553 5593 8

headline
review

Jill Mansell

Books

straight through your letterbox...

The Unpredictable Consequences of Love	£7.99
Don't Want To Miss A Thing	£7.99
A Walk In The Park	£8.99
To The Moon And Back	£8.99
Take A Chance On Me	£8.99
Rumour Has It	£8.99
An Offer You Can't Refuse	£8.99
Thinking Of You	£8.99
Making Your Mind Up	£8.99
The One You Really Want	£8.99
Falling For You	£8.99
Nadia Knows Best	£8.99
Staying At Daisy's	£8.99
Millie's Fling	£8.99
Good At Games	£8.99
Miranda's Big Mistake	£8.99
Head Over Heels	£7.99
Mixed Doubles	£8.99
Perfect Timing	£8.99
Fast Friends	£8.99
Solo	£8.99
Kiss	£8.99
Sheer Mischief	£8.99
Open House	£7.99
Two's Company	£8.99

**Simply call 01235 400 414 or visit our website
www.headline.co.uk to order**

Free delivery in the UK.
For overseas and Ireland £3.50 delivery charge.
Prices and availability subject to change without notice.